Praise for *The Sweetheart*

"[An] impressive coming-of-age novel."

—*The New York Times*

"Spunky and colorful. . . . *The Sweetheart* is a smart and touching romp through the history of women's wrestling, and it just may give you more respect and understanding for those spangly WWE Divas."

—Bustle.com

"*The Sweetheart* is well-balanced in its humor and pathos . . . full of seamless sentences and surprising swerves of action."

—*Minneapolis Star Tribune*

"A wonderfully straightforward coming-of-age story that's set against a backdrop that's anything but."

—Goop.com

"A heartwarming novel about love, relationships and lady wrestling debuts. Yep, Angelina Mirabella's *The Sweetheart* is about the unforgettable lady wrestling circuit in the 1950s, and it's a hands-down winner."

—*Fort Worth Star-Telegram*

"The setting is based in historical fact—actual "lady grapplers" performed in matches that were staged much like professional wrestling is today. But this isn't just a book about subverting stereotypes (although that'd be enough to make it a worthy read); it also examines the impact Leonie's pursuit of fame has on those close to her."

—*The Huffington Post*

"An unusual coming-of-age novel with a focus on being true to oneself."
—*Booklist*

"An engrossing portrait of the little-known world of women's wrestling with questions about the nature of stardom and showing love. Leonie will fascinate teens, especially girls, as she makes her own way in a male-dominated sport."
—*Library Journal*

"Debut novelist Mirabella delivers a powerful blow with her coming-of-age story set in the world of women's professional wrestling in 1953. Leonie Putzkammer is a 17-year-old who's primed to reinvent herself. . . . The novel is bursting with colorful characters who are far more complex than the heels and faces they portray in the theater of professional wrestling. A powerful tale of a person's capacity for reinvention, without the fakery."
—*Kirkus Reviews*

"Told from an unusual retrospective second-person perspective and perfectly evoking 1950s culture, *The Sweetheart* is often hilarious but also filled with the wholly realistic yearnings and heartbreak of young-adult reinvention, and is peopled by familiar, sympathetic characters. Mirabella's impressive debut offers laughter, tears, failure, redemption, striving, success and a sweetheart we can't help but love."
—Shelf-Awareness.com

"Like Gwen Davies' signature dropkicks, Mirabella gives the reader a few jolts and some well-scripted writing. If you're an old-school wrestling fan, this book will resonate. And newer fans will get a taste of what wrestling was like before it became simply glitter and cartoonish. And that's no illusion."
—*The Tampa Tribune*

"Readers will find this backdrop refreshing, unique and an interesting look into the world of wrestling. . . . Life is complicated and messy, and as Leonie learned, it is impossible to play a part forever."

—*The Emporia Gazette*

"Leonie's journey, including the depictions of her wrestling training and matches, is written so realistically. It is almost inconceivable that Mirabella is neither a huge wrestling fan nor a fellow wrestler. Wrestling fans, both males and females, looking to read about wrestling and this incredible time in its history will be impressed and entertained."

—*SLAM! Wrestling*

"*The Sweetheart* pulls off that rare task of being an engaging novel in its own right that will appeal to a general audience, but being credible for pro wrestling fans, with the wrestling scenes an integral part of the storyline and themes rather than merely being a backdrop . . . anyone who has a keen interest in wrestling and also enjoys reading fiction will certainly find it a worthwhile purchase."

—ProWrestlingBooks.com

"Wow."

—PaperbackHeart.com

"You would be forgiven for thinking Angelina Mirabella had herself been a star lady wrestler in the 1950s, given how authentically detailed her debut novel is. Fortunately for us, she's a fiction writer—and a superb one—who has penned *The Sweetheart*, bringing all her glorious gifts of empathy and language to bear on its unforgettable heroine."

—Teddy Wayne, author of
The Love Song of Jonny Valentine

"Smart, funny, and poignant, Angelina Mirabella's *The Sweetheart* puts a hammerlock on one of literature's most important themes, the search for an identity, and makes it cry 'Auntie!' This is a delightfully original novel by a champ of a new writer."

—Robert Olen Butler, Pulitzer Prize–winning author of
A Good Scent from a Strange Mountain

"Like Gwen Davies, its deeply loveable heroine, *The Sweetheart* is a delightful combination of beauty, brawn, and heart. Angelina Mirabella revives the entertainment of 'lady wrestling' from its black-and-white age and raises it to the level of art. This is a bold, agile, and breathlessly exuberant debut."

—Eleanor Henderson, author of
Ten Thousand Saints

"Why haven't there been more novels written about the lady wrestling circuit of the 1950s? Thank God the talented Angelina Mirabella has opened up this fascinating world for us in her mesmerizing debut novel, *The Sweetheart*. Its heroine—Gorgeous Gwen Davies—is the most feisty and vulnerable character you'll ever meet. Once she leaps from the turnbuckle and takes the competition to the mat, you'll find yourself out of your seat and cheering. *The Sweetheart* made me downright giddy."

—Elizabeth Stuckey-French, author of
The Revenge of the Radioactive Lady and
Mermaids on the Moon

The SWEETHEART

a novel

ANGELINA MIRABELLA

SIMON & SCHUSTER PAPERBACKS
New York London Toronto Sydney New Delhi

Simon & Schuster Paperbacks
An Imprint of Simon & Schuster, Inc.
1230 Avenue of the Americas
New York, NY 10020

First Simon & Schuster trade paperback edition January 2016

SIMON & SCHUSTER PAPERBACKS and colophon are registered trademarks of Simon & Schuster, Inc.

For information about special discounts for bulk purchases, please contact Simon & Schuster Special Sales at 1-866-506-1949 or business@simonandschuster.com.

The Simon & Schuster Speakers Bureau can bring authors to your live event. For more information or to book an event contact the Simon & Schuster Speakers Bureau at 1-866-248-3049 or visit our website at www.simonspeakers.com.

Interior design by Aline Pace

Manufactured in the United States of America

10 9 8 7 6 5 4 3 2 1

The Library of Congress has cataloged the hardcover edition as follows:

Mirabella, Angelina.
  The sweetheart : a novel / Angelina Mirabella.— First Simon & Schuster hardcover edition.
    pages cm
    1. Women wrestlers—Fiction. 2. United States—History—1953–1961—Fiction.
I. Title.
PS3613.I745S94 2014
813'.6—dc23
                              2014001457

ISBN 978-1-4767-3387-6
ISBN 978-1-4767-3390-6 (pbk)
ISBN 978-1-4767-3391-3 (ebook)

For the Zeds

PROLOGUE

The Turnip and I have a history.

Many decades ago, when he was a little boy and his folks were newly split, my sister left him with our parents and came to Memphis to live with me for a short while. It was only two months and just the medicine she needed, quite frankly, but he has held it against me ever since. It seems Sis and I prodded at this still-sore spot three years ago, when we sold our respective homes, pooled our resources, and purchased this new place, with its senior-friendly amenities—No steps to enter! Grab bars everywhere!—and traditional Queen Anne architecture. I thought the Turnip would be glad I moved up North to be with her rather than the other way around, but instead he is as resentful as ever.

Sis and I are still in our pajamas when the Turnip arrives with lunch. We've been up for hours, but it is a fog of a morning—our bodies still making the slow cruise-ship U-turn back to Eastern time, our machine-brewed coffee both comfortingly familiar and suddenly pedestrian. We have only just returned from Bologna, where we visited her granddaughter, Riley, who is spending a semester abroad studying illustration against the wishes of her father, the Turnip. No doubt he is here not only to make sure the old ladies made it back in one piece but also to learn a few secondhand details about Riley's plans for the future. I say if he really wanted to know, he should have gone with us and gotten it from the horse's mouth.

"Your mail came," says the Turnip. He hands me the stack, and I start going through it with much more interest than I really have. This is how I usually handle his visits—I occupy myself with some mundane task to keep our interactions to a minimum.

While the Turnip pummels Sis with questions—Was Riley seeing anyone? What did she say about her summer plans? Is she still talking (God forbid!) graduate school?—I sort the mail into piles, one for bills, another for more interesting stuff. The circulars go directly into the recycling bin. As you might expect, the bills stack up quickly while the interesting stuff remains thin. Nobody mails interesting stuff anymore. Only toward the end of the pile do I find something worth opening. It is plain white and high-quality stock—clearly a card or invitation of some sort. A wedding, maybe? No, the return address says PWHF, which has to be a business of some sort. Only one way to find out.

I slip the letter opener in just as Sis throws up her hands. "If you really wanted to know so much, why didn't you just go with us?"

"That," he says, "would have been a tacit endorsement of this cock-amamie dream of hers."

That kind of statement is exactly why I can't attempt interactions with the Turnip. Is Riley likely to find fame and fortune as an illustrator? Probably not. But what is the point of youth other than to dream big and go for broke? Goodness knows I did. Life is long. There is plenty of time for pragmatism.

Sis and the Turnip agree to disagree and start setting up lunch—cheesesteaks, the last thing I need—while I get my first good look at this invitation:

THE SWEETHEART

You are cordially invited to the 12th annual
Professional Wrestling Hall of Fame induction banquet

Honoring Sandor Szabo, Dick Shikat, Bill Watts, Baron Von
Raschke, The Assassins (Jody Hamilton and Tom Renesto),
Tito Santana, Dick Murdoch, J. J. Dillon, Joyce Grable, Mimi
Hollander, and El Santo

Saturday, May 18, 2013 at
Holiday Inn
308 Comrie Avenue
Johnstown, NY 12095
7:00 PM TO 10:00 PM

"*Professional Wrestling Hall of Fame induction banquet?*" says the
Turnip, close to my ear. I had no idea he was looking over my shoulder.
"Why would anybody send that to you?"

"They probably thought I was somebody else," I say in a way I hope
sounds tossed off.

"I don't think so. Look," he says, snatching it from me and turning
it over. "Dear Leigh—"

"Give me that," I say, snatching it back and scanning down to the
end of the handwritten note for the signature: Mimi. I put the invitation in the pocket of my bathrobe. I'll read the rest later, when the
Turnip is gone.

"You don't know everything about your aunt Leigh," says Sis. She is
forever pestering me to make peace with the Turnip, so it is a nice surprise to find her on my side for once.

He takes a seat and claims a sandwich. "Maybe one day she will do
me the great honor of enlightening me." He takes a big bite and chews
in silence. I am almost moved to explain myself to him. But then I hear
his voice in my head saying "cockamamie dream" and decide it is better
to keep my cards close.

3

Soon enough, Sis and the Turnip return to their conversation, which lets me slip out of the kitchen and into the bedroom, where I can read the rest of the note in privacy:

Dear Leigh,

Don't you think our old pal Gwen Davies ought to make an appearance on my big night? She is one of the few among us who can still put on a suit and look respectable. I say it's time to let all that old shit go and have some fun. Because it all worked out, didn't it? I'm happy, you're happy, everybody's happy. Let's not let too much more time pass before we get together. We're not getting any younger.

Yours in sports,
Mimi

Gwen Davies—now that is a name I haven't heard in a while. Life is funny that way. One day, someone means the world to you, and then, before you know it, you've been out of touch for years. Truth be told, I don't know if *our old pal* is around anymore. And even if she can be found, I'm not sure I have it in me to find her. Talk about history. My issues with the Turnip pale in comparison. But Mimi is as old and dear a friend as I have in this world, and this is her big day. If she wants Gwen to be there, I should probably suck it up and see what I can do.

I get dressed in my walking clothes and fill a water bottle in the kitchen sink while the Turnip tells his mother that this afternoon, he has an appointment to tour a place for sale in the old neighborhood. There's been some new construction in the area, and with it all the usual hopes and fears of gentrification. Too soon to place bets, if you ask me, but the Turnip, who has been ridiculously nostalgic about this pocket of the city ever since we sold the family home, seems ready to double down. I head toward the door.

"Look at you," says Sis. She sits at the kitchen table, her fingers laced around what might well be her fourth cup of coffee. "We haven't been home for a day yet, and already you're back in action."

"You know me," I say. "I always do my best thinking when I walk."

"What do you need to think about?"

I shouldn't have said that. Sis doesn't know as much about my past as she lets on, but she knows enough. If I don't say something to ease her mind, she will fret the whole time I am gone. It would be easier if the Turnip wasn't here, but he is, and he doesn't seem to be going anywhere soon.

"Mimi wants Gwen Davies to come to her induction ceremony."

"And what do you think of that idea?"

"I think I'm going to look for her. That's what."

"Is that so?" she asks, propping her feet on a nearby seat. "Just how do you plan to do that?"

"I don't know. Same way you look for anything that's lost, I guess. Retrace your steps."

"Sure you don't want to stay for dessert?" says the Turnip, holding out a box of MoonPies. In our family, there has been a long-standing debate over which snack cake is superior: the Turnip's choice, Butterscotch Krimpets, or mine, chocolate MoonPies. I more or less won this argument a few years ago when the Tastykake factory closed its doors for good, but this is the closest I have come to receiving a concession. He's making an effort. This is not lost on me.

"Leave me one," I say. "I'll eat it when I get back."

"Suit yourself." He drops the box on the table and gathers the empty plates.

That's my cue. I give a little wave, head out the door, and take off down the sidewalk. I have no idea where I am going, but at least I know where to start.

Okay, Gwen. Let's see if I can dig you up.

ONE

You want to be somebody else. You don't know who this person might be; all you know is that she should be confident, beautiful, *beloved*. This isn't what makes your story special—every lonely, awkward teenage girl in the history of American adolescence has wanted to be someone else. But unlike those girls, you, Leonie Putzkammer, will have the marvelous opportunity to wholly reinvent yourself: a new name, a new persona, a new life. Right now, you don't aspire to anything better than the likes of ultrapopular Cynthia Riley, your next-door neighbor and once-upon-a-time best friend, but your life is about to take an amazing turn, one that will transform you (albeit fleetingly) into Gorgeous Gwen Davies—aka The Sweetheart. None of the peaks and valleys that follow this extraordinary year in your life (and believe me, there will be plenty) will come close to the height and depth you are about to reach. And it all starts now, one Saturday afternoon in April 1953, as you are quietly living your unassuming life in the sooty, evenly plotted city of Philadelphia, when you open the front door to the row house you share with your father and find high school teen queen Cynthia standing there, a lock of hair twisted around a finger.

Your response—startled brow, parted mouth—betrays your amazement. It's been a long time. During your early girlhoods, you were the best of friends: brushing and braiding each other's hair, wearing matching jumpers, sharing a crush on Frankie Laine. When your father, Franz, had to work a late shift rubbing powdered color into hats at the Stetson factory, you trucked over to Cynthia's in your pajamas for an evening of Truth or Dare?, séances (your long-dead mother was frequently summoned, but, to your heartbreak, never appeared), and all-night giggling. One afternoon a week, at the insistence of your father, a former Turner himself, you went to tumbling classes at Turner Hall to build *a sound mind in a sound body,* and when you returned home, Cynthia would run from her own row house, take you into her arms, and cry, "Darling, I thought you'd *never* come home!" as if you were a homecoming soldier and she your long-suffering war bride. Once, the two of you even conspired to unite Franz with Cynthia's divorced mother. You cared little for the facts: your father strongly disapproved of Ms. Riley's many admirers, and Ms. Riley considered herself much too full of life to entertain the thought of a sad old widower like Franz Putzkammer. You could only see the rightness of this vision, so you felt assured your *Lisa and Lottie*–inspired adventure would bring you all together into nuclear perfection and officially solidify your sisterhood.

Anyone looking at the two of you standing on the stoop would have a hard time imagining you as sisters. Now in her senior year, Cynthia is petite, with approachable girl-next-door beauty: dark, snappy curls and a tiny, squeezable wazoo. Beneath her fuzzy sweaters bounce pert apple-sized breasts. It's an enviable body, easy to drive and poised for privilege. With it, she manages a flock of friends and two boyfriends— dreamy Freddy, who is high school royalty in his own right, the kind of boy you might cast as the romantic lead in the perfect version of your life, and the older, more enigmatic Wally, whom you sometimes see parked down the block, his dog tags hanging from the rearview mirror, his tattooed forearms resting on the steering wheel as he rolls cigarettes, biding his time until Cynthia can make her escape.

Compared to Cynthia, you are a Viking. Your Nordic blond hair swings behind you in a waist-length ponytail. You are obnoxiously tall: five foot eleven, to be exact, and nearly all of it leg. Your breasts are frightfully ample. When they arrived four years ago, your father insisted you take the only bedroom of your row house and stopped making eye contact with you, which made the distance between you that much more difficult to bridge. You are alarmed by what you see in the mirror, an image as lurid as the Peter Driben illustration taped up in the locker next to yours at school, your body parts best described by sound effects: *va-va-voom!* gams, *a-woo-gah!* breasts, and a total effect of *homina homina!* This body is incongruent. You are a pensive girl who listens to Georgia Gibbs, reads dime-store detective stories, and likes Ike. Your speed is slow; you shouldn't look fast. You don't know how to handle the catty gossip and taunts your body provokes other than to shrink away. In the hallways at school, you walk hunched over, eyes downcast, a large stack of books ever present in your arms. You are a mouse inside of a tiger.

You don't know if there's a connection between the changes in your bodies and your relationship to Cynthia; you only know that after your mutual dream of sisterhood faded, so did your actual sisterly union. In these last four years, the two of you have gradually disentangled from each other's lives. You were too old to need supervision while your father worked late and not young enough to avoid more household duties, while Cynthia's hormonally driven extracurricular activities frequently led her away from the neighborhood—and from you. In other relationships, you will do the leaving, but this time, you are the one who has been left behind. You are now at a stage of being only acquaintances, your communications reduced to passing waves and quick hellos. She usually grants you this much, but you always wait to be acknowledged by Cynthia first; you do not want to take the chance that your salutation will hang in the air, unrequited.

But now, here is Cynthia on your doorstep for what might be the first time in years. You hope that your initial expression (here it is again: brow up, mouth open) is still there, revealing only your curiosity and surprise. You pray the torrent of excitement that courses through you remains invisible.

"Say, Leonie," says Cynthia, "I was wondering. You still know how to do a back handspring?"

Do you know how to do a back handspring? True, you haven't been to Turner Hall in years—tumbling was a lot easier when you were shorter and less curvy—but every once in a while in your physical education class, you horse around on the mats enough to knock the rust off. Tumbling is the one activity that allows you to harness your body's potential and power, the one physical arena where you are confident and in command. Without tumbling, you might not have the coordination, let alone the courage, for all that is to come.

"You know it." You barely recognize your own voice; you sound uncharacteristically self-assured.

"Great!" Cynthia barrels into the house, as if she held as much dominion over it—and you—as she did four years ago. "You *have* to teach me."

You should be taken aback by her audacity, but instead you feel bloated with joy. Might this be a reigniting of your friendship? You know better than to be optimistic, but it's too late: you're already imagining a rekindling or, better yet, a fresh start.

You close the door, point to the coffee table, and say, "Help me move this out of the way."

After two hours in the cramped space of your living room going through the same motions—Cynthia holding her arms over her head, you by her side with one hand on her navel, the other on her spine, coaxing the anxious girl back, back, back—Cynthia is no better than she was when she first knocked on your door. Even after hundreds of attempts, several near injuries and lots of giggling, she still can't land it. For her last effort, she jumps but then panics, her arms backstroking through the air as she tries to right herself. You lunge forward, but you are a beat late: she falls through your arms and lands with a thud on her back. Cynthia may lead most of your high school around by the nose, but she is no match for gravity. You're secretly glad you still have this one advantage over her. Besides, anything that brings her back down to earth puts her that much closer to you.

"Forget it. It's no use," she says, remaining flat on the ground.

"Come on." You reach down so Cynthia can take your hand, but she is right. Still, you're enjoying yourself; you're not ready for this to be over. "Don't give up yet," you beg, hoping you sound encouraging but not desperate.

"I can't do it. Not unless you loan me your body."

"Are you kidding?" you say, taking a seat on the floor and stretching your atrociously long legs out in front of you. "I would trade bodies with you in a heartbeat."

"Really?" Cynthia lifts herself up onto her elbows, incredulous, and pushes a finger right into your breast. "You'd take my bird chest in exchange for those gazongas?"

"You can have them," you say, although you shy away from the interrogating finger. You are terribly unpracticed in sorority. "Don't forget, you'd be stuck with these stork legs, too." You fold over at the torso, running your arms down the length of the offending body parts to emphasize their monstrosity. "You'd hover over Freddy on the dance floor."

This, Leonie, you know all too well. At the sock hops you dared attend, you sat alone and swayed, the boys too frightened of having to rest their heads on your shoulder (or worse, your chest) to ask you to dance. Cynthia never sits at a sock hop. On top of her likable, got-the-world-on-a-string vibe, the girl can cut a mean rug, which has earned her a card-carrying membership on *Bob Horn's Bandstand* and a minor degree of celebrity. She and Freddy's last period of the day is study hall, so they can leave early and catch the subway to WFIL's studio B on Market Street. Freddy is not only her dance partner but also, and more importantly, the other half of *Cynthia and Freddy*. It is a favorite romance of *Bandstand* viewers, a bug-in-a-rug courtship born of the show and played out on the airwaves. This, you learned shortly after Cynthia usurped your afternoon, is what this handspring lesson is all about: Freddy wants her to learn the move so they can make a splash during the next *Bandstand* dance competition.

"Puh-lease," Cynthia says. "Freddy can bite it. I can't believe I even went for this birdbrained idea of his. Besides, I'm getting sick of *Bandstand*. It's *soooooooo* square. Those old geezers should take their heads out of the sand and pay attention to what the kids in this city are *really* listening to. I'll tell you one thing, Leonie. It ain't Eddie Fisher and Georgia Gibbs."

"What's wrong with Georgia Gibbs?"

"What's wrong with . . . see? We *should* switch. You and Freddy can dance your hearts out to that razzmatazz." She cocks her head; it seems a thought has come to her. She sits up, tenting her knees and wrapping her arms around them. "You really like Georgia Gibbs?"

You shrug, self-conscious. You think Georgia Gibbs is the cat's pajamas, but you are loath to admit it now. "I think she's all right."

"She's going to be on the show Wednesday. If you want to see her, you can be my guest. My way of making up for wasting your afternoon."

Your first impulse: disappointment. You certainly don't think of the afternoon as wasted, and you don't want Cynthia to, either. But slowly you begin to recognize the potential of what's been laid out in front of you—*Bandstand*, Freddy, an up-close encounter with Georgia Gibbs, and, best of all, another afternoon with Cynthia—and you swell with delight. Maybe your initial optimism wasn't misplaced; maybe this is a new beginning. You are young and still believe in such things. Just in case, you cover your bets and play it cool. "I don't know. I may have plans."

"Oh, who are you kidding? The only time you ever leave this house is to go to school or buy groceries."

"That's not true," you say.

"Geez, Leonie, lighten up." Cynthia stands up, smooths out her skirt. "If you can't go, you can't go. I just thought—"

"I can go," you sputter, jumping to your feet. "I just remembered. My plans are for Thursday, not Wednesday."

"Then, it's settled." She has one hand on the doorknob already. "I'll come get you from your last class. Dress like a good girl, no tight skirt or nothing. And thanks for trying to help me today, even though it was a lost cause."

You try to think of a way to entice her to stick around for a while, but you come up empty. You have nothing to bait a trap with, nothing to offer but your wide-yawning loneliness.

"It was fun," you venture.

Cynthia laughs. "You got some weird idea of fun, Leonie, but okay," she says, and is gone.

On Tuesday afternoon, the day before your visit to *Bandstand,* you rush home, climb out of your school clothes, and hide your embarrassing legs away in dungarees before you flip the dial to WFIL. The television—a Philco with a seventeen-inch picture tube and mahogany console—was an uncharacteristically imprudent purchase by your father last Christmas. It took nearly an hour of futzing with the rabbit ears to get a reasonably clear picture, which made you question the whole endeavor, but then your father patted your shoulder and said, "What do you say,

Leonie? Maybe now you'll come out of your room once in a while." You stared at the screen, seeing nothing, only marveling that your father had not only wanted you closer but had done something about it.

There is Cynthia, on the dance floor, under the lights. She is a peach: soft dark curls springing from her head, legs kicking out from her full skirt as she jitterbugs to Ray Anthony and His Orchestra. Together, she and Freddy, in his flat-front pants and preppy vest, are Cute with a capital C. The day will come when you will understand what Cynthia was talking about, how she could have all that she has and still feel unsatisfied, but at your tender stage, it is hard to believe. You would salivate with envy except that tomorrow, you'll be out there, too. You prepare by grabbing the handle of the refrigerator and pretending you're in front of the cameras, stepping up and sugar pushing with your own perfect complement. In this daydream version of yourself, you have an easy smile and a pair of manageable, just-right legs. Your whole life is made in the shade.

Seventy-five minutes later, this daydream ends, and you realize you've let your *Bandstand* fantasy take too much of your time. You have to rush to get dinner in the oven so you can finish your geometry homework and have a meal on the table before your father gets home. Shortly after you inherited the bedroom, you assumed this job without ceremony or complaint. It is, to your mind, a tedious chore, but also a fair exchange. The person who wins the bread deserves the small reward of a hot meal. Tonight, you're making beer-braised beef brisket with potatoes, a real stomach-padding meal and Franz's unequivocal favorite. This particular meal has purposes beyond nourishment: you haven't told your father about *Bandstand* yet. Franz has strong and sometimes idiosyncratic notions about what people should and shouldn't do, and you can't begin to guess what side of the line *Bandstand* might be on, so you do everything you can to make sure he's primed for leniency. Besides, you know tomorrow you won't have enough time to get home from the studio and get dinner together, and though your father balks at leftovers, he never turns his nose up at a second helping of his favorite meal.

You put the brisket in the oven and check the clock again. As you feared, you haven't left yourself much time. You worry that you may have preempted all the goodwill you hoped to build by mistiming the meal. Sure enough, when your father gets home, washes his dye-stained hands, and kisses your forehead—a gesture that requires him to raise himself up on his toes—the table is empty.

"Sorry," you say. "Dinner's going to be a little while longer."

Your father nods, but you feel guilty. This is the worst possible night for dinner to be late, and not just because of *Bandstand.* On Tuesday nights, the two of you like to eat early and get the dishes cleared away in time to watch Franz's newsmagazine show *See It Now,* and then your favorite, *I've Got a Secret,* where panelists like Kitty Carlisle and troublemaker Henry Morgan (who works close to blue at a time when blue can get you blacklisted) try to guess the secrets of the celebrity contestants.

"Why don't we eat in front of the television tonight," you offer. You smile brightly—maybe too brightly. He squints at you, suspicious. "Just this once," you say. To slather it on even thicker, you take a can of beer from the fridge and twice plunge the church key into its flat top before holding it out to him. Franz angles his head to look at you sideways. It takes some effort to meet his gaze, keep your grip on the cold beer, and maintain your neutral expression, but somehow you manage to pull it off. You're not going to blow it—not yet, anyway. Finally, he takes the beer from your hand.

"Okay," he says. "Just this once." He heads to the living room, plops in his chair, and takes a long, steady pull from his beer before he turns on the television. In the privacy of the kitchen, you breathe a sigh of relief.

• • •

Half an hour later, dinner is ready. You hand your father his plate and take a seat on the couch, the television glowing in front of the both of you, a modern hearth.

"This looks terrific," Franz says.

"I'm glad you think so," you say. You have heard these words countless times, and yet they still send a ripple of sadness through you. You do not think of your mother often, but when you do, it is usually in a moment like this, when you are accepting a compliment that should be hers. You don't have many memories of her; you were so young when she died. The most persistent one is from an afternoon some months before her death, when your father came home from the factory and surprised her with a hatbox. She sat up in bed to open it and pulled from its depths a brown felt hat trimmed with black grosgrain: a Musette, from Stetson's Freedom Fashions line. She placed the hat on her head at a jaunty angle and admired herself in the vanity mirror. "Look at that," she said. "I look like Betty Hutton." Even at your young age, you understood that she was being ironic, and yet her words seemed true and always will.

Perhaps it is this sadness that makes the possibility of another, much more trivial loss occur to you: what if your father says no? This had not crossed your mind before now; you had not imagined him denying you one afternoon of ordinary adolescence. What if, after this terrific meal, after all the terrific meals, he forbids you from going? You have never withheld anything from your father, but this is a risk you cannot take. It is in this moment that you decide you won't tell him about your plans for tomorrow afternoon after all. Even on the off chance that he makes it home before you tomorrow evening and has to put his own foil-wrapped plate in the oven to warm, he wouldn't begin to guess that it was the trivial pleasures of music and dance that took you away from home. From your favorite quiz show, you have developed this understanding of secrets: they are most easily kept when they run completely counter to expectations (Boris Karloff is afraid of mice) or are so obvious as to be invisible, as plain as the nose on your face (Desi Arnaz? He loves Lucy). Your secret, Leonie, will be both: a self-conscious girl seeking a spotlight; a teenager acting like a teenager.

Before Edward R. Murrow can usher in the show in his distinctive way ("This . . . is *See It Now.*") and before the two of you dig into your terrific-looking plates, you bow your heads, as you do every night, so that Franz can thank Almighty God for his job, this food, your health, and each other. You tack on a silent addendum: for tomorrow to give you a taste of the life you've been missing, a life that reunites you with Cynthia Riley, a life that more closely resembles hers.

The next afternoon, Cynthia, true to her word, rescues you from your last class of the day so that you can accompany her and Freddy to studio B, where there is already a line of kids at the door, all of them white: twelve-year-olds in too much makeup and their mother's padded girdles, Catholic schoolgirls with sweaters over their uniforms so that only their Peter Pan collars are exposed. At the door, a short, stocky doorman sends a boy away for not wearing a tie. "How can I expect you to behave right when you don't dress right?" he asks.

When the three of you reach the door, bypassing the line, you hover in the background while Cynthia and Freddy flash their membership cards.

"This is our friend Leonie," says Cynthia.

You are a steadfast rule follower. You've heeded Cynthia's warning and worn a full skirt, and you ditched your chewing gum a block ago, per Freddy's instructions. The doorman, a bulldog in uniform, still frowns with disapproval. "Your skirt seems a little short."

"It's not," you say, perhaps too quickly. "I'm a little tall."

"C'mon," says Cynthia, hinting at a smile. Her smile is a weapon and she knows it. "Give her a break."

"I still say it's too short, but for you, I can bend the rules."

Cynthia shifts her smile into full throttle. You can hardly believe it is this easy. If you'd been forced to rely on your own charm, you'd be headed home along with no-tie boy.

The studio is surprisingly small, much smaller than it looks on television and not much bigger than your own row house. The live broadcast is shot by three cameras that have been strategically placed to make the dance floor look bigger, but from your behind-the-scenes vantage point, it seems they take up a good deal of space themselves. The seats for the audience are only pine bleachers, the record store merely a painted canvas. Bob Horn stands by his podium, a paper bib tucked into his collar, while a bored-looking woman applies powder to his already heavily made-up face. A few of the star couples mill about in pairs, holding hands.

"Disappointing, isn't it?" says Cynthia.

Not exactly, you think. True, you can already sense there's no way the day will live up to your hopes, but, you have to admit, your hopes were high. If nothing else, you suspect there's something to be gained from the experience, some lesson that can be learned only from fly-on-the-wall observation. And you don't want to appear ungrateful, so you say, "It's terrific."

Freddy puts his hands in his pockets. "Want me to introduce you to Bob?"

Before you can say yes, Cynthia rolls her eyes. "Why would she want to meet that old creep?"

"He's not a creep."

"Trust me, Leonie. You don't want to meet him. One look at your jugs and he'll be inviting you back to his dressing room for a sip of schnapps and one of his 'dance lessons.' "

You cross your arms reflexively. In the little time you've spent with Cynthia recently, there's been an unusual number of unabashed references to your breasts. "Maybe I should just try to get a good seat."

"Sure thing, Leonie. You don't want to get stuck in a corner for the big thrill of Miss Nibs in the flesh." Cynthia uses her index fingers to draw a square in the air.

Freddy lets out an exasperated huff. "Why do you have to be such a wet blanket?" He talks through gritted teeth and makes none of the wild hand gestures someone else in his position might; it seems he doesn't want the audience to guess there might be trouble in *Cynthia and Freddy* town. "Bob's a creep, the music's square. What about me? I guess I'm a jerk, too, right?"

"I don't think you're a jerk, Freddy," says Cynthia. "I just think you take all of this a little too seriously."

You take a step backward, out of the crossfire. Maybe if you inch your way to the bleachers, they won't notice your departure.

"I'm just trying to be professional," says Freddy.

"Good." Cynthia's all-charm smile comes back, fully powered. "You heard him, Leonie. If no one else asks you to dance, Freddy will, because he's a *professional*."

Freddy is obviously horrified by the idea, but he has boxed himself in. "Sure I will," he says obligingly. "I bet I won't have to, though. Someone will ask you to dance. I'm sure of it."

The two take their places with the other dancers by Bob's podium, leaving you to take a seat. A man wearing headphones quiets the audience. The lights on the bleachers dim while the dance floor brightens under the spotlights, and "Leap Frog," the show's theme song, signals the start of the program.

Seventy-five minutes is a long time to sit and watch other people dance, even when you're well rehearsed in that particular activity. By the time they get to "Bunny Hop," a novelty song that cues the teenage heartthrobs to take one another by the hips and wind around the confined dance floor in a series of bounces, your restlessness has grown to a full squirm. When Georgia Gibbs appears from backstage—the petite, big-voiced singer looking like her own little party in a strapless dress, her hair pulled back tight and secured with a flower—and launches into her mournful, vibrato-filled version of "Autumn Leaves," all the dancers pair up, lean into one another, and sway their little hearts out. You try to content yourself with swaying alone, in the dark, but even that, it seems, is too much. Someone behind you whispers, "Give it a rest, Stretch. Some of us are trying to watch." You freeze and try to make yourself as small as possible—and then, it gets worse.

The show breaks for commercial, and the room, spectators and dancers alike, quickly separates into cliques, all thoroughly engrossed in conversations. You have no one. You stare out at the dance floor, first at Freddy, who stands, hands in pockets, at the podium, chatting up a storm with Bob Horn and another boy, and then at Cynthia. She is at the center of an animated girl-gaggle, laughing and rolling her eyes. At one point, she looks up into the stands, and so you wave—*Here I am*—because who else could she be looking for? She sees you, you are certain of it, but she doesn't come over. She doesn't even bother to return your wave. Instead, she gives you an embarrassed little smile, wiggles her eyebrows, and then says something to the other girls that results in hearty laughter, perhaps not at your expense but it might as well be. You've done the one thing you've managed to avoid for years—made the opening gesture—and, just as you feared, it's fallen flat.

And you thought this experience would have something to teach you. What have you learned that you didn't already know? Some people are stars, and some people are spectators, and the general consensus is that you, dear girl, are the latter. You wish the show were over so you could just go home, where everyone seems to think you belong.

Toward the end, when it comes time for the popular Rate-a-Record spot, Bob Horn summons three people from the bleachers to his podium to offer their opinion on a new Essex 45: Bill Haley's "Crazy Man, Crazy." It's an adventurous choice for the show, as close to the burgeoning genre of rock 'n' roll (too loud, too fast, too black) as they've dared to go. Before the record begins to spin, Cynthia drops Freddy's hands, leaving him open-mouthed on the dance floor as she trots over to the bleachers to fetch a new dance partner, settling quickly on the rangy, easily accessible boy sitting in front of you.

"Now this is more like it," she says to you. "Freddy's coming for you, so get loose, Mother Goose."

You have no interest in dancing anymore—you don't want anyone's pity—but you don't see how you have any choice. Sure enough, Freddy represses his scowl, takes your hand, and leads you onto the dance floor.

"Let's keep it simple," he says. "Just follow me."

When the song begins to play, you try to oblige, but it's an effort. You're not an experienced dancer, but you can hold your own. The problem is that Freddy's lead isn't clear, a side effect of having one consistent dance partner, and the turns are awkward and sloppy because of your height. As a result, you step on his feet twice in the first minute. When you do it a third time, he doesn't bother to stifle his groan. Instead, he dances the two of you over to Cynthia and her partner and stage-whispers to the considerably taller guy, "Hey, fella. I think you're more this girl's height. Why don't we switch?"

The boy glances over, looks you up and down. Your heart's in your throat; you can taste it. "Get bent," he says to Freddy.

Your cheeks flush with mortification. "Freddy, we can just stop if you want. Let's just stop."

Freddy, clearly exasperated, pretends he doesn't hear you—obviously, that wouldn't be very *professional*—and makes a new plea, this time directly to Cynthia. "C'mon, C. Be reasonable. Let's switch."

Cynthia meets Freddy's eyes, her glare sharp enough to puncture. She seems to be weighing her options, an action that takes a torturous amount of time. Finally, she says, "Good idea." Before you know what is happening, Cynthia has disengaged from her partner, embraced not

Freddy but *you*, and led you into the middle of the dance floor, leaving the two guys standing next to each other in a daze.

"Get a load of their faces," Cynthia says, dancing you around so you can see. The tall boy appears stunned, but Freddy is clearly humiliated. Not only have you come out of this unscathed, but for once, you are positioned to look down on someone else's embarrassment. Oh, Leonie, isn't it simply delicious? You can't help yourself; you have to laugh.

"I know!" says Cynthia. "Isn't it a hoot?"

Cynthia's lead is more intuitive, more confident than Freddy's, remarkably, and the two of you fall into a surprisingly natural (although exaggerated) groove. The other dancers fall away until you are the only couple dancing amid the bewildered stares of your former partners, the wide eyes of the other dancers, and the dreamy grin of Bob Horn. Your blood is electric with alarm, but Cynthia radiates cool. Toward the end of the song, Cynthia guides you into the sweetheart position, and when you look down at your friend (and it does seem that she is your friend again), the two of you lock eyes, and she whispers, "Do it, Leonie!"

Ordinarily, you wouldn't do a thing except get out of the spotlight as quickly as possible, but you've somehow managed to absorb enough of Cynthia's confidence to do the unimaginable. After Cynthia spins you out, you break away and show off the one talent that you have and she does not by launching into a series of back handsprings. You go over one, two, three times, ending directly in front of one of the cameras, your arms in the air. A sound bursts out of the spectators and echoes riotously throughout the studio. It is a sound with a life of its own, its own heartbeat; a sound you find yourself craving the instant it begins to subside.

Here it is, Leonie: your defining moment. It will not last long (not in real time, at least), and soon you will be disciplined for it. The bulldog doorman will make it clear you are not to come back—you've gone and shown all of Philadelphia your bloomers, for goodness' sake—and your father, who will make it home ahead of you after all, will interrogate you until you confess, and then punish you with a week of disappointed silence. Even Cynthia the snake charmer won't walk away unscathed. Her membership card will be taken away, which will effectively end her relationship with Freddy. Of course, as the two of you walk home that evening, she will declare triumphantly, "I'm free!" but in the next month, she'll realize she's pregnant with Wally's baby. But your whole life pivots on this event. Perhaps you cannot yet articulate just who it is you want to be, but you know that when that person makes herself known, she will be accompanied by that sound, the music of thunderous applause.

TWO

Four months later, the performance still plays on a continuous loop in your memory. It is easily the wildest time in a life that has otherwise been a total drag, a state to which it has since returned and seems destined to remain. If not for this dread, you might have been unreceptive to your father's unusual proposal: on this hot night in August, your father comes home from work, sits in front of another dinner you have prepared for him, and announces that on the following evening, he wants the two of you to attend a wrestling match.

Your face betrays your surprise. Ordinarily, you would be thrilled to get an invitation of any sort from your father, but wrestling? If ever a thing should go against his sense of propriety, you would assume wrestling would be it. In response, Franz shrugs his shoulders, swallows his food. "Some of the Italian guys on the line really like this one guy who's wrestling tomorrow night. Apparently, he does these flips through the air." He makes demonstrative circles with his fork. "They say you've got to see him to believe him."

In a million years, you never would have guessed your father could be so easily persuaded to do something so frivolous. The only signal you've ever been able to read clearly is the one he uses when he seeks solitude, an itch that a man who has to sleep on his own couch doesn't often get to scratch: *If I turn the radio on, leave me alone.* And while your father remains a mystery to you, on rare occasions, as he unwinds to the sound of Rosemary Clooney or Perry Como and you are trapped in your bedroom, he turns up the radio and calls out, "This one's for you, Leonie."

Lately, you could use a little of that tenderness. You've seen Cynthia only once since that fateful *Bandstand* performance, when you were returning home from your new job, serving breakfast at a chromed-out diner on North Broad, a pie balanced on your fingertips. Cynthia and her mother were outside on the stoop. You offered your pie; they invited you in for coffee. Cynthia looked radiant, the luster of her hastily formed new life not yet tarnished. Ms. Riley, her hair in rollers, appeared weary and disappointed. Just months ago, it must have seemed Cynthia had heeded all her warnings and was barreling toward a brightly lit future. Instead, she was repeating the follies of her mother's youth. You put your hand on the barely protruding abdomen, which was as incomprehensible to you as the act from which it came, and congratulated your friend with as much sincerity as you could muster while Ms. Riley looked away. Returning home to an empty house, you wondered if the fixedness of Cynthia's course was in fact worse than your own rudderless existence. It seemed you were headed toward nothing at all. So now, even though you would probably take more pleasure in reading a book than watching a wrestling match, you agree to go along for the ride, appreciative of your father's gesture and open to anything out of the ordinary.

The next evening, the two of you pack into the arena at 46th and Market with thousands of others. Wafting through the densely populated, un-air-conditioned auditorium are the manly aromas of spilt beer and Brylcreem. There is little light—the better to focus the audience on the spotlit ring, you figure—and you have to force your way through the crowd of men and the occasional pencil-skirted woman to find seats. When you find two together, you start to squat into one, but Franz stops you with his arm and uses a handkerchief to wipe it off. The gesture strikes you as both old-fashioned and dear, and it fills you with tenderness. When he's done, he motions with his arm—*Now, you can sit*—and you follow his command with as much elegance as you possess.

The first match on the card is the midgets. The one with the scruffy beard and blue briefs is Short John Silver; in the other corner is the hairy-chested and unfortunately named Willie Weeman; the two men toss each other over their shoulders while the spectators laugh and shout insults and obscenities. At one point, the referee, a giant by comparison, separates the wrestlers by palming the top of each of their heads while they swing viciously at the air. And if this sight, and the crowd's responsive chuckles, weren't enough to break your heart, this finishes the job: just two seats ahead of you, one man turns to his friend and whispers something in his ear, and the friend responds by silently holding up his right hand and measuring an inch of space with his finger and thumb, sending both of them into spasms of laughter.

You press your fingers to your worried mouth and turn to your father. Franz continues to stare ahead at the ring, but his mouth hangs open. "Maybe this wasn't such a good idea," he says.

It will be disappointing if you have to cut short this rare time together, but you would be alarmed if your father drew any other conclusion.

It takes another five minutes for Willie Weeman to pin his opponent's shoulders. The ref pounds the canvas while Short John Silver's legs bicycle above him. Mercifully, Willie holds the pin. The match is over.

Franz lifts his hat off of his lap and places it on his head. "You want to get out of here?"

You should say yes. You *want* to say yes. So, why don't you? Perhaps you are hoping this night can still be redeemed, perhaps you want to believe the audience can redeem itself. So, instead you say, "Let's just finish out the card. We haven't seen that guy you were talking about yet." Your shoulders lift and drop. "Who knows? Maybe he'll change our minds."

That guy you are referring to, Leonie, the headliner for tonight's event, is none other than high flyer Antonino Rocca. Rocca, you will later learn, is an Argentinean of Italian descent, a combination that makes him a big draw with two of the Northeast's largest ethnic populations. He might rightly be credited with reviving wrestling in the New York territory. He regularly sells out Madison Square Garden, often the biggest draw on the card even when there's a headlining championship bout, and yet he will never win his own world belt; the promoters fear that the very thing that makes him a hero in this region, his ethnicity, simply won't translate in the National Wrestling Alliance's two biggest territories: the heartland and the Southeast. When he climbs into the ring, you decide that he's built something like Burt Lancaster—broad in the shoulders yet narrow-waisted—but with hairier legs, bushier eyebrows, and a more sizable schnoz. His feet are bare. When his name is announced, the large Italian contingent stomps its feet; their collective scream is passionate and primal.

If anyone can redeem the evening, this is the man. Two people who appreciate the athleticism of tumbling can't help but be mesmerized by someone who can leap into the air and deliver back-to-back slaps to his opponent's face *with his feet,* which causes Franz to leap onto his own.

"Did you see that?" he says.

"Yeah." You stand up beside him, along with most of the crowd. "Yeah, I did."

From that moment on, you and your father are transfixed, balanc-

ing on the tips of your toes to take in as much as you can over the sea
of heads. At one point, Rocca drapes his opponent—a man, it should
be added, of considerable size—over his shoulders, spins around, and
helicopters him into the air, and then slips artfully out of the way before his opponent crashes to the ground. The two of you howl with
approval.

After this, it becomes difficult to see anything. Some of the women
have taken positions on the shoulders of their husbands and boyfriends; others stand on the seats of their chairs. You stare at the seat
of your own chair, but the echoes of your past prevent you from taking
the first step. *Give it a rest, Stretch. Some of us are trying to watch.* You
would remain on the ground if not for your father, who sees you waver-
ing and makes a face.

"What's stopping you?" he says. "Go ahead."

Franz offers you his hand, and you take it, squeezing it a little as you
let him bear your weight. He steadies you until you are in position, and
then you return the favor and help him climb onto his own seat. The
two of you raise your heads above the crowd just in time to see Rocca
work the ropes for his finishing move, which happens so quickly, you
can hardly tell what occurs: all you see is Rocca leaping from the top
turnbuckle *over* his opponent's head, and a series of legs going over
heads, until the hapless goof is pinned to the mat. And then, miracle of
miracles, your father momentarily forgets to feel self-conscious about
being physically close to you. He puts his arm around your shoulder
and pulls you roughly to his side with the congratulatory one-armed
hug of a true fan, which would stun you if you weren't so transported
yourself.

After the match, the two of you walk out of the auditorium to the
subway and hop onto the Broad Street line, talking nonstop for the
entire ride in excited, sputtering half sentences ("Did you see the . . . ?"
"Yeah, but how about when he . . . ?"). You get off at your stop and
walk a block or so before your father asks if you want to go back to the

subway station and wait for the rain to pass, and you turn your face to the sky.

"It is raining, isn't it?" you say. "I hadn't noticed."

Franz smiles and drapes his jacket over your head, and you clutch it closed beneath your chin. By the time you walk the ten blocks to your home, you are both soaking wet. But you hardly notice: you are both still busy reliving all of Rocca's amazing feats. For the rest of your life, you will remember this conversation as the longest and most intimate the two of you ever shared.

You are still reveling in the moment the next morning, when local wrestling promoter Salvatore Costantini steps into your diner in search of breakfast. For the time being, you want nothing more than to do it again—to sit in the audience, your father by your side. But this man will give you reason to dream much bigger. As it happens, you arrive at his booth—blue-and-white uniform crisp, ponytail swinging—to drop off a plate of scrapple just as he finds the article about the bout in the paper, along with a photo of Rocca midair, legs and arms spread, fingers touching toes.

"Isn't he amazing?" you say, pointing to the photo. "Were you at the match?"

Costantini looks up from the paper with an expression that is starting to become all too familiar. This figure of yours, the one that keeps the boys your age away, also has a way of attracting the attention of a particular kind of man. Your body is both a force field and a magnet; you're not sure which is preferable, but in this case, it serves you anyway: Costantini might have given you a curt response to shoo you away so he could get back to his paper—he is surely anxious to see how the match played in the *Inquirer*—but it seems he can't resist the opportunity to impress a pretty girl.

"It was my promotion," he says, grinning.

"No kidding!" you say. "You want a warm-up?"

Of course Costantini wants a warm-up. When you return with the coffee pot, he says, "You look familiar. Have I seen you before?"

In the few short months you've worked here, you've heard this line and dozens of others enough times to see through them. You were prepared to like the guy for putting on a good show; now you decide your initial impression was on the money, so you say, "I don't think so," and turn on your heels. But then Costantini snaps his fingers loudly, which can only mean (a) he is being genuine, and (b) the answer has come to him.

"I know where! You were on that show, with the dancing. I remember you—you and the other girl, doing the flips."

"Yeah, that was me," you say, more than a little embarrassed.

"You were really something!" he says, wagging his finger at you. "Where'd you learn that? You some kind of athlete?"

"Why?" you ask, still suspicious. "You writing a book?"

Why? Because Costantini is always on the hunt for talent, not only for his Pennsylvania territory, where it is still illegal for women to wrestle, but in DC, which is decidedly pro-woman. And a woman like you, a woman who can get attention with both her looks and her physical skill, might be just what he needs to lure spectators away from rival DC promoter Vince McMahon. Costantini slurps his coffee, his eyes fixed on you.

"No," he says, "but I do think you could be a wrestler yourself."

This statement is so ludicrous that at first, you laugh it off. But his expression doesn't change; it seems he's serious. You listen to the sentence again in your head, first breaking it down into digestible parts—*I, think, you, wrestler*—and then putting the parts back together again. He thinks you could be a wrestler.

"So, women wrestle, too?"

"Not around here they don't, but in lots of other places they do."

For all the pleasure last night brought you, at no point did you imagine yourself in the scene. But when Costantini plants the seed, it quickly sprouts. Why couldn't you be the one in the ring, on the ropes? You are in need of direction. Maybe this is the way to go. "And you think I could do it?"

"Not everyone can move like you did on that show," he says. He pulls a money clip from his pocket and peels off a twenty-dollar bill. When you tell him you'll be right back with the check, he holds up a hand to stop you. "This isn't for the food," he says, slapping the bill on the table. "It's for you, if you can show me another one of those flips." He taps his finger on the table and smiles. "Let's see it."

You don't know whether to congratulate or kick yourself. If you take a spill in front of the regulars and the line cooks, you will never live it down. And you're still not sure about this guy; you don't know what he's after. But twenty dollars is a lot of bread, more than you bring home most weeks. So go ahead. Step back from the booth; slide your tray onto the counter. Warn the nearby diners to stay in their seats. Breathe in, breathe out, and then bend your knees, swing your arms, and go over, body arched, muscles strained, skirt opening to the world, before coming right side up again and landing squarely on your saddle shoes. Hold your arms up in a V: *victory*. Revel in the applause.

The only person who doesn't cheer audibly is Costantini, who slurps his coffee and stares shamelessly. After accepting the congratulations of the diners, you return to his booth to collect your money.

"Impressive," he says, handing over the twenty. While you pocket the dough, he reaches inside his coat and retrieves a fountain pen and a notebook, which he flips open. "Do you think you could write your name and address down here for me? I want to tell someone I know about you."

"I can't tell you where I live," you say, thankful that, despite your excitement, you can still exercise some common sense. "I just met you."

"How about just your name, then?" This much, you can manage.

You write your name in your clear, precise hand. He attempts to read it aloud, and you correct him twice before he gives up.

"Yowzah," he says. "If you do become a wrestler, first thing we're doing is changing your name."

"We are?"

"Young lady, I can see you signing a lot of autographs, and trust me," he says, waving the little pad in the air, "when that happens, you're going to want a lot less name."

The days that follow are the longest and slowest of your life. Wrestling, it now seems, may be the solution to all of life's problems. One, it could give the sole bedroom of the little row house back to your father, a gift you aren't sure how you might give him otherwise. Two, it's *something*. What have you got going now? A whole lot of *nothing,* that's what. But most of all, the memory of Rocca's riveting performance is still fresh enough for you to imagine that this could be more than something: it just might be *it*. If you never hear from Costantini or his friend, you may never recover.

Thankfully, by the end of the week, a large envelope postmarked Otherside, Florida, arrives at the diner. When the owner hands it to you, eyebrow raised, you offer no explanation before shoving it into your bag, hurrying home, and ripping it open in the privacy of your bedroom. Inside is a letter from Mr. Joe Pospisil, trainer, manager, and proprietor of the Pospisil School for Lady Grappling, in which he dangles the possibility of your coming to the Florida Panhandle (on a trial basis, of course) to learn to wrestle so that you might join the pantheon of lady grapplers he has personally trained and managed. In addition to outlining the careers of the most notable figures (Kat Fever, Screaming Mimi Hollander, and, of course, The Ragin' Cajun), he has included a half-dozen publicity shots of wrestlers he manages: strong, beautiful ladies in pinup attire—bathing suits, platform heels. Some flex biceps and smile, their mouths stained with lipstick; others stand with their hands on their hips, staring aggressively back at whoever dares look their way. The most mesmerizing of the lot (not one of his girls, he admits, but meant to inspire) is photographed in this latter pose: a petite, brawny brunette with a deep V in the front of her suit, upswept bangs, a cleft in her chin, slightly pointed ears, and a large belt around her waist, a trophy that "with hard work and a little luck, might someday be yours."

This, you will soon learn, is Mildred Burke, the former (and, by some accounts, current) Women's World Champion. True enough, the belt—a reported twenty-four-karat-gold accessory studded with seven diamonds, six amethysts, and four sapphires and weighing roughly the same as a four-month-old child—is still in her physical possession, as it has been for nearly two decades, but it is currently at the heart of a fierce custody battle. Make no mistake: Mildred Burke is one tough old broad. She is a tenacious road warrior, spending up to six nights a week defending her title, all the while suffering nose fractures, knee injuries, and the loosening and subsequent removal of *all of her teeth*. But in anything as duplicitous as wrestling, it takes more than grit—or talent, for that matter—to be a champion. Burke has kept the title this long for one reason, and one reason only: she's married to Billy Wolfe, her manager. Wolfe had a vested interest in keeping his wife on top and enough force to make it so. But now, after years of exploitation and public humiliation, Burke has finally decided to part ways with him, which has led to fierce contentions over the belt and caused an already dubious championship to become even more suspect.*

But it will be a long time before you know this history, or under-stand anything resembling the truth about wrestling. What matters now is that in this image, all of your vague longings find their form. You tape Mildred's glossy to the back of your bedroom door, a place

---

* In wrestling, even the asterisks have asterisks.

where it should not draw your father's attention but can continue to inspire. Now you know who you want to be. You want to be the champion.

Last but not least, the letter invites you to answer a few questions in order to see "if you have what it takes" to be a professional wrestler. The enclosed questionnaire is brief and perplexing. Oh, it begins straightforwardly enough, with questions about your experience with athletics in general and wrestling in particular. The next few are more peculiar and more personal—questions about your relationships ("Do you have a serious boyfriend whom you intend to marry in the foreseeable future?"), your domestic skill set ("Do you cook?"), your personal habits ("Do you practice good hygiene?"), and your characterization of yourself ("Would you consider yourself a feminine woman?"). It is hard to see what any of this has to do with your qualifications to be a wrestler; still, you answer the questions easily and honestly. The only real snag you hit is when it asks for your measurements, including your height, which apparently has to be between five foot two and five foot nine.

It was possible to imagine from the previous questions that you might in fact "have what it takes" to be a wrestler, but there is no way around this problem: you are simply too tall. But you cannot let a couple of inches keep you from realizing your destiny. And so, after scrawling a 5 in the space allotted for "feet," you press the pen against the paper, loop around and, hand shaking, come down, creating a 9 in the space for "inches."

When you failed to tell your father about *Bandstand,* you didn't exactly lie; you simply withheld information. This action, however, is unmistakable: you have represented yourself as something you most certainly are not. But what is the alternative? It seems a reasonable and justifiable move, but so will many that you will take over the next year, until you find yourself neither where you meant to go nor where you might turn back. Of course, that is impossible for you to imagine now, in this early leg, with all that is familiar just a turn of the head away. Only those of us burdened by hindsight can see this act as dangerous. You fold the completed questionnaire three ways, stuff it into an envelope, and send it on its way.

It takes ten excruciating days for Pospisil's response to arrive, but it is everything you hoped it would be. He is convinced that a career in wrestling is in your cards and hopes you'll take the next southbound train so you can attend his school and get this career off the ground. When he gets the green light from you, he will wire the money for a train ticket. Not only that, he will pay you fifty dollars a week plus room and board for the first month. If, after a month, you want to return home, he will pay for that ticket as well and wish you a happy life. And, of course, he is happy to answer any questions that you or your parents might have, as he is a father himself and understands that fathers often need personal reassurances on these kinds of things. A business card is provided for this purpose.

As thrilling as all of this is, there's an element of ice-water-to-the-face about it. What reassurances could Pospisil possibly offer that would convince your father, a man who doesn't even believe in eating in front of the television, to let you just pack up your bags and travel unescorted to *Florida* for the purpose of becoming a professional wrestler? It takes a day, and another brisket dinner, for you to summon the courage to broach the idea with him.

His response is definite: "Women don't wrestle."

You provide him with the only evidence you have to the contrary, fanning the publicity shots out in front of him like a winning card hand. As you should have expected, Franz stares at them in saucer-eyed horror.

"This is what you want?" he says, gesturing toward them. "To parade in front of a bunch of men you don't know in a suit like this?"

"I want to be a wrestler," you say with forced patience. "I want to give it a try, at least."

"I don't understand," he asks, his face pained. "Why?"

Why? It's an impossible question to answer. The reasons are complicated and unspeakable. Eventually, you say, "I can't stay here and take care of you my whole life."

"I think you've got this backwards, Leonie. I'm your father. I go to work, I pay the mortgage, and I keep my daughter from making bad choices. *I* take care of *you*."

You've put your foot in it now. You feel your opportunity slipping away; you have to blink your eyes and look up at the ceiling so you won't cry. "What else can I do, Father? This is my best chance."

Franz looks down at his feet; you are still looking up. In another minute, you are sure, he will slam his fist on the table, and that will be that. When moments later this still hasn't happened, you dare to look at his face, one that has always looked old to you but now seems even older. He looks up at you. You are prepared for him to say anything. You've never crossed your father, no matter the stakes. If he says no, you will accept it and never mention it again.

Who can know what he is thinking in the minutes before he says his next words. I have always imagined that in this moment, he understands how little he knows about what the world has to offer, what you might need from it, and how you might get it. You are as mysterious a creature to him as he is to you and me, and none of us will know much about what is or isn't a best chance until it has been taken.

"I will call this man," he says. "I'm not promising anything, but I'll call."

Your father has plenty of questions for Mr. Pospisil. How safe is it? How often will you have to travel? How far? Who will go with you? A number of his questions concern men: at the school, on the cards, in the audience. Apparently he believes his entire sex is bad news from which you must be shielded. This conversation is difficult for you to endure. Complicated negotiations regarding your future are in process, and you are barely even a spectator. You have no idea what Mr. Pospisil is saying, or whether your father finds these answers satisfactory; his flat expression reveals nothing.

At the end of this torture, Franz asks, "Tell me, Mr. Pospisil, would you let *your* daughter do this?" Franz listens to the answer, stone-faced, and then wordlessly hands the phone to you and steps outside. Once he is safely out of earshot, you thank Mr. Pospisil for his patience.

"It's my job," he says. "I love it when I get that last question. It's my ace in the hole."

"So you think he'll say yes?"

"You know that better than I do. But I hope so."

You would not typically follow your father outside, but you do it this evening, sitting quietly beside him, your arms wrapped around your knees, while he puffs on a Winston. Somewhere nearby, a group of men sit in a living room playing an improvised jazz number, and the muffled notes drift into space. A door opens; the sound has drawn Ms. Riley out of her house. She puts her hands on the small of her back and arches, thrusting her chest forward. She sees the two of you sitting there and waves down at you.

"Leonie. Franz. How goes it?"

Your father gestures toward you with his thumb. "My kid here wants to move to Florida and be a wrestler. What do you think of that?"

Ms. Riley gives you a curious look and laughs in a way that strikes you as more than a little sad before turning to your father. "My kid got herself knocked up by a meathead bum. Want to trade?"

Your father says nothing.

Soon, the engine of a sedan drowns out the music, and Ms. Riley waves her good-byes and returns inside. When it is just the two of you,

you dare to ask your father, who stares ahead, his eyes glazed, what he is thinking.

"I'm thinking," he says, "that you are going to Florida, and nothing will be the same."

He has decided; he will not give you his blessing, but he will not stand in your way. You could burst from relief, but, to your credit, you keep your feelings under wraps. This is big—as much as you could hope from him. He deserves your gratitude, which you attempt to demonstrate by following him inside and drying the dishes after he washes them. When you finish, Franz gets a beer from the refrigerator, turns on the radio, and lies down on the couch. You take your cue and disappear into your bedroom, excited by your father's decision, but saddened by it, too. You understand his fear, that he will lose you, and this scares you as well. Not enough to drive you out of the bedroom and into his arms (if you had any idea just how complete the loss will be, you would do exactly that), but enough to keep you up well into the night, so that you are still awake when Franz turns up the volume on Perry Como and cracks open your bedroom door.

"This one's for you, Leonie," he whispers into the darkness, barely audible above the crooner.

THREE

A nd so begins your unlikely transformation into an icon of the golden age of wrestling.

Perhaps the only thing more incredible than the wild success you will achieve is the amount of faith you place in this possibility. You know almost nothing of the sport, and yet you are so capable of imagining yourself as its champion that before the week is out, you bid your father good-bye, board a train, and head toward an alien world on the invitation of a stranger. On the first leg of the journey south, this dream sustains you. You see nothing of the passing landscape, only the bright future you are headed toward. Your surroundings begin to come into view only after you cross the Mason-Dixon Line, when the passengers with darker skin are relegated to the cars farthest from the engine, the shoeboxes carrying their dinners bouncing in their laps. Later, when your books are read, your sandwiches eaten, and sleep is still eluding you despite a restless night, you watch the sun set over endless fields of farmland. In this moment, it occurs to you that the only givens are that it is late in the day and you are far from home. By the time you step out onto the near-empty platform, the vision that propelled you here is almost impossible to recall.

One of the few people waiting is a square-shouldered, jut-jawed gentleman with dark-rimmed glasses held up by cauliflower ears. While an attendant heads off to retrieve your trunk, he approaches you with an outstretched hand.

"Leonie Putzkammer, I presume," he says.

"Hello, Mr. Pospisil." He gives you a quick once-over, as he might any newly acquired merchandise. You hope that in whatever assessment he is making, he isn't wondering about your height. You might have some newfound doubts about your decision, but you don't want this man to tell you that you don't belong.

Whatever conclusions he draws, he keeps to himself, offering instead a well-rehearsed "Hot enough for you?" Soon after, the attendant arrives with your trunk, and in no time, you and Joe have hauled it into the back of his DeSoto and are heading down the highway. In the quiet of the car, you try to recall the sights and sounds of Rocca in the ring, details that might reinforce your faith and steady your nerves, but it is difficult to ignore the endless miles of slash pines. Just as you begin to wonder if you will ever again see anything besides trees, a light appears in the distance.

"Welcome to Otherside," says Joe as he rockets past the illuminated sign.

It is hard to believe this place merits identification. When you finally see houses, they are few and far between, and set so far back from the road they seem like shadows of themselves. Those old Victorians must retain a hint of what made them grand in their day, but all you can see are the sunken porches, the boarded windows, the yards littered with trucks and boats in various stages of repair. The only signs of life are a few mangy dogs and the occasional scratching chicken. To you, it seems like the land that time forgot, halfway between nowhere and nothing.

Shortly thereafter, Joe's car turns off the highway, crosses over a

set of train tracks, and rattles along an old shell road that takes you
through a scrubby forest into a clearing, where the dozen weather-worn
cabins that make up the Pospisil School for Lady Grappling stand in a
semicircle near the river. Not that you can see much. It is dark out here,
purple dark, which makes it difficult to see anything other than whatever lies directly in the path of Joe's headlights. Eventually, these are
aimed toward your new home: something more than a shack but less
than a motel room, its wooden siding scabby with green growth. As Joe
nears the cabin, he spins around and backs the DeSoto up to the door,
which sweeps the headlights toward the cypress knees in the river.

After he parks, you step out of the car to investigate. You have lived
near the Schuylkill all your life, but this belongs to another category of
nature altogether. You can't see much in the dark, but you can smell its
ripeness and hear its laps against the boat ramp. You also hear something chirping—frogs, or maybe crickets.

"Why Otherside?" you ask. "Other side of what?"

"I guess that depends on who you ask."

You slap at a mosquito. "I'm asking you."

"Me?" Joe walks around to the back of his car, unlocks the trunk.
"I think this place is the other side of heaven, but I suspect some of the
girls will say differently. Hey, you going to help me with this or what?"

Joe lifts one end of your trunk out of the DeSoto and motions for
you to take the other. "Your training begins now," he jokes, and the two
of you hoist it out of the car and into the dark, wood-paneled room
where you will live. Joe wasn't lying about the heat. It sure doesn't feel
like September in that room—not any September you've ever known,
anyway. By the time Joe locks the room up and hands you the key, your
dress is drenched in sweat.

"Living out here might be a bit of an adjustment for you. Was for
me, too. I'm from Cleveland myself. But I love it now. Winter's a lot easier, and living on the water has its perks. Mullet will be running soon.
Sometimes I catch ten, twelve with one throw."

"I have no idea what that means," you say, and Joe laughs.

"I didn't used to, either. Here's something else that's nice."

Joe points over your head and you look up. Through the flags of Spanish moss, you discover one more thing that makes it clear just how far you are from home: a hazeless sky thick with stars.

It is easy for me to imagine you in this moment, your mouth open, your ponytail stretching down your back as you tilt your head back to look at the universe above. I only wish that I could see now what you saw then: the water in front of you, the sky above, and your whole life ahead of you, sparkling.

After Joe walks you quickly around the grounds to orient you—the gym is this concrete-block building *here,* his office is in this cabin *here*—he escorts you into the diner, which, believe it or not, is even drearier than your room. Black paths are worn into the heavily trafficked carpet. The orange vinyl booths are outlined in greasy nautical rope. All of these are empty save one, where three young women chat over the remnants of their dinner. As you follow Joe past their table, you sense furtive glances.

"I was just about to give up on y'all," calls a woman from the flattop.

Joe walks you over and introduces her as Betsy. "My girl Friday," he says, but she is hardly a girl. There are faint lines around her eyes and some of the hairs that have escaped her hairnet are gray. Betsy wipes her hand on her apron and extends it over the counter. "Looks like you made it in one piece."

"I think so."

Betsy's smile gets your attention. Not just because it is unusual— one of her front teeth is significantly larger than the other—but also because there seems to be some maternal concern embedded in it: *I sure hope you know what you've gotten yourself into.* She seems like someone who will look out for you, which is one more reason to feel good about being here. "You must be starving. What can I get you, hon?"

Moments later, a plate of meatloaf and mashed potatoes arrives at the booth where you and Joe have taken up residency, and for a while, everything and everyone else disappears. You don't just eat this food: you inhale it. It is not until you lick a finger that you remember where you are and who is watching. When you look up, Joe stares back. "You have a healthy appetite," he says. No kidding. You had no idea you could devour so much so quickly. You slow down and chew your food at what you hope is a reasonable pace. "I meant that as a compliment," he says, laughing a little.

A bell on the front door signals another arrival, and when Joe looks up and waves over whoever has arrived, you can't help but turn to see for yourself. The woman entering is stocky, with a dark complexion and a heavy, textured mane of hair she has attempted (and failed) to confine to a ladylike bob. Perhaps you do not immediately recognize her—in her publicity shot, taken years prior, she is crouched and snarling—but from the way the other girls labor at continuing to talk without making eye contact, you understand that she is someone to be reckoned with. She walks toward you with a forced stride, its power restricted by her high heels and pencil skirt. She seems a wild animal restrained, a trained bear balancing on a ball.

There is no single person who will feature more prominently in your life as a wrestler than this woman. She will be in the opposite corner for your first bout, a modestly attended card (just weeks away!) at the local armory, and the last one, just a year later, when the two of you will make history in the Memphis arena under the watchful gaze of over nine thousand marks.

"Joe," she says, "can I talk to you for a moment?"

"Can you at least say hello to my newest protégé? I'd like you to meet—"

"Yeah, yeah. The gymnast. You told me." This mockery is the only acknowledgment you get. It seems you are not worthy of either end of an introduction. She doesn't care to hear your name, nor does she bother to share hers. "It's important, Joe," says the woman.

"Fine, fine," he says, sliding out of the booth. Before he leaves, he turns to you and says, "It's on the house tonight, so get some pie or coffee or whatever you want. Tomorrow, come by my office around ten so we can talk before you head to the gym. Bring your suits. All of them."

All of them? You are lucky to have one.

Once the bell rings them out, you relax and return to your plate, anxious to finish and head to your room for some much needed rest. But before you can shovel in the last bite, you find yourself encircled by the women from the other booth, who, judging by their Capri pants and wide eyes, are closer to you in age and experience than the woman who spirited Joe away. With these girls, you feel less need to put up your guard.

"Hi," says the blonde. "You're the new wrestler, right?"

You nod, even though it still seems strange to think of yourself in these terms. "Leonie," you say.

The girls slide themselves into your booth uninvited, introduce themselves quickly—the blonde is Peggy; the brunettes, Bonnie and Brenda, are sisters—and begin bubbling with questions for you and anecdotes from their own lives and recent adventures. All of this girl-friendliness makes you nervous. Previous experience has taught you that groups of women don't easily welcome new members into the fold. To be sure, the sisters do seem to be sizing you up, but Peggy has a smile that would be suspicious only to the thoroughly jaded. She slurps her vanilla Coke and tells you that tomorrow night will be Bonnie's first match.

"I have to fight that cow you just met," Bonnie whispers. "That's how it works around here. Your first match is always against Mimi, and she always wins."

At last, you have a name. "*That* was Screaming Mimi Hollander?"

"In the flesh," says Bonnie. "I should know. She plays a starring role in most of my nightmares."

"You worry too much," Peggy says to Bonnie. "You'll be great." She slaps her on the thigh before turning to you. "Brenda and I are going to the match tomorrow night to cheer her on. It's about an hour out of town, but Brenda has a car. Want to tag along?"

"I guess so," you say. "I've never actually seen women wrestle before."

"What? Then you have to come. You have to!"

Betsy swings by the booth to ask you if you want some pie. What you really want is to go back to your room and fall into bed, but Peggy begs you not to go just yet, the coconut cream is *to die for.* The possibility of friendship is too appealing to say no, so you stay for another half hour, growing dizzy with sleepiness and sugar.

When you finally wish them good-night, you walk back to your dank little square of a room and open your trunk. There it is: the gift from your father, a little Philco Bakelite AM/FM radio. He'd given it to you just the night before, mumbling something about your mother and music and summer nights. You pull it out from its nest of sweaters and set it on the nightstand, but you don't plug it in. Instead, you lie on your bed, head spinning, listening to the frogs and crickets, absorbing the weird world into which you have just leaped.

The next day, Betsy waves you into Joe's office, and you walk in, holding your bathing suit in a sweaty hand. Joe tosses it in a bag, explaining that his wife will need to do some work to it before you can use it in the ring, and pulls out a contract. He reiterates his original offer: salary and expenses for the first month and, if you change your mind, a train ticket home. If you decide to stay after that, you'll have to pay your own way, including travel. He has a hard and fast rule against advances, and he's heard every sob story out there, so don't bother. Finally, his booking fee will be forty percent of your purses.

"Standard," he assures you, and hands you the pen.

Had you been listening, you might have found this gasp-worthy, but your attention has moved to the area behind his desk, which has been wallpapered with wrestling pinups that flap with each periodic blast of the oscillating fan. This morning, waking up to your depressing new home, your only connection to your father and your former life a radio you had yet to turn on, you felt homesick and once again plagued by doubt. But here, surrounded by these confident, hard-thighed women, your sense of opportunity returns. Many of these images are the same ones that lured you here; now, they seem to beckon you into their ranks. You take the pen and sign on the dotted line.

Once you're done, Joe whisks the contract away and deposits it in his desk. "Good," he says. "Now that you're officially one of us, we can discuss the rest."

The rest can be boiled down to these two syllables: KAY-fabe. The origins of the word are sketchy at best, part carny slang, part pig Latin. Kayfabe. Be fake.

That's right, Leonie. It's fake. It's not sport, it's story. The rivalries are manufactured, the outcomes predetermined. The athleticism is real—you've seen this with your own eyes—but the rest is scripted. From this moment on, your primary responsibility will be to protect wrestling's first and only tenet: never, ever break character. After all, that's what you've been admiring up there on the wall. Not women, characters. There are "faces," the heroes, and "heels," the villains. That's it. Women are too messy, too complicated, Joe explains. Characters are simple. And now, you're on your way to becoming one, too.

• • •

Last but not least, Joe lays out his strict code of conduct. The women he manages are, first and foremost, ladies, by which he means both "classy" and "feminine." That means gloves, heels, and nylons to and from matches and no "loose behavior" on the premises or on the road. Relationships with men should be discreet; relationships with women should not exist. If he gets wind of any questionable behavior, you are out. Get married and congratulations but you are out. Get pregnant and you will be out before the door can hit you. Deviate from the script in any way and guess what. Out.

"But I won't have to worry about you, will I?" he asks. "You're a good girl, right?"

"Of course," you say, shocked that anyone might assume otherwise.

"Good." Joe slaps his desk. "I've got a promotion tonight, so I won't be able to start you on the program until tomorrow. See if Mimi will show you a few things. She knows up from down better than the rest of them. If she's stubborn about helping you, just do what she does."

As he says this, Joe looks up at Mimi's publicity shot, the one he included in his first letter to you. It is just as ferocious as you remembered, her jaw set, her body poised for attack. Her ensemble is similar to all the others in every way except for one: instead of wearing heels, she wears wrestling boots. Black boots stitched in white, to be precise, just like her suit.

"So, go to it," he says, waving you on. "Get to work."

The gym is a swirl of activity: girls drop-kicking medicine balls, punching heavy bags, pushing each other back and forth into the ropes. You will discover that the number of residents here changes by the hour, but at the present moment there are eight others, all of whom are here, obediently heeding Joe's imperative. (In case it has been lost somewhere on the short journey from his office, there is a hand-stenciled banner

47

on the wall to remind you: GET TO WORK). The cinder block walls echo the sounds of contact, human and otherwise, and the air smells of used towels, Hypnotique perfume, and boot-clad feet. Peggy and the sisters are there, as is Mimi, who's on a mat in the corner doing sit-ups. With more than a little trepidation, you walk over to her.

"Mind if I join you?"

"Yeah, actually, I do," says Mimi, counting under her breath "seventy-two, seventy-three, seventy-four . . ." You look up to the ring, and Peggy, leaning against the ropes, waves at you. You should blow off Mimi—what was it that Bonnie called her? Oh, yes: *that cow*—and join your new friends, but Joe's advice rings in your head. You wave back, but then you get down on the mat beside Mimi and begin doing sit-ups yourself, trying your best to crunch in unison with her, finishing at Mimi's count of one hundred. You flop back on the mat, hoping to catch your breath before your real instruction begins, when Mimi flips onto her stomach and begins to do push-ups. Seeing no alternative, you turn over and start your own set—a slower, less graceful, and notably shorter set (you barely pump out half as many) but a series nonetheless.

"Fine," says Mimi. "Over here."

She picks up a medicine ball and throws it to you. You fold under its weight but retain your grip.

"Well?" says Mimi. "Throw it back."

It takes an incredible amount of effort, but you manage to oblige her, and the two of you go back and forth like this a number of times. After the ball, you jump rope for what seems like an eternity. You try to keep up, but your arms begin to feel like molten lead, and you are forced to drop the rope and massage your shoulders. While you rest, you watch Bonnie ride Brenda's chest across the mat as Brenda struggles in vain to keep one shoulder up, groaning all the while.

"Come on, Brenda," yells Peggy. "Dig deep!"

"Any chance I'll get in the ring today?" you ask Mimi, your eyes locked on the ring.

Mimi stops and wipes her brow with the crook of her arm. "Not if you have a lick of sense," she says. "Wait for Joe. He'll start you off right, with falls."

"Falls?"

Mimi takes a long drink from her Thermos. "Yeah, falls. You know. How to go down, hit the mat."

"I have to learn how to fall down?"

"Well, no. You don't *have* to learn anything. You could just stay stupid." She follows your gaze to the unfolding drama of the ring. It seems Brenda is finally succumbing to Bonnie's pressure, and they both grow louder and shriller as they realize the pin is inevitable. Mimi sighs. "I really don't have time for this," she says. She takes the jump rope from you and throws it with hers into the corner. "I got to get in some bag work. Why don't you go up there with the fruit flies, since you know so much already."

Mimi heads over to the heavy bag. You should join her there, but you just can't quite bring yourself to do it, not with more exciting possibilities available. And so, after Peggy slaps the mat three times, signaling the younger sister's victory over her sibling, you make your way over to them, eager to be where the action is.

Later in the evening, while you are in your room waiting for the girls to come for you, you keep yourself busy by straightening the clothes in your drawers. You haven't brought much with you, so this is about as much as you can do to make it feel more like home. At the appointed hour, three energetic raps arrive at your door: Peggy, just as she promised. "Hello again," she says. "Long time no see."

Yes, it's been all of an hour. You spent most of the day watching her practice hammerlocks and toeholds with Bonnie and Brenda. One by one, you retreated to your rooms to doll up for the evening, as you've been instructed—gloves, heels, the whole nine yards. When you climb into the back of Brenda's car, you are wearing your best dress, bright red and belted with a full skirt and darted bodice. The dress was an impulsive purchase, made only days ago when you spotted it in a department store window after your last day at the diner, your apron pocket unusually full from the generous farewell tips of the regulars. It seemed reckless at the time, but now, you're glad of it.

"You look darling!" says Brenda.

"Doesn't she?" says Peggy. "Here. I have just the thing to finish it off." She pulls a lipstick from her clutch and offers it to you. After you lean over the seat and use the rearview mirror to guide yourself as you paint your lips in a matching red, you hand it back to Peggy, but she waves it off.

"Keep it. It's just one of those new plastic-cased ones. The color looks just smashing on you. I never could pull it off."

The compliment makes you blush, but the gift makes your day. You've never made friends this quickly. You spend the hour-long drive hearing the girls bemoan the dearth of date-worthy boys in the area and share the gossip of your new world—the boss is cheap, and Lacey Bordeaux is dumb as dirt for not realizing Johnny is stepping out on her—but listening to little of it. The warm buzz of conversation is enough for you; its substance hardly matters.

The venue is nothing like the arena in Philadelphia. This is small-town, make-or-break wrestling, where a fruit fly like you will either hone her craft or pack her bags. It takes place anywhere and everywhere: a park, a high school gymnasium, a hotel lobby, an Elks lodge, or, in this case, a brick National Guard armory surrounded by browning palmetto trees. You and the girls file in with the rest of the crowd—locals mostly, men and women who work on the water, whose lives are routinely turned upside down by the elements, and who are likely glad for the chance to wear their best clothes, to forget about their own lives and lose themselves in a different story, one where justice is doled out with more frequency. Eventually, you reach the ring, where Joe stands on the apron, speaking directly into the ear of the ref. The three of you find seats near what will be Bonnie's corner, and you settle in for your first ladies' wrestling match, absorbing the enthusiasm of the audience. You feel your own sore hamstrings ache with possibility.

The women's match is the first on the card. The names come over the PA system, and the women run down their respective aisles. First is Bonnie, smiling and pumping her fists, waving to the three of you as she gallops along. She garners polite applause from the crowd merely for being pretty and representing the forces of good. As you're going to learn, an audience does not give up its heart lightly. Before any wrestler can expect a more enthusiastic response, she will have to earn it: she will have to entertain. If she can successfully accomplish that, they will cheer for her until the end of time. Tonight is Bonnie's chance to prove her worth.

Next is the heel, the scapegoat for their deepest rages and disappointments. She is draped in a fur-trimmed robe, her face a steely scowl despite the rising tide of insults. A few reach your ears. "Bulldog." "Ugly-ass bitch." "Goddamn man with tits." When she climbs into the ring, into her corner, and slides off her robe, she remains stone-faced, as if none of it has registered. Nonetheless, something inside you twangs with pity. I don't suppose it's easy being Screaming Mimi Hollander.

The bell rings. The wrestlers begin pacing panther-like in their suits, waiting for the other to blink. This will be a three-fall match, the first of which is over in a flash. Bonnie manages to get Mimi in a hammerlock, but Mimi gets out of it by ramming the amateur backward into the turnbuckle. The veteran spins out and deals an audible slap to the chest that knocks Bonnie to the ground and prompts you to flinch in sympathy. It is a real slap, not a staged one—you can tell from the sound and the color spreading across Bonnie's collarbone—which cancels out any compassion you might have felt for Mimi. This woman has no vulnerabilities; she hardly needs your pity.

"Come on, Bonnie!" you shout. "Look alive!"

Too late. Mimi flops Bonnie to the mat and quickly pins her for the three, and you join the chorus of hisses and boos as the women head back to their corners to catch their breath for what soon amounts to the last round of Bonnie's career.

After the signal, the two women lock into the ref's position and stay that way, neither making any headway until Mimi sweeps the girl's leg out from under her. Bonnie crashes, twisted and awkward, to the mat. Peggy gasps; Brenda turns her face and covers her eyes. You, on the other hand, can't tear yourself away. Mimi hasn't yet registered what has happened; she is locked and loaded, primed to pin the girl and take both the fall and the match, when Bonnie's scream stuns her to stillness.

The ref rushes in, followed by Joe and the ring doctor. You crane your neck but can see nothing but the three of them hovering over the girl's leg. After some debate, Joe climbs out of the ring and waits for the ref to slide the injured wrestler under the ropes and into his outstretched arms. He walks through the crowd, past you, with Bonnie's arms wrapped about his neck, the girl sobbing openly as he carries her up the aisle and behind the stairwell, away from the crowd, the history books, and your life forever.

When the ref declares Mimi the winner, the crowd erupts into venomous jeers. But she is impervious; she raises two defiant fists into the air and rotates around the ring, daring them to call her anything other than victor. Over all this noise, you hear Mimi's own voice rattling around in your head: *You don't have to learn anything. You could just stay stupid.* Eventually, Mimi turns in your direction and meets your gaze. You search her eyes for remorse, but there is none. Months from now, when you are at the height of your fame, you will be asked by a reporter to recall your initial impressions of Screaming Mimi Hollander. There will be many things you cannot say, but this question will provide one of the rare moments when you won't have to choose between the truth and the script. When you respond, you will describe this moment and conclude by saying, "It was clear to me that I was looking at the meanest bitch that ever walked the face of the earth."

FOUR

The sun is up but the moon is still faint in the sky the next morning as you drag your aching body across the grounds to the gym. Being awake at this time usually gives you the feeling that you have a jump start on the rest of the world, but not today. Here at the Pospisil School for Lady Grappling, there have already been plenty of comings and goings—mostly goings. It was still dark when an unfamiliar car rolled up to Mimi's door, pausing only long enough to collect her and her suitcase before rolling back out. And at the first sign of light, Bonnie and Brenda, who had packed her bags along with her sister's, drove off the premises. Even the girls who are still here are a few steps ahead of you: Peggy, the only other rookie left, and a few of the vets are already pushing against the exterior walls—right legs bent in front, left legs extended straight behind. You hurry toward them and follow suit.

"What are we doing?" you whisper to Peggy.

"Stretching," she says. "Today we do roadwork."

"Today *they* do roadwork," booms Joe, who strides toward you, a limp tangle of fabric dangling from his clutch. His presence is jarring enough, but seeing him dressed in the same gym attire as the rest of you—T-shirt and shorts—seems unreal. If it weren't for the mosquitoes, you might wonder if you weren't still in bed, dreaming all of this. "You and I are getting in the ring. You can join them next time."

"I thought—"

"Don't think. Bad habit." He turns to the line of girls. "*Well?*" he shouts, visibly startling them. "Go on! Get out of here!" And with that, the four young women shuffle toward the shell road that leads to the highway. Peggy turns her head just enough to shoot you a sad smile and a wave, and then she is gone with the rest of them, leaving you and Joe alone.

"Here," says Joe. It is the bathing suit you handed over yesterday, the straps now reinforced with surgical tubing and the legs with strings of elastic, necessary measures, Joe explains, to ensure that all the kicking and clawing won't result in any riding up or falling out. The industry is walking a fine line between titillation and obscenity, one that shifts depending on the state. Some have gone so far as to ban women from the ring. To the degree he can, Joe intends on keeping his girls on the right side of that line. "What are you waiting for?" he asks. "Get dressed and meet me in the ring."

It is quiet in the gym, not like yesterday. And while the dressing room is sufficiently private this morning, there is something uncomfortable about undressing with Joe just meters away. You shimmy into your suit as quickly as you can, pull the top up and the seat down, and, once you are as covered as possible, pad out in your bare feet, your arms crossed in front. There is a mirror before you reach the door, but you shy away from it. If you see how exposed you are, you won't be able to leave the dressing room.

"Come on, come on," Joe calls from the ring. "I don't have all day." Dutifully, you hurry across the gym, hop on the apron, and thread yourself through the ropes. After he leads you through a series of stretches, he jumps to his feet and claps his hands together. "Now. Last night you saw what can happen if you don't know how to take a bump. So we'll start there."

For the next half hour or so, Joe shows you how to go down in a way that is supposed to lessen your chances of injury. He models a dozen or so falls, his figure seemingly suspended in the air before he hits the mat with a loud clap, and then, in testament to the effectiveness of his technique, quickly rolls on his side and jumps to his feet. The trick, he says, is to "level out"—to distribute your weight over your whole body, to flatten yourself into a plane rather than attempt to break the fall with a limb. "Pretend the mat is a bed of nails," he tells you. "You got to hit 'em all at once, or it's going to hurt like hell." On top of that, you have to "work loose" to keep your muscles from tensing.

"Go ahead," he instructs. "You try it."

As you soon discover, falling is more difficult than one might imagine. The first time isn't bad; the lesson is fresh and you are in your prime. But as soon as your body hits the mat, it begins to have the real experience of pain. Even with all of this working loose and leveling out, you are still a falling body crashing into a solid surface, and every subsequent fall is preceded by less capability and more fear. You fall again and again, but rather than get better, you get clumsier and fall harder. It probably doesn't help that you can't quite shake the self-consciousness of wearing so little. Every time you hit the mat, Joe kneels down beside you to offer his critique, pointing to the places where you hit (the small of your back) and where you should have hit (the whole of your back), or, even worse, physically moving your body into the correct position (feet flat, palms up). Work loose? Fat chance. Whenever he makes contact, you turn to stone. On your final attempt, the back of your head ricochets into the canvas hard enough for you to cry out.

"You're thinking too much," Joe says, standing over you, hands on his hips, elbows cocked. "You can't think it; you have to feel it."

You might have managed one good fall if he had just given you an inch of space. You remain flat on your back with your hands fisted and your neck throbbing. You would stay like this for the rest of the day if you could, but after a while, it becomes clear that Joe is not going to budge until you respond, so you roll onto your side, push yourself up—this much of the drill, you can manage—and say, "I'll work on it."

When you are upright again, Joe grabs you by the bicep and jerks you to attention. This time, his grip is more than intrusive—it's downright menacing. His face is close enough for you to see the hairs missed during his morning shave, just under his nose. You understand that he means for you to meet his eyes, but that is asking too much, so you stare instead at the hairs.

"Was that sass?" he spits.

"No."

"Because it sounded suspiciously like sass. And I will not tolerate sass. Is that clear?"

"Yes."

Joe throws down your arm and nods toward the locker room. "Go on. I think we could both stand to take five." He climbs out of the ring, grabs a clean towel from the top of a stack, and dries his hands while you silently rub your arm, your feet glued to the canvas, your eyes on the exit.

Here is the sad truth about lady wrestlers, Leonie. Their careers are roughly the same length of time as the average life span of a fruit fly: four weeks. Will this be your fate as well? You have been here less than two days, and already, two friends are gone, the prospect of injury has become frighteningly real, and your boss is just plain frightening. So far, all signs point to yes. You could just cut your losses and follow Brenda's skid marks out of here, but for that, you will need to enlist Joe's help. That would mean initiating a conversation with him, and you will have to summon a lot more courage before you will feel ready for that.

The next week is the most physically grueling of your life. Joe's program includes hours and hours of weight training, calisthenics, and roadwork. But it is the time in the ring that is truly punishing. Joe works with you for an hour every day. During a typical session, he might show you how to work the ropes safely, or he might teach you a simple hold or two—a hammerlock, a wristlock—and make you practice on Peggy or Mildred, a spring-loaded wooden dummy with stubby, offset arms. But mostly, you fall. On your back, on your front, after a flip. For the next several days, you practice falling over and over again, attempting to disconnect your brain not only from your muscles but from everything around you: the remoteness of this place, the nakedness of your body, the fear that grips you every time Joe wrenches your arm behind your back or easily breaks free from your hold. These sessions burn off all of the physical and emotional fuel you possess and then some. As a result, you eat ravenously. Each morning, you drink a glass of milk with two eggs stirred in along with your breakfast, and at night, you have an extra scoop of potatoes with your dinner, and then you head back to your room to soak your sore muscles in the tub before falling into bed, having neither time nor energy for anything else. On Friday, when you climb into the ring and Joe asks, "Ready?" it is all you can do to nod your head.

"Good," he says. "Let's see what you got."

And with that, he fires his forearm into your chest hard enough to knock you straight down to the mat. Joe hits you, you hit the canvas—there is no time for thought between these acts. You are pained and dazed, but still in one piece, still able to roll over and jump to your feet, so you must have done something right. But just as you begin congratulating yourself, you are promptly thumped again. This time, you go wheeling backward, gasping for breath. You manage to grab hold of the ropes and bounce back, a maneuver that you might be able to put to good use if you knew what you were doing. Since you don't, you catapult yourself straight into Joe's awaiting clothesline and go down like a brick. You are still seeing stars when his shadow crosses your face.

"Not bad," he says. "Now that I know you can take it, I'll teach you how to deal it."

In the tub that evening, you press the fingers of one hand into the darkening bruise on your chest while the other holds aloft the first letter from your father, a brief note that amounts to little more than a few jagged lines, hastily dashed off on a sheet of browning stationery. *You are missed,* it says, not *I miss you,* but coming from such a reserved, stolid man, it feels like a substantial outpouring of love. It's enough to make you want to lace up your Keds and run straight up the East Coast and into his arms. For all his faults, he has never laid a hand on you. Never. Not once. You read his letter over and over, until you are pruned. When you are ready for bed, you tuck it into your pillowcase, pull up the covers, and turn the radio knob until you settle on a familiar crooner. You close your eyes and wish that you were back at home, listening as the song drifted into your bedroom from the other side of the closed door.

At least you are not the only one in this foxhole. Every day you thank your lucky stars for Peggy. This whole enterprise would be intolerable if she weren't there to crack wise during roadwork, moan and groan over the day's extra reps and additional weights, and swap complaints over cold shakes and hot fries. And when Sunday, the day of rest, finally rolls around, and all the girls who aren't off to paying gigs have been rescued by their dates, she is there to keep you company. In the afternoon, you smear each other in Coppertone and lounge on the dock, your ankles cooling in the river as you flip through last month's *Confidential,* Peggy arguing that Marilyn should ignore her boss and marry Joe.

"That's what I'd do, at least," she says.

"You mean you'd give up all this?" you say, waving an arm. "For a ballplayer?"

"Oh, no, not this. A studio contract, sure, but not this glamorous life." Peggy laughs, and then combs your hair with her fingers, begins working it into a loose braid. "I'm telling you, Leonie, for all that Joe's put us through, we better end up with fur coats and rings on every finger."

"And ragtops," you say, one eye toward the unpaved road.

The next day is Monday, a roadwork day, and since all but you and Peggy are on the road, Joe decides he will go along, joining you for stretches before leading you both off of the grounds. This is the only part of the program you genuinely enjoy. Running allows you to pull deep inside yourself, your most familiar and comfortable environs. You would be happy to wear down the rubber on your Keds (*The Shoes of Champions!*) on the endless highway, but Joe says, "Let's change the scenery," and turns right, toward town, where you usually turn left. Before long, you are on the waterfront, running past the seafood houses, the pier, and the marina, where there is decidedly more to pull you out of yourself: the ripe, salty air; the pelicans standing sentinel on pylons from a long-destroyed pier; the glares and whistles from the shrimpers and oystermen. At the public dock, a couple of boys around your age load an ice chest into a boat. One takes notice, slaps his buddy in the chest with the back of his hand, points at the two of you.

"Hey, you!" he shouts. "You with the curls! What's your name, sugar?"

The smile on Peggy's face makes it clear she'd like to tell him, but she looks ahead anxiously, gauging the distance to determine whether Joe is in earshot. Even though he is well ahead, she seems reluctant to test his hearing, or his temper, so you do it for her, cupping your hands around your mouth and shouting, "Her name's Peggy!" She gives you a playful shove, and you shrug in mock innocence: *What did I do?*

"Peggy!" he calls, his voice growing more distant with each syllable. "Where ya going, Peggy?"

An emboldened Peggy opens her mouth to shout her answer, but she clamps it shut again when Joe spins around and shoots her a look that chastens you both. Reflexively, your head snaps down, your eyes fix on the asphalt in front of your toes. When the boy yells, "You can't run from me, Peggy Lee! I know where to find you!" you risk only the quickest of glances, which is just enough to see her reddened cheek, an upturn at the corner of her mouth.

Peggy normally grumbles through roadwork, but for this last mile, she is jubilant, occasionally jarring you out of your thoughts and braving a question. "He was cute, right?" "Do you really think he'll try to find me?" Even back at the gym, when Joe tells you both to clean up and meet him in the ring, she is still bobbing around on another plane: humming a tune while she showers and dresses in the locker room, checking and rechecking her hair in the mirror before she walks out. Only when you're all in the ring and Joe says, "Okay, ladies, let's see what you got," does she plummet back to earth.

"I'm sorry. What do you want us to do?" she ventures.

"What do you mean, what do I want you to do?" Joe asks, his hands extended in front of him. "This is a match. You are opponents. So wrestle, damn it."

"Oh," you say, blinking back at Peggy. The two of you stare at each other for a while, each waiting for the other to begin, to offer up some clue as to how this might go. Thankfully, Peggy steps forward and takes you by the shoulders, granting you permission to do the same. It is a strange sensation, to be locked in ref's position with her—not just another woman, but a buddy. It is a decidedly tentative press, and it makes you tentative, too. How real should this be? What are the boundaries? And what is she to you, exactly? Is she your colleague or your rival?

"Well, this is boring," says Joe. "Would either of you care to do anything that might keep a paying customer from walking out?"

"Like this?" says Peggy, and she drops down and grabs your legs out from under you.

"Better," says Joe. "Nice fall, Leonie."

Yes, it was, you realize, already back on your feet, crouched and ready to go. You hadn't even thought about it, just let your body unfurl and meet the mat as you'd practiced so many times. Maybe you were getting somewhere after all. Peggy, similarly crouched, snarls ironically, which further deflates the tension. *It's a joke,* she seems to be saying, and you acknowledge your understanding of this by comically baring your teeth. You feel confident enough to take her by the arm and launch her into the ropes.

From the other side of an open window come the snap of twigs and the crunch of pine straw.

"There's no free shows," shouts Joe. "You want to come in here and buy a ticket, or should I go out there and bang your skulls together?"

At first, there is stillness, but then the sound starts again, recedes from the window, and picks up again by the entrance, where the two boys from the boat—olive-skinned, sharp-nosed boys with wiry muscles—stroll in with cocky smiles. You do not have to look at Peggy to know her reaction; the exhilaration radiating from her is palpable.

Peggy's admirer, his ball cap tucked into his back pocket, digs into his pocket and pulls out a fistful of change. "Oh, we'd never try to cheat you, Mr. Pospisil. What's the going price these days?" he says, examining the contents in his palm, his hair clinging damply to his head. "Seventy-five cents, right? Here you go. Four, five, six quarters." He pinches the short stack and walks toward Joe, the price of admission extended in front of him.

Joe eyes him warily but accepts the money. "Sit on that bench," he says, pocketing the change before pointing to a far corner of the gym. "Tick me off and you'll eat these quarters." He returns his attention to the ring, claps his hands together rapidly. "Let's go, let's go, let's go."

So it's back to the awkward two-step of ref's position, and the frantic wracking of your brain. What next? Just as the rules of engagement were beginning to become clear, the presence of Peggy's would-be admirer muddied them. You should care only about Joe, of course: he is your boss, and this is your work. But for Peggy, it has also become some strange dance of courtship, one you want to help her with but aren't sure how. When she takes your wrist and wrenches your arm behind your back—this time, she means business—you simultaneously work to free yourself and worry over the sight of your extended chest. Should you try to turn away, or will that only obscure their view of Peggy? You manage to walk her back into the ropes and knock her off, but when you spin around to face her, she throws an arm forward and slaps you on the sternum. It is a feeble hit—if it weren't for the sound of her exertion, you might have thought that was intentional—and so you are at least a beat too late when you cry out and fall back.

"Atta girl!" comes the cry from the bench. "Don't hold back, honey. I like a strong woman."

"Try that again, Peggy," says Joe, firing a look at the boys that dares them to say another word. They clam up but keep their smug grins: they will not be chastised. "Put your whole body into it," Joe says to her. "Like this." He demonstrates for her in slow motion, and indeed, the movement is a fluid rushing-up from the sole of his boots through the heavy palm that strikes the air. For perhaps the first time since you first stepped in the ring with him, you feel something for this man besides abject fear. Not affection, but something akin to it. I might call it respect. "Go ahead, Leonie. Come at her again."

This time, when you walk toward Peggy, she plants her feet, rears back slowly, her torso moving back in unison with her arm this time, and then hurls her hand at your braced chest. It is still not enough to force you down of its own accord, but you are more prepared this time, so your fall is timelier and more convincing.

"Now you hit me," says Peggy.

"Okay," you say, and you do, but the hit is halfhearted and Peggy is not inclined to be generous in the same way you were: she rocks backward but stays on her feet. "That all you got?" she jeers. Before the taunt even registers, let alone the shock that might rightly accompany it—is she serious, or is this part of the act?—she rears back and takes aim at you again, catching you off guard and legitimately knocking you down. "Get up, weenie."

Now you're confused. Is this a real competition now? And for what? Her expression is hard to read, as is Joe's—he's not sure what's going on, either. "Come on," growls Peggy. "Hit me. I can take it."

Okay, she asked for it. You close your eyes, stop attempting to understand the dynamics at work among the people in this room, and give yourself over to the strength and knowledge of your limbs. Your intention is to strike her in the chest and send her flying into the ropes, clutching her sternum and struggling for breath: potentially embarrassing but not unforgivable. Just enough to show everyone that you can hold your own. But what happens is this: when you throw your arm out, you hit the considerably shorter girl in the bull's-eye center of her pretty face. Again, it takes you a while to pick up on what is happening. You don't hear the crunch of bone; you don't feel the warm rush of her blood on your hand. You begin to come around when you see Joe dive for a fresh stack of towels, when you hear Peggy's pitiful wail, but you do not feel the full weight of your action until you catch sight of those feckless boys slowly backing out of the gym, their self-satisfied expressions fully gone.

So now you know what it's like to play the heel, to prove your might only to send the audience toward the door. No one enjoys her first bite of this, Leonie. It takes time and experience to acquire the taste, to savor, even crave, its complexities. Even then, not everyone gets there. I certainly didn't, and I would guess the connoisseurs are few and far between.

Peggy does not wait until morning to leave; she is gone before night falls. She would have none of your comfort, none of your apologies. She does not even say good-bye. That makes three girls gone in less than a week. Tomorrow, you will make it four. You have no intention of staying beyond this evening, not when you've driven the only other girl currently in residence—and your only friend—away. You might as well go home, where the love is imperfect but still measurable. Besides, if there's anything you've learned, it's that disaster is inevitable. Better get out now while the getting's good.

When Joe knocks on your door that night, having just returned from the train station, you attempt to speak to him through the thinnest of cracks. You don't want him to see that you are packing your things. Maybe he would try to talk you out of it, maybe he wouldn't, but you don't want to take a chance. You want your farewell speech written and rehearsed before you approach him with the news.

"Yes?" you ask, pressing one eyeball against the gap.

"Can you come out here, please? I want to show you something."

"I don't know, Mr. Pospisil. I'm so tired—"

"Just open the door and come out here, Leonie."

Despite your misgivings, you do as instructed, closing the door behind you to keep the tornado-tossed room and half-packed trunk out of view. Once outside, Joe holds up a pair of emerald-green wrestling boots. "These are for you," he says, dangling them by the knot of their white laces. You watch them swing back and forth, forgetting that you have no need for such things, since you are never setting foot in a wrestling ring ever again. "If you didn't lie about your shoe size on your application, then they should fit."

What does that mean? That he knows you lied about your height, or that everyone lies about something? Either way, this small shame refreshes the day's bigger one. You shake off their trance and return to your senses. "Why are you giving these to me?"

"Why do you think? I just put you on the schedule. You can't go barefoot in a real match."

"A real match? But I just got here!" *And tomorrow I am leaving on the first train out.*

"I think you'll be okay, kid." He thrusts the boots at you. "Go on. They're yours now."

You take the boots by their soles and hold them out in front of you. They are not new—the toes scuffed, the tongues wrinkled—but still, they are a possession worth prizing, so much so that you can't quite bring yourself to hand them back, to give voice to the sentence spinning around your head like a train on its tracks: *Thank you, Mr. Pospisil, but I think you better save these for someone else.* "These weren't—who did they belong to?"

"A really terrific wrestler—Kat Fever. Katerina. My daughter."

"Your daughter?" *I love it when I get that question,* he told your father. *It's my ace in the hole.* Most people would not treat a dog the way that Joe has treated you this past week. Could he really have put his own flesh and blood through this same demanding and humiliating program? What does that say about him? And what does it say about you that he would give you these boots? He wouldn't give them to just anyone, would he? You thought you had the man figured out; now you don't know what to think. "Your daughter is a wrestler?"

"Not anymore. That was a long time ago." Joe gets a funny look on his face. "Look, there is nothing symbolic about this, okay? This is practical. You have big feet. So did my daughter. That's it."

"I didn't think—"

"Good." Joe turns to walk away without so much as a good-bye or even the barking of an order—but after a few paces, he stops and rubs the back of his neck. "Peggy was going to leave sooner or later," he says to the dark line of trees in front of him. "If you hadn't scared her off, something else would have. And if you ruined her chances with that joker, then believe me, you did her a favor." He continues on his path and is soon swallowed by the night, leaving you alone under the light above the door, the boots still cradled in your hands.

It is only when he is long gone, after you have been sitting at the foot of your bed for some time, neither packing nor unpacking your wide-yawning trunk, that you decide to slip on the boots and lace them up. It doesn't hurt to just try them on. It doesn't mean you are staying.

And, even if you do stay, you are not betraying a friend—if you can give that weighty name to the brief relationship—by accepting these boots. They did not fit her; they fit you. And they do: they are soft and snug and perfect in every way. How could a pair of secondhand boots be so particularly suited to *you*? Much of what you will keep of this era will be too imbued with multiple meanings for you to feel anything but ambivalence. These boots will be the one exception. Forever and ever, they will say only what they say in this moment: *You belong*.

Joe is wrong. This has to mean something. Fate has brought you here; fate has sent Peggy away. There are forces bigger than you at work here, you suppose, returning a stack of folded clothes from the trunk to the dresser. You might as well see how far they will take you.

FIVE

Leonie Putzkammer, I am sorry to tell you, is no name for a wrestler. It is certain to be spelled wrong on cards, to be stumbled over by announcers, and to take up valuable time during introductions and autographing sessions. It is also too ethnic, too *German,* and the powers that be (men, I feel obliged to point out, who continue to use names like Costantini and Pospisil) want everyone to think you are an all-American girl. Luckily, David "Monster" Henderson, the man Joe pays to take publicity photos of his girls, has a special talent for ring names. He has named dozens of wrestlers over the years, including not only Joe's daughter, Katerina (Kat Fever), but also Joe himself (Cleveland Joe) many decades prior. All of this you learn from Joe on the way to Mr. Henderson's house for your photo session. What he neglects to mention is the man's size. Henderson is a giant, and not in the figurative sense. All the classic features are there: the big forehead, the large jaw, and the staggering height. The scant literature from his days in the ring puts him at an impractical and cartoonish seven and a half feet. If this is an exaggeration, it isn't much of one. When

Monster Henderson answers his door, you forget your manners and say, "Wow."

Who could blame you for this response? It isn't every day that someone makes you feel small. Besides, this is surely not the first time Monster has gotten this reaction. It's clear from his smile that he's good-natured about it, which makes it easier for you to recover. You consciously make the effort to look into his eyes and allow him to take your comparatively tiny hand into his own. Joe does the introductions—"Leonie, Monster. Monster, Leonie"—and Monster stoops down to briefly hide all of your knuckles with his lips. Then, a final shocker: the voice.

"Hello, Leonie," says Monster, the words surfacing through gravel.

"Hello," you squeak, and follow the sweep of his massive arm into the house.

Inside, Joe asks, "Anything leaping out at you?"

Monster runs his thumb and finger over his chin. "I don't know yet. I have to think," he says, lending the task more seriousness than you might have expected. "Let's start with the pictures."

Monster offers you a spare bedroom. It doesn't make much sense to use it—you've worn your suit under your clothes; why do you need privacy just to strip down to it?—but you accept the offer anyway. The room's decor is outdated, the muted greens and browns of two decades prior, and startlingly girlish: wall vases filled with silk peonies, a vanity crowded with celluloid brushes and dusty glass atomizers, a shelf lined with felt cloches, feathers rising jauntily from their bands. A tape measure belts a headless dress form that stands in the corner; next to it is a cube-shaped leather trunk with brass accents. As fine a space as any in which to unbutton your blouse, step out of your skirt, and take a few calming breaths before presenting yourself.

Monster, standing by a tripod-mounted Bolsey, nods toward the white wall and you take your place. Your bathing suit is simple: black with boy-cut legs and a halter top with a shallow V and a bit of a ruffle.

Your heels are black, too. You wanted to pose in your beautiful new boots—the Green Goddesses, as you have come to think of them—the way Mimi had posed in hers, but Joe insisted that this deviation from the script was particular to Mimi and instructed you to bring your pumps.

"I know, it's stupid," he told you. "But this is how it's done."

Monster takes a seat behind the camera, puts his eye up to the range finder, and begins to offer instructions. He snaps photos of you with both biceps flexed, with fists on hips, in profile, looking over your shoulder. Over and over, he holds down the shutter and raises the film wind knob to advance to the next frame. You've worn your hair down, long and wavy, instead of the usual ponytail, and parted it far to one side so that it dips over your forehead. You are not used to all the hair in your face. You tuck it behind your ear time and time again, but it refuses to stay put.

"Here," says Monster. "I have an idea."

He opens a wooden box on a side table. Inside, interwoven like mating water moccasins, is a collection of what appear to be ribbons. He walks over to you, combs your hair into his hand, and curves the ponytail over your collarbone. With the other hand, he winds a ribbon around the stick of hair. He tries to tie the ends, but struggles; he is clearly in pain. "I can do that," you say, taking the ends from him.

He sighs his relief. "My hands aren't so good anymore," he says.

The truth, you will learn, is that while everything of Monster's is *great,* none of it is so good anymore. Carpal tunnel syndrome isn't even half of it. Vision deteriorating, diabetes settling in, the heart losing its will to pump. Monster is a giant who is about to fall.

Seconds later, Monster snaps the photograph that will adorn wrestling cards across the country for the next few months. Your later photos will be of better quality, with all the benefits a studio and a professional can bring, but this will be the one most prized by collectors. The washed-out black-and-white image will feature your hands resting just behind the small of your back so that the elbows bend into little wings, your front leg raised so the knee is at the barest of angles, your mouth toying with the idea of a smile, your head thrown back, the floppy bow sagging in your band of hair. But the real moment in history happens once the image is committed to film, when a look—recognition, perhaps?—comes over Monster's face. He cocks his head, as if turning something over in his mind until, finally, he smiles and nods.

"Gwen Davies," he says to you. "Your new name is Gwen Davies."

Monster, it turns out, is a collector of kink. You won't see the items that are more difficult to explain (issues of *Eyeful* and *Wink,* photos of bondage models Tempest Storm and Blaze Starr mail-ordered from Irving and Paula Klaw, other photos taken with his own Bolsey) for months, when they are pulled from the trunk where they are normally kept under lock and key. Today, you see only the more socially palatable material, like his eagerly anticipated and hot-off-the-press copy of Kinsey's *Sexual Behavior in the Human Female,* which is displayed on the bookshelves that line one wall of his living room.

Unlike many bibliophiles, Monster doesn't sort or discriminate by genre. His only concern is subject matter. Not that this is apparent to you. Perusing his bookshelves as Joe takes his time in the bathroom, you also see *Lady Chatterley's Lover* and *Tropic of Cancer,* which seem to have the wholesome ring of literature. You forgo these, instead leaning in to examine a row of paperbacks, Bantam and Gold Medal titles, their prices (25 cents each) prominently featured in one corner. You stop at one and gently coax it from where it is wedged: *Halo in Brass.*

"Is that the sort of book you like?" Monster asks.

You stare at the cover, on which a lone blonde holds a smoldering cigarette beneath this phrase: *She expected her lover, but death walked in.* "It looks like my kind of book," you say.

"That's interesting," he says. "I wouldn't have guessed that about you."

You are much too naive to know what it is that he has assumed or why it might amuse him. If you knew what I know now, you would shudder. From this, I can fairly guess the picture he has created in his mind: you, on the floor, hair fanned around you, a darker, more domineering woman straddling your chest.

"I like my name," you say, purposely moving the conversation toward surer ground. "What made you think of it?"

Monster doesn't answer right away. It can't be because he is having difficulty remembering. This only happened moments before. His silence can mean only one thing: there is something unpleasant about the answer.

"You reminded me of Sweet Gwendoline. But you probably don't know who that is."

"Can't say I do." And why would you? When would you ever have occasion to come across John Willie's cartoon serial or its busty blond protagonist, a girl always bound, in peril, desperate for rescue? You might have gone your whole life without knowing if he hadn't given you reason to seek it out.

"What about Davies?"

"Well, now," he says, eyes twinkling. "That's my name, isn't it? A bit of vanity on my part, I suppose. I hope you don't mind too terribly."

David. His name is David. You'd forgotten already.

"No, of course not," you lie. The truth is it is rather uncomfortable to be so intimately connected to someone you have just met, especially this particular someone. Over time, you will come to read something else into this gesture. You will see it as a need to pass on some part of himself that he otherwise couldn't, impotence being, as you will later discover, another cruel side effect of his condition, and you will be glad to have been honored with this task. Remembering this about him—*his name was David*—will help to fill out your memory, help him remain the man he was instead of the caricature he could so easily become.

Henderson looks down the hall—no sign of Joe—and leans in. "Just so you know, I sometimes take . . . other kinds of pictures. Just for my personal collection. No one sees them except for me. I pay well, and I'm very discreet." This time, you understand him perfectly. It is hard to hold such a bold proposition in your head. Before this moment, no one has so much as asked to hold your hand. He searches your face, like he's expecting—maybe even hoping for?—a reaction. But while you are feeling many things (shock, anger, and fear, to name a few), you keep your eyes locked on the book cover, your lips sealed shut. This is the only strategy you have for dealing with this kind of attention: withdrawal.

When Henderson speaks again, his voice is an octave higher. Perhaps he hopes to sound friendly and jocular, but that's hardly the effect—his bass is a weight too heavy to lift. "Sometimes the girls find the extra money useful."

Ignoring him is clearly not going to work.

You turn to him with wide eyes and say, "That's something to consider, Mr. Henderson."

"Please," he says, attempting to smooth things over. "Call me David." He takes the book from your hands and returns it to the bookshelf, pulls down another one. "This is a much better book. I'll just put it in a bag for you so Joe won't ask questions."

The two men return at the same time, Joe smoothing his trousers with his hands, Monster—David—holding a paper bag.

"Okay, we're gone," says Joe. He points to the bag. "What's that?"

"A birthday gift." David places the bag in your hands. "Welcome to the world, Gwen Davies."

SIX

Inside that bag, you learn after returning to your room, is a book entitled *The Price of Salt*. While the title reveals nothing to you, the cover is decidedly more explicit: a young woman sits canted, legs crossed at the ankles, lips curled into a slight, mischievous smile; behind her, an older woman reaching out adoringly; in the background, a lone, excluded man. Scrolled across the top, leaving nothing to the imagination, are these words: *The novel of a love society forbids.*

You wondered why Monster treated the book like contraband, why he feared Joe asking questions about a dime-store novel. Now, Leonie—Gwen!—you have your answer. When he asked you if you liked *that sort* of book, you thought he meant *detective stories*. (To be fair, the cover of *Halo in Brass* is subtler than most. No girls lounging together, no "odd" or "warped" or "queer" in the title.) Under other circumstances, you would spend the next few hours replaying the events with Monster Henderson, looking for meaning in the gift. The newly dubbed Gwen Davies, however, is too focused on adopting this new persona. You throw the book on top of your nightstand, strip back down to your suit, kick off the silly heels, lace up the boots, and stand in front of the mirror, your balled fists resting on your hips.

Here we are, you think. *Gwen Davies and the Green Goddesses.*

This clicks your new name into place with a satisfying snap. Despite your earlier protests, you are now glad to be rid of your old one. A new woman has emerged from the shell of the pitiful girl from Philadelphia. Where is Leonie Putzkammer now? Serving eggs and sausage to salesmen? Spending another Saturday night in front of the television with her father? Holed up in her room in want of any kind of love, forbidden or otherwise? No, that girl's *gone, gone.* It hurts my heart that you can say good-bye to her with such haste and so little care. But that's just me. As far as you are concerned, this is exactly as it should be. You came here because you wanted to be somebody else. And now, you are.

You will not win your match against Mimi. Joe makes this abundantly clear to you on the drive to the arena. It will be a best-of-three match, with Mimi winning the first and third falls. Your only goal tonight, he tells you, is to make them *want* you to win, and for that, you must build some goodwill, some underdog lovability. He parks the car next to a defunct old cannon in the lot adjacent to the armory (the site of Bonnie's career-halting injury) and clamps his hands onto your shoulders.

"Timing is everything," he tells you. "Play the game, and your time will come."

Your match is the first on the card. You are standing in the doorway of your dressing room, staring at your boots and trying to settle your swirling emotions, when the announcer calls your name: "Ladies and gentlemen, making her first appearance in the squared circle, a young lady with a mean dropkick and a face that will drop-kick you in the heart, put your hands together for *Gwen Davies!*"

Here it is. You've read it on the mimeographed wrestling cards and heard it in a trio of voices (Monster's bass, Joe's tenor, and your own alto), but now, it fires out of the PA system like it's straight out of heaven, propelling you down the aisle and through the crowd of winks, raised eyebrows, pats on the back, and what might be encouraging words if only you could hear anything but your own interior voice: *work loose, level out*.

And then, you are through the ropes and into the ring for the first professional match of your career. One look out at the crowd—the hands cupped over the mouths hooting and hollering, the showers of embers produced when the spectators clap while holding their cigarettes, the tiny whirlpools made in the cups of beer as the men who hold them stomp their feet—and you feel Leonie returning. Who are you kidding? These are hard-core fans who will see right through you. They will know you are a fraud, and they will call you on it. You wave quickly and retreat to your corner, overwhelmed to the point of near paralysis.

"In the opposite corner," booms the announcer. "The girl you love to hate, Screaming Mimi Hollander!"

Mimi—resolute, pitiless—emerges and strides toward the ring, pounding her way across the floor. Red-faced men bark at her. They hurl their plastic cups of beer; she swats these away like flies. One goes so far as to spit on her boots, and she reflexively shoves him back down into his seat. When Mimi finally climbs into the ring, she stands in its center, rounds her substantial arms to bring her fists together, knuckles kissing knuckles, and lets loose her hallmark scream.

Before the scream ends, Mimi is hit in the chest by a flying object, something black and square, about the size of a satchel. She picks it up by the handles—it *is* a satchel!—twists the metal clasp, climbs up on the turnbuckle, and sprays the crowd with its contents. Marbles fire out of the bag like bullets, landing in beer cups, ricocheting off metal chairs, and smashing painfully into the bony parts of men, women, and children.

"That'll teach you!" she shouts at the crowd.

You have no real interest in trifling with this woman. But the referee signals the start of the first fall, which doesn't leave you much choice. Everything that was true for Bonnie is true for you, too. If you want to win over the crowd, you will have to perform.

There is no choreography to the match, no script: only a predetermined outcome. You begin in ref's position, pushing each other back and forth across the ring as if sawing logs. Before you can think of a maneuver, Mimi sweeps your leg out from under you. *Work loose, level out.* You land on your back and roll away before her boot meets your stomach. Mimi backs into the ropes to spring into you, but that gives you just enough time to deal a forearm blow. It is more exhibition than power—you barely make contact—but the veteran performer knows how to sell it and she flies backward into the ropes.

A congratulatory whistle slices through the indeterminate screams, and you draw power from it. Suddenly juiced, you manage to get airborne and land one of those mean dropkicks (now *this* has some ferocity to it) into the chest of the returning Mimi. The strike yo-yos her back into the ropes, where she remains for a satisfying second, long enough for you to see her expression change—*That's all you'll be getting this fall, fruit fly*—and before you can get out of the way, Mimi slams you face-first into the mat.

While you lie there, dazed, Mimi straddles you, and before you know it you have been headlocked, rolled over, and covered for the count. After Mimi climbs off, you work your way onto your hands and knees, and then, eventually, back onto your feet. You are down, but not out. Sore, but injury free.

The next fall begins much like the first, the two of you locked against each other until Mimi falls back into the ropes. But this time around, you fire an emerald boot at her head. Mimi simulates disorientation, hamming it up and dragging it out long enough for you to climb onto the top rope. It is your moment, and you intend to seize it.

Once you are up there, however, you begin to think that you have made a terrible mistake. You were propelled into this position solely by your Rocca memories. There has been nothing in your training to prepare you for what you are about to attempt, and very little chance that you are going to pull this off. But you can't very well climb back down. And now, your balance has become precarious, so if you want to avoid an embarrassing and painful spill in the wrong direction, you'd better go ahead and do it.

So do it, Gwen: take the leap.

Once airborne, elevated above the fans and hurling yourself toward a lone yet savory victory, you are aloft for a mere second, but it is long enough to look down at the crowd in its various poses: arms in the air, mouths open, hands cupping mouths, all thrilled. Before you even begin your descent, you are already plotting how you will return to this great height.

You land squarely on Mimi, toppling her over and pinning her to the mat. Once the ref makes it final, you return to your corner, clutch the top rope with one arm, and pump a fist into the air with the other while crowd cheers. They love it. They love you. And you love them right back. Already, you are developing the appetite that will be your downfall. I know this, and yet, I take nothing but pleasure in remembering this moment. Go on, Gwen. Keep pumping. We may as well enjoy this while it lasts.

When the third fall begins, you quickly maneuver Mimi into a headlock, trying in earnest to choke the wind out of the woman.

"Let up, will ya?" hisses Mimi. It seems you want this fall and the victory so much that you have temporarily forgotten Joe's orders. It takes this directive for you to come to your senses and comply. When you do, Mimi puts you in your place by resorting to a catfight tactic: grabbing you by the hair and yanking you forward over her shoulder. Before you can get up, she deals a retaliatory kick to your jaw, and you startle at the crack and the subsequent pain. Instinctively, you cup the side of your face with your hand. You're not sure what just happened, but you can tell that it's serious.

Mimi bends your other arm around your back. "It's over," she whispers. Fine by you; you are now as ready as she is. You drop to your knees and fall to your side.

Pin. Fall. Match. The ref lifts Mimi's arm to the sky while you gather yourself, defeated and wounded, your heart throbbing painfully in the right hinge of your jaw.

Once you've returned up the aisle—Mimi ahead of you, Joe behind—and the three of you disappear into the dressing room, out of the audience's view, Joe spins you around.

"Let's see," he says, cupping your jaw in his hands. This doesn't cause you any more pain, but still, you flinch. "Yeah, I was afraid of that. Nice work, Meems."

"Sorry, Joe, but she choked the bejesus out of me."

"I can pop it back in," says Joe, "but I got to do it now, while it's still hot."

"Pop it back in?" yells Mimi. "Don't be such a goddamn cheapskate. Get the ring doctor in here to do it right."

Color creeps into Joe's neck; he doesn't raise his voice, but his fury is palpable. He does not like to be second-guessed, especially by Mimi. "I'm not paying that hack to do something I can *do right* all by myself." He turns to you; his voice softens. "Okay?"

You nod, unsure of your options, and take a seat.

"Open wide," says Joe, wriggling his fingers. "You're going to want to tense up, but try to keep your mouth as slack as possible. Got it?"

You open your mouth as best you can and try not to go rigid.

Joe hooks both thumbs into your mouth, fits them behind your back teeth, and presses down on your mandible. The pressure is merciless, unyielding. You attempt to focus on something outside of this moment, try to relive the feeling of weightlessness you'd had earlier that evening when you'd been aloft and confident of the pin, but all you can feel is the overwhelming pain. Finally, Joe fits the condyle into the TMJ with a loud and startling pop. He removes his thumbs, wipes them on his jacket, and rests his hands on your thighs.

"That's it. No walk in the park, but at least you're back together. I'd take you home, but I can't leave before the card is over, so I'm going to bend the rules and let your opponent here take you back. Just try not to let anyone see you both get in the same car, okay?" He gives your thigh a quick pat, and then he is gone.

"Don't bother changing," Mimi says. "Just grab your things."

An hour later, when you return to the grounds and open the door to your room, a blast of stale, humid air socks you in the face. You have never been this hot in October. You flip on the light and sink onto the bed, your hand still encircling your chin. The heat, of course, is the least of your problems; your whole face throbs. Moments later, Mimi, a pair of shorts pulled over her wrestling suit, lets herself in. She is carry-ing a bowl of ice and a bottle in a brown bag. "Do you want to get into something more comfortable?" she asks. "We're going to get you good and drunk, and I doubt you'll want to do anything once that happens."

Here you are, late at night in a room with a bed, a bottle of whiskey, and a woman who can knock the average man to the ground. This has all the trappings of the monkey business you've been instructed to stay away from. You would like to change out of your suit—the elastic in the legs cuts into your flesh—but making yourself vulnerable in front of Mimi is out of the question. You wave your hand and shake your head. *No.*

"Suit yourself." Mimi unscrews the cap to the booze and thrusts the bottle toward you. "Let's get this into your system." When you protest, she wraps your hand around the bottle's neck. "Drink," she says, re-leasing the bottle. "Trust me on this one."

You comply. This is your first swig of whiskey, and the peppery, almost chemical taste makes you cough.

"Again," says Mimi, searching the room. "You got a washcloth or something?"

You point to a set of hooks and take a reluctant second sip while Mimi finds the washcloth hanging under a towel and loads it with ice cubes.

"One more," Mimi says, and after you take it, she takes the bottle from you and gives you the ice pack. "Now hold this up to your face." She tilts her head a bit, gives you a long, soft look, and wrinkles her mouth into a kind of smile. "Lie down. Try to let your mind go a bit."

Again, you wave. *I'm okay.* You're decidedly not okay, but you have no intention of letting your mind go to any degree. Instead, you sit on the corner of your bed, pressing the quickly dampening rag to your face.

"Suit yourself." Mimi plunks her fists onto her sides and slowly pans the room. She spies something on your nightstand and picks it up—the book Monster gave you, *The Price of Salt*. She looks at you with surprise and then opens a drawer, sweeps the book inside, and shuts it tight. "I wouldn't leave this kind of stuff just lying around if I were you."

You want to tell her that it's not what she thinks, but even if you could form a sentence, you're not sure you could explain it. *Once upon a time, as I was looking for a detective novel, a seven-foot man asked if I wanted him to take naked pictures of me and then handed me this book.* The moment passes, and Mimi turns her attention to another item on your nightstand: the radio. "How about some tunes?"

She turns it on without waiting for a reply, and when the room fills with the sounds of Sinatra, she makes a face and mutters, "Yeesh." She twists the knob until she settles on a station playing Faye Adams's "Shake a Hand." She moves a stack of laundry from the chair in the corner and takes a seat, swaying with romantic exaggeration to *the little gal with the big voice.*

In another context, you might still feel wary. You have been warned about Mimi from day one, and the woman herself, with her hard-nosed ways and outlandish ring behavior, has seemed so intimidating, you've had no trouble believing there was something sordid and predatory about her. Knocking your jaw out of the socket hasn't exactly discredited this notion. But now that she is here, in your room, moving to the music, her expression dreamy and wistful, you can see how it might not be as simple as that.

"Sorry about this, kid," she says. "It's happened to me more times than I care to count, but it always hurts like all get-out." Before you can decide whether this is merely an obligatory apology, she breaks out in a smile and gives her knee a swat. "That was some stunt off the ropes there. Most of the new girls just pull hair and try to yank you down by the waist or something, maybe take a kick at you. Getting up on the turnbuckle like that your first fight? That shows me something."

You hope she is being sincere. You're not sure you want much from this woman, but you would like to have her respect. And after all you've been through tonight, you deserve it.

The song ends; a new one begins: Varetta Dillard's "Mercy, Mr. Percy."

"Here we go," says Mimi, getting out of her chair. "I think this one requires a little dance action."

You hope you are not expected to participate in the "little dance action": just the thought of rhythmic movement produces renewed anxiety and pain. But Mimi pays you no mind as she stands and puts on a one-woman show—eyes closed, shoulders bunched, hips shaking—while Dillard belts out her song. Did you look this silly when you were on the *Bandstand* dance floor, following Cynthia's lead? Probably. Mimi opens her eyes long enough to read the bemused smile on your face and amps up the irony, rolling her pelvis as if spinning an imaginary Hula-Hoop. You clutch your chin more tightly with one hand to stop yourself from laughing and wave her off with the other. *For the love of God, stop.*

Mimi obeys, wipes the sweat from her brow, and hands you the bottle again. "One more sip while I freshen up your ice pack." You do as you are commanded before taking the ice pack back from her. "Don't work your mouth too much for the next few days," she tells you. "Fill up on milkshakes and soup. Keep a hand under your chin if you've got to yawn."

Just the mention of the word makes you yawn, so you follow protocol.

"Good girl. And do this for me, too. Don't go home yet, okay? Stick it out. This is as bad as it gets. If you make it through this, you'll make it through the rest. I'll see if I can't get Joe to take it easy on you while you heal up. How's that sound?"

It sounds just fine to you. In this moment, Mimi seems like someone who knows what she's talking about, someone you can trust. But that's easy to feel when someone is saying what you want to hear. After all, you have no intention of leaving. Gwen Davies was born in Florida and came of age in the celestial space that hovers over the squared circle; Gwen Davies *is* home. You wink your response: *I'm not going anywhere.*

Mimi winks back. "Right. Sleep tight." And with that, she turns off the music and slips out, and you, following orders, topple onto your side and fall asleep, your suit digging trenches into your thighs, the Green Goddesses still laced to your ankles.

SEVEN

People like the Turnip have a hard time understanding the appeal of professional wrestling, but I get it. During a match, the audience can make absolute judgments about the people in the ring, something that can hardly be done in real life. Every character falls neatly into one of two categories: face or heel. In the early stages, your character was allowed some ambiguity while Joe decided what he was going to do with you. But now, a plan has been hashed out: you and Mimi will pair up for several tag team matches in various regional venues starting two days from now. This is Joe's idea. He explains that after a significant injury, a wrestler can become nervous about getting back on the horse. The best cure for this, he believes, is to remount as soon as possible, before you overthink all the ways the horse might throw you again. And, in case you are skittish about reentering the ring, he wants you to have the fortification of a seasoned partner, someone who will take the reins should you get bucked off. You are joining forces with Mimi, a heel; therefore, you must be one, too.

Welcome to the dark side, Gwen.

Joe explains that heels come in all shapes and sizes, but an unfortunate number of these archetypes are condescending, mean-spirited, or outright intolerant: delinquents, giants, nut jobs, clowns, freaks, butches, and brown-skinned savages. During Joe's five years of managing lady wrestlers, his stable of heels has included his daughter, Kat Fever; The Angel of Death, whose face is mottled with scar tissue from burns she suffered when her PT-19A crashed during WASP training; dragon lady Kim Korea (played by a Chinese-Canadian); a bitch from the Bayou known as The Ragin' Cajun, and, of course, Screaming Mimi Hollander. Now, Gwen Davies will be joining their ranks.

But what kind of villain are you supposed to be? You need a persona that wrestling spectators will be prone to dislike, and with your figure, there's only one answer. The new Gwen Davies will be an ice princess: self-important, obsessed with her looks, and supremely frigid. The men will long for you but hate you for your inaccessibility, and the women will hate you because the men long for you. You are instructed to sneer at any man who whistles or catcalls. When you enter the ring, you're supposed to pull a tiny compact from the pocket of your robe and use it to primp—fluff your hair, kiss the air, etc. And the pièce de résistance: an adjective tacked to the front of your name.

From now on, you are not just Gwen Davies, you are *Gorgeous* Gwen Davies.

If only it were that easy. It takes more than a name to make a heel. You've got some work to do. And so, one morning after you finish your workout, already looking forward to a bath and a hearty lunch (you have to cut your food into the tiniest bites, but at least you can chew again!), Mimi asks if you can stick around for a while to work on your program. You readily agree, thrilled by her willingness to teach you what she knows. But when you ask her what you're going to be working on today—Full nelsons? Flying scissors? Backbreakers?—she presses the compact into your hand.

"We'll work on plot another time," she says. "Today, we're working on character."

And work you she does, sending you up and down the aisle for a solid hour while she critiques your stride and your nose-powdering technique.

"Here's the deal," says Mimi, her voice echoing in the empty gym. She hops up on the apron and leans against the ropes. "You have what they want, but you're not going to give it to them. You don't need them. You don't need *anybody*. Got it?"

"Got it," you say, belting your robe for the umpteenth time. Your stomach growls; lunch service will be over soon. "Let's go eat."

Mimi checks the clock at the back of the gym. "We've got time. Don't get lazy on me now, Gwen. Thursday will be here before you know it. Now try it again, and this time, *convince me*. Make me *hate* you."

Thursday night will be your first match since the injury. Joe granted you a full two weeks (unpaid, of course) to recuperate and allowed you to run a tab for your room and board to be paid back (with interest) at a later time. But he made it clear that you were to keep up your daily regimen, which you did despite your diminished caloric intake. Otherwise, you did nothing but drink egg creams, fall under the spell of the radio—how did you go this long without hearing the Orioles or Big Mama Thornton?—and write out a long, earnest reply to your father in which you shared the events of your life since leaving. You described the gym and your daily routines; you told him about your suits, your photographs, and your new name. You proudly recounted the story of your first match, how your jaw was knocked out and then popped back into place. Last but not least, you tucked in one of the cards from your first match, autographed with your new moniker, no less. It was all too much—he would not approve—but you wanted to be clear about what was happening: you were transforming.

Toward that end, you will attempt the ice princess routine one more time. She is hardly the character you imagined for yourself—why would anyone want to be a heel?—but she has more championship potential than Leonie Putzkammer. Besides, you are in no position to protest.

You finger the compact in your pocket, inhale through your nose, and gather together every dastardly instinct you have.

Here goes nothing, Gwen.

At this point, keeping a smile off your face isn't exactly a challenge, and keeping your stare forward-facing isn't hard, either. No, the stride is what's tricky. When you walk toward the ring, you start off in the way you've been instructed—short, powerful steps with flexed legs, hips swaying, arms swinging in the wake of the hips—but the minute you feel the fluctuation of your breasts, you seize up. Striking a confident, slightly hammy pose was easy enough in the privacy of your room, when the only spectator was your own reflection, but out here is a whole different ball game. Despite your best efforts, you cannot overcome the years of instinctive defensiveness: your spine curves, your shoulders drop forward, and even the remotest appearance of rhythm drains out of your pelvis.

Ice princess? Not even close.

"Stop!" yells Mimi. "You had it! What happened?"

"I don't think I can do this," you say. "I'm just not like this."

Mimi closes her eyes and pinches the bridge of her nose. "Am I a screaming maniac?" When she says this, she is in fact speaking rather loudly. "Let's see the rest. Just the last bit with the compact."

You pull the compact from the depth of your pocket, snap it open, check your image, and halfheartedly dab at your nose with the cosmetic puff.

Mimi slaps her forehead with the heel of her hand. "Gwen," she says, her voice small and impatient, her eyes closed. "Go to lunch."

"I'll work on it tonight," you lie. You are sorry to be a disappointment, but you have no interest in mastering this character. This is something to be endured, not enjoyed. "I'll show you tomorrow."

"I'm busy tomorrow." Mimi is already on her way out of the gym.

"But we haven't worked on the program."

"I'll tell you the program." Mimi turns around and cups her hands around her mouth to direct the next words toward you, to make sure you hear them. "Don't blow it."

Two nights later, your first performance as a self-absorbed evildoer is, to put it mildly, lacking. Despite all the time spent coaxing out your inner heel—the expression, the strut, the *intensity*—you haven't managed to pull her out from the hard shell of your self-consciousness. If anything, the venomous reaction from the fans makes you feel more like a mouse. True, their collective moan of disapproval is largely for Mimi, but you are guilty by association.

The result? You guessed it: body curled into itself, compact left in your pocket, inert and unused. Mimi mutters "Jesus Christ" as she takes her place in the ring.

You don't want to anger Mimi by blowing the match, but the heart-rattling disapproval of the audience, as well as some residual anxiety over your jaw, results in a limited, stilted performance consisting only of defense and reaction. In fact, the first time Mimi tags you in, all your opponent has to do is charge and you drop right down and spend a good five minutes turtled on the mat. Even over the noise of the audience—the villain has shriveled up before their very eyes, to their great delight—you are sure you can hear Mimi's exasperated sighs. When you finally manage to kick off your assailant, you race to the corner and tag out. The other team has been guaranteed the victory, and Mimi is forced to lose it for you both by somersaulting in the air as if this smaller wrestler has flipped her, and landing on the canvas with a deafening clap.

"Young lady," she tells you after the match, "that's one. There better not be a two."

"Right," you say, but she doesn't hear you; she's already gone.

This is only your second match, but it is a horribly low point, especially considering the heights you reached during the first one. *That* was the way it was supposed to go. Not like this. Not with everyone against you. You cross your arms on the surface of the makeshift vanity and put your forehead down on top of them.

"How's it going?" asks Joe. Mimi must have left the door open. You hadn't noticed him walk in, but now, he leans in the doorway.

"It's been better."

"Come here for a minute," he says, which you do. "Turn around."

You're not sure what this is about, but you follow instructions and turn your back to him. From this position, Joe grabs your bicep with one hand and presses his fist against your back, between your shoulder blades. You try to stay loose, but it's an effort—you still aren't used to Joe's manhandling.

"Imagine there's an apple, and you've got to hold it right here," he says, twisting his knuckles. "You can't let it drop. Your life depends on it."

You close your eyes, nod your head, and squeeze. An apple. Okay.

"Now," says Joe, removing his fist. "Hold it. Don't let go." Your eyes are still closed, but you can feel him walk around you. He pinches your chin between his thumb and fingers. "This is okay, right? Not still sore?"

"No," you lie.

"Good. Now tilt this up like this"—he gently pushes your chin toward the ceiling—"and keep it there. Pretend you've got a penny resting up there. You don't want your penny to fall, do you?"

You shake your head only slightly, so as not to drop the penny. No.

Joe lets go of your chin. "One last thing. Every character can only be one thing. You have to be that thing, and only that thing, as big as you can. That's all they want. One thing. And your thing is to be vain. So, act like it. Think about a time when you felt gorgeous. Keep that in your head. Keep everything else out. Don't listen to anyone. Don't think about anything." Joe holds out his hand, extends three fingers. "Apple. Penny. Gorgeous. Say it."

"Apple. Penny." Your voice lowers to a whisper. "Gorgeous."

Joe shoves his hands into his pants pockets, rolls onto his heels and back. "Modesty is a nice quality in a young lady, but it's a fatal flaw in a grappler. People won't pay to see modesty. Got it?"

"Got it," you say, understanding that for the second time this evening, you've been threatened. You will have to pull it together, and fast.

In your room, you turn on the radio and pace. *Think about a time when you felt gorgeous.* When might that have been? It's not a word your father ever used, that's for sure. The boys at school? Forget about it. The guys at the diner looked at you some kind of way, but not one you cared to analyze. There was Cynthia running down the sidewalk— *Darling, I thought you'd* never *get home*—but that didn't exactly make you feel *gorgeous.* Loved, sure, but not gorgeous. And there are faraway memories of being in bed with your mother, her fingers combing your hair back against the pillow. *My pretty little girl,* she'd say. Closer, but that isn't right, either.

Someone knocks on your door. It's The Angel of Death, otherwise known as Mabel Hubbard, her skin flush and dewy from a recent soak, a laundry basket propped on her hip. "How'd it go tonight?"

"Lousy," you say. "I wasn't gorgeous enough."

"No?" Mabel scratches her head, which has apparently just received a fresh shave: a spot of shaving cream jiggles on the curve of her ear. "Well, we can't all be gorgeous."

Nice work, Gwen. Sure, Mabel's developed a thick skin and a quick, tension-defusing humor, but that just makes your thoughtlessness seem all the worse.

"I need to do some wash in the morning, but I've only got half a load," she says. "Got anything you want to add?"

The laundry basket is on the floor of the closet. From the corner of your eye, you size it up: half full. "Sure."

Mabel holds the basket out in front of her. "Toss it in." After you fetch the basket and dump its contents into her own outstretched one, she adds, "If you pay, I'll bring it back to you folded and everything."

"Fine."

While you fish a precious dime from the corner of your change purse, Mabel rifles through the pile. "Not this," she says, handing you back your red dress, the one you wore to Peggy's match on your first full day here. "The last thing I need is a drawer full of pink socks."

But the dress is the thing. Once you've submerged it in a sink of cold water and begun scouring it with a bar of soap, you recall the events of the day you wore it, the day you climbed into the backseat of Brenda's car and Peggy passed her lipstick back to you.

The color looks just smashing on you.

You sling the water from your hands and dry them on the nearest towel. Where is that lipstick now? It must be in the clutch you brought that night. But where is that? Not in the closet, not in the trunk. It's in the nightstand, in the little cubby beneath the surface that holds your radio. Open the clasp. Look inside.

There it is, Gwen. There's your answer. The next time you cruise down the aisle and climb through the ropes, apple and penny held firmly in their respective places, you will flip open the compact, pop the cap off the lipstick, and pretend to paint your lips with it. What could be more positively ice princess-y? The crowd will go wild.

Two nights later, when you and Mimi return to the ring for another battle, you chicken out. You'd gone so far as to tuck the lipstick into the pocket of your robe, felt the weight of it bouncing along beside you, but on your way to the ring, it was all you could do to keep the invisible penny balanced on your chin, to clutch the imaginary apple between your shoulder blades while the spectators taunted you. As soon as you are on the canvas and lock eyes with the same opponents who roughed you up last match, you let the apple drop, the penny slide, the lipstick lie idle. Tonight, you are slated to win—evil has to triumph over good occasionally, to keep things interesting—but still, you can't help worrying about what your opponents might have in store for you. At the last minute, you shove the lipstick into the top of your boot, hoping perhaps to draw power from its proximity.

What's worse, the girls, hard-core catfighters, resent having to lose to the likes of you. Tonight, they plan to make you earn it. Right after you are tagged in, short stuff takes a fistful of your hair, and, rather than simply pretend to sling you around the ring by your hair, she launches you into the ropes. After you land, dazed and panicked, she slaps you across the face with the back of her hand, hard.

So much for faking it.

Your first instinct is to tag out. Your jaw hurts and your confidence is nonexistent. But if you tag out, you can kiss your partnership and tenure good-bye; you can hang up your boots and scatter the ashes of Gorgeous Gwen. This is your last chance to prove that you are no fruit fly. After your boastful letter to your father, you can't very well go home. But more than that, you can't let Joe lose faith in you; you can't let Mimi be right.

It's now or never, Gwen.

You swallow your fear, roll onto your back, and steer every atom of your strength into firing the Green Goddesses into your opponent's stomach. And what do you know? It works! As your opponent flies backward into the ropes, her round eyes grow rounder—an immensely satisfying sight. This is just the mental turnaround you need, a victory of will over dread. By the time she returns, you are ready with one humdinger of a clothesline. As soon as she's down, there you are, pressing her shoulders into the mat. She struggles against you, but you have just enough juice to hold her while the ref counts.

One!

Two!

Three!

You are on top again, at least for the time being. Better yet, you have shown Joe that there is a reason you are here, that you are a worthy investment of his time and resources. High on your own bravado, you stand, rest the sole of your boot on her chest, fish out the lipstick, and pretend to apply it to your lips.

The audience responds with howling disgust, but for now, you don't hear it. It is enough that you have won, that you have proven yourself. That you can stay.

But wait, there's more. There's one last and potent victory of the evening, and this is it: Mimi comes to the center of the ring and, while the referee raises both your arms, says out of the side of her mouth, without making eye contact, "That's more like it."

This is as clear as it gets, Gwen. This is real triumph—as much as anyone can ask for. I only wish that it were enough for you.

EIGHT

It is just two months into your stay, and already, you have shown that you can do anything that is asked of you. You can deliver or take a bump; you can charm or rile a crowd. You have come a long way, but you still have a long way to go. "If you really want to be a champion," Joe says, "you have to prove yourself out on the road."

Now that your partner is sold and your story solidified, it is time to venture out of Florida and into the great nation. Getting to this stage has been a feat in its own right, but it remains to be seen how you will play in other arenas, whether you can convince and impress the die-hard fans in heartland states like Ohio, or, perhaps more treacherous for a girl from the urban Northeast, the Southern states: North Carolina, Tennessee.

"Just follow the rules, no matter what you think of them," Joe warns you. "And, whatever else you do, don't forget to say 'ma'am' and 'sir.'"

Your tour begins in a Tallahassee auditorium. After the match, you and Mimi creep through the dark parking lot, gear-laden suitcases thumping into your sides, until you arrive at the car—a Hudson Hornet—that will take you to the Carolinas for a spell before picking up the Great Lakes to Florida route and following it all the way to the Ohio territory, run by Joe's brother, Leo Pospisil, and the home base of the car's owner, Johnny Bordeaux.

There is something suspect about these travel arrangements. Earlier in the day, when Joe pulled up to the curb in front of the auditorium and opened his trunk to retrieve your suitcases, he handed yours right over but kept Mimi's, holding it against his chest with both arms.

"If you can't obey my wishes," he said, "the least you can do is be discreet."

"I don't know what you're talking about," she said, and wrested her luggage out of his arms.

More details emerge when the stocky, pinch-faced wrestler who will be your chauffeur hustles through the parking lot toward you, his motions rushed and jumpy as if his actions were criminal, and Mimi straightens and smiles. He tosses his bag into the trunk, slides into his seat, and, before even acknowledging your presence, says, "Finally," and covers Mimi's mouth with his own.

So that's it.

As it happens, Johnny is returning home after having been loaned out to Joe and other Southern promoters for a few weeks. Arranging the schedule so he will be wrestling on the same cards—and therefore traveling with you and Mimi—has taken a good amount of strategizing, negotiating, and cajoling at several levels. Mimi worked hard for this deal, not only because Johnny lives far away, but also because he is married to someone else, someone he can't leave because she recently gave birth to his son. This trip is a rare opportunity for them to be together.

Are you staring? You might be staring. The shock of seeing Mimi in this light—smitten, almost girlish—is too mind-bending for you to even give the pretense of caring about anything else. Mimi in love! Who would have guessed? Perhaps the only thing that can capture your attention now is the thing that happens: someone slams the trunk closed, opens the car door, and pops his long face into the backseat.

"Got room for me back here?"

Spider McGee: a wrestler who gets his name from the extraordinary length of his limbs, which he must now attempt to fold into the backseat. "I think so," you answer, sliding over. It only makes sense that Johnny's tag team partner would be joining you, but the thought hadn't crossed your mind. This trip has been full of surprises and you haven't even left the parking lot.

It takes a few awkward moments, but finally, there he is, beside you, his bent knees nearly level with his chest. He straps a bag of ice to one; the other grazes yours in the barest of ways. When he realizes this, he pulls it back, apologizes, but there is no need: already, you are hoping there will be occasion for it to drift back into your space.

Johnny manages to turn the ignition even though Mimi is practically in his lap, and the four of you are off, bouncing along through the still-alien Southeast, bound, ultimately, for Cleveland. There is no place you would rather be than in this seat, in this car, pointed in this direction. You are quite certain that from here, you are poised for all sorts of victories.

Shortly after you leave Point A, a debate breaks out over the location of Point B. Mimi and Johnny are eager to call it a night. Spider, however, is in no such rush, and neither are you. The two cents per mile you are supposed to pay Johnny for his services seems a reasonable fee for the pleasure of sharing a small space with Spider McGee.

Once a compromise is reached, Spider loosens his tie, pulls a loaf of sliced bread and a package of bologna from a paper bag, and sets about making sandwiches for all who are interested, which turns out to be only the two of you. (It seems Mimi is getting all the nourishment she needs from Johnny's collarbone, and Johnny, humming his approval, is too occupied with this activity to respond.) While you attempt to nibble and not wolf your sandwich, he opens a couple cans of beer—this time not bothering to extend his offer to the front seat—places one in your hand, and then brushes his against yours. "Cheers," he says, and you watch the bob of his throat as he takes a long drink.

What is there to like about Spider? It can't be the crooked nose; it certainly isn't the too-big ears. Maybe it's his minor celebrity, and his age. Six or seven years your senior, you suppose, which gives him a certain cachet. Also working in his favor: proximity and novelty. You can't remember a time when you sat this close to a boy for so long, and never in a backseat. More likely, you are drawn to him for his mood (blue) and its cause (heartbreak), which he is surprisingly and endearingly eager to talk about. Not long into the trip, he is recounting for you The Story of Spider and Debbie, a girl who smells like almonds and walks with a slight polio-induced limp, who has not only left him for a soda jerk—a soda jerk!—but didn't even have the decency to wait until he got home so she could tell him in person even though he *treated that girl like she hung the moon* and *offered her a good life where she'd never have to worry about a thing.*

"'It's not you, it's me,' she says." He rolls his eyes in exasperation. "Why do chicks always *say* that? A man can only hear it so many times."

This is your cue; it is when you are supposed to explain why women operate the way they do. The problem is, you haven't a clue. But Spider is speaking to you as if you are a knowledgeable peer, and you are anxious to maintain this appearance, so you say the only thing you know to say, "Maybe it's true."

Spider sighs. "No, it's me. It's got to be me."

Before you can offer up the compliment he's fishing for, Johnny chimes in: "Yeah, you're right." The sound of his voice startles you;

you'd forgotten all about the world beyond the backseat. "It's probably you. Now, for the love of God, will you please talk about something else?"

Spider turns toward the rearview mirror, gives it a hard stare, as if preparing for a challenge, but Johnny's eyes are no longer there to meet it: he's already returned his attention to Mimi and, to a lesser degree, the road. The skin around Spider's eyes slackens; he looks away and exhales through his nose: a little puff of laughter. "Yeah," he says to you. "I'm starting to bore myself on the subject. Let's talk about you."

And then, another reason to fall for him: his round eyes, the way they open wide, their whites visible both above and below the dark irises, and, best of all, the way they look at you attentively while you answer his questions. *Where are you from?* Philadelphia. *When did you start wrestling?* This summer. *What inspired you?* Antonino Rocca. *How'd you learn about Joe's school?* Sal Costantini. *What's your real name?*

You start to tell him. Your tongue is already on the roof of your mouth, ready to push out the first L. But you stop yourself. That is who you were, not who you are. And right now, you have no interest in being that girl. You want to be the kind of girl who might be given a chance to mend his wounded heart. So, you tell him the truth: "Gwen Davies is my real name."

Spider raises an eyebrow. "Come on."

"It *is*. The *gorgeous* part is new, of course, but the rest is all me."

He doesn't look convinced, but he doesn't press. "What about your parents?" he asks. "What do they think of all this?"

"My father's not crazy about it."

"And your mom?"

"Dead," you say. There is a moment of dread; strangers never know how to respond to this news, and you often get some kind of awkward sympathetic gesture that seems ill timed. But it's too late to say anything else; you're committed to the truth.

ANGELINA MIRABELLA

"Geez, doll, that's awful."

When you look up at his expression, you see those crush-inspiring eyes shine with earnest sympathy. Even the *doll* sounds comforting coming out of his mouth, not the slightest smack of condescension to it. This leads you to produce a sad little smile, which encourages him to lay his arm over your leg, soft side up as if he's offering you a vein to tap. Go ahead, Gwen: slip your hand into his. Revel in the sensation as he grips it once, too firmly; marvel at the way it lingers long after he releases. Sure, accepting this compassionate squeeze feels a bit fraudulent—after all this time, you are hardly in need of consolation—but this time together has made you want precisely the thing he is offering, so who are you to refuse?

Before you know it, Johnny pulls off the highway and into a novelty auto court outside of Jacksonville, rolling past the welcome sign and down the semicircle of wood-and-stucco teepees, darkness mercifully disguising their precise degree of wear and tear, to a larger teepee advertising vacancies. He puts the car in park and hurries off to acquire a room for him and Mimi. Know what that means, Gwen? You won't be able to count on her for a roommate this evening or, for that matter, the entire trip to Cleveland. Consequently, travel costs are about to take a ravenous bite out of your meager profits.

Just as this realization is beginning to dawn, Spider, suffering the same dilemma, asks, "Care to split a wigwam?"

This sounds exactly like the high jinks Joe's warned you against. Not that any of your fellow passengers would make this situation known to him, but the thought of his knowing is enough to strike you with fear. And what about the other disapproving man in your life? You don't even want to *think* about what your father would say.

Either your hesitation is apparent or Spider means to alleviate it before it appears, because he quickly follows with "Two beds, of course," and then holds up a hand in pledge. "I'll be the perfect gentleman." This is not the kind of thing a good girl like you does, even with such assurances, but it sure beats ponying up for your own room. Besides, you are weary from the Tallahassee match and a little drunk to boot, conditions that sand the edges off of your reservations, so you nod in agreement. After a series of complicated maneuvers, he extracts his reedy frame from the backseat and heads into the office to make the arrangements.

Soon, there you both are: standing, suitcases in hand, in a cloud of dust, Johnny and Mimi having sped off, anxious to rattle the poles of their own teepee.

Spider sets his suitcase down, fits a key into the door. "Hope you don't mind," he says, "but I told the desk clerk you were my wife. Didn't want him to get the wrong idea."

"No. Of course not," you say, letting yourself get a bit swept up in the romance of this, wondering if someday these words will seem prophetic.

"So, the good news is"—he pauses while he plays with the uncooperative key, eventually managing to pop the lock—"Johnny and I got the last two rooms."

You realized from Spider's awkwardness in the car that he was a tall man, but it's only now, as he stands upright, looking down at you with that sad, moony countenance of his, that you realize just how tall he actually is. Not Monster tall, of course, but tall enough that if you were to embrace him just now, you could comfortably place your cheek against the open collar of his shirt. Eventually, you force yourself to stop picturing this and think to ask, "And the bad news?"

He flings the door open, revealing not the two promised beds but one large one. "But don't go getting any ideas. If you think you're going to use this to take advantage of me, you are sadly mistaken." Perhaps he sees the color draining out of your face, because he quickly follows with "Sorry. Bad joke." He points to the head of the bed. "Look. There's lots of pillows. We'll build a wall between us." And then, when that clearly hasn't diminished your alarm, "Or I could sleep on the floor."

Spider plops his suitcase down, takes a seat at the foot of the bed, and toes the heel of one shoe off, then the other, making himself at home while you remain in the door frame, frozen in place. In the backseat of a car with two other passengers, where there were limited possibilities and low expectations, Spider seemed innocent enough. Here, with him seated in a private room on a freshly made bed—one you are expected to share, no less—you aren't so sure. Perhaps you should be reassured by his status as the recently jilted, but this only makes you all the more anxious.

Spider wrinkles his face; a curious smile spreads over it. "Would you like me to carry you over the threshold?"

This time, the marriage reference has an altogether different effect. "You know," you say, grabbing the handle of your suitcase, "I think I'll just go stay in the car."

"Gwen, don't be silly."

But you don't respond: you are already on your way.

An hour later, stretched out as much as the backseat of the Hornet will allow, you give up on sleep. There is too little room and too much on your mind for that. You rifle around in the glove compartment until you find a flashlight and try to concentrate on *The Price of Salt,* a last-minute addition to your suitcase—a girl needs something to distract and entertain herself, doesn't she?—but you are not really taking much of it in. Mostly, you are absorbing the strangeness of your situation. You are so far from any experience you can recognize. Earlier this evening, you would have happily driven all night; now, you wonder if you aren't beginning to drift off course.

Rapping knuckles on the car window cause you to startle, and then, instinctively, you shove the book under your blanket and point the flashlight toward the sound: Spider. He moves his fist in a circular motion—*roll down the window*—and you oblige before lying down again.

"Hey," he says. "Whatcha reading?"

"A book," you say, a bit more tersely than you intend.

Spider rolls his eyes. "Okay. Don't tell me. Can I at least come in and talk to you for a minute?"

There's good reason to be annoyed. After all, you are currently trying to sleep in the backseat of the car that brought you to this forsaken part of the world. But Mimi and Johnny are to blame, not him. Go ahead: wave him in. Hear him out.

Spider reaches in through the opening, unlocks the driver-side door, and lets himself in, propping himself up against the passenger-side door, his knees bent so that he can fit on the upholstery parallel to you. His short hair is still damp from a shower—a shower: now that would be nice right about now, wouldn't it, Gwen?—and his shirt is misbuttoned so that a bit of fabric balloons out beneath his collarbone. "Here," he says before reaching into his shirt pocket and pulling out something wrapped in cellophane. "I brought you a peace offering."

For all the time you will spend here, the South will never feel like home. Most of what you have seen so far—tenant farmers, white lightning, stock car racing—makes you long for the Northeastern peculiarities you know. The only exception is the food. On this tour, you'll discover chicken-fried steak and fried catfish plates at drive-ins along the way, some of them so new as to be unpaved and un-canopied, and you'll learn the pleasures of peanuts: both the hot-and-meaty boiled variety and the standard roasted-and-salted puppies, the latter being best poured into a bottle of ice-cold Coca-Cola. But you will fall most deeply in love with this graham cracker goodness, filled with heavenly marshmallow and bathed in chocolate.

You pinch off a bite, pop it into your mouth, and close your eyes: *yum*.

"Pretty nice of me, giving you my last MoonPie."

What can you say to that? Not much. Maybe you've been a little rash, but if he thinks you're going to be reassured with snacks, he is sadly mistaken.

"You can't be comfortable out here," he says. "Why don't you come sleep in the bed for the rest of the night? I'll take the car."

"Don't be silly." You look over the bench seat, point to his tented legs. "You don't fit in here."

"And you do? Come on, Gwen. You're making me feel like a jerk."

"It was my choice."

"What are you going to do? Sleep in the car the whole way up?"

"Of course not." No, your plan is to stubbornly hemorrhage money. "I'll get my own room next time."

He makes a face at this—brows pinched, lips turned out—as if trying to determine what it is he doesn't know that would help all of this make sense to him. He takes a stab: "Are you worried about what your boyfriend will think?"

What you should say is this: "I don't have a boyfriend." But what you say, reflexively and carelessly, is this: "Yeah. Like I've ever had a boyfriend."

Spider cocks his head. His dark eyes flash as he registers this new information. "*Really?*"

In the car, you'd managed, however imprecisely, to give the impression of being someone with comparable experience in this realm. Sure, you've probably already tarnished this image by taking up residency in the Hornet, but now, with this admission, you have confirmed that you are not only young and naive but also incredibly pathetic. The last thing you want to do is have a conversation about your nonexistent love life, so you give the shortest, most benign answer you possibly can: "Really." Then, curious, you say, "You've probably had a lot of girlfriends."

"More than I would like." Spider sighs. "What I really want is to go on my last first date. But that's not going to happen anytime soon. For most chicks, this going out on the road thing gets old fast." There is weariness in his voice when he says this, and, for a minute, it looks like he might say more, but then he changes his mind, steers away from this downer of a topic, perks up. "What if I tell you a secret? Maybe then you'll know you can trust me."

"Depends," you say, sorry that you ever thought him capable of ill intent and glad that, despite his new knowledge about you, he has continued to grace you with his company.

"My name isn't actually Spider McGee."

"No kidding."

"I know. Hard to believe, but true. My real name is Sam. Samuel Pospisil."

Pospisil? "You mean—"

"Yep. Joe's my uncle. Leo's my dad."

How about that: a bona fide member of the Pospisil dynasty. "Why is that a secret?"

"It never helps things, in my experience, when people know. *They* do"—he points out the windshield at the teepee Mimi and Johnny currently occupy—"but most people don't, so I'd appreciate it if you'd keep it just between us."

Just between us. You like the sound of that. It's not like you've been entrusted with government secrets or anything, but it is nice to be taken into his confidence, even in this small way. Maybe he does think you a little naive, but perhaps he hasn't written you off altogether. The right thing to do, it seems, is return the gesture.

"Mine's Leonie. Leonie Putzkammer."

Spider—Sam—closes his eyes. "Leonie Putzkammer," he exhales. "Leonie, Leonie, Leonie."

I can't be sure of his motives on this evening, if the feelings he will develop for you are already taking shape. But your revelation has led to this tender reward—the whispering of your name, as if he's holding it delicately in his hands, leaving room for it to breathe—and it pulls you toward him with the force of gravity. Whatever has happened, it feels like intimacy to you, and this rare and fleeting taste of it makes you hungry for more.

"I should get to bed." Sam puts a hand on the door handle. "Sure you want to stay out here?"

There is nothing you'd like more than to go with him, to toss off more of your boundaries and reservations in pursuit of this feeling. But you are paralyzed by the same fear that sent you to this car and a stubborn need to save face, so you nod.

Sam slides back down the bench seat, lets himself out, and, before closing the door, says, "Can't say I didn't try." Once he has disappeared from sight, you brush the chocolate crumbs off your chest, pick up your flashlight and book, and flip to where you left off, with the arrival of Therese's Christmas card in Carol's mailbox, signed only with her employee number. But instead of moving forward, you read the same page over and over again, unable to absorb the words, too preoccupied with the sound of your name—*Leonie, Leonie, Leonie*—and the man who spoke it.

NINE

Nineteen fifty-three might well turn out to be a perfect season for Cleveland's resident NFL team. That's the word from Sam, at least. As he pilots Johnny's car toward the stadium on this mid-November Sunday, he rattles off both recent history and future predictions, more than you care to know about Automatic Otto Graham and the thorough routing he expects today of the San Francisco 49ers to keep the Browns' undefeated season alive. "I'm telling you, Leonie," he says, pulling into a parking spot, "this is our year."

"Sounds like it," you say, but you haven't a clue, really. You are just happy to be here, with him. In your weeks together on the road, Sam was a pleasant fixture in your life. He was easy company in the back of the car and over prematch sandwiches or postmatch drinks, which loosened you both up enough to talk freely of your lives. When money finally grew so tight that you had no choice but to share a room, these conversations went late into the night. It felt like you were unspooling parts kept tightly coiled. But then, shortly after the four of you rolled into Cleveland, he disappeared back into his life, leaving you semistranded in a strange city and, worse, abruptly ending what you'd foolishly assumed was courtship. It was only Johnny's eagerness for an afternoon with Mimi, and the ready alibi that the game provided, that made this ticket available to you. Still, when Sam stopped by your dressing room and asked if you wanted Johnny's ticket to the game, you accepted, not entirely sure what game he was talking about but grateful for one more afternoon with him. You tell yourself that this is only an opportunity for a proper good-bye, nothing more, but you can't quite fool yourself. In your heart of hearts, you still hope.

Sam comes around to open your door, offers his arm, and escorts you into quite possibly the worst place to be if you want to survive a Cleveland winter: the bleachers of Cleveland Municipal Stadium. In this exposed section positioned in the gap between the ends of the horseshoe-shaped stadium, you feel particularly vulnerable to the winds blowing off of nearby Lake Erie.

"This has got to be the coldest place on earth," you say.

"Trust me, it gets worse," he says, lacing his fingers together in front of him. "This stadium is the pits."

"Is it? I don't have anything to compare it to." You pinch the neck of your coat together in your fist and try to burrow down into its collar. "I'm not much of a sports fan."

Sam laughs. "That's pretty funny, coming from an athlete."

Much of the first half goes this way, your conversations centered on the smallest of subjects: the temperature, the crowd, and, of course, the action on the field. It is a stark and disappointing contrast from the cozy chitchat of the road. Sam talks endlessly about the game—explaining rules and penalties, describing plays and their justifications—but you don't have a lot of interest, and it's hard to fake it. But just when you are ready to abandon hope, he changes tack, mercifully ditching the narration and asking, "So, you've been in Cleveland for what, three nights now? What do you think of our fair city?"

"Seems okay to me," you say, hoping he doesn't ask for a more precise description. The truth is, you haven't ventured beyond the corner diner, which limits your understanding of your current locale to lake-effect snow and chicken paprikash.

"Oh, yeah? What have you been up to?"

If only there was something to tell. Mostly, you've been holed up in your hotel room, listening to the radio and feeling blue. But in this time, you've grown enamored of Alan Freed, King of the Moondoggers, and you say as much. This admission prompts him to entertain you with the tale of his harrowing experience at the Moondog Coronation Ball, which you follow with your own mishap on *Bandstand*. This exchange feels more like the return to form you were hoping for, which prompts you to share some of the human details you might otherwise keep under wraps: your loneliness in the stands, the humiliation of getting passed off by Freddy. It feels a little risky, sharing this with him, but he rewards you for it with his attentiveness. He seems to like this version of you, as do you. If only you could always be so easy and pleasant, so charmingly self-deprecating.

When you finish your story, Sam slides toward you on the bench, and suddenly, the possibility of Something Happening seems very real. You are more than ready for it, whatever form it takes—an arm around your shoulders, a hand on your knee, even (dare you imagine?) a kiss. Anything is welcome. When his face moves toward yours, the rest of the world peels away.

"Leonie," he breathes, "what's a nice girl like you doing wrestling?"

This is not what you were hoping for. It takes a moment to return to the present, to find your voice and use it. "I want to be the champion. Same as everybody else, I guess."

A savvier gal would understand this is not what he wants to hear. If you had been paying attention these last few weeks, you might have picked up on the fact that he is indifferent to wrestling, that he is only following his father's plan for him to learn the family business from the bottom up. He is merely hanging on until he makes it to the other side, where he can wake up each morning in the city he loves, wear a suit to work, and serve as his father's right hand. And if you were not just savvy but worldly, you would see the conflict here, enjoy the afternoon for what it is, and move on with your life—without him. But you are you, hopelessly clueless and overly smitten, which means you have no idea what you have said.

Sam looks at you for a long time, as if carefully measuring his words before cutting them from the cloth. Eventually, he straightens up and smiles in a way that is not unfriendly, but not exactly encouraging, either.

"Not everybody," he says quietly. "I guess that's one more way we're different."

Something worrisome happens on the field that gets everyone on their feet, including Sam, which gives you a blessed minute to hide in a cave of legs while you process what he has said. *I guess that's one more way we're different.* That can only mean one thing: he liked you well enough to do the math, but found you didn't add up. You wish you didn't know this. If he had merely disappeared, as it first seemed he would, you could have convinced yourself you'd misunderstood, that any connection was all in your imagination. Now you are left to mull over all the ways you might have come up short.

I can't be sure about Sam's calculations, of course, but from what I have come to know of him, and men in general, I might guess that he has come to a reasonable conclusion: you are not the right girl for him. More likely, he is looking for a girl who is a little more traditional, someone who won't object to frying up the bacon he brings home. That glorious, imposing figure of yours probably isn't helping matters, either. As you will soon learn, he can be overprotective. No, what he needs is a girl who is pretty enough—who needs ribbing from the guys?—but not so pretty that she often lands the attention of a man's wandering eye. You might not notice how men react when you come into view, but he's sure to have taken note and guessed that getting involved with you would mean for him a perpetual brawl with the rest of the male world. In short, he knows himself. This will be true for you, too, someday. Just not today.

Above you, the murmurs grow more frantic. When you stand up to see what the hubbub is about, Sam says, "This is heartbreaking."

"What is?" you ask, hopeful beyond reason.

He points to the field, where a player—14, Browns—is being helped off the field. The quarterback, Sam informs you. That sleazebag Michalik elbowed him in the face.

Sam adds his voice to the worried mumblings of the crowd. What will this mean for their promising season? Since you, having no investment in this player, this team, or this sport, have little to contribute, you drift off into your own more self-centered melancholy while he starts sinking into the collective one of the crowd. "This is it," he says. "I can feel it. This is the beginning of the end."

Your sentiments exactly.

As the end of the half slips into halftime, you are so deep in your thoughts that you almost don't hear a voice say, "Pardon me." When you turn around, you find a married couple standing nearby. The husband sports a gruff bit of stubble and a tweed driving cap, while the wife holds a pen and pocket-sized pad. "Could we get an autograph?" asks the man. "The missus is a big fan."

"Really?" you ask, grateful to these blessed souls for salvaging what would otherwise be a miserable afternoon. "You want my autograph?"

The woman hesitates, and her husband says, "Actually, ma'am, we were asking Spider here. No offense, of course."

"Oh, no, of course," you say, shoving your hands deep into your pockets. "My mistake."

While Sam takes the pen, you stare at your feet and wait for the heat to drain out of your cheeks. Maybe this should be your strategy for the rest of the day: keep your eyes down and your trap shut. That way, nothing else will blow up in your face.

Once they are gone, you shake your head. "I'm an idiot."

Sam laughs. "Why?" he says. "Because you expect everyone to know that you're the hottest thing in lady wrestling? That you've razzed every audience in Ohio and the Southeast, and now you're about to do it across the nation? Listen here, Gwen. Those folks are going to kick themselves one day when they realize what they did."

"Those people don't even know who I am."

Sam puts his hands on your shoulders and says, "Then those people can just get bent."

You shouldn't let this get your hopes up. If Sam still had any romantic interest in you, he would probably be annoyed by your eagerness for attention. The fact that he is ready to humor your desires and bolster your confidence suggests he is prepared to be your fan, maybe even your friend, but nothing more. But you hear only earnest praise, and this gives you something to cling to. There is still time. Perhaps you can convince him he has not considered all the variables.

When more fans approach with pens and pads, Sam draws you in and says in a low voice, "Want to get out of here?"

"Yes!" You cross your arms over your chest and clutch yourself. "It's miserable out here. I don't know how you can stand it."

Sam helps you down the bleachers, escorting you away from the spot where you both might have witnessed history: Graham will return to the field with fifteen stitches and a helmet wrapped with plastic, and the Browns will continue their season's winning streak. Not a big loss for a girl with an aversion to team sports, but one that is sure to plague Sam for years to come. Thankfully, something he might find equally memorable is about to come of it.

Before you can make it safely out of the stadium, a voice calls out, "Hey, Spider! Spider, wait up!" Jogging up behind you isn't another autograph hound but a twitchy young man wearing what looks like his father's sports coat and fedora, a camera in his hands. When he catches up, he points to the press credentials stuck in his hatband. "Can I get a picture of the two of you for the *PD*?"

"Fine," says Sam, who turns and asks, "You?"

Once you nod your approval, he leaves his arm outstretched until you join his side and he can rest a supportive arm around your shoulders. It fits beautifully there, even better than you might have guessed. Emboldened, you place your arm around his waist and hold firm. "Thanks, Spider," says the reporter, letting the camera dangle about his neck while he reaches inside his jacket for a notebook and pencil. "And what's the young lady's name?"

"I'm Gorgeous Gwen Davies," you say, suddenly bristling with bravado. "The hottest thing in lady wrestling."

The reporter, his smile forced, his eyes flecked with annoyance, turns to you. "Is that so?"

"It is," says Sam. He presses a finger into the man's notebook. "Write it down."

First, there was the cheerleading, then his arm around you, and now this. It is hard to stand still; every physiological response in your body is in overdrive. This feeling is just too good to let slip into *good night, and good luck,* roll credits. No, you have to try. The quarterback might be out, but that doesn't mean you can't throw your own Hail Mary.

The reporter does as he's told, but he will take some creative license before the words make it into the paper. The next morning, under a messy newsprint photograph in which the both of you have brilliant, open-mouthed smiles, there will be this sentence: *Also in attendance was one of professional wrestling's hottest couples, Spider McGee and Gorgeous Gwen Davies.* In the years to come, every time you see the clipping, you will wonder whether this was something the photographer intuited or something he set into motion, if that glare of his wasn't the toppling domino, the car spinning on black ice that made Sam defensive, and you, in turn, uncharacteristically bold. Because the moment the reporter is gone, you burn up the last of your bravado by smashing your mouth into Sam's.

"Thank you for saying that," you say when it is over.

Even by your own very low standards, this was not a great kiss. Not even close. In fact, it was precisely the kind of kiss that would be delivered by a girl who has only practiced on pillows. But there are real feelings behind it: adoration, gratitude, and urgency. Perhaps these are factors enough for Sam to rework his careful calculations. Or maybe there are no calculations. Maybe that kiss, however clumsy, scrambled his brain. In any case, the effect is game changing. This could easily have been the last conversation you ever had with Sam Pospisil. Instead, it is a new beginning.

"So, there's a new RKO flick playing at the Palace," he says. "*The Big Heat*. Interested?"

TEN

Early the next morning, you watch Sam wave through the window of a Greyhound Scenicruiser, Mimi firmly settled into the seat beside you, as it pulls away from the platform. This begins your long journey to Memphis, one of the most rasslin'-passionate cities in the nation, where you will kick off a tour that will take you through Tennessee to Nashville and into Pinky George's Kentucky-West Virginia territory, after which you'll pull a U-ey and head back to Ohio, where your darling Sam will be waiting. Over the last three months, you've had to (a) recover from a serious injury, (b) overcome performance anxiety, (c) win over a lukewarm partner, and (d) spend all your meager earnings on travel expenses, but this is the first time you've questioned whether the benefits of your vocation outweigh its disadvantages. You would like nothing better than to stay right here with him. You press your nose against the cold window glass and wave back until he is no longer visible, already counting the days until he will be again (20).

"Aren't you a cute little puppy?" says Mimi without looking up from her magazine. "Don't worry. We'll be back soon."

Could she be any more irritating? It's bad enough that she is the intermediary for all your bookings—just once, it would be nice if Joe would call *you* with some information—or, more frustrating, that she insisted on her own room in Cleveland just so she could have privacy on the afternoons that Johnny could sneak away (which added up to a grand total of *one*), forcing you to live off milkshakes for the past couple of days. At least she was able to sweet-talk Joe into booking you both in Ohio again. You will benefit from that as much as she will.

"Not soon enough."

"Oh, come on. You're days away from your first title bout. Aren't you even a little excited?"

This gets your attention. "Title? You never said anything about a title."

"I didn't? Well, then," she says, closing her magazine. "Allow me to fill you in."

And with that, Mimi tells you how it is. What better way to convince the average consumer of the relevance, the *importance,* of a match than to raise the stakes and make it a *championship*? Maybe said working stiff wants the security of being on the side of the incumbent; maybe the rugged, up-by-your-own-bootstraps individualist in him prefers to pledge his allegiance to the contender. Either way, the evidence is indisputable: a surefire way to boost ticket sales is to include, before a wrestler's name, that eye-catching designation *champion*. And so, when the Tennessee promoter discovered a void in the wrestling pantheon, he decided it was high time he fill it and booked four up-and-coming girl grapplers—Vera Blake, a former roller derby champion with hammers for thighs; Kay Pepper, a charismatic ex-actress; Mimi Hollander, a wild-haired heel; and Gorgeous Gwen Davies, the filly from Philly—to vie for this new title: the Tennessee Women's Tag Team Championship.

In this game, it is just that easy. Not that you're complaining. No one has to explain the appeal of a champion to you. And now, you have a chance to be one. That's the catch.

"Please tell me we're going to win it."

"Dunno. It's a shoot."

"What does that mean?"

"It *means* it's for real. We'll have to fight for it."

Fight for it? Once upon a time, you'd been shocked to learn about the engineering of the victories, but when Mimi tells you this, you are even more shocked—and, to be completely honest, disappointed—to learn that there are still occasions when they aren't.

"Don't sweat it," she says, sensing your anxiety. "Vera is tough, but Kay's nothing but a pretty face. And you know how to hold your own now."

"I do?" There's no way you heard that right. It almost sounded like a compliment.

"You've got good technique." Mimi licks her finger, flips the page of her magazine. "Your instincts aren't half bad for someone so green, and you've definitely got the moxie. You wouldn't believe the silliness I've seen over a broken toe, but it hasn't stopped you."

Mimi is referring to an injury you sustained from your heavy-heeled opponent in last night's match. She buddy-taped it for you between falls, and although you were forced to steer clear of your signature dropkicks, you'd managed to finish the match. Now, you wiggle your toe, refreshing the pain and reminding yourself how tough you really are.

"You got a long way to go, though," Mimi continues. "You know what you need to do?"

"Travel with someone I can share hotel costs with so I won't go broke?"

Mimi ignores the comment. "You need to embrace your persona."

This makes you laugh. Fat lot of good your persona's done you. If you weren't already weary of being a heel—who besides Mimi could put up with the soul-crushing symphony of boos and insults night after night?—you certainly are now.

"I'm serious," says Mimi, folding her magazine closed and focusing her attention on you. "You think you want to be a face. But you see how it is when we walk in. They're on top of their chairs, right? They're tearing their hair out, beating their chests. You can *hear* their blood boiling. They can't get enough." Her mouth spreads into a self-assured smirk. "They want to rip the faces' clothes off, but us? They want to tear us limb from limb."

"I want them to love me, not assault me."

"*Love* you?" she repeats, incredulous. "You're a heel, damn it. Love should be the last thing on your mind." You turn toward the window and close your eyes. Everything Mimi says makes you weary. "You don't like my advice," says Mimi. "That's okay. You'll see. The heel is the *show*."

She opens her magazine again, snapping it forcefully to make her point: *This conversation is over.*

Later that night, you and Mimi check into the most posh of your hotels thus far, The Maxwell House Hotel, its coffee *good to the last drop*, at the same time that Kay and Vera step out of the elevator carrying a bottle in a paper bag.

"Hi, ladies," says Vera. You've never seen Vera—short-haired, hard-jawed, and bullet-eyed—in anything other than her wrestling gear, so it's a little jarring to see her in street clothes at all, let alone the ones she's in now: trousers, saddle oxfords, and a man's blazer. "We're going to catch up with some of the guys for a few cocktails." She slides the bottle out of the bag a few inches—rum—and rattles it. You can't help but stare at the hand on the neck of that bottle, in particular the nails: long, manicured, and lacquered; strange, considering the rest of the getup. She returns the bottle to its paper sleeve. "Care to join?"

"No thanks," Mimi says quickly. "Joe will kill us if we're caught out in public with you two."

"Oh, get off it, Meems," says Vera. "We're just going to the local watering hole. Besides, no one knows who you are, anyway."

Mimi's posture steels; her eyes narrow. "Don't you ladies have kind of a big match tomorrow?"

"Sure do," says Kay, "but if we all have a drink, then we'll all be in the same position, now won't we?" She turns to you, eyes flashing. "What do you say, fresh meat? Want to go for a cocktail, or you want to sit in your hotel room watching the paint fade?"

The warning look Mimi gives you—wide eyes, puckered lips— makes it painfully clear what you're supposed to say. And she's right: you should say no, not only to stay in her good graces, but also to take every advantage you can get over these two. But this sounds harmless enough. It might even be fun. At the very least, it could be a pleasant diversion from the usual monotony of holing up in your hotel room and suffering through Mimi's gloating and know-it-all-ness. Besides, why should *she* get to call all the shots? This last thought is what clinches it for you; it's time to claim your rightful position as full partner in this arrangement.

"One drink," you say to Mimi. "And then we'll take a cab home."

Mimi points her finger at you and opens her mouth. She's about to let you have it, but, instead, she stops herself, takes a quick look at Vera and Kay, and changes her mind. Mimi takes the business of wrestling narratives more seriously than most. As mad as she is, she has no interest in presenting anything less than a united front; there will be no argument in front of the enemy.

"Fine," she says. "One drink."

The bar, a real hole-in-the-wall on Printers Alley, leaves a lot to be desired, but it does have a jukebox and a small parquet dance floor. After the bartender makes your drinks from Vera's bottle, you and Mimi take seats at a table on its edge and watch as a giant Austrian repeatedly slings Kay through his legs and over his shoulders. Mimi drains her glass in short order.

117

"That's my one," she says, standing up. "Finish up. I'm going to the ladies' room. When I get back, you better be ready to go."

You take small, purposeful sips of your drink. Screw Mimi. You don't want to hurry up and hurry out, and you're not going to. Instead, you swing your foot in time to the music. Too bad your toe's broken. It might be fun to cut in and show the Austrian there's nothing Kay's got that you don't. Plus, Kay might welcome the reprieve; she looks flustered and dizzy. Sure enough, before the song ends, she says a quick word to her partner and then falls into Mimi's vacated seat.

"I can't do it anymore," she says.

Kay waves to the bartender, signals for him to mix her another drink, and starts talking your ear off. Turns out she is a former actress, with bit parts in *Ladies of the Chorus* (chorus girl), *Life with Father* (maid) and *Gentleman's Agreement* (party guest). She went by Lila Garner back then, not that she was ever credited for her roles. Do you remember her? You don't, but nod and say you thought she looked familiar.

Someone is at your back. You assume it's Mimi, but when you turn around, you discover the Austrian: barrel-chested, sweat-drenched, and ready for more. Kay waves him off and sticks her thumb out at you. "Ask fresh meat here."

The Austrian extends his catcher's mitt of a hand. "What do you say?"

"Can't," you say, and point down at your foot. "Broken toe."

He rolls his eyes and heads to the bar to hit up someone else.

"Good one," Kay says.

"Good nothing. I broke it last night."

Kay reaches behind her neck, cups her hand around her hair and pulls it over to one shoulder, all the while leaning in, lowering her eyelids, looking down her nose, like she is sharpening her focus on you, or, rather, something lurking just beneath the surface of you. "Which one?"

You wiggle your left foot. "This one." Kay's eyes brighten; her laugh is shrill. "Well, then. That's a rather convenient injury. Now you don't have to suffer through that ogre pulling your arms out of their sockets."

You look toward the bathroom. Mimi still hasn't come out. Should you go check on her? No. Mimi can take care of herself. Besides, Kay seems sweet. You understand why you are not supposed to be friends with your rivals, but what harm is there in just talking?

"Why did you stop acting?" you ask.

"It wasn't exactly my idea." She searches your face. "What about you? You're a pretty girl. Ever think about it?"

"Acting? Who, me?"

"Why, with a little haircut, you'd look just like Marilyn Monroe! Here." Kay snatches the elastic out of your ponytail, releasing your hair, and then combs the ends into her hands before holding them up, simulating a bob. It will be years before you can unpack everything that is going on in this moment, to understand that there are lots of ways a girl can be seduced, and many reasons for it. For now, you are only pleasantly surprised at this gesture of intimacy, much as you were when Cynthia marched into your house for tumbling lessons. You try not to be hopeful in the same fruitless way, but you can't help but think it *would* be nice to make a friend.

"Very glamorous," Kay says. "Just one more thing."

Kay opens up your clutch, somehow knowing what she will find in there: the lipstick Peggy gave you when you first arrived in Otherside, the one you use every night as part of your ice princess routine. Kay twists the tube until the well-rounded end appears and hands it to you.

There's a loud, purposeful cough behind you, and then Mimi says, "I hate to interrupt this lovefest, but it is high time we got the hell out of here. Kind of a big day tomorrow, wouldn't you say, Gwen?"

Your stomach flops nervously. You might not feel the need to adhere to kayfabe quite as religiously as Mimi, but even you can admit this is

119

over the line. Kay, however, isn't the least bit rattled. "Gorgeous," she says. "Just like your name."

Calling Kay Pepper a pretty face is a serious understatement: the woman is a total knockout. The next evening, when you see her entering the Hippodrome skating rink (*For Health's Sake, Roller Skate!*) for the big match, she is cloaked in a mink coat—actual *mink*—even though it's sixty degrees. The flips on the ends of Kay's ebony pageboy bounce as she preens for the Converse-clad boys and their slightly less sex-dazed fathers, who all but accost her, thrusting pens and pads into her manicured hands, clamoring for her to pose with them. When she begins rewarding them for their patience and loyalty, Mimi makes a derisive noise and mutters, "Miss Hot Shit," but you are soaking it all in: the alluring gait, the charismatic flounce, and, most importantly, the adoring fandom. What you wouldn't give to spin heels like Kay Pepper. You stand there, enchanted, until Mimi breaks the spell with a slap to the back of your head.

"Hey," you say, rubbing the spot. "What was *that* for?"

"I think you know," says Mimi, her brow and mouth two horizontal lines. Kay's reception contrasts quite starkly with the treatment you and Mimi receive. Later in the evening, when the two of you step into the aisle, you are greeted with the fiercest disapproval of your short career. This goes beyond the usual tunnel of booing spectators; for the first time, the crowd dares to make its threats physical. Mimi is pelted with an egg, and then a beer can. Most of their hatred is directed at her; it seems you might reach the relative safety of the ring unscathed, until, just steps away from the apron, you take a tomato in the chest.

You should know better than to stand there, dumbfounded, staring with disbelief at the wet stain on your suit. If you're going to make yourself a target, then don't act surprised when someone takes advantage of it: in this case, a teenage girl—one or two years younger than you, by the looks of it—with an aisle seat, who is perfectly positioned to give you a fierce push. There's not much to it (in addition to years, you've got some inches and pounds on her, too), but it's hard enough to force you back a step and leave you standing there with a dumb look on your face. That leaves everything up to Mimi, who steps in front of you and gives the girl a quick lesson in the art of the shove, sending her straight to the floor, before grabbing your elbow and leading you to the ring.

"Was that necessary?" you ask, hoisting yourself onto the ropes.

"Please," says Mimi, rope in hand. "I gave her exactly what she came for."

Once you are both in your corner of the ring, Mimi explains your role: to give her short, occasional reprieves, and then to tag out as soon as you get her signal. You might be insulted by this reduction of faith if your stomach hadn't been colonized by leg-thumping rabbits. This is the big one, after all. Tonight, you could go home with a belt. So you stick to the plan, and Mimi pins Kay in the first fall while you lift nary a finger. But during the second fall, Vera launches her over the ropes, and when you see Mimi hit the front-row spectators, a party of red-faced, soft-bellied Kiwanis club types who push her off and onto the floor, you know it's time to make the switch. You jump down to help her up.

"Stay in as long as you can," she whispers. "I hurt all over."

"Yeah, okay," you say, and climb over the ropes. There, waiting in the ring, isn't Vera but Kay, wiggling her fingers at you. "Hello, fresh meat," she says.

What a relief. Vera is a monster, but Kay—if you can't handle Kay, then you can't handle anyone. She confirms as much with her first hit, a paltry open-handed slap to the head. So go ahead, Gwen: show her what you're made of. Knock the wind out of her with a judo chop. Grab her by the hair; toss her over your shoulder. While she crawls around on the mat, trying to catch her breath, climb to the top of the turnbuckle, and the minute she's on her feet, fly at her. Take her down.

After you both hit the mat, you are sure you hear a noise of real misery issue from beneath you. When the ref begins to count, you whisper, "You okay?"

"Gee, Gwen," says Kay. Her face registers pain, yet her hushed voice drips with playfulness. "I thought we were friends."

You shouldn't care about being Kay's friend, of course—not here, not now—but for a moment, this gets to you, and, however unconsciously, you ease off a bit. It is only a moment, but it costs you big: before the last count, Kay works her shoulder off the mat, and then kicks out of the pin. You hurry onto your feet, but she's ready for you, first with an elbow to the stomach.

"You really shouldn't make it this easy," she says. While you are still doubled over, she grinds your toe into the mat with the heel of her heavy-soled boot.

That toe. The left one, the one you told her about last night. Kay never wanted to make nice, you moron. She wanted to disarm you, and she succeeded because she is a master at falsifying a connection. She knows how to leverage her assets and create the illusion of love. Usually, she relies on those bedroom eyes and pouty lips, but for you, she shifted her tactics ever so slightly, putting away the come-hither stare in favor of a friendly smile and a compliment. She saw a lonely girl in need of a friend, and she played the role. And you fell for it hook, line, and sinker.

Now, you hit the mat, reverberating with pain from the elastic of your ponytail down to your battered little toe. Out of the corner of your eye, you see Mimi at the ropes, her arm stretched out. You summon all of your willpower to get to your knees so you can crawl over to her, but before you get anywhere close, Kay kicks you once, hard, in the stomach. You fall over onto your back, and she's on you in seconds.

That's it for this fall, Gwen: you're toast.

After the ref calls it, you return to your corner. Mimi spits over her shoulder. "What the hell just happened?" she says, and you lie through your teeth: "I have no idea."

Meanwhile, across the ring, Vera throws an arm around Kay's neck and pulls her close, knocks Kay's forehead with her own. This is as much public affection as they allow each other, as you will ever see between them. You don't think anything of it, but I have heard every rumor. I know history. For me, that gesture has only one meaning: *I love you.*

It is a hard way to live, getting paid to publicly roll around with other women for the pleasure of an audience who would condemn you for doing the same behind closed doors; to make sure those doors stayed firmly closed. And yet they will do it. They will love each other as quietly and invisibly as possible, insisting they are only friends, only roommates. It's instinctive kayfabe, deeply ingrained by a lifetime of fear and reprisals.

If you ask me, the secret to Kay Pepper's success is linked to this secret. It all boils down to one word: survival. She doesn't want to work the boys into a frenzy; she has to. These are track-covering, throw-off-the-scent tactics. This role has been the longest acting gig of her life. This is what I wish you could see, Gwen. I understand why you admire her sex appeal and self-possession, but it is not as simple as it seems. It never is.

It could go either way now. One more fall and you will either go home with a belt or with your empty hands stuck in your pockets. You are in bad shape, but you are angry and in need of redemption. Before Mimi can climb back into the ring, you grab her arm.

"Let me lead this time," you beg.

She makes a face and pushes you off. "Not on your life."

That's as much action as you see for the rest of the match. Mimi does not let you off the ropes. Instead, you are left to stew in your own juices while she wins the fall and the match herself with her new finishing move, grabbing Vera behind the knees, knocking her onto her back, lifting her from the mat, and swinging her repeatedly in circles before dropping her and covering her for the pin. Even in your self-involved state, you can admit that it *is* an exquisite move. Still, it's hard to watch from behind the ropes, knowing what it means. She has won this match all by her lonesome. You were more hindrance than help. When it is all over, you let the ref lift your arm along with hers, but you feel like a hypocrite.

The crowd denounces the verdict with a chorus of scoffs and heckling, which only grows louder as you head up the aisle. A grandmotherly woman in a floral-print dress even has the gall to strike you with her cane. Another day, you might just stand there blinking. Not today. You reflexively snag it from her hands and throw it into the crowd. This wins you a brutal scolding from the audience ("She's an old lady, for Christ's sake!"), more derision from the injured party ("You'll get yours, bitch!"), a fresh helping of self-loathing, and, perhaps worst of all, Mimi's admiration.

"That a girl," she says, patting your back. At the beginning of your partnership, any praise from Mimi was a real triumph. Tonight, it feels like yet another loss masquerading as victory.

When you return to your room, Mimi is not with you. She has gone off in search of a late-night bite. She did not invite you along and you did not tell her to get anything for you. Under the circumstances, it seemed unreasonable to ask for a favor of any kind.

So tonight, you will starve, but you will also have a blessed moment alone, which you use to drag the monstrously heavy phone with the mercifully long cord into the bathroom. Back in Cleveland, it's time for all the boys and girls in the Moondog kingdom to tune in. You aren't sure that Sam will be home yet—didn't he have a match in Sandusky this evening?—but you could stand to hear a friendly voice right about now, and so you have the hotel operator connect you to the Cleveland operator, who connects you to the Samuel Pospisil residence, where you hope you will find him, fresh from his shower and tuned in, bopping his head in time to the music. To your great relief, the phone is picked up in the middle of its third ring and a familiar voice arrives in your ear: "Sam here."

He sounds breathless and chilled. Is it possible he's hurried out of the shower to catch this call? You imagine him drying his ear with the corner of a towel. "Have I called at a bad time?"

"Leonie!" More sounds: the moving of furniture, it seems. Perhaps he is positioning a chair to ready himself for a long, interstate chat. "No, no. It's not a bad time. In fact"—there is a pause as he settles into his seat—"I was just thinking about you."

This is exactly what you need: the pleasure of Sam's enthusiastic response. You stare ahead at the gauze and circle of tape on your two buddy-wrapped toes, still pulsing with pain. You are a champion now with the battle scars and belt to prove it, but this is not how you imagined the experience: your partner indifferent and the crowd hostile. More than anything, you want to be with someone who cares about you. You want to be with Sam. Fourteen days to go, and already, you sense they will be the longest fourteen days of your life.

When you come out of the bathroom, Mimi's stretched out in her bed, holding the corner of a burger in a paper napkin. She's still dressed in the requisite feminine pre- and postmatch attire, although she's kicked off her pumps and stripped off her nylons. She pops the last bite in her mouth, chews twice and swallows it down.

"How is Spider?" she asks.

"How did you know who I was talking to?"

"I'm not stupid, you know," she says, wiping her mouth. "Why else would you hide away like that? Be careful with that one. That's all I've got to say."

This strikes you as hypocritical. "You're one to talk."

"Johnny's different. It's not serious. It can't be. So I get all of the fun and none of the fuss. Trust me, Gwen. You do *not* want to get serious about Spider."

"How do *you* know what I want and don't want?" You might owe Mimi for tonight, but you have had it with her advice.

Mimi tosses the napkin across the room and misses the trash can by a mile. She says, "I don't know anything about you. But I know this much. The surest way to get derailed is to get caught up with a man. Even the good ones bring you down. *Especially* the good ones. They don't mean to, but they do."

Mimi jumps up and walks the napkin's wayward trajectory, deposits her trash where it belongs, and gathers her cosmetic bag and nightgown. It is only after she closes the bathroom door behind her that you notice the grease-stained paper bag sitting on your bed, with your own burger inside.

I like to think that I have untangled every emotion you've had—that you will ever have—toward Mimi Hollander, but now that I have come to this part of your story, I am not so sure that's possible. Your character might be one thing, but you are many.

ELEVEN

The gears of time turn slowly, but they do move along, and eventually, fourteen days have passed and you are where you want to be: back in Cleveland, headed up the walkway to Sam's pad. Instead of spending the night in Charleston and taking the first bus in this morning, as any reasonable person might have done, you and Mimi raced from the arena to the depot and caught the last bus out. The noisy, slow-jostling sleep you got on the ride could hardly be called restorative. You could use a long tub soak and an even longer nap, but these can wait. For now, you are content to run on the adrenaline of your first crush.

If you weren't so mission-oriented, so eager to take each next footstep, you might notice the familiar car parked kitty-corner from Sam's apartment and suffer privately the shock and disappointment of realizing you won't have Mr. McGee all to yourself this afternoon. But no, you are too honed in on your target to see much more than the apartment landing, which has been shoveled and dusted with rock salt in anticipation of company, and the front door beyond it. A couple of knocks result in the sound of heavy, even footsteps. Your heart falls in sync with their pace, forming a countdown to your long-awaited reunion, but, when the door bursts open, the man that pours out of it isn't Sam: it's Johnny Bordeaux, beer in hand.

Despite all your recent travel together, you haven't paid much attention to Johnny. Now that you follow him inside the narrow hallway, streaked in mud and littered with galoshes, you realize that he's not a big guy. In fact, he's probably half a foot shorter than you. He's fat-muscled and strong as an oak, though. I suspect he's spent his whole life compensating for the measurement he couldn't fix with the ones he could. You've seen enough of these parts to know the man's got *Midwesterner* written all over him, too, well-insulated with antifreeze in his veins. Why in the world the Pospisils gave him a Cajun shtick is beyond you.

Johnny says, "The game will be on any minute. Just throw your coat on the bed"—he points through the open door of a bedroom off the hallway—"and come join us."

Now that he's gone, you are free to make a noise of disappointment over what lies ahead—not the much-anticipated private reunion you imagined, but instead the long-established, companion-filled ritual of Sunday football at Sam Pospisil's house, a tradition that began well before your time and will continue with or without you.

In the living room, Johnny sits on the couch while a woman who can only be Mrs. Bordeaux burrows into one of the torn and threadbare armchairs, stirring her drink with a maraschino cherry, her legs kicked over one of the arms.

"Gwen," says Johnny, talking through a mouthful of popcorn. He motions to the armchair. "This is Lacey." And then, after a few more crunches, he adds, "My wife."

Even from across the room, you can see that Lacey is surprisingly like Mimi in many ways: dark hair, squat build, camel-colored skin. Her face is younger, prettier even, but with stark blue crescents under her eyes and a galaxy of freckles across her nose. Despite Lacey's baggy sweater, you can make out a bit of a belly. She looks weary, defeated, but still, her presence scares you. You are afraid of being transparent, that she will somehow guess that you know something important about her life and will needle you until you slip and spill the beans. Good thing you are too far away to offer your hand and only have to wave. "Nice to meet you."

"Likewise," she says. She lifts the cherry out of her drink, drops it into her mouth and yanks it off the stem with her teeth.

"Where's the little one?" you ask, not really caring but attempting small talk.

"At home, with my mother," says Johnny.

Lacey rolls her eyes. "Here we go." She kicks off her flats; they hit the ground in two little thuds. "He'd just mess up everyone's good time. Plus, I don't like taking him out in this weather."

"You see, Gwen"—you startle at the sound of your name coming from Johnny's mouth; the tense turn of the conversation has put you on edge—"no matter how many days or weeks of his life I miss, my wife can *always* come up with some reason for us to go off without him."

"Ha! Suddenly, you're worried about missing out."

You're not sure where this is going, but it's clear that things have taken a dangerous turn. And you thought the jeopardy was over when you entered the apartment without injury.

"Is she here?" calls Sam, stepping out from the kitchen, a dish towel tucked into the front of his pants, unwittingly striking the couple silent. (That's a relief; there's no telling what Lacey and Johnny might have said next.) When Sam sees you, he breaks out in a smile and shoots across the living room. He extends his arms straight out in front of him, fingers spread wide.

This gesture, you assume, is meant as an invitation to embrace, and so you walk into it, arms rising, but instead of sweeping you up into his too-long arms, Sam takes your arm and extends it over your head, referee-style. Alas, your reaction time isn't quick enough, so you take one step too many and bump into him while he says, "Please welcome Tennessee Tag Team Champion, Gorgeous Gwen Davies!" and then widens his mouth and exhales in that way that is meant to imitate the roar of a crowd.

He means well by this display, Gwen. He wants to celebrate you, to be your loudest and most ardent fan. But you don't feel like celebrating. This championship of yours has become a sore spot. You've been introduced by this title for the last two weeks, but you haven't enjoyed the new distinction. In fact, the abuse from the spectators is getting worse. Here is a partial list of items that were thrown at you in Kentucky alone: an empty snuff can, an assortment of overripe fruit, eggs, a plastic doll, and a chunk of coal. And Mimi is just as vexing. Since the title bout, she's taken to calling you *champ*. Every time she says it, it seems more condescending, more ironic. Perhaps the only plus in this is that you're learning how to let your shame burn on the inside, out of view. You've learned how to stay in character, which is exactly what you do now, posing for your audience, bending a knee and flexing the muscle on your other arm. You are sure you hear Johnny make a slightly derisive noise, but you let this go, just as you've let go of the idea that this is a romantic greeting, or that there will be anything remotely romantic about this afternoon, for that matter.

"That's great, Gwen," says Lacey in a tone you can't quite decipher. "Congratulations."

"Good stuff," says Johnny. "I mean, you're no World Junior Heavyweight, like our friend here, but hey, we all got to start somewhere."

Sam's jaw sets; the tips of his ears grow red. When these fade, his face slips into something that looks like resignation. He drops your clasped hands. "Surprise," he says, his voice flat.

This time around, you share his indifference. Once the belt is in his possession, he will begin its perpetual defense, which means he will be on the road as much as you are. And, since women aren't supposed to wrestle on the same cards as the major titleholders (wouldn't that be insulting?), there will not be many opportunities for your paths to cross. You swallow the bad taste building in your mouth and say, "That's terrific."

"Yep," says Sam.

"Don't downplay this for my sake," says Johnny. "This is it, man. This is what it's all about." He leans into the couch and pats his stomach. "My time will come later. It would be too much right now anyway. What with the baby and all."

Lacey scoffs loudly at this, walks her stockinged feet up the wall. Johnny cuts a look at her, but she pays no attention. "But it's not too much to send you to Minnesota in the middle of winter?"

Johnny answers her with stone-faced silence. Sam grips your shoulders with his long fingers; his eyes sparkle with exasperation. "Why don't you come help me in the kitchen? I mean, if you're tired, you're welcome to stay out here—"

"I'll come with you," you say, ready to do anything to get away from those two.

In addition to being a refuge, the kitchen is the staging ground for Sam's hospitality. A food-splattered copy of *Joy of Cooking* lies spread-eagled on one end of the counter; a small metropolis of liquor bottles stands on the other. Between these, hard-boiled egg whites sit on a platter with fans of radish roses and celery sticks. After offering to make you a Tom Collins, which you decline—with the lousy night of sleep you've had, one drink and it will be hard to avoid a face-plant—Sam asks if you'll finish off the crudités. This is the word he uses, too—crudités—and, after he clarifies, you get to work washing and peeling the carrots while he sets about filling the eggs with yellow dollops.

Sam seems to be in his element in the kitchen, occasionally wiping his hands on his makeshift apron before taking a swig of beer. This is not something you would expect from the soon-to-be Junior Heavyweight wrestling champion, or any man, for that matter. The kitchen has never been a natural fit for you, but it seems to be for Sam. While he works, he taps his foot in time with the unfamiliar tune he's humming. Wouldn't it be something if it were always this way—you coming home from the road, exhausted and famished, and Sam in the kitchen?

"This is a nice place," you say, a pile of carrot ribbons forming in front of you.

"It has its charms," says Sam. "I'll take being here over being on the road any day of the week, that's for sure. I'm kind of a homebody." He doesn't look up from his eggs when he says this; he's got a two-spoon technique and he's on fire with it. "Can you look in the cabinet over the oven and grab the paprika for me?"

A spice rack in a bachelor pad seems out of place to you, but sure enough, there's a full carousel, packed tight enough to make locating the paprika a major undertaking. After considerable rifling, you find what you're looking for and toss it over. "You must do a lot of entertaining."

"I like having people over. I did, at least. Believe it or not, those two used to be a lot of fun." Sam takes a pull of his beer and wipes his mouth with the back of his hand. "I'm glad you're here, though."

"For the moment, at least." You have a bout here on Wednesday, and then nothing before the holidays, but Joe will surely do something about that. Last you heard, he was trying to work out something in Baltimore. That would be nice; it would certainly make it easier to get home for Christmas, a trip that seems long overdue. The last phone call with your father did not go well. *This was a mistake,* he said. *I want you to come home.* Not *you are wanted,* but the more active, possessive *I want you.* You can't grant him this, but you can go for a visit, reassure him in person that all is well, that you are still the same girl he knows and loves. Perhaps in return, you will be able to enjoy a little of this newfound demonstrative love. "What about you?"

"The title match is in St. Louis. Next month." He puts the finishing touch on his eggs, dusting them with the paprika. "I'll be here until then."

If Sam takes any pleasure in knowing the title will soon be his, he is keeping it to himself. He's grown up in this sport, so he must already know what you will soon learn—that any perks come with some steep costs. There will be crazed fans and police, not to mention a dizzying amount of travel and publicity. But I suspect the thing that is really bumming him out is the terrible timing, which is certainly going to place a burden on the budding relationship between you.

"I almost forgot." Sam wipes his hands before reaching into a drawer and pulling out a couple of paper rectangles, one of which he hands to you. "I got you something."

It's a road map. At first glance, there's nothing special about this one. On its cover, a couple stands in front of their car consulting their friendly Esso gas station attendant. Open up its accordion folds, spread it out, and still, it seems perfectly ordinary: an index, a legend, the Information for Sightseers (*Gulf Coast: Popular vacation playground with miles of white beaches against background of moss-draped oaks*), and the nation, crosshatched in red and black. But then you notice the inky spots dotting the landscape, all in familiar places: Tallahassee, Orangeburg, Charlotte. The blue stars, Sam explains, represent your solo travels; the purple ones are for the places you've been together. He shows you the one he's kept for years to document his own travels; it is well-worn and littered with stars, mostly red, but some purple ones, too.

"The first night you called—Memphis, I think—when I got off the phone with you, I got out my map and figured out the distance between us." He makes a face. "Is that goofy?"

Nothing could bring you more pleasure than the image of him

curled over the spread-out map, searching for you. "I don't think so," you say, taking his hand and squeezing it.

Sam takes a breath and begins: "Leonie, I know it's going to be hard for us to have a relationship. Most of the time, we will literally be going in opposite directions. But I'd like to try."

Now *that's* goofy. Luckily, you know that a person can be clumsy with words and genuine in feeling. All that matters is that he's all yours. So, what are you waiting for? Tell him as much. Kiss the tops of his knuckles, the back of his hand; turn it over, kiss the lines of his massive palm. You mean this as a promise that you are on board. No matter where you are, you will never be too far away.

Sam says nothing, but when you look at him again, the tension that made his eyes shine dissolves. He thanks you by grabbing you around the waist and, at long last, pulling you in for a slightly clumsy and beer-washed but nonetheless blood-pumping kiss.

This is the reception you hurried here for. Remember the fondness you've retained for those memories of a school-age Cynthia, the ones where she races toward you as you return from tumbling class? Instantly, that fondness dulls; the recollections themselves recede into a more obscure, less easily accessed area of your brain. From now on, when you imagine a homecoming, this scene—Sam's face, pinked and medicinally scented from a recent shave, moving quickly toward your own—will be the one that plays in your mind's eye.

As much as you both might dread it, you will eventually have to leave the kitchen and return to the war zone, so you might as well get hopping. Already, there is popcorn on the floor and a forest of Erin Brew bottles (*All you have to do is . . . pop a cap!*) on the boomerang-shaped coffee table. Sam pushes the bottles aside to make room for the tray of crudités. While he nestles into the empty seat, you hold on to the platter of deviled eggs, surveying the room. This bachelor pad isn't the most spacious and comfortable place to host a party, even one this small. The couch, the armchairs, the coffee table, and the massive television are crammed into the tiny, carpeted space. Apparently, it is the last of these that makes Sam's home the hub of their football viewing, and from the looks of it, everyone's position is long-established: Lacey in one armchair, Sam in the other, and Johnny on the couch, which doesn't exactly leave much space for you. (Surely the aforementioned Debbie took part in these shindigs. Where on earth did she sit?) You'd think Johnny would offer the couch to the two of you, or at least make some room—somehow, he manages to take up the entire thing—but the man appears clueless. Eventually, you make a space for the tray on the coffee table, snag a pillow from under Johnny's foot, and settle down on a plot of carpeting next to Sam's chair. He leans over the arm and looks down at you, his face wrinkled with confusion. "Don't you want to sit with me?"

Was this supposed to be the arrangement all along? How could you have guessed that?

"Is there room?" you ask.

Sam extends his hand down. "*Is there room,* she asks. Come on."

You have your doubts, but it's hardly an offer you can refuse, so you hike yourself up on an elbow, take his hand, and let him pull you onto your feet. While you wait for the impending coin toss, you try to situate yourself in Sam's lap in such a way that each of you might be comfortable and able to see the screen, but it's impossible. Just as you thought: you are too tall, too ample. Story of your life.

From the chitchat, you gather that this game is a done deal. The Eagles may be second in the conference, but they've lost their last two games, including one against the Giants, for Christ's sake. Besides that, even if the Browns roll over and play dead today, they've already won the Eastern Conference by a country mile and will move on to Detroit for the national championship.

"Just so everyone knows," you say, "I'm rooting for the Eagles."

In an instant, all the goodwill you have earned by playing the hostess dissipates. Everyone, smitten Sam and indifferent Lacey included, stares with incredulity. It is up to you to break the long silence: "What?"

Sam shrugs. "I guess I can live with hometown loyalty. Tell you what. If by some strange fluke of fortune the Eagles take this game, I'll take you out tonight and buy you a big fat steak, nice and bloody. What do you say?"

"You're on," you say, mouth already watering. "And if the Browns win, I'll buy you a steak."

"That's okay," says Sam, looking at you with pity.

"Why not?" you ask. "Fair is fair."

"Maybe you could just *cook* him a steak," Johnny volunteers.

"Maybe she doesn't *want* to cook him a steak," says Lacey. She sucks on an ice cube and spits it back into her glass; it clanks against the bottom. "Maybe she prefers to *buy* him a steak. She makes money, too."

"All right, then," Sam ventures. He offers his hand; you give it a shake. "You're on."

As uncomfortable as Johnny and Lacey have made you today, Sam's lap is worse. In each position you attempt, you are both only momentarily at ease. The pillow you took from the couch is still on the ground, beckoning. "I really need to stretch out my legs," you tell Sam, sinking down to the floor. Perhaps that is how he and Debbie watched the games, but you are not Debbie. He nods, clearly a little hurt but also, you suspect, a little relieved. You fold the pillow over to prop up your head and close your eyes. *Just for a second,* you tell yourself, but you are no match for this exhaustion, so you give in to it and proceed to sleep through the entire game. Hours later, when Sam gently shakes you awake and informs you of the result (42–27, Eagles), he will still be incredulous, but you will take more pleasure in a victory of other sorts: a quiet house, with Sam all to yourself.

· · ·

Early the next morning, you step outside Sam's apartment and pull up the collar of your coat, which you managed to get on despite Sam's playful unfastening of the buttons. Above you, the sky is a clean, watery gray. The street is plowed clear; on the sidewalk, the snow is still white and piled high. If you had time to think, you'd feel a stab of guilt for being the one who has to do the spoiling. But you don't have time. You were supposed to call your father last night. You will have to hurry to catch him before work, so you race as fast as your galoshes and your still-sore toe will allow.

There's a good chance you're already too late. You should have left at first light. Scratch that: you should have left *last night*. The snow was a flimsy excuse for you to stay, but Sam played the card, and who can blame you if you were quick to fold? You will have to hit the road again soon, and this time, without the same assurances. Even if you could sweet-talk Joe into returning you to Cleveland, Sam might well be off on his own tour. The only thing that made leaving palatable was the knowledge that you will see him again tonight for that promised steak.

By the time you get to the hotel, you are breathless and a mess, not in a state to see anybody. But Mimi is already in the lobby, on her way to Leo Pospisil's gym for a morning workout.

"Just getting back from the game? Must have been some serious overtime."

There's no need to kiss and tell, Gwen: it isn't any of her business. Besides, there probably isn't much hope that she will believe the truth—that, by just about anyone's standards but yours, it was all fairly tame. Clothes were loosened, hands traveled and lingered, but that was as far as it got. It wasn't too terribly square of you to stop things there. We are talking about a more conservative, cautious age, after all—one with stricter social mores and less reliable birth control. Besides, you are still

137

getting to know each other. Still, it will have to happen sooner rather than later. He likes you, but the man is a star, one that is about to burn even brighter. Women will be readily available to him. You cannot afford to be a prude.

"It was," you say. "Longest game in football history."

"Lots of quality time with the usual suspects, I reckon. You get to meet the Ragin' Cajun?"

"Who?"

Mimi laughs. "Exactly."

It is this harshness that helps you make the connection between the character Mimi has just named and the other Bordeaux. No one bothered to tell you Lacey used to wrestle. As far as you knew, her perpetual fight with Johnny was her whole story. You can only imagine Mimi would enjoy hearing about the hostility you witnessed last night, but you aren't keen to trot out Lacey's troubles for Mimi's pleasure. Whether this is because you feel protective of Lacey or hostile toward Mimi, you couldn't say.

"What about you?" you ask, changing the subject. "What've you been up to?"

"Me? Oh, I caught some shut-eye, and then I got Leo to open the gym for me. I was overdue for a workout."

You have a vision of Mimi alone in a cinder block gym while others enjoy their Sunday meal or, like you, gather with friends to watch the game. She hits the bag; the sound echoes in the empty building. What was it she said to you? *I get all of the fun and none of the fuss.* She can't believe that. You certainly don't.

"By the way," she continues, "I spoke to Joe last night. We leave for Minnesota on Thursday."

"Minnesota?" This is not what you want to hear. The train ride from Baltimore to Philly would have been short and relatively inexpensive. Minnesota is a completely different story. "What happened to Baltimore?"

"This came up and Joe gave me a choice. Minnesota pays better, so we're going to Minnesota."

"Why do you get to choose?"

Mimi narrows her eyes. "Are you kidding me?"

All your nerves tie into knots. On top of being an economic hardship and cutting into what will undoubtedly be a short holiday, Minnesota makes no sense to you. For the life of you, you can't understand why Joe would—but then it hits you—*send you to Minnesota in the middle of winter.*

Right.

"Deal with it, Champ. It's a done deal."

In the pockets of your coat, you make two fists with your gloved hands and release them.

Mimi pulls up her coat collar and confirms what you already know. "Johnny's picking us up here Thursday morning. Be in the lobby by nine." She drops her chin into the neck of her coat, steels her posture for the cold, and pushes her way through the glass doors of the lobby. You should hurry upstairs and make that phone call before it's too late and then get on with the day. There is plenty to be done before Sam picks you up and you have to tell him you'll soon be inking blue stars in the North Star State. You need to send some clothes to the laundry, pack your bags, get a long nap. You can take that bath. But for now, you stand in the lobby and watch the other Tennessee Tag Team Champion walk up the street and against the wind, alone.

TWELVE

Minnesota takes another eight days out of your life, but at the end of it lies a sweet reward: one week of long-anticipated, richly deserved time off for the holidays (unpaid, of course), which begins as soon as you step off the train and into the 30th Street Station. Maybe you're biased, but if there's any place on earth better for a homecoming, you'd like to know where it is. Even on an evening like this one, when the terminal is teeming with seasonal travelers, their arms filled with sleeping children and shopping bags overstuffed with holiday gifts, the space feels light and airy; the art deco chandeliers cast a warm and welcoming glow. Here and there, weary voyagers catnap on the wooden benches, which might be long enough to accommodate even your lengthy self. Tempting, isn't it? After Minnesota, you are bone tired. You were right to be reluctant; it was everything you feared it would be: cold, expensive, lonely, and demoralizing. Three days ago, a spectator struck you with a folding metal chair. When you threw up an arm to protect yourself, you caught most of the blow on the jutted palm of your hand, and it has throbbed ever since. You haven't been able to make a complete fist for days. Now, as your feet click swiftly across the terminal, you practice opening and closing the injured hand, the other firmly gripped around the handle of your suitcase. You don't know what to expect from this visit home, if anything, but at least you can spend a few days out of character. You're tired of this heel business. Something's got to give.

You look over the crowd for your father. You told him not to bother; it would be late and besides, even if you weren't as travel-savvy as you are now, this is your hometown. But he is the kind of man who thinks young women should have escorts—and so, despite the late hour, there he is, standing underneath the arrivals-and-departures board, just as he said he would be. He looks more slight than usual in his plaid coat. When he sees you, he smiles without restraint and opens his arms wide.

"Leonie!" he says.

And then, it happens: that feeling that pestered you early in your adventures, the one you thought was gone for good—something like homesickness, but more like loss—breaks loose, and the combination of everything that's been difficult since you left home (Joe, the audiences, Mimi) quickly flanks and complicates it, producing a surprise multifronted physical attack. Nausea. Chest pain. Dizziness. Tears. This, sweet girl, is what happens when you ignore your feelings. They didn't disappear; they were only tucked away, compounding interest. Now, they overwhelm you. You enter your father's arms and fall apart.

"Come on now," he says, his hammer-strong hand cupping the back of your head. He takes the suitcase from your hand. "Is this it?" You nod against his shoulder, and he sighs. "All right then. Let's get you home."

It is a half block to the subway station, and the two of you walk it side by side, your head on his shoulder. You collect yourself on this walk and, sensing you no longer need propping up, your father gradually lessens the force in the arm he's locked around your waist, eventually releasing you entirely but only after you've taken hold of the subway pole. It is here, rumbling toward the old neighborhood, your father seated in front of you with your suitcase on his lap, where it dawns on you what he'd meant when he'd asked that question—*Is this it?*—and what was implicit in the subsequent sigh. You press your forehead against the pole.

"You thought I was coming home for good."

Franz Putzkammer rolls his lips into a forced smile. Behind him, the darkened tunnel whirrs past.

"No, I didn't really think so," he says. He turns his face toward the blackness, as if to confess to it. "But I hoped."

The next morning, you stumble out of the bedroom—while it is your father's now, he insists that it's yours while you are home—and into the main room, where, despite the fact that it's well into his workday, he sits in front of the Philco holding a half-finished can of beer in his hand and a half-smoked Winston in his lips.

"Look who's alive," he says as you make your way to the kitchen. You open the refrigerator—more beer, a wedge of cheese, and a lot of empty space—before checking a canister on the counter where, mercifully, you find enough grounds for a partial pot of coffee. You prepare the percolator, put it on the lit stove eye, and stand there for a minute, warming your hands over the flame. This has never been a warm house, but this morning it seems particularly drafty.

"You don't have to be at the factory?" you ask.

"I'm on vacation," he says. "It's Christmas, isn't it?"

"I guess. How long you get off?"

"I go back right after you leave."

You head over to the couch and plop down beside your father. "A whole week? What's gotten into you?"

Franz shrugs and stubs out his cigarette. "Why not? My only daughter comes to visit me. Why shouldn't I take a week off?" He strokes the back of your head, rougher, more playful than he had just the night before. "Enough about me. What about you? Tough stuff, the wrestling? You get hurt much?"

"Not too bad." You resist an urge to practice fisting your injured hand. "It's mostly show."

"The travel, though. That's hard."

You see an opportunity to explain away last night's episode and take it. "It's tiring. That's what you were seeing last night. Exhaustion." This claim is not completely off base—you can't yo-yo across the country the way you have without growing bone weary—but, you admit to yourself, it is incomplete. The weariness makes it harder to deal with the problems of life; it is not, in and of itself, the problem. When your father nods his understanding, you yawn, additional evidence for your claim. "I really needed that sleep."

"You like it?"

"Sleep?"

"Wrestling."

"Sure," you say, because it's the easiest answer. He won't understand the more complex one: that it's also lonely and taxing; that while you like playing a persona, you hate being a heel and being Mimi's underling; that it was good in the beginning, and you're hopeful things will change, that it will be good again.

"I'll show you something," you say, and disappear into the bedroom. Five minutes later, you return, wearing the half-laced Green Goddesses beneath your flannel nightgown. The suit you will keep under wraps, but the boots might be appreciated. "What do you think?"

Your father stares at your feet and sips his beer. "They're green."

"*They're green?*" you say, returning to your spot on the couch. It wasn't exactly the reaction you'd hoped for. "That's it?"

"What am I supposed to say?"

"I don't know. Something else."

"Okay then. They're great. They're exactly the kind of wrestling boots a father would want his daughter to have."

A long silence follows. To cover up the awkwardness, you get up to check on the coffee. Just as you figured—not quite ready. Instead of returning to the couch, you stand by the window, one boot resting on the other. Outside, in front of Cynthia's house, is Wally's truck. Has Cynthia had her baby yet? You fish around in your memory and do the math. No, she should still be pregnant, but due very soon. Perhaps you should stop by to say hello. Now that the tide has turned and Cynthia is the one stuck in banal domesticity while you are out on the open road, it might be very satisfying to regale your old friend with tales of your new life.

"Someone named Sam just called for you," your father says. He stares at the television while he says this, and you get the sense that he's tiptoeing up to something. "Is he your boyfriend?"

The question catches you off guard. Your father has never once asked you about boys before, and you are hesitant to discuss the subject with him now. But you will have to tell him sooner or later, won't you? You might as well go ahead and spill the beans.

"Yes, actually. Some of your buddies might know him as Spider McGee."

"Spider? You're dating an insect?"

"That's just his wrestling name." Finally, the coffee finishes. You pour yourself a mugful and rejoin him on the couch. "You can call him Sam."

"Am I going to approve of this Sam?"

"I don't know," you say, allowing yourself a fleeting thought of Sam, and lean against his shoulder. "Maybe."

You will end the day in this position, too. At present, there's no snow or ice outside, so after you finish your coffee, you will put on your Keds and go for a run, reacquainting yourself with your neighborhood, before cleaning up and going off to buy groceries. When you return, you will scrub down the kitchen and bathroom, make a hearty dinner that your father will gulp down in appreciation, and once again settle into the couch (where your father will spend most of the day) for your regular Tuesday night programming. But the present moment is what's important: the small community of father and daughter together, staring ahead at the screen, where Jean Corbett and Bill Hart create a casserole with condensed soup on *Home Highlights,* you dressed in your wrestling boots and cupping a coffee mug, your father polishing off his beer, both of you awash in misunderstanding yet still able to provide each other some measure of comfort, still finding a small way—a head against a shoulder, the short press of a kiss against the scalp—to connect and sustain, to accept love in the form that it comes, not the one you wish it would take.

I wish I could say the rest of the week was more of the same. Rather, it is all downhill. Sure, it's nice to relive the familiarity of a night in the company of your father and Edward R. Murrow's authoritative presence, but you soon realize this is all your father does anymore—sit in front of the television, watching everything from the superbrainy archaeological quiz show *What in the World?* to the inane children's serial *Atom Squad*—and, as a result, this is all he expects the two of you to do in your short time together. You try to keep him company, but being together like this, in front of the television, makes you painfully aware of how inadequate it is to the task of closing the distance between you. Even when you are both parked right in front of it, you are miles apart. This is not the kind of love that seemed promised in your father's phone calls. It feels more like your familiar pattern, but worse. On top of all this, it's difficult to see your father, formerly healthy and athletic—*a sound mind in a sound body*—now completely sedentary but for the occasional raising of a cigarette or beer. Each morning, you invite him to run with you, and he steadfastly refuses.

"Why should I run?" he asks. "Who is chasing me?"

Feeling guilty for whatever part you've played in creating this shell of your father, but unwilling to stay cooped up and frustrated, you spend your afternoons shopping for the food you forgot you missed. Each afternoon, the two of you spoil your appetite: Amaroso's rolls stuffed with grilled beef and Cheez Whiz from the suddenly popular Pat's King of Steaks, a baker's dozen of warm *laugenbrötchen*, the saccharine pleasures of Tastykakes (Butterscotch Krimpets, Kandy Kakes, and Chocolate Juniors) that all but bury your memories of MoonPies. It's the best part of the day, the two of you sitting across from each other at the table, teasing each other about how the other eats, you in small pinches or cut-up bites, Franz practically inhaling the food, your view of each other slightly obscured by the *weihnachtspyramide,* the wooden Christmas pyramid that has served in place of a tree every year of your life. Usually, your father is the one to unpack it from a trunk of your mother's things, but this year, when you didn't see it in its rightful place, you dug it out and set it up yourself.

On the morning of your last full day home, Christmas day, you sit in these same seats, the gifts you've bought for each other—one bulky and rectangular, the other small, thin, and square—lying to each side of the *weihnachtspyramide*. You pour two cups of coffee while your father lights the candles and then take your seat as the heat and smoke rise, turning the propeller and spinning the nativity. It's as pleasant a morning as you can hope for: hot coffee and comfortable silence, save for the occasional wham of the radiator. Your father pushes his gift to you across the table.

"You first," he says.

You're careful with the gift wrap so it can be used again, as you've been taught to do, peeling the self-stick ribbon off, running a finger under the tucks and easing the tape off the paper. The gift is a 45, which you guessed correctly by the shape, but not one you might have purchased for yourself. It isn't Faye Adams, nor is it the Drifters' "Money

Honey." No, it is "Rags to Riches" by Tony Bennett. Earlier in the week, you considered bringing your record player and albums back to Florida with you, but it only took a cursory glance at the artists—Patti Page, Peggy Lee—to realize there was no point: they'd be just as inert and purposeless in Florida as they were here. Now, you'll have to take Tony back with you when he really belongs here, among that clan of boring crooners and pop singers. You have no use for a Tony Bennett record. But this isn't what saddens you; it's what the gift *means*. Few things make better yardsticks for measuring the gap between two people than a present. Although he'd been spot-on with the Bakelite radio, this one proves that the gulf is not only titanic but continuing to widen.

"It's not much," your father says.

"It's great," you say, and force an expression that matches that sentiment. You hope he does not read through you. You *are* grateful for the time, energy, and money that went into its purchase. You reach across the table to squeeze his hand and make this known. "Thank you."

"It's nothing. Now this," he says, pulling his gift toward him. "This looks like too much."

"Not too much. Just enough."

Shopping for your father was an impossible task. Despite how barren and slovenly his life seems now, you couldn't imagine him wanting or needing any particular thing. Finally, in the men's section of Wanamaker's, you spotted a pair of warm flannel pajamas. It was the only thing you'd seen that made any sense to you, so you counted the few bills in your pathetically thin wallet, confirmed that you had enough for your train fare and the pajamas, too, and made the purchase.

Franz goes through a similar process of unwrapping. When he gets to the pajamas, he hoists the top half out of the box, holds it up by the shoulders in front of him, and frowns. "What is this?"

"Pajamas. You don't like them?"

He sighs. "You think your father is dying."

"What? I don't think—"

"You think my life is over." He refolds the pajama top and puts it back in the box. "You think I am ready to put on my pajamas and watch television until I die." He pushes the box back across the table. "I don't want them."

There is no point in denying this accusation. He will not be convinced, and besides, he might be right. Instead, you say, "I can't take them back."

"Then you can wear them yourself." When your father stands up, his hand brushes the box, knocking it onto the linoleum floor you'd scrubbed on your first full day home, where it lands upright, flannel exposed. "You think you know me, but this"—he points a finger at the contents of your gift—"this is not who I am." He walks into the bedroom and closes the door.

You can hear him in there, banging around. Unsure of what else to do, you stoop to retrieve the box and return it to the table, and then sip your coffee and wiggle the foot of your crossed leg incessantly as you wait for him to reappear. Finally, he does, wearing a sweatshirt, soft woolen pants, and low-top Chucks. Your foot stops. You freeze with your coffee cup at mouth level, your lips midblow.

"We're going running," he says. "Get dressed."

When you finally unfreeze, you say, "You don't have to do this."

"Yes, I do."

You are not ready for a run. You like to wait until later in the morning, when it's warmer outside. Besides, you still have half a cup of coffee to finish. But your father's stance makes it clear that the choice is not up to you, so you take one last gulp and walk past him into the bedroom.

Outside, in the chest-stinging chill, you say, "Let's just stay in the neighborhood."

"Don't be easy on me."

"I'm not," you lie.

He points down the street, and says, "Let's go."

• • •

As you and your father run, your joints stiff with cold, your breath visible, your mind wanders and a surprising thought comes to you: perhaps *you* are the one at fault for the events of this week. Perhaps Franz did park himself in front of the television, but why did you let yourself be so easily disappointed in him? Your father is who he is; wanting him to change isn't doing either of you much good. Besides, under the circumstances, you couldn't exactly expect him to be different. Really, to let your feelings be hurt over a 45? Are you really so petty? Here is your father—thinning, aging, wheezing, and half-crazy with the need to prove himself—and all you can think about is yourself.

Wait: *wheezing?* You look up and over at him; his face is scrunched in pain.

"Are you all right?"

He puts a hand to his chest. "It's a little tight. It will go away."

"Stop," you say, and follow your own command. He jogs a few more steps and stops as well. You point to the steps of the row house in front of you. "Sit down."

"Just a minute," he says, still standing, his breath labored. "I just need to catch my breath."

"So have a seat."

"Really. It's not that bad."

"Please sit down. I would feel better if you sat down."

"I won't." Franz takes quick, shallow breaths and spits in the grass. "Don't ask me again."

You turn your face to the sky and press your fingertips over your eyelids. "You're so stubborn," you say.

Your father leans forward, his arms bracing against his thighs. He seems to be commanding his breath to slow, effortful work that causes him to wince. When, eventually, he has enough air to speak, he says, "Don't leave."

"I'm right here, Father."

"Not now," he says, looking up at you. "I mean tomorrow."

"Father, I—"

"Don't you remember the first night you got here? How upset you were? Why do you want to go back?"

"Please don't ask me to stay." It's true, your life as Gwen Davies leaves much to be desired, but at least that life has promise.

The next time your father looks at you, his face slackened, you see what he has never let you see before: his unchecked fear.

"I'm not on vacation," he says, his voice quiet and controlled. "I got laid off."

You start to think this might be part of some elaborate joke, but your father isn't exactly a kidder. He sits down on the steps and says, "I guess guys aren't wearing hats too much these days."

He's serious. He's been laid off. It explains his leanness and the empty refrigerator, the chill in the house. "What are you going to do?"

"I don't know," he says. "I don't know."

"I've got some money socked away," you say. The outrageousness of this lie frightens you. Minnesota wrung you dry; what little money you had left evaporated in the past few days. You'd spent more than you could afford on indulgent food and those stupid, trouble-causing pajamas. "It's in Florida, though," you say, hoping this is true. Maybe Joe will advance you money from your upcoming bouts. You can ask, at least. "I'm not sure how soon I'll be able to wire it to you."

Your father shakes his head and stands upright. "Don't do that. I'll be fine."

You adjust your position so you can meet your father's gaze. He is not fine, it's clear, and while you haven't the slightest idea what you can do about it, you want him to see the forthrightness of what you are about to say, the honesty of it. "I'm not going to let anything happen to you."

"Your mother—" he starts, but doesn't finish. How had he intended to end this sentence? *Your mother would want you to stay,* or maybe *Your mother is probably turning over in her grave.* Other possibilities: *Your mother would be proud of you, Your mother would not understand this,* and *Your mother should be here.* You will always wonder and never know because your father is who he is. But you don't blame him, really. You can't expect him to be anyone else, or to do anything differently than he does, which is to leave his thought incomplete, unshared, and begin the silent walk home, where he cleans up, puts on his new pajamas, and parks in front of the television, that suffocating box on which he'd blown precious rainy day cash.

That afternoon, while you pack your suitcase, you look out the window; Wally's truck is still parked outside Cynthia's house. You are no longer interested in the opportunity to crow, you decide, but the polite thing to do would be to say a quick hello, wish everyone a Merry Christmas.

When you knock on the Rileys' door, someone cracks it open and cautiously peeks out for an initial assessment. Once you are recognized, the door opens wide and Ms. Riley puts her hands to her face in surprise.

"Leonie! Look at you!"

Look at you? Look at *her*! Ms. Riley is decidedly more pulled together than she'd been the last few times you'd seen her, her hair pulled behind her into a neat chignon, her wool slacks smart and crisp. Perhaps she has decided that becoming a grandmother prematurely isn't the worst of fates. She opens her arms and draws you in with a fierce hug, nearly puncturing you with the hard points of her bullet bra.

"Cynthia's taking a little nap."

"I'm up!" cries a voice from the bedroom. "I'm coming!"

Ms. Riley waves her arm toward a man perched on the edge of the couch cushion, hunched over the copy of *Life* spread open on the coffee table. "Leonie, have you met Cynthia's husband, Wally?"

Wally's tattoo peeks out from the rolled-up sleeve of his grease-streaked navy-blue uniform; his name is stitched over his breast. The young husband scans the strapping silhouette you cut, part athlete, part Amazon. This full-body size-up lingers too long; it feels judgmental and invasive. "Nice to meet you, Leonie," he breathes, which further puts you on edge. "Merry Christmas."

Once you are safely in the kitchen, Ms. Riley whispers to you, "What a meathead. If he's not at work, he's sitting on that couch taking up space. I must have lost my mind, letting them move in here."

When Cynthia finally enters the room, you can't help but eye the hearty bump that precedes her. Here is the girl you knew, now weighed down by maternity. She is breathing heavily; her prettiness is distorted with effort. You pull out a chair for her, and she smiles her gratitude at you.

You ask the ladies about themselves, but they both declare that for them, it's the same old same old; they want to know what's going on with *you*. You tell them what you want them to know about—your press, your belt, Sam—and keep the rest to yourself.

"That's some life, Leonie!" Cynthia punches you on the arm. "What a life!"

When you'd imagined this moment, you'd expected (and, let's be honest here, eagerly longed for) a smidge of jealousy. Unfortunately, it doesn't appear. Cynthia means to be supportive of your choices, of course, but there's something exaggerated about this gesture, something forced. Your choices are not ones she would make for herself.

"What about you?" you ask. "This is good, too, right? You're happy?"

"Are you kidding?" Cynthia's hands rest on her belly; she smiles down at it. "I couldn't be happier."

Is that a note of effort in her voice? Is it possible that she is not as confident in her decisions as she was this past summer; that she simply wants to prove her mother wrong about Wally? That would be comforting, wouldn't it: to believe that ambivalence is settling in for Cynthia, just as it is for you. But one look at that face and you know the truth. This isn't a character she's playing; this is what she feels. And here you were hoping to impress her. Instead, you find yourself envying her contentment, her certainty. You could surely use a little of that these days.

"It's too bad you have to head back so soon," says Cynthia. "Are you sure you can't stay until the New Year, watch the Mummers Parade? I'm sure your father would like that."

The possibility of seeing a band of men in blackface playing "Oh, Dem Golden Slippers" on banjos is not much of an incentive to stick around, but the idea of staying has its appeal. After all, you and your father have heedlessly squandered valuable time. You try to mask your real emotion with a smile. "Unfortunately, no."

"Speaking of your father," says Ms. Riley, "he came over here a few months ago with your contact information, said he wanted me to have it in case anything happened to him. Just a precaution, he said, but it worried me a little. Is everything all right?"

You remain silent for a while, shuffling your feet beneath the table, trying to decide where your responsibilities lie. This is your father's business; he wants to handle it his way. But you are frightened, and it seems to you that he is, too. Before you can frame a sentence, Ms. Riley cocks her head to the side, gives you a thorough examination. "Something's wrong, isn't it?"

"Maybe you could just keep an eye out," you say to her. This seems to you a reasonable compromise, one that provides a measure of protection without revealing much. "Drop in on him once in a while?"

"Why?" asks Cynthia. She senses drama, and she wants in. "What's wrong with your father?"

Ms. Riley silences her with a look, and then takes your arm at the crook of your elbow. "Sure thing, Leonie. I can do that." She pats you twice there, at the soft fold of your arm, before pulling away.

There was a time when you had so wanted this woman to be your mother, when you and Cynthia had pulled all matter of silly stunts in an effort to persuade her and Franz to fall in love. Now, you are just grateful that she hasn't let this keep her from extending a little much-appreciated maternal affection to you.

The next morning, back at 30th Street Station, in front of the spinning numbers of the arrivals-and-departures board, Christmas with your father comes full circle, with you falling apart and your father providing the fortification of his arms. A moment like this provides relief for two people who want to show each other love but never quite get it right. Perhaps most of your time together has been strained, but whenever you are within the walls of this station, you are both at your best. You've got your hellos and good-byes down pat; the only thing you need to work on is everything in between.

"You never told me about this boy," he says. "If it keeps up with him, you know you have to bring him here. I need to look him over."

You understand what he is doing, that he is as frightened as ever but eager to hide his fears away. Even in this moment, just before you hop on board, the one person who still matters to him disappearing into the world outside of Philadelphia, a world outside of his reach, he keeps any pain he is feeling to himself. For all the problems with this, its familiarity is reassuring. This is the father you know.

"I know," you tell him. "Don't worry. I know."

For now, you will go back to Florida. Somehow, you will get money to send to your father. You and Ms. Riley will get him over this hump, and then something will come through for him. It has to. You will return to your life as Gorgeous Gwen Davies with new energy and purpose; you will make something happen. But you will come back soon and let your father give your boyfriend the once-over, let him participate in your life the way a father should. On this trip, you will be better. He will be better. Next time, you will get things right. You are sure of it.

THIRTEEN

In Joe's office, as you sit on the edge of a chair in front of his desk, waiting less than patiently for him to finish tallying the results of your most recent efforts—it's payday—your eyes rake over the backdrop of publicity shots. Eventually, they settle on your own, the one Monster Henderson took all those months ago. It seems tacked up hastily and forgotten, too low and far on the perimeter for your liking. What will it take for Joe to move you up? Perhaps these latest numbers will get his attention. Your recent bookings have been plentiful and attractive, and the longer he takes, the more encouraged you feel.

This should be good. You hope it is, at least—for your father's sake. The two weeks since you returned from Philadelphia have afforded you the best possible opportunity yet for saving a little dough. By some small measure of fortune, all of your bookings were located between central Florida and north Georgia, so you've been able to spend more nights than usual at the school, which runs you half the price of a motel room. There's no Johnny around either, so when you do have to sleep on the road, Mimi's willing to share, which significantly boosts your coffers. Joe's also been generous enough to let Mimi drive his DeSoto to many of the matches. He charges for the gas, of course, but it ends up being less than, say, a bus ticket, and decidedly faster and more comfortable. For once, everything has been working in your favor.

Your stomach rumbles.

"Hungry, eh?" Joe laughs. "I'm not surprised. You've been eating like a bird lately."

"I'm okay," you say, fingering the heads of the brads in the uphol-stery, but you aren't. The truth is you are running on fumes. In an effort to pinch every possible penny, you've cut back on your meals, making the occasional lunch out of ketchup and saltines, skipping breakfast altogether. No matter. You are sure that Joe is about to put a fat stack of bills in your hand, and you will be able to wire money to your dad before you leave tomorrow—Joe is driving you and Mimi first to St. Louis, where he has somehow managed to finagle a match with the biggest names on Billy Wolfe's roster, the tomboyish and technically proficient June Byers and *the Betty Grable of the Mat World,* Nell Stewart, for the Women's World Tag Team Championship, and then to Nashville to defend *that* title. Once the money is safely on its way, you will go to the diner to enjoy the most satisfying hot dog and egg cream of your life.

"Here you go," says Joe, beaming as he lifts a crisp fifty out of his cash box and holds it out like a prize.

"That's it?" You are going to need every penny of that just to eat, sleep, and get where you are supposed to be for the next two weeks. "That just doesn't seem right, Joe."

"What do you mean? Of course it's right. See for yourself." Joe hunches over his calculator, pulls his glasses down to the end of his nose, and starts typing away, narrating as he goes along. He adds the price of the purses first, and then quickly whittles this number down: first his commission, then your expenses. Not only do you owe him for gas as well as your most recent evenings here and charges at the diner, but, according to his records, you are still paying off expenses from the previous month. You've been behind the eight ball ever since that convalescence for your jaw; you were never paying off the most recent debt, but the debt from the month before, which, of course, means Joe has to punch in a few more numbers to add the interest. When it is all said and done, he says, "Here," and turns the calculator around so you can see. "Take a look."

You pull up the tape and inspect it for yourself. "Here," you say, pointing to what is surely an error. What a relief. You just *knew* something had to be wrong. "You only gave me twenty bucks for each match. Purses for tags are around a hundred, right? If you get forty percent and Mimi and I split the rest, I should be getting thirty."

"Gwen," Joe says, his voice dropping down to that low tone he reserves for bad news. He even goes so far as to put his hand over yours. "Mimi is a more established wrestler than you. She's the reason I can book you as often as I can."

"Are you saying"—how is it you have gone this long without knowing?—"she makes *twice* as much as me?"

"For now." Joe gives your hand a little pat, and then picks the calculator up and returns it to its rightful place on the desk. "On the bright side, you and I are completely square, and you're booked up for a while. That pile's only going to get bigger."

That may be true, but you need that pile to get bigger *right this minute*. You didn't want to ask for a handout—you have a vague memory of him ixnaying advances when you signed your contract—but you don't have much choice. All you can do is hope he will find it in his heart to make an exception.

"I'm sorry, really I am," he says at the end of your sob story, "but I have a strict policy about this. I don't break it for anyone."

If only you could stop there. You don't want to press the issue, but you are desperate enough to play this card: "My mother is dead, Joe. I'm an only child. There's no one else who can help my father. I'm it."

Joe goes into lockdown: his jaw sets, his eyes go flat. He needn't say anything—what's left to say after that expression?—but after a long pause, he says, "I'm sorry, Gwen, but it's a hard, fast rule for a reason, and I've been clear on it from the beginning. I expect you to take care of your own business and be ready to leave tomorrow."

"Got it," you say, refusing to let your voice crack.

"Tell you what." He pinches another dollar out of his box and places it on top of the fifty with a magnanimous smile. "Go get some lunch. Can't have you starving yourself to death."

It would feel good to refuse that dollar—to be too proud to accept this meager offering, to refuse to be paid off so easily. But you can't go on like this—that much you know—so you swallow hard, snatch the bill, and shove it into the pocket of your coat.

On your way out, Betsy, who is seated at a desk, the phone receiver pressed against her ear, flashes one of her lopsided, motherly smiles at you. This one is not of the typical variety you have come to expect, neither sanguine (*don't let it get you down*) nor cautionary (*take care of yourself out there*). No, this one seems more matter-of-fact, more like the one you remember from your first night here: *no one said it was going to be easy.*

How are you going to manage to get the money you promised your father? Joe's refusal puts a fork in one of your very last options. As you walk toward the diner, you flirt with the notion of hitting Sam up for the dough. You will see him in a couple of days in St. Louis, but can you really go to your new boyfriend for a loan, especially when you haven't seen him in over a month? If he felt you were overreaching, he'd either have to refuse you or concede, both of which could create additional stress your delicate long-distance arrangement couldn't handle. No, you decide: it is too much to ask. You don't want to save one man only to lose another. The only other person you know who might be in a position to grant you a loan is Mimi, and that is a nonstarter. Under no circumstance will you ask Mimi for charity in any form. Perhaps you should simply trust that you can scrimp and starve yourself for another few weeks, this time with better results.

Oh, who are you kidding? All it takes is the sound of those patty melts sizzling on the flattop to deflate that idea. Your father needs help now, which means there is only one thing to do.

When Monster made his offer to you all those months ago, you filed it not in your memory's active records but in its dead storage as if it were an old tax return, the kind of thing you never expected to retrieve but kept around just in case. Now, here you are, desperate enough to consider ignoring your values and risking all of your relationships.

You've spent most of a lifetime attempting to hide your body from the world. It took weeks of deprogramming just to walk upright into the ring and drop your robe with some semblance of confidence. Even now, at the end of a match, when you return to whatever makeshift space you've been given for a dressing room, you often spend a few minutes with your head between your knees, fatigued not from the physical exertion but the monumental effort of pretending to be comfortable in your own skin. How might a girl like you, nearly paralyzed by self-consciousness, pose without at least the minimal protection of her wrestling suit? The very thought of it now, as you return to your room and close the door behind you, makes you draw your arms into your body.

But as you stand there, patty melt weighing guiltily on your belly, the record player you brought back with you sitting idly on the dresser, Tony Bennett at the ready, you understand that this is not your real problem. If it were, you would just harness some chutzpah and get to work. No, the real problem is not the event but its aftermath. There is no way to control what happens to the pictures, which mattresses they'll be hidden under or what locker doors or garage walls will display them. There is no way of preventing them from passing under the eyes of anyone—Joe, Sam, or even, God forbid, your father. Anything is possible.

You place the needle in the groove, turn the player on, and sit cross-legged on the floor. The music fills the small, wood-paneled room. You close your eyes and try to imagine what your father might say in such a scenario, but the man you conjure cannot speak. He can only wheeze and clutch his chest on your neighborhood sidewalk.

If Henderson is willing and able to let you pose for him tomorrow, you could wire the money before you leave and buy yourself at least a month's worth of peace. You will just have to do it and hope the pictures get lost among the many distractions available out in the big, noisy world. The record skips and crackles to its finish, and then continues to spin in near silence, as you pick up the telephone.

Later that afternoon, while you wait for Mr. Henderson to answer the door, a gust of wind makes its way under your coat, lifting the hem. When you rush to cover yourself, you get a glimpse of your legs, wrapped in slightly pilled, out-of-season white nylons, which you have worn at his request. *I have to learn how to fall down?* When you said those words to Mimi on that first day in the gym, you could not imagine a need for such a lesson. Now, you get it. If this isn't falling down, you aren't sure what is.

To your surprise, Joe's secretary, Betsy, opens the door wearing a shapeless, somber-colored shirtdress. She squints and smiles at you, but if there's any message in today's smile, you can't read it. "Betsy?" you say, panic setting in by degrees. Is Betsy staying for the photo shoot? If so, isn't there a risk that this will get back to Joe? "What are you doing here?"

"Just helping out, dear." She takes you by the elbow and rushes you in, out of the cold.

"What's in the bag?"

She's pointing at your hands, which are in front of you, cupped around the front of a wrinkled paper bag. "This? A book. Mon—Mr. Henderson's book, actually. He gave it to me, but I think it was kind of a mix-up." Betsy reaches down and gently pulls the bag from your hands. She slides the book out while you chatter on. "He may have gotten the wrong idea about me."

"Did he?" Betsy hurries the book back into the bag. "Tell you what. Let's not say anything about that today, shall we? Our secret."

You squint your eyes. "I'm not catching your drift."

Betsy opens a coat closet and removes a wooden hanger from the pole. "I just think we should let David believe what he believes for the next little while, okay? Here. Let's get your coat off."

It's a curious tone, like the gentle prod of a mother coaxing a forgetful child. You have half a mind to keep your coat just to show that you can, but it seems uncommonly warm to you inside, so you hand it over. Betsy hangs it carefully on the rack, shoves the book into the pocket, and ushers you down the hall.

In the living room, all of the lamps are on, the heavy drapes pulled closed. The Bolsey is already set up on its tripod with, you are certain, a fresh roll of film already loaded.

Monster comes in from the kitchen carrying a silver tea service. "There she is!" He sets the service on the coffee table, pours the tea, and asks if you take cream and sugar. You do. "I can't tell you what a delight it is to have you here," he says, handing you a delicate-seeming cup and saucer before settling into a stuffy-looking wingback chair. "A delight, but, I have to say, something of a surprise. I hear you have a big match coming up."

You blow over your tea: the surface ripples; steam escapes. There's a question beneath this observation. *Why are you doing this?* You're not sure what the fishing expedition is all about or why he should care; perhaps he's trying to gauge your desperation level in order to aid the negotiations. Maybe that's why the heat's cranked up: for interrogation purposes. You stay close-lipped on the implied question and answer only the overt one: "Tomorrow."

"We shouldn't waste time, then. Do we need to talk money?"

"I need to leave here with a hundred dollars."

"But you know I only pay fifty an hour."

"Right. Two hours."

"Two hours is more than I need," he says, leaning back into the upholstery, "but I'm willing to pay more for a little something in particular."

"Mr. Henderson," you say, "that is *not* on the table."

David chuckles at this; Betsy smirks. Apparently, your naivete is hilarious. David smiles and waves his hands in front of him, showing his desire to resolve a misunderstanding. "No, no. That's not what I meant," he says. "I'm afraid those days are long over for me."

He is no sexual threat—his disorder has made certain of that—and it seems important to him that you know this. This is likely one of the reasons Betsy is here: to make you comfortable, to contribute to a safe, amiable atmosphere. But, as you will soon learn, it's not the only reason.

"No," he says, smiling at Betsy. "I had something else in mind."

Once the deal is struck, Betsy escorts you into a spare bedroom, the same one you used when you were here the first time. Everything is just as it was before—the atomizers, the dress form, the trunk—and yet different, their connotations now sordid. She closes the door, squats in front of the trunk, and unlocks it with a key she retrieves from her dress pocket.

"Let's see if we can't find something that will work for you in here," she says.

From the recesses of the trunk, she retrieves an assortment of props and tosses them haphazardly onto the quilt-covered bed while you take inventory of the items: underbust corsets, garters, a riding whip, a dark-haired wig, a pair of patent leather knee-high boots. With every new item, you reach a new level of anxiety. This is most definitely *not* going to be the kind of photo session you imagined last night, one inherently more benign, with you lounging in a restful, if nude, pose. Alone. The best you can now hope for is that the boots, one of which you pinch by its tongue and hold out in front of you, aren't intended for you. On top of looking horribly uncomfortable—pointy toes, stiletto heels—they are certainly made for a much smaller woman. You doubt you could get more than half of your foot into it.

"Everything okay?" Betsy is by your side now, watching with concern as you absorb the scene.

"I don't know," you lie. You are decidedly *not* okay. You drop the boot, take a seat on the corner of the bed, and put your head between your knees.

"Take your time," says Betsy. She takes a seat on the bed next to you, extends her legs out for a minute and relaxes them again. When you still don't surface, she begins rubbing your back.

It shouldn't be surprising that Betsy treats you with this level of patience and maternal tenderness. She is probably old enough to be your mother—her own teenage children aren't much younger than you. What *is* surprising is that, despite all her compassion and borderline goody-two-shoed-ness, she will be posing for these pictures as well, and with what appears to be utter comfort and poise.

"You're awfully calm," you say, resting the side of your face against your knee. "Have you done this before?"

"Nope." She stops rubbing your back and leans back onto her extended arms. "First and last time, just like you."

"But you're not nervous?"

Betsy shrugs. "I'm flattered, to tell the truth. Seems like an exciting thing to do while I still can. I don't see what the big deal is, really. Lots of people do it. Here." She springs off the bed, reaches into the chest, and pulls out a thin paper bag. "I'll show you something," she says, sliding out a new men's magazine and flipping through its pages, past the editorial describing the magazine's intended clientele (gentlemen who enjoy *inviting in a female acquaintance for a quiet discussion on Picasso, Nietzsche, jazz, sex*), past the story purchased from the estate of the late Sir Arthur Conan Doyle, until she finds what she's looking for. When, finally, she hits pay dirt, she turns the magazine around and holds it open, spread wide and at your eye level. "Check this out."

There it is: Tom Kelley's five-year-old photograph, a once-anonymous bit of calendar art entitled "Golden Dreams." The backdrop: plush red velvet. The subject: Norma Jeane Mortenson.

"Is that—"

"Uh-huh."

You reach up to take the magazine and lay it out over your knees, incredulous and awestruck. It's her, all right. And just look at her, Gwen. Angled across the fabric, her still-long, not-yet-platinum hair waving behind her, her leg and arm extended toward opposite corners. She looks like an angel, or a superhero in flight. She seems the very picture of self-possession, and why wouldn't she? As far as you know, everything is coming up roses for her. Very soon, *Photoplay* will name her Best Actress; before that, she'll walk down the stairs of a San Francisco courthouse with her new superstar husband. In time, you will learn that the real story is much different. Waiting on the perimeter of all those yards of fabric are more than her fair share of demons. But you don't know this yet. As far as you can see, she's as invulnerable and assured as any woman has ever been.

You toss the magazine onto the pile on the bed, walk over to the vanity, and hold your hair up behind you, the way Kay did the night before she ground your toe into the mat. What was she talking about? You don't bear the faintest resemblance to the popular actress. If anything, you are built more like Jane Russell and sweater girl Lana Turner than the petite star of *Niagara* and *Gentlemen Prefer Blondes*. If it weren't for the naturally fair hair, she would never have made the association. Plus, Kay wasn't exactly concerned with truth, was she? She was only doing what she does best: saying precisely what her audience wants to hear.

"Tell you what," says Betsy, putting her hands on your shoulders, her image joining yours in the mirror. "Don't pay attention to all that stuff behind you, okay? Let's start smaller. Maybe you could just take off your top and see how you feel."

"Just my top," you repeat.

But *just your top* is a lot, of course, and so you snail-pace your way through its removal while Betsy takes a seat on the bed and busies herself with those painful-looking boots. In the time it takes you to unfasten each button, remove your arms from the sleeves, and fold your blouse neatly over the top of the vanity, she has managed to pull both boots over her thin calves, yank the laces taut, and secure them with bows.

"Ready?" she says.

"No," you say, but you close your eyes and reach behind you regardless, and, on the count of three—*here goes nothing*—unhook your brassiere.

"Look at you!" you hear Betsy say. "You're such a knockout, Gwen. What I wouldn't give to be young again. Not that I ever had your assets."

You open your eyes again and look first at Betsy's reflection in the vanity mirror. She pulls her shoulder-length blond hair tightly behind her and ties it into a bun while she smiles down at you, her face dominated by that oversize front tooth. Eventually, you shift your gaze and sneak a peek at your own image.

"What do you say?" Betsy asks, holding up the brunette wig. "You think you can do the rest?"

You're too busy fighting off the urge to put your top back on to even consider removing anything else, so you avoid the question by pointing to the wig and asking, "Is that yours or mine?"

"Mine." She pulls it on over her own pinned-back hair and studies herself in the vanity mirror. "I'm Secret Agent U69. You're the damsel in distress." She straightens the wig, tucks a stray tuft of blond hair out of the way, and returns her attention and imperfect smile to you. "Today, you get to be the face."

"The face?" you ask, crossing your arms over your chest. You're beginning to understand the white nylons now, how they fit into the narrative. "That's a change of pace."

"See?" Betsy grabs the collar of her shirtdress and yanks; the snaps pop open one after the other, as swift and disquieting as machine-gun fire. Out from the shapeless dress comes someone else entirely: half flesh and half patent leather, round in the hip and severely cinch-waisted. You bleat out a hard, fast gasp and quickly cover your mouth. Betsy shoots a cross stare at you, but when she looks down at herself, she sniffs a little laugh.

"Yeah, I guess it is pretty outrageous. Better get it out now, though. When we walk out of this room, we have to be these women." She takes a seat on the edge of the bed and rests her hands on her knees. "Go ahead, hon. Get undressed. When you're done, I'll help you with the corset."

She's exactly right, Gwen. You'll have to do more than just take off your clothes; you'll have to become someone else entirely, however temporarily. You know what David Henderson wants, and if you want him to pay you, you'll have to give it to him. But if you can pull this off—if you can play this role for this moment—you can pull off anything. You'll be able to do what Kay and Marilyn do: be anyone and anything that anybody could ever want. Sure, nearly every instinct you have screams for you to stop here, get dressed, and get out, but if you've learned anything from all your training, it's how to put your natural instincts in their place. So, after another breath or two, you stand up and begin to remove your skirt.

. . .

In the short time you will be in front of his camera this afternoon, Monster Henderson will fill two rolls of film. The set of pictures he develops from them will survive intact into the next century, largely because they will be held by very few hands, nearly all of them women's. When I last looked at them, decades after they were taken, I was surprised by how precious they seemed—the tone no more overt than might be found in an advertisement for, say, cologne or blue jeans. More than that, I was struck by their amateur quality. The subjects, always in the dead center of the frame, were washed out from overexposure. In one, the faces were obscured by a giant finger. But the product isn't what matters. Not yet, at least. What matters now is the process. This experience will change you, and not in the soul-crushing way one might have assumed, given both the era and the girl. This will be a much more remarkable transformation.

FOURTEEN

The next morning, you are physically standing outside of your room and in front of the car trunk, the dawn-lit pine straw crackling under your feet, your suitcase hanging from your fist, but in every other way, you are still in Monster Henderson's house, simulating acts you hadn't known existed but now will never forget. All these hours later, the session—the bite of the corset, the sweat at your hairline—are still so immediate, so palpable, it seems hard to believe it is over. And yet, it must be. The cash that Monster Henderson pressed into your hand last night is on its way north, and soon, you will be, too.

"All set?"

When Joe says this, his gloved hand clasps your shoulder, his eyes peer through his dark-rimmed glasses and search yours. If he is seeking reassurance, if he wants to know how you are faring after his especially harsh dose of tough love, he need not worry. As far as you are concerned, he has done you an enormous favor. Sure, he could have been your hero; he could have bought your goodwill and loyalty for the low, low price of a hundred stinking bucks. Instead, you got to be your own hero. You are expected to take care of your own business and, as it turns out, you can. The icing on the cake: you don't owe anybody a damn thing. And so, after you slide your suitcase on top of his and Mimi's and seal up the DeSoto, you have no trouble meeting Joe's gaze and saying, with conviction, "All set."

He leans back and breathes. "Good." He yanks on the end of your ponytail in his playful way. "Okay, then. Let's get rolling."

Joe heads in one direction; you take the other, walking around to the passenger side. As you expected, Mimi is already firmly planted in the front seat, her head pressed against the window. It's the backseat for you, Gwen. But that's okay. You don't mind climbing back there today, because this is the last time you're going to take a backseat to Mimi Hollander. After all, you left Monster Henderson's house with something better than a hundred bucks: you left with a plan.

At the beginning of your photo shoot with Betsy, portraying the emotions of Sweet Gwendoline, desperate for rescue, did not require a monumental stretch. The concern etched into your face would have been there even if it didn't fit the character. The getup certainly wasn't putting you at ease: heels wobbly on the carpeting, underbust corset tight-laced. Still, you were doing it. Despite all your reservations, you remained composed through the entire first roll of film. While David switched it out for a fresh one, Betsy stepped into the spare bedroom to tuck a few stray hairs into her wig, and you pretended to adjust your nylons while you took a few calming breaths. When you looked up again, David had finished preparing the camera and was staring at you.

It was not the first time you'd caught someone staring at you and it wouldn't be the last. People have always stared at you, men in particular. You are used to being (pardon the pun here, Gwen) sized up quickly.

But this: this was different. Perhaps it takes a man like David Henderson to understand that a person can play the role to which her body lends itself, and yet be more than this caricature would suggest. His gaze was not reduced to lust. Yes, that was part of it, but so was curiosity, compassion, admiration, even gratitude. If posing for him cost you anything, it was a fraction of what you got in return. In that moment, you felt confident, beautiful, beloved. And all of this is to say nothing of the money you would receive. The roll of film David switched out represented the halfway mark, which meant you'd already earned fifty dollars: the same amount of money you'd been paid, post expenses, after two grueling weeks on the road.

Maybe you've been thinking about this all wrong. For better or worse, you are stuck with your figure. Isn't it high time you turn into this skid?

You intend to answer this question here, in St. Louis.

The plan, like all good plans, is both simple and elegant: you're going to take advantage of the national appetite by copying the looks and manners of a certain blond bombshell. After all, there were droves of men out there who couldn't care less about the sophisticated lifestyle *Playboy* advertised, but had nonetheless paid their fifty cents for Hef's definition of *Entertainment for Men* because they simply could not resist the revelation of Marilyn Monroe. What better way to show off your new attitude than to pay homage to the woman who most epitomizes it? By your own admission, the resemblance is shaky at best, but if Kay could con you into seeing it, who's to say a few subtle suggestions wouldn't be enough for everyone else?

And that's why, on your first morning in St. Louis, you sit in a beautician's chair in a downtown salon, fingering your ponytail for the very last time.

"Sure now?" The stylist talks to you through the mirror, her scissors hovering in the air. She's feeling you out, ensuring you're not making the mistake many women do when they can't change anything else in

171

their lives. She doesn't like the mournful way you're stroking your hair; she doesn't need any tears today.

"I'm sure," you say, planting your hands firmly on the arms of the chair. "Do it."

"Here goes." The stylist gathers and smooths the first lock of hair, clamps it with her fingers, and snips; it falls onto the floor.

Sure, you're sure. You've never been surer of anything in your life. No more driving the tiger. From now on, you *are* the tiger.

Later in the afternoon, you race along a narrow, one-way street clogged with cars. You're late. You were supposed to meet Sam (it's been forty-three days!) ten minutes ago. After the beauty salon, there was one more matter of business to tend to, which took much longer than you imagined. But when you get to your meeting place, he's not there. Have you missed him? You check the hastily scribbled note in your pocket, the one he slipped beneath the crack of your door sometime late in the night, which included his schedule for the day (nonstop press appearances all morning), a window of time when he'd be free (perfect for a late lunch), and the street corner where he would meet you. While you search for confirmation that you are in the right place, a convertible, shiny-new except for the occasional bug splatter, honks two, three times as it creeps past. The window rolls down and a head pops out, followed by a long arm, which scoops the air.

"Quick! Get in the car!" Sam yells. "There's no place to park in this city!"

You break into a run. Your heels clack against the sidewalk; the shopping bag from Stix, Baer & Fuller bangs into fellow pedestrians. Sam stalls at the yellow light at the cross street. You barely have enough time to hurry in and close the door before he turns off. The light turns red as you roll beneath it. Angry motorists yell and shake their fists.

"I almost didn't recognize you," he says, reaching over to take a fist-ful of your new bob.

"What do you think?" you ask. When the stylist spun you around to see your new do in the mirror, she said, "Now *this* is some serious glamour." Not that you needed convincing; it had been obvious to you, too. But Sam seems to be grasping for phantom wisps. Maybe he doesn't like it. You hadn't considered that possibility.

"What do I think?" he says. Instead of answering, he drops his hand from your hair to your shoulder, draws you in and covers your mouth with his own. When he finally pulls away and returns his eyes to the road, he says, "I think I'm going to lock you away so I don't have to pulverize every guy in St. Louis."

It's exactly the response you wanted—so it took him a minute; at least he came around—but it doesn't make you feel quite the way you'd imagined; it swims around in your gut. You ignore the feeling and run your hand over the Crestline's two-tone upholstery. "Wow. This is some car."

"Not bad, eh? The guys razzed me about getting a ragtop consider-ing where we live and all, but I figure, hey, if I have to be the champion, I should do it in style, right?" Sam points to your bag. "Looks like you've been doing some shopping yourself. Whatcha got there?"

What do you think, Gwen? Should you let him in on the plan?

No. Better not take the chance.

"Socks," you say, clutching the bag to your chest.

It takes a large chunk of your time together just to find a parking spot; you burn up most of the rest looking for a place to eat. The first place you try, a department store cafeteria, is embroiled in a sit-in: currently uneventful but thick with tension and the looming threat of cops and press. St. Louis, you will come to learn, is just beginning what will be a long, slow, painful process for the country: ridding itself of the laws that give you access while keeping others in the corners, under the shadows. While you might be on the right side of this argument, you have little interest in being here, where, for perhaps the first time in your life, you feel conspicuously white. No, better to settle at the lunch counter at a five-and-dime, where the stools are only half full and you don't have to worry about troubles any bigger than your own.

An annoyed-looking young man in a paper hat chews on a toothpick, but spits it out and perks up when the two of you walk in. He drops menus in front of you. While you look over your options, the attendant turns around and begins rifling around for something in a rucksack that hangs off the back wall. He finds what he was looking for—a magazine—lays the magazine on top of Sam's menu, and speed-flips through the pages.

"Hey, ain't this you?" He stops on a page and points to a picture. "Ain't you Spider McGee?"

"I am." Sam leans conspiratorially toward the boy and mock-whispers, "And as you can see, I am in the midst of a supersecret rendezvous with the evil temptress Gorgeous Gwen Davies. It's imperative that word of this exploit not leave this lunch counter." Sam turns to the woman on his right and raises his eyebrows with mock seriousness. "Can I trust you?"

The woman rolls her lips into her mouth to suppress a smile and nods her head a little. Eventually, she raises her pinched fingers to her lips and gives the universal sign for *your secret is safe with me*, pointedly flicking the "key" in the attendant's face.

"Excellent!" Sam returns his attention to the boy, who hasn't taken his eyes off you. "How 'bout you, Junior? Can I trade an autograph for your silence?"

The boy already has his pen out.

Sam dashes off his autograph and flips one page of *Wrestling Revue*, where there is the faintest image of you hovering behind the ropes while Mimi, the photographer's true target, swings her opponent around the mat. "Lucky you," he says to the boy. "Two for the price of one." He slides it over to you and hands you the pen.

This is not the right time to try out your new persona. You still have to get through tonight; you still have to convince Joe. But you're feeling brave. Anything seems possible. You take the pen, draw a heart around your unrecognizable head, and quickly scribble this for an autograph: *XOXO, Gwen.* And then, an inspired impulse: lifting the magazine to your mouth, you press your red lips against the page, leaving souvenir prints. The boy's mouth cocks into a funny little smile, which he aims first at the magazine, then at you. When he turns toward Sam, he is met with a flat glare and his smile evaporates. He takes your order and shuttles off to put the magazine back in his rucksack before assembling your sandwiches.

"What was that?" There's an edge to Sam's voice. You don't like the tone he's taking—too much fatherly scolding to it—and steel yourself against it.

"I'm trying something new."

"Are you sure it's such a good idea?" He scratches his head, softens his voice. "It's not exactly something your character would do."

"I know," you tell him. "But I'm working on that."

Sam looks sideways at the counter attendant. "I don't like the way he looked at you. If it turns out that I *do* have to beat up all of St. Louis, I'm definitely starting with that kid."

Poor guy. If he thinks that's blood-boiling, wait until he sees what's sitting in the bottom of your shopping bag: a two-piece suit as red as Norma Jeane's velvet backdrop.

Over the next decade, the two-piece will make way for its more daring little sister, the bikini, and never look back. By that standard, your new suit, which doesn't so much as expose your belly button, seems embarrassingly conservative. In fact, when you debut it this evening, the only difference between it and the suits of the three other women in the ring will be the mere two-inch-wide band of torso flesh yours will reveal. Such a small amount of exposure—a glimpse of the ribs, really—but hopefully enough to make sure you are noticed.

Finding a bathing suit in January took forever. There wasn't time for a tailor to add any precautionary reinforcements, so you have no choice but to shimmy into the unaltered suit, tape the back clasp as tightly as you can, and hope for the best. Doing this in the makeshift dressing room you share with your partner is an operation that requires both speed and stealth. (If Mimi gets one whiff of this stunt, she will surely nip it in the bud.) Thankfully, you finish the job and slip into your robe before she can pay you any mind.

Before you know it, you are following her down a darkened aisle, flanked by dozens of dart-eyed, heel-hating spectators, to the ring. Now that it is time to put your plan into action, you don't feel much like a tiger. You are half-inclined to run back up the aisle and out of the auditorium. There are a million things to worry about—some you can articulate, some you can't—but the worst and clearest one of all is this: *Can I really pull this off?*

Of course you can, Gwen. You will not flinch now, just as you didn't flinch when David Henderson put you into a pose: turning your face with his enormous hands, pulling down your corset, easing your legs further apart. You met his eyes and held them while he worked. When he was ready for the last shot, he stood back beside the tripod, nodded his approval, and smiled. "You know something, Gwen? I don't think you're the same girl you were the first time you came here."

"Mr. Henderson," you answered, the very picture of self-possession, "I'm not the same girl I was half an hour ago."

No, you aren't that girl anymore. And now it's time that everyone knows it. Hold up your chin, drop your robe, and strike your pose— one hip cocked and supporting a propped hand, the opposite arm resting against an athletic leg. Pretend to look at the crowd, but make sure you can see the corner of the ring, where Mimi is standing. You will want to catch her reaction when she sees the gift you have made of yourself: the red-lipped smile, the green boots, the new do, the suit, and those extra inches of sex.

It seems to take a minute for Mimi to realize what is happening. At first, she appears far, far away. She is probably too lost in her imaginings of the future to think of anything else, her eyes too glazed by stardust to see what's right in front of her. It is only after the initial stir—a few frenzied yelps, shrill whistles, guttural *yeaaaaaah*s, and even various sisterly approvals like *Flaunt it, honey!*—becomes an all-out hullabaloo, complete with a lightning storm of flashing cameras and the thunder of the audience's response, that her expression begins to turn. Soon, there will be a few minutes of flabbergasted debate by the officials before they eventually decide there is no official rule against two-piece suits. You expect there will be a scolding from Joe and maybe even from Sam. But the possibility of these threats are tempered, if not altogether drowned out, by the look on Mimi's face *right now* when she finally registers what is happening, the one that says her carefully plotted career has just hit a serious bump in the road.

There is no way the story of the evening is going to be the Hollander Helicopter, or even, for that matter, Byers and Stewart's successful defense of their belt. This is The Sweetheart's story now.

FIFTEEN

While Byers and Stewart preen, belts aloft, in the center of the ring, you and your partner slink back up the aisle. The crowd is disturbingly quiet. Not exactly the exit you were hoping for, is it? You can't blame them, really. They're not quite sure what to think about you, the recently defeated heel, and your out-of-place bedroom eyes and rosy-lipped smile. Mimi, on the other hand, is easy to read. She stays two paces ahead of you, choosing instead to direct her rage at random spectators by reaching into the crowd and shoving them to the ground despite (or, perhaps, because of) the complete absence of provocation.

As you expected, Mimi is not the only person who is less than enamored with your performance. After she disappears in a huff behind the door to your dressing room, Joe, coming seemingly out of nowhere, steps in front of the doorway to prevent you from following her inside.

"When you take off the suit," he says, "I want you to come out here and hand it to me."

He hasn't raised his voice, but you almost wish he would. Perhaps that might be less frightening than the undercurrent of rage you sense in his tone. He moves to let you through, and you disappear into the dressing room. Minutes later, you return to the doorway with the suit and hand it to Joe. He surveys the legs on the briefs. "You didn't even have it altered."

"There wasn't time."

"You could have—" he says, and stops himself, regroups. "What if you'd been disqualified?"

"But I wasn't."

"But you could have been. This was a title match, Gwen! It was too big to gamble on a stupid stunt."

Your lips purse as if you've sucked on something tart. He has some nerve chastising you like this. So he doesn't loan money. Fair enough. But if he is really so worried about morality, why doesn't he pay you a fair percentage? Why does he charge his struggling protégés interest on their debts? If he were really looking out for you, perhaps you would have been less inclined to take matters into your own hands. "You're the one who said modesty has no place in wrestling," you say in a voice flattened with spite.

Joe stares at you, incredulous. "Let's make something clear, young lady," he says. "This is my game, and there is only one way that you can play it: by my rules."

You knew Joe and Mimi wouldn't be the only ones upset with your stunt. Sam was certain to be peeved, and probably more than a little, given his strong reaction at lunch earlier today. But all of that will disappear, you are sure, when he realizes what you have in mind for the rest of the evening. Later tonight, when he comes by your room, he will find you still dewy from your bath and ready to lose what is left of your innocence. What better way is there to confirm, without ambiguity, that you are his? It will be a fitting end to your triumphant day.

Of course, in real life, you are too silly with anticipation to stay in pose, and then, when the hour comes and goes, too unsure of the plan to do so. It will be enough, you think, pulling on your gown, to find you in your nightclothes—that will speak volumes. But then more time passes, and eventually, dewy becomes damp and cold, so you climb under the comforter. He's an hour late, then two hours. There is no reason to fret—it's a big night, and it will be hard for him to get away. Still, it is your only night together and it is slipping away. You pick up a book and look at the words until your mind shuts off.

The creaking of the door wakes you. Light shoots in from the hallway and disappears again. The room is too dark for you to see any of Sam's features, but the silhouette that walks toward you is unmistakably his. When he gets to the bed, he stretches out beside you on top of the comforter, fully dressed. The mattress shifts as he slips his hands beneath his head, crosses his ankles. You wait for him to say something. When he doesn't, you say, "You made it."

"Sorry, did I wake you?"

"I was hoping you would. What took so long?"

Sam lets out a long, slow breath. "Well. First I had to win a title I didn't want. Then I had to talk to a lot of people I don't care about. Then I got waylaid by my uncle, who wanted to know why I didn't stop my girlfriend from going through with her little exhibition this evening, and I had the great pleasure of admitting to him that I didn't know anything about it because she didn't bother to let me in on it."

Some emotion gathers in his voice as he speaks, but you don't bother to identify it. Whatever it is, you are sure you can placate him. You slip a finger into an empty belt loop on his slacks.

"Sam—"

"And then, when I finally got back to the room, my knees were killing me, so I popped a few pills and waited for those to kick in while I iced them down." If he has noticed your hand, he hasn't let on. "Then I cleaned up and came down here, but I had to circle around a few times

so no one would see me sneak into my girlfriend's room. Like a school-
boy or criminal or something. And now, I am so, so tired that I don't
even want to take off my shoes."

So that's all it is: exhaustion. Well, then, you will just have to ener-
gize him. You give the loop a playful tug.

"Sam—"

"Did you buy socks today?" he asks quietly.

This gives you pause. Maybe this is not going to be so easy after all.
You search his face in the dark. Maybe he is asking an earnest question.
But you are hesitant to give an earnest answer, so you buy some time.
"What?"

"You said you had socks in your bag. Did you?"

You still have a lot to learn about the language of relationships, its
nuances, but this, you understand. *You lied to me,* he is saying. *You don't
trust me.* And he is right. You have not met your basic obligations to him.
You put the plan first. Knowing Sam, I suspect this is the great problem
of his life—everyone's plans always come before his own. If you want to
assure him you are not just more of the same, you should come clean.

"No," you say, and retract your hand.

Sam nods and closes his eyes. "I didn't think so."

There are footfalls in the hallway, and the hum of voices. They recede and then disappear while your own heartbeat picks up pace.

"I'm falling asleep," he says. "I need to, anyway. No way I'm making it to Lincoln tomorrow if I'm not out of here by first light."

First light? You knew this evening would be a race against the clock,
but you didn't know it would be rigged. Hours have been stolen from
you; now even the precious minutes are gone.

"But we haven't even—don't you want to—" There's no right way
to say it, or to express the panic you are feeling. You need this. Com-
pleting this act would assure you both of the other's importance, would
carry you through the long weeks ahead. Desperate, you kick off the
comforter and thread one of your legs through his.

This time, your gesture registers: Sam looks down at the tangle of your legs. But that is it. He looks and thinks; he doesn't move. It is terrible to lie here like this. To wait. Worse, though, is when he props himself up on his elbow, pats your knee, and moves it gently back to your side of the bed.

"Maybe we should see which way this thing goes first," he says, his eyes soft and kind. "Okay?"

He says this gently. Still, it is rejection. Tonight it seemed every pair of arms in St. Louis drew you in—just not the one that could hold you until morning. Who knows how long you will have to wait for that?

"Okay," you lie.

"Let's say good-bye now," he says, resting a hand on your shoulder. "Just in case I have to slip out before you get up."

"You could wake me," you say, but when he presses his lips to your forehead, you understand that he won't. Soon he is asleep. You stay up as long as you can, hoping you can outlast him. And for a while, it seems you might. Your churning thoughts keep you awake while he softly snores. But you have reasons to be weary, too, and eventually, you run out of gas. When you wake the next morning, he is gone, just as you knew he would be.

That night, you stretch across the bed of a different hotel room and ink two new stars in your map: a purple one in St. Louis and another blue one around Nashville, your current location. Mimi's suitcase, still packed, sits at the foot of the bed. Joe is gone, too, having rushed off for a meeting with the promoter. Not that either of them was much company on the road. Normally, you don't mind silence, but right now, the last thing you want is to be left alone with your thoughts, which are growing more panicked by the minute. As exciting as it is to make the papers, you can't help but worry that you have gone too far to get there. By the time someone knocks on the door, you are convinced that Mimi is going to pummel you, Joe is going to fire you, and you have lost Sam forever.

It's Joe, his overcoat still buttoned to his neck. Rather than wait for an invitation, he brushes past you, stops at the foot of your bed, and points at its corner, where you dutifully sit, washed over with dread. While he drags a chair across the carpeting with one arm, popping open his coat buttons with the other, you imagine all the directions this conversation might go, none of them good. He's going to punish you by giving Mimi an even higher percentage of the purses. He's going to make sure you are never booked within two hundred miles of Sam, that you never have the chance to win him back. No. He's done with you altogether. By the time he sheds his coat and settles into the chair, you're certain he intends to put you on the first bus home.

Joe leans in until the two of you are almost nose to nose.

"Just tell me why you did it," he says. "Give me a reason. And make it good."

"I just wanted some attention." You rub the back of your neck and look just above his eyes. "I needed to show that I had star power."

"It was a national title match." He speaks with exaggerated restraint: quietly, slowly. He is a muzzled Doberman. "What. More. Do. You. Want?"

"They didn't book *me*," you say, just above a whisper and with all the hesitancy of a confession. "They booked Mimi. I just happened to be her partner. You said so yourself."

"You want to go solo then?"

"Yes," you say, finally lowering your eyes to meet his.

Joe, satisfied that he's gotten the truth out of you, reclines into the chair and drapes his arms over the back. "You got me in trouble with the boss. You embarrassed me in front of my colleagues."

Your eyes wobble in their sockets, but they don't break their gaze. "I didn't think—"

"Exactly," he says, nostrils flared. "You didn't think."

"Am I—" you say. "Is this—"

"No," he sighs, "but we have to change plans. People are already talking. Costantini wants you in DC next week, alone and with the suit. Others will, too. You wanted attention. Well, you got it. I think the best thing we can do is just go with it. Tomorrow, during the match, you'll make a public break with Mimi."

"Does that mean—"

"Yes," he says. "You're going clean."

This should be a relief, and it is, but it also serves to release all of the day's pent-up angst. You close your eyes, cup your hand over your mouth, and will yourself to stop trembling.

"What's wrong with you?" Joe sounds more frustrated than sympathetic. "This is what you wanted."

"I know." You let out a long, slow exhale. "It is. I just thought . . . I thought you were going to say something else."

"I'm not done being mad," he says. "This is a major hassle. Everything has to be reworked. I'll have to call promoters, change bookings. But, first things first—and first, we worry about tomorrow. Mimi is working out the new program. She'll walk you through it in the morning. Here." Joe fishes around in the pocket of his coat, and then slaps the red suit, now heartily reinforced, on the top of the bed. "I just hope you know what you're doing."

You close your eyes again and do not open them until he is gone. You do not want him to see that you haven't the foggiest. You are not even sure about what you have already done. St. Louis may prove to be a shrewd move that will pay off in the end, or it could be the biggest mistake of your young life.

Just past sunrise, Mimi shakes you awake. You didn't even know she was here; you'd fallen asleep before she returned to the room. She wants to get to the local gym before anyone else needs the ring. "Let's get going."

The orders don't stop there. For the next half hour, she is a flurry of directives. *Get dressed. Walk faster. Hop up.* You do as you are told, waiting until you are more than half-awake and on top of the apron before bothering to ask, "What did you have in mind?"

"I think you should do that thing off the ropes again," she says, stretching her hamstring and looking past you at the empty gym, hard-eyed and resolved. "Like you did in that first match. Only this time, do it better."

You aren't sure what exactly she is after. It is entirely possible she is trying to trick you into breaking a bone before the match just to teach you a lesson. Perhaps sensing your reluctance, she says, "You started this." Her breath is hot against your skin. "It's better for us both if this thing makes some noise."

You are all for noise. If there is no noise, then everything is for naught.

The match that follows is the most tightly scripted of your career. The entire bout will clock in at twenty-five minutes, but it is the final ones when you climb up and balance yourself on the top rope that really matter. Mimi hits her mark, and you make your move: not the higgledy-piggledy jump-and-hope-for-the-best maneuver you attempted in Florida, but an infinitely more assured top-rope dropkick, which now lands within reasonable proximity of the middle of Mimi Hollander's chest.

Later, in her postmatch interview, Mimi will tell the local reporter that she doesn't understand why you did it. All you had to do was kick back, wait for her to finish things off, and then enjoy the spoils of victory without having made even the most minimal of efforts: no sweat broken, no finger lifted. But for some mysterious reason, you opted to join forces with your opponents. She will then wipe the back of her neck with her towel and say, "She really dropped a bombshell on me." By *bombshell,* she will mean your treasonous act, when you surprised her with an explosive blow that resulted in the loss of your shared title and your partnership. And maybe that's how the reporter will understand her. Maybe it's simply a coincidence that her quote will be printed beneath a picture of you—midair, about to deliver said blow—and change the meaning of this term from the emotional act of double-crossing a partner to the physical act of jumping from the ropes and drop-kicking her in the chest. Either way, the fusion of Mimi's words and your image will have an important lasting effect. Without it, that dropkick might have remained a nameless maneuver. Instead, it will become the Bombshell: the signature move of wrestling's newest star.

And as satisfying as that will be, what really matters to you is what happens *now.* At first, there is nothing. Not a peep, not even from Mimi. But then, finally, the audience catches up to the shifting plot— it's true; you're on *their* side now—and there it is, Gwen. Just as you hit the mat, you are surrounded by a towering wave of noise. Nothing you've ever heard before—not your rousing ovation at *Bandstand,* not Sal's prediction (*Young lady, I can see you signing a lot of autographs*), not Mimi's approval (*That's more like it*), not Cynthia's attention, not Kay's compliments, not Sam's affections, not even your father's sporadic overtures (*This one's for you, Leonie*)—has sounded so pivotal, so transformative, so absolute. It is true love doled out in decibels, and it's all for you. It crashes down around you, washing away the jeers, Sam's rejection, Mimi's ironic *champ*s, and, most importantly, all of the miserable silence you've ever suffered.

SIXTEEN

Two days later, you arrive in DC, where you have come to perform for the first time as a face. This, you are sure, is the character you were born to play: the object of everyone's affections, the girl of their dreams. Unfortunately, everyone around you seems oblivious to this truth. At the bus depot, the other passengers rush past you as if you had no more presence than an I beam. The driver of the cab that takes you to Sal Costantini's gym cannot be bothered with eye contact, let alone pleasantries. Only your host seems happy to see you. Shortly after you walk through the door, Sal spots you and walks briskly over, his smile unrestrained, his arms spread wide.

"Huh?" he says. Costantini brings you in, satchel and all, gives you a few claps on the back, and then holds you out at arm's length. "Did I tell you or did I tell you?"

"You told me," you say, more than a little thrown. Joe is a lot of things, but demonstrative is not one of them. Not with affection, at least.

"Here. Check this out." He turns you toward the mimeographed card hanging on the wall. There you are, but it is not the image you have grown accustomed to seeing in these advertisements, the glossy Monster snapped all those months ago. Instead, Costantini has used the most revealing image of you that exists, a newspaper photo from the St. Louis bout that is both grainier and fleshier. He has also given you a new title. In small print, just above your name, are these words: THE SWEETHEART OF THE RING. Your mind moves immediately to the magazine at Monster's house and the actress who will be the first and only Sweetheart of the Month (the term *Playmate* won't be coined until the second issue). Is this his intention? If only you could ask. Instead, you press your finger against the wall and run it beneath those words.

Sal points you toward the locker room. "Go get changed, and then we'll get started. I've got big plans for you, kid. Big, big plans."

Another kind of girl would want to hear a few of the details, maybe ask a few questions, but you have already heard enough. Whatever Sal has in store, you are sure there is more to be gained than lost. I can understand why it might seem this way, given recent history. And I suppose you can't be expected to see how these transactions are still in motion, their final tallies yet to be counted. If you understood that, you might not be so quick to hook your satchel over your shoulder and walk in the direction Sal is pointing.

This evening, you share the card with a bejeweled, leopard-skin-clad heel. She will take the one-fall-to-a-finish match with an exquisitely executed flying mare, but it is you who will win over the crowd. As soon as the thunder-voiced announcer calls for "the Sweetheart of the Ring, Gwen Davies!" you climb over the ropes and enchant the audience with the act Costantini had you polish this afternoon, his personal spin on your lipstick shtick. The mirror is long gone now. There is only the lipstick, which you pull from your pocket and uncap *with your mouth*. You spit the cap out over the ropes, where it is fought over by frenzied fans, and proceed to paint your lips red, all the while staring down the referee with a pulse-racing look of *come hither*. And then, the kicker: the robe hits the mat, revealing your extra splash of milk-glass skin. The audience pounds its feet, while the referee follows the script and pretends that this look is enough to knock his legs out from underneath him. He swoons onto the mat.

Good thing Joe's not here to see this. It isn't hard to imagine his reaction. Too bawdy, he'd say. He'd tell you it was over the line and put the kibosh on it right quick. And maybe he'd be right. After all, you are pretty sure the important-looking man in the front row is Senator Kefauver—you recognize him from his appearances on *See It Now* and *What's My Line?*—and if it is, you'll be lucky to get out of here without an obscenity charge.

But Costantini, perched only seats away from the Senator and his entourage, doesn't seem concerned in the least. When the ref hits the canvas, Costantini shoots you a double thumbs-up. Later, when the card is over, he comes by your dressing room, beaming with pride.

"You're a hit," he announces.

"Am I?" you say. "I was afraid that maybe it was too much."

"I sure hope so." Costantini checks himself in your mirror, straightens his tie, and settles a wayward tuft of hair. "That's the only way to break through. But I don't have to tell you that. You figured that one out on your own."

"I don't know. I don't want to cross the line."

Costantini snorts. "All lines are arbitrary. Drawn by little men who don't think you've got the guts to cross. Well, you showed them who's who. And now, you're reaping the benefits. You know who I just talked to?"

"Who?"

"Arlene Wilson, the gal who writes the DC Dispatch column for *Wrestling as You Like It*. She wants to do a profile for the magazine."

"Now?" you ask, trying to sound cooler than you feel. A profile in *WAYLI* could be a game changer.

"Tomorrow. I took the liberty of booking an appointment with a photographer, too. You really need a new glossy to go with the spread."

You can't afford new glossies. The investments you made in St. Louis took what was left of your cash. You are only just beginning to replenish the coffers and need every penny you make to cover expenses. "How much will that run me?"

Costantini knots his brow. "Why? Is it a problem?"

"Kind of. Things are a little tight right now."

"Then it's my treat." He smiles and offers you his arm. "So don't think about it again, okay?"

It takes a minute for his offer to sink in, so unaccustomed are you to this kind of generosity. This man, who has been your employer for less than a week, has not only made a significant investment of his time and energy into your character, but now he is offering to pay for new, professional-grade photographs. And you didn't even have to ask. You doubt Joe could be coaxed into such an expense, but even if he could, he would have gone a few rounds with you first. He would have made you beg.

"Okay," you say, taking his arm. "Thank you."

"My pleasure. Now, let's go greet your fans. I can't wait to see the look on your face when you get a load of the crowd that is waiting out there."

Before, you were simply slow to process Costantini's words. This time, you don't hear a thing he says. A national interview! New photographs! These are the thoughts that crowd your mind as he escorts you to the exit, not the possibility of a more immediate gratification lying just on the other side of the door. But then Costantini flings the door wide and thrusts you forcefully out of the future and into the present, where a dense throng of arena rats stands huddled. Earlier today, when you first arrived in this city, no one would give you the time of day. Now, it seems they have all shown up, hoping for some tangible contact:

autographs, photographs, *proximity*. When the crowd catches sight of you, they erupt into a frenzy of noise and gesture.

With time and practice, you will learn how to maintain kayfabe in moments like these, how to enter the arms of a fan mob with Kay Pepper's poise and charm. But this is a first, and you can hardly contain your delight. Despite your best efforts, you can't stop your eyes from rounding, or the corners of your mouth from curling up.

"This is for me," you whisper.

"All for you," says Costantini. "Here's a tip—don't overstay your welcome. It's best to quit while there's still a crowd. I'll call them off in ten minutes, fifteen tops." He urges you forward. "So go on. Don't keep them waiting."

This is all the encouragement you need. A beat later, you are taking up the nearest pad and pen, thrust into your hands by a young girl who is only slightly more ecstatic than you. Before you know it, you have given yourself over fully to your fans. In the short time you are allotted, you wear your lipstick down to the nub by replenishing your lips every few minutes so you might press them against another autograph pad. When Costantini takes your arm to whisk you away, you are so dazed that you have stopped recognizing your body's desperate needs for rest and sustenance. There is nothing you need that isn't right here, in front of you.

Before you make it very far, you are stopped by a young woman—a girl, really, a teenager—with T-zone acne, her chin-length hair white-blond and stiff from peroxide.

"Oh, Miss Davies, do you mind?" she asks, pulling a pen and folded page of newspaper from her clutch. "Just one more, please?"

"I think I can manage one more. Who should I make it out to?"

"Vicky. Vicky Darnell."

You scrawl your name across the paper before pressing your weary lips against it and handing everything back to the girl. "There you go, Vicky."

"Thanks so much for making time for me," she says, clutching the paper to her chest. "I just *had* to meet you."

"Did you?" asks Costantini. "How come?"

"Because," says the girl, who can't seem to take her moony eyes off you. "You're who I want to be."

What do you know? Not only have you become *somebody else,* you have become the very *somebody else* that others want to be. In all your life, you have never heard so bald a sentiment expressed anywhere outside of the pages of a book. I can't help but feel embarrassed for her and a little frightened for you, but in this moment, all you feel is the unequivocal rapture of self-actualization.

"Here," you say, suddenly inspired. "Let me give you something."

You press the capless lipstick into your overzealous fan's hand. The girl closes her fingers around it, looks up at you, and, without prompting from any script, slumps to the ground.

Security guards rush over and push the crowd back while you kneel down beside the girl, her eyelids already fluttering open, but Costantini stays standing above you both, his thumbs looped in the pockets of his well-pressed trousers, his smile assured.

The publication of the January 30, 1954 issue of *Wrestling as You Like It* is a pivotal moment in your career, one that signifies the next transition, the shedding of yet another skin. Notably, there's Arlene's column, the DC Dispatch:

Meet Gwen "The Sweetheart" Davies, one of the bright new stars of the mat show. Gwen was discovered at a diner in her native Philadelphia by promoter Sal Costantini. "He bet me twenty bucks I couldn't do a back handspring in front of all those people. It's the easiest twenty bucks I ever made." Gwen trained with Cleveland Joe Pospisil in Florida but can be seen up and down the East Coast. Let me tell you, the statuesque blonde sure gets attention when she sashays down to ringside, throws off her robe, and shows off her swell figure in that provocative two-piece suit of hers. But Gwen is not just another pretty face. No sirree, Bob! Gwen took on Slave Girl Moolah three times while she was in the DC territory and proved that she can sure pack a punch! Up until recently, Gwen was wrestling rough as part of a tag team with Screaming Mimi Hollander. When I asked her about the breakup, she said, "I decided to quit listening to Mimi's big mouth and start listening to my heart." I couldn't have said it better myself. I for one am glad to see that she has hung up her bag of dirty tricks.

Now add to that one humdinger of a cover shot. The session Sal set up for you was scheduled for late morning, which gave you just enough time to hit the makeup counter at the closest department store for both products (what were you *thinking* giving your only tube of lipstick away?) and instruction. Your skills in the art of cosmetology were exactly what one might expect in a motherless girl, but the patient, heavily made-up salesgirl gave you a crash course in the magic of the eyelash curler before selling you a tube of the cleverly marketed Revlon Fire and Ice. (*Do you sometimes feel that other women resent you? Do you think any man really understands you?*) At the studio, the photographer dug out a footstool draped in black velvet, seated you on it sideways with your legs out toward one side of the frame, and instructed you to bend the one in the background while you flexed and fully extended the other, pointing your bare foot. That accomplished, he had you twist your exposed torso around to the front, and your head even further around so that you weren't looking at the camera but rather at something off to the side, out of the frame. Whatever it was must have been scandalous and enticing: in the photograph, your mouth is curled into an intimate, secretive smile. Arlene submitted the new publicity shot with her copy, and the editors found it so magnetic, so luminous, that they placed it not in the confines of the column but a more prominent place, its highest place of honor: the cover.

So long, Gorgeous Gwen. Viva la Sweetheart!

But wait: there's more! In what can only be called an act of incredibly serendipitous timing, this letter is printed on the very last page of this same issue, all but buried in a section known as Voice of the Fan:

Dear Mr. Axman,

I am a big fan of your column and I hope you will print my letter. I am writing to share my feelings about a certain lady wrestler who goes by the name Gwen Davies. I saw her when she was in DC and I thought she was tops. Now I have been a fan of Mildred Burke for many years and also Television Champion Nell Stewart but I think Gwen blows them both out of the water.

I would also like to invite other girls like me who think Gwen is tops to join my fan club, the Gorgeous Girls. In case you didn't guess, it is just for girls, so boys need not apply. Just send a letter and one dime to the post-office box listed below and you will receive my newsletter, the *Gorgeous Girls Gazette,* which contains lots of useful and enlightening information.

> Sincerely,
> Vicky Darnell
> c/o The Gorgeous Girls
> PO Box 72355
> Washington, DC 20055-72355

Even the most calculated marketing campaigns have unexpected and extraordinary side effects. While it's clear that Sal was targeting lust-driven men when he began molding your character, the two of you managed to garner attention from at least one impressionable young woman, inspiring her to create the *Gorgeous Girls Gazette,* a one-page newsletter, which she distributed to anyone who cared to read it. In the first installment, she included a brief history, a few how-to tips for girls who wanted to look more like you (*Gwen's signature lipstick color is Revlon Fire and Ice*), and a list of suggestions for fans who wanted to demonstrate their unflagging loyalty. One proposal encouraged

Gorgeous Girls to make buttons out of their authentic Gwen Davies lipstick prints to wear on a purse strap, cardigan buttonhole, or jacket lapel. But for those who were truly ready to make the leap, there was this simple, elegant call-to-arms: *Prove Your Bond by Going Blonde!*

This extraordinary issue hits the stands while you are in the second state (Louisiana) of a five-state tour, and you couldn't need it more. Strange things are afoot with your father. It takes days to get him on the phone. When you finally do, he informs you that Cynthia has given birth to a little boy. *His name is Harold and he is a little turnip, just like you were.* But the real news is that he has sold the television to Cynthia's mother and is now spending every Tuesday evening at her home, eating dinner and watching Murrow. *Maybe I have been too hard on her. She is not such a bad lady.*

It is difficult to know what to make of this, but at least it is information. You haven't heard from Sam since St. Louis—not one word in seventeen days. To the best of your knowledge, he's currently somewhere in the Great Plains and perfectly content with both silence and distance. At night, when you spread out your map, locate yourself, and mark the spot with a blue star, you calculate the miles between where you are and Cleveland, which seems as accurate a measure as any of the space between you. And while the *WAYLI* issue does help to rally your flagging spirits, having no one to help you celebrate only amplifies the quiet of yet another strange hotel room.

So don't stay there. You've got time to kill before the evening's match and some money in your pocket, even after another substantial wire to your father. Why not venture downtown and poke around in the stores? There: at that corner boutique. Check out the dangerously low-plunging blouse on that mannequin. Sure, blowing a wad goes against your better judgment, but you have a new character to cultivate. That requires some initial investment, doesn't it? Besides, you deserve it, don't you?

Go ahead, Gwen: live a little.

Amazing, isn't it, how much clothes actually *can* make the person? Outside of the ring, people are typically indifferent to you, happy to let you fade into the wallpaper. But this afternoon, while you are out and about in your new duds, persona a-blazin', everything seems a little easier, everyone a little nicer. Doors are held open when you are still yards away from an entrance. When was the last time that happened? And have you ever been able to get a plate of scrambled eggs so many hours after a diner stops serving breakfast? Not that you can recall.

Later in the evening, when you step into the ring, you feel cosmically powered, able to turn every spectator into an autograph hound. The crowd calls for your signature move by name: "Drop! The! Bomb! Shell!" Once it is delivered, and your enemy vanquished by it, they seem to feel the same exhilarating wallop in their chests that you do. But, best of all, when the match is over, there they are, waiting for you, their copies of WAYLI held aloft along with uncapped pens.

Who's got the world on a string now?

Gorgeous Girls will turn up soon enough in Texas. You'll spot the first of them in Lubbock, after soundly defeating Esmerelda Martinez (played by a deeply tanned Nebraskan farm girl named Esther Horton) by pulling her floppy sombrero over her eyes and slinging her around by her serape-striped suit. Here they are: a trio of girls sporting chemically gained white-blond bobs sitting in a nearby row. At the end of the match, they'll be waiting outside, clean squares of white paper in hand, one chomping nervously on her thumbnail while another bounces on her toes.

They are a bit of a mystery to you. You know what the men want; you're not so certain about the women. If you want to understand them, just think back to your own girl-crushes. These girls only want what you wanted from Cynthia, and then Kay, and then Marilyn. You didn't want them: you wanted to *be* them. That's what Vicky said when she sought you out in DC. And now, it seems Vicky's letter has intrigued a surprising number of girls who see, in that same photograph, something they want to capture for themselves.

You're who I want to be.

I know, Gwen. It's hard for you to imagine anyone looking to you for guidance when it seems you're still trying to figure it out yourself, when it all still feels a bit awkward and ill-fitting, like the too-big shoes your father always bought for his perpetually growing daughter. But that's exactly what this dark-rooted, slightly punch-drunk threesome is after. They seek your confirmation and approval; they want you to tell them they've figured it out. This much, you can do. All it takes is to cruise up and say, "Looking good, ladies." Before they can answer, you slide those little papers from their slightly damp hands, leave dark-red lip prints under your signature, wink your good-bye, and sashay over to the next set of pens and autograph books.

The next evening, all three girls show up again in Midland; this time, they sport lip buttons pinned to their sweaters. They've also brought reinforcements. They've doubled in number and, to your delight, don't hesitate to make their abundant support clear. For the first time in your life, love comes easy. All you have to do is doll up and be generous with your affection, which you are all too happy to do. And if you win the match, too, however scripted it might be, well, that doesn't hurt, either.

Tonight, back in your room, you will be as lonely as ever. You will tuck yourself into yet another infrequently washed comforter, and hope against hope for the phone to ring (it won't). You will pull your map out from beneath your pillow, where you hide it every evening, and look at the stars, feeling farther away from Sam than ever. But for now, you are not alone. In this moment, your fans are all that matter; they're everything.

SEVENTEEN

Your rapidly increasing fan base is not limited to adolescents with low-self-esteem-driven girl-crushes or harmless gents. In Lawton, Oklahoma, one of the last matches of this tour, you meet a wholly different breed of admirer. At the exit stands a man with his ten-year-old son in tow, both of them holding issues of *WAYLI*. The man introduces himself as Earl: an oilman, a single father, and your biggest fan.

"It's an honor," he says, tipping his big white Stetson.

"I like a man in a hat," you say, grabbing it by the brim and shaking it back and forth.

You don't mean anything by it. This is your character speaking. Plus, you say this to any guy you see in a Stetson these days. It is part of your plan: a quiet one-woman campaign to inspire a Stetson renaissance and help your father get his old job back.

But then Earl, his son, and his hat show up outside the auditorium in Oklahoma City. When you spot them in Muskogee, too, you get a sneaking suspicion that he knows something about you. Perhaps David Henderson wasn't completely honest about his intentions and those pictures have made their way out of his massive clutches and into Earl's smaller but equally ready ones. This is not the first time this notion has crossed your mind. It's a fear that presents itself on random occasions. It's a ridiculous thought, of course—you've been reassured, and you have no real reason to suspect otherwise—but that doesn't stop pearls of sweat from forming on your forehead.

After the Tulsa match, you spot them in your hotel lobby, the son slumped into a chair, bored and exhausted, Earl pretending to read a newspaper. He straightens his bolo, removes his hat, and steps between you and the elevator. Despite your concerns, you stay in character, expressing pleasure in his persistence, calling him your most loyal fan, and telling him you hope you'll see more of him again soon, expecting that to be the end of that.

"You could see more of me tonight," he says. "After I put the kid to bed, I could come knock on your door. What if I came by around"—he checks his watch—"midnight?"

"I don't think so," you say, dropping the routine. Earl has ceased to be amusing.

"One?"

Is he serious? "No, Earl."

"Two?"

"I don't think you understand me, Earl," you say, adding some steel to your voice. "I don't want you to come by my room at any time, day or night. Not ever."

He puts his hand on your arm and hisses into your ear, "Then why did you flirt with me all week, you goddamn cock tease?"

He isn't gripping you, exactly. He's just holding on, insisting that you hear him out. He's gone to a great deal of time and expense to be here tonight, and for what? You'd call it a misunderstanding; he'd call it a lie. Are you in any real danger? It is late, but the lobby is still full of people. At the front desk alone, there stands a clerk, three traveling salesmen, and a bellhop loading their suitcases onto his cart. Surely they'll provide you with backup if you need it; surely Earl isn't foolish enough to try something in front of an audience. Still, you aren't taking a chance. You fall right back into character: smiling, taking Earl's other hand in your own and squeezing it affectionately.

You see right through me, Earl, the gesture says. *You know what I really want.*

It works. Earl, effectively disarmed, releases you. As soon as he does, you clamp down on his hand and twist until you have him in a wristlock. His legs buckle; his knees hit the floor with a loud crack. While the salesmen elbow one another—*Get a load of that!*—you crouch low and put your mouth up against Earl's ear.

"If you knock on my door," you say, "I will knock you straight back to Lawton."

The elevator bell sounds, and you let go of Earl's arm. You are exhilarated, suffering only the smallest twinge of guilt when Earl's son comes over to help him up off the floor. But when you get back to your room, you lock the door and prop a chair beneath the doorknob. For the next half hour, you think about the bath you'd like to take, but you can't get up the nerve to remove your clothes.

A phone call to Joe and two nights later, you are by his side in his DeSoto, rambling up the shell road to the property in Otherside. To his credit, he has not made you feel the least bit guilty about canceling a couple of matches and taking some time off. This morning, far removed from the episode by both time and distance, you wondered if calling Joe wasn't a rash decision. Now, you are grateful for it. Four weeks of touring as The Sweetheart have caught up to you. Your muscles are sore, your body bruised, your energy long gone. Now that you are here, all you want to do is crawl under the covers for the remainder of your stay. In fact, you are so exhausted that when you first spot a familiar car across the way, top down and ghostly in the moonlight, you are sure that you are seeing things. And yet, when you rub your eyes and look again, it is still miraculously there.

"Sam's here?"

"Uh-huh." Joe slams his trunk closed. "I just happened to talk to him the other night and mentioned your little incident. Next thing I knew, he was here. Back injury, he says."

It seems Earl has done for you what you could not do on your own—bring Sam back.

You are wide-awake now, rehearsing the words you weren't sure you'd ever get to say. Joe cannot leave fast enough. When Joe's taillights disappear completely, the door to Sam's room opens.

How many times have you been in this scene already, standing across from Sam, a doorway between you? In this version, he is a bigger presence than you remember, more disheveled and desirable, and you more desperate. Later, you will see how the intensity of this moment—the vulnerability, the anticipation—is not unlike the seconds before a match begins. This observation will be underscored by his next move: he clutches your shoulders and squeezes you in a grip that could crush bones.

"Are you okay?" he asks. "Tell me you're okay."

"I'm okay," you say, grateful to be touched again, even in this death grip.

"Tell me what happened. I want to hear it from you."

Once you are both settled into your room, you tell him a slightly embellished version of the story, one that makes the encounter seem harrowing enough to merit this response. He has come a long way, after all.

"Say that again," Sam interrupts. "He called you *what*?"

Careful, Gwen. You want to stoke the fires, not set him aflame. "Cock tease," you say, this time tempering slightly what you'd just repeated verbatim.

"Then what?"

Then, you handled it. It's too bad you can't share with Sam the feeling of triumph—*real* triumph—this gave you. But what good would that do? You have more to gain by his panic, so you skip this detail.

"Did you call the police?"

"No. I called Joe."

Sam shakes his head. "He *followed* you. To your hotel." He chops the air with his open hand as he lectures. "You should have filed a report."

Maybe, but you're not so sure. The man was delusional, yes, and highly inappropriate, but ultimately harmless. Not that you are going to argue this point. The last thing you want is an argument, so the best thing to do is just let him play the wise protector.

"You're right," you say, "and if it ever happens again, I will."

The suggestion that this encounter might not be a one-off seems to set Sam's gears in motion. Before you know it, he is on his feet. "I should teach you something." He begins rolling up his sleeves. "You can use it the next time you're in a real emergency. It will give you some time to get away."

Your heart drops. So he is not here to reconcile. He has only come to protect you from the creeps of the world. This is not what you wanted to hear. You are hardly in need of another father figure. You have more than enough as it is.

"Show me tomorrow, Sam," you say. "I'm too tired."

"So am I," he says. He closes his eyes, takes a deep breath, and tries again. "I haven't slept since Joe told me what happened. Now I won't sleep until I know that you know this hold."

You try not to read too much into these emotions. You can always hope, but if you are going to do this, you should be ready to go through the motions and then say good night and good-bye.

"Okay," you say, kicking off your shoes. "Show me."

· · ·

Sam fancies himself a *technical* or *scientific* wrestler. He takes great pride in describing for you the mechanisms by which the hold he wants to teach you—the sleeper hold—will work, how it puts pressure on the carotid arteries, resulting in unconsciousness. When you ask him to explain it again in regular words, he tells you it will cut off the blood to your assailant's brain until he passes out and drops like a stone.

"Now," he says, rubbing his hands together before turning his back to you. "How about you give it a try."

"No way." He can't seriously think you're going to do this to him.

"It's okay. You're not going to hurt me."

It's a pitiful sight: his chin lifted slightly, his throat vulnerable. You want to press your lips against that throat, not clamp down on it with all of your might. But there is no way for you to refuse him, not under these circumstances. No, there's only one thing to do: take a long, deep breath and get to work. You snake your right arm around his throat and pinch it in the crook of your elbow, just like he showed you, and then push against the arm with your left hand, applying additional pressure.

Sam goes limp. When you release him, he slumps to the floor.

"Sam?" You drop to your knees and slap his face lightly with both hands. "Sam!" Finally, his eyelids flicker. "Oh, thank God," you say, pressing your hands against your face. "I thought I suffocated you."

"I told you," he says. "It's not suffocation. You just cut off the blood to my brain."

"I don't care what it is. It's dangerous."

"I know," he says, meeting your eyes. Despite his still-short breath, he offers up a sad little smile. "That's the point."

If there was ever a time to apologize, Gwen, this would be it. If you want to avoid regret—and, trust me, Gwen, you do, as much as you possibly can—then do it now, while he is still holding your gaze. The words have been spinning silently for weeks. At long last, you can slip the needle into the groove and press play.

ANGELINA MIRABELLA

"I'm so sorry. For St. Louis, I mean. Not for this. I mean, I'm sorry for this, too. But I'm really, really sorry for St. Louis."

Sam says nothing for a long time, and then ventures a question: "Why didn't you just tell me?"

"Because you would have talked me out of it," you say. "You would have tried, at least."

"Probably."

"I didn't want to be talked out of it. I wanted things to change."

"Being a heel was that bad?"

"Are you kidding? Everyone hated me. I was killing myself night after night, and they all hated me. Even Mimi. Even my own partner."

"I didn't." Sam rubs his lips together; his eyes dart over your face, as if looking for some evidence, some assurance. "I didn't," he says again. This time, his voice is soft but certain. He clutches your shoulders, pulls you into him. "I don't," he says before covering your mouth with his own.

And then he is fumbling with your nylons, and you, more timidly, with his belt. This is it. This is how it will occur: his slacks pulled midthigh, your skirt yanked up, the prophylactic opened quickly, out of your view, and without your assistance. Maybe this is how it is supposed to go—you on your back, your shoulders pinned. What do you know? You have half a mind to roll him over, to turn this into the victory that it should be—you have won him back!—but you are too unsure of yourself to attempt it, too inexpert to do anything but submit.

Later in life, you will not be able to recall many of the details, but the scattershot ones that remain will be sharp, forged by heat like iron. They will never be subjected to willful or subconscious editing; they will not grow dim or fuzzy with age. And this will have little to do with the hold you have learned, or the other milestone that has been reached. What you will remember most is what happens once you sit up and rest your back against the foot of the bed, when Sam gingerly places his head on your lap, and the usual quiet of your last waking moment is broken by his snores after he drifts off to sleep. These are the things you will keep: the weight and the sound of this man.

The note you find the next morning includes an explanation for Sam's absence—there are reds to catch, not to mention appearances to keep up—and a promise to meet for lunch. You are just beginning to wonder what you should do with yourself when there is a knock on the door. It's Joe, his damp face shadowed under a wide-brimmed hat, a clean burlap sack, stuffed full, hung over his shoulder.

"Special delivery," he says, slinging the bag just inside the doorway.

"What's that?"

"Fan mail," he says. "Something, isn't it?"

"Fan mail," you repeat, letting it sink in. "That's all for me?"

"Yep. Glad to be rid of it, finally. It was taking up too much space. Oh, and one more," he says, pulling an envelope with a Philadelphia postmark out of his shirt pocket. "Didn't want this one to get lost in the pile."

"Thanks, Joe," you say, touched but wary. It isn't like Joe to be this tender.

Joe shoves his hands into his pockets. "I saw Sam for a bit this morning. He doesn't want you out on the road by yourself. He's asked me to book the two of you together for the next little while. What do you think of that?"

You can't imagine anything more perfect. But the way you understand it, there are rules against such things—the NWA's rules, and Joe's personal rules for women and how they should conduct themselves on the road. Surely he can guess what Sam is up to, that he is interested in more than just your safety. "I could ask you the same question," you say.

Joe exhales. He looks over at the water and says, "You know, after I said good-bye to you in Nashville, I drove to Cleveland. See my brother, tend to business. You know. Anyway, when I was there, I stopped in to see an old student of mine." Joe turns back to you and swats something away from his face. "You ever heard of Lacey Bordeaux?"

"You mean Johnny's wife," you say. Just hearing her name out loud has put you on edge. You already know too much about this woman's troubles and aren't sure you are ready for more. "The Ragin' Cajun."

"Exactly. Best wrestler I ever had."

"Thanks."

"That's no slight to you. I'm just saying. The kid could take a bump. And she was a great student. You never had to tell her twice. Anyway, just when it seems like she could be the next big thing, she meets Johnny, and in no time, he asks her to marry him. Now, I don't think the road is any place for a married woman. So I give her a choice: wrestle for me, or settle down with Johnny. 'I don't know,' she tells me. 'I'm crazy about this guy, but I really think it could happen for me. What should I do?' You know what I told her? That wrestling was a flash in the pan; a solid marriage will take you through eternity. If she loved him, she should get married and not look back. That's what my Kat did, and she's as happy as a clam. I didn't want any less for Lacey."

"Oh."

"Yeah, oh. I guess you know how that's turning out. Of course you know. Everybody knows. Even Lacey knows. And you know who she blames? Me. First I gave her lousy advice, and then I rubbed her face in it by letting Mimi have her wrestling career and her husband."

"That doesn't seem fair."

Joe shrugs. "Maybe it is, maybe it isn't. The truth is, I don't like much of anything you're up to these days. I don't like where you're going with this character. And I definitely don't like the idea of you living on the road with a man like you're married when you're not. But I am officially out of the business of life counseling. I am not your father; I am your manager. I'm sure we can get you onto some of Sam's cards, and I know we can make some money in the process. So if that's what you want, that's what I'll do."

You have never been affectionate with Joe. You have seen other girls grace him with a hug at the news of a first or prime booking, but you, while polite and (until recently) deferential, have kept your distance. Seeing Joe like this inspires you to step into that gap. It is not easy to admit that the world might not work in the way that you imagined. And for this gesture, you want to give thanks in a way that is clear and genuine. You place your hand on his arm, lean in, and plant a tiny kiss at the top of his ear.

"Okay then," he says. "I'll keep you posted."

You wait until Joe has disappeared into the office building before sealing off your room and tearing into your letter. You are tempted to rip into the bag, but first things first. Besides, you are more than a little curious about what is happening on the home front. This should give you the latest in both subplots: your father's diminishing assets and his increasing estimation of Ms. Riley.

February 17, 1954

Dear Leonie,

I got your letter yesterday, and all of the clippings you sent. I have to say that I did not think it was you at first with that short hair but then I realized it was you and I was alarmed. What has happened to your suit? I don't want to see my daughter like that. I am an old man and my heart can't take it.

I appreciate the money you sent, but don't worry about me. I am fine. Ms. Riley got a job for Cynthia as a receptionist in her office and she is paying me to watch little Harold during the day. Nappies are the pits, but he is a good baby and I can watch television while he sleeps. Also I make dinner and heat up the leftovers so they are hot and ready when Patricia comes home for lunch. Can you believe it? No, you probably cannot. Anyway it is just until I get a real job.

Call me once in a while, okay? I think about you going all over the place by yourself and I worry. When will you come for another visit? You are missed.

Your father,
Franz

PS: I should not have said that thing about my heart. I haven't had any more pains, so there is no need to be worried.

You are not sure what to make of these latest developments. Patricia? In all your life, you have never heard your father refer to Cynthia's mother as anything other than Ms. Riley. And now your father is *working* for her? As a *babysitter*? You will have to talk to Joe about taking some time off soon. This you have got to see for yourself.

You could use a distraction from these thoughts. So you turn the bag upside down over your bed and let its contents spill out into a large pile, some of the envelopes sliding down onto the spotted carpeting. Valentines: hundreds and hundreds of them. There are 367 in all; you count them twice to be sure. According to the postmarks, they've come from DC, Texas, Louisiana, Minnesota, Tennessee, and even states where you've never appeared. (Apparently, you've got fans as far away as Wyoming.) Most of the valentines are store-bought but some are handmade, and all of them full of maudlin sentiment and illustrated in some stereotypical manner. There are gold doilies and silver ribbons; bluebirds holding banners; watercolor violets, roses, and pansies; cards with scalloped or lacy borders; cartoon Injuns beating out their love on tom-toms; monkeys beating theirs out on cymbals; cards that stand up; cards with parts that pivot, rotate, or pop up; chop-licking foxes; plaid puppies with textured ears and paws; and cowboys with lassos at the ready. Each of them displays at least one heart of some shape, size, or texture: red plastic hearts, gold foil hearts, filigreed hearts, hearts with cutout middles that peek through to the picture on the other side.

Hundreds and hundreds of hearts, all of them offered up to you.

For the rest of the morning, you sit on your bed poring over the cards. There are some blue ones in the bunch—several offers to father your children, plus some references to specific body parts—but not that many. Not really. The vast majority are sweet, innocent, and worshipful: just the pick-me-up a road-weary wrestler could use.

Part of you feels guilty for reveling in the attention of strangers on a morning like this. Then again, it's not every day that you receive a truckload of valentines. You worked hard for this outpouring. So go ahead. Read on. Just be sure to leave yourself enough time to stuff them back into the sack and pack it away in your trunk. You do not want Sam to ask you what is inside this bag. You cannot lie again and you do not want to risk the truth.

EIGHTEEN

Before you know it, it's time to hit the road again. You couldn't order a more perfect day for a road trip, or better company. The Southeast is currently in the midst of an early spring, and you and Sam roll through its small towns with the top of his snazzy, mostly new convertible down. Along the way, roadside stands showcase their wares, including early strawberries. Sam, enticed, stops and buys a basket, and you eat the fruit as you follow a path of purple stars, quite certain it is taking you both to your rightful place at the top of the world.

Life is good. The brief respite in Florida has renewed your energies and reaffirmed your affections. Now, just before you hit the South Carolina border, Sam puts his hand on the back of your neck and rubs. It is a gesture you've come to adore—part massage, part affectionate pat—and you respond by propping your bare feet up on the dashboard and offering him the last strawberry, holding it out by its green cap. He slows down to look at it, and then at you: the wisps of hair that have escaped from beneath your scarf, the freshly shaved ankles peeking out from the bottom of your Capri pants, the arches of your feet. Before you can interpret the look, he pulls over, rumbling over gravel, and plants one on you: a long, unyielding kiss, ripe with all the anticipation and promise of a honeymoon.

You aren't simply headed to the top of the world, Gwen: you have arrived.

The act of dressing has become an important ritual, an essential part of the mental and spiritual transition that allows you to fully embody your character. From pulling up the second skin of your nylons to brushing on your mascara, you draw power from the outfitting. In preparation for the first match of this blessed tour, you complete the final part of this ceremonial act, smearing on your lipstick, before checking yourself in the mirror and smiling mightily.

When you emerge from the bathroom, Sam rubs his hand down the back of his neck, his eyes wide and darting from one of your extremities to the next. "That's what you're wearing?" he asks, a note of alarm in his voice.

"This?" You smooth the wrinkles out of the front of your skirt. "This is what I always wear to a match."

"I've never seen you wear it before."

"Sure you have. This is what I was wearing when I got back to Florida." And that he clumsily peeled off of you later, you might add.

"I wasn't exactly thinking about your clothes then. Don't you think it's a bit . . . much?"

This concern seems a little silly, seeing that you'll be wearing a lot less before the night is over, but given recent circumstances, you can hardly blame him for feeling a little possessive.

"I have to give them a little," you say, and kiss his lips just enough to reassure him without smearing your lipstick. "But I will save everything else for you."

Later in the evening, on your way down the aisle to meet the villainy that awaits you in the ring, someone pulls the top strap of your suit away from your body, which you feel only moments before the sting of its return. It is enough of an attack to prompt some mild fright, and you spin around and assume a defensive position: legs braced, hands up. "What's the—" you say, but then stop cold. The end of that sentence: *big idea?* The reason you don't say it: the perpetrator is only a child. Doe-eyed, crew cut, and freckle-faced. Eleven, twelve tops.

You stroll over, wry smile and all, and take his chin in your manicured hand.

"Is that any way to treat a lady?" you say. "Where are your manners, young man?"

"I'm sorry," he says. He is clearly delighted with the attention.

This is the whole encounter: no harm, no foul. He's done nothing bad enough to merit punishment from you or anyone else. And yet, after the match, when you come back up the aisle, you can't help but notice a small but conspicuous absence: in the spot where the boy and all of his friends should be sitting, there is a short stretch of empty chairs. Why are they gone? Did management escort them out? Your heartstrings twang at the possibility.

Later that evening, back at your motel, you make good on your earlier promise, sliding your naked body under the covers and offering it to Sam. This is the extent of your seductive powers. You might play a character who sells this stuff, but in real life, you aren't altogether sure how to deliver it. However, you have already learned two important truths: it is sometimes the simplest way to heal a rift, and even the faintest promise of it on your part is enough to initiate action on his.

"So tell me," he asks afterward, half-asleep with contentment. "What's your plan for life after wrestling?"

"I don't know," you say, hoping to sound casual. Gwen Davies isn't going anywhere. Not if you can help it.

"Really?" Sam puts his hands behind his head and stares up at the ceiling. "It's all I think about these days. I hate living on the road like this. I don't know how you stand it."

This is not a conversation you want to have. These concerns should be swept into the dark corners of your mind with all of the others, where you hope they will somehow work themselves out. Thankfully, Sam gives you an out by turning onto his side and pulling you toward him. "It's definitely nicer with you here. How many days left?"

"Twenty-nine."

In a month, Sam will head to the big arenas of New York, where the ladies aren't welcome, and you'll jog over to Boston before some much-deserved time off, which you plan to spend in Philadelphia. When you called to tell your father you were coming, he suggested there might be some surprises waiting for you but would not confirm what they might be. You understand what possibilities you should brace yourself for, but who knows? He could be talking about a job, maybe even his old job at the Stetson factory, and you will return home to find the life you knew fully restored.

You peek over Sam's shoulder at the clock on the bedside table, which ticked past midnight some time ago. "Scratch that. Twenty-eight."

Sam follows your eyes and then reaches behind him, pulls the clock's plug out of the socket. "There." He settles back into place, pulls you against him. "That takes care of that."

"Nice work." You pull away from his embrace just enough to create some room for yourself, settle into the pillow, and close your eyes. "Now we never have to leave this room."

"If only." The weight on the bed shifts as Sam tents himself up on one elbow, causing you to roll into him. "You know what we *could* do, though? I was thinking that instead of going to Boston, you could come to New York with me. After that, I could finagle another short break and go to Philadelphia with you."

"Mmmm." You close your eyes and say, already half-asleep, "Tempting."

"I'm serious. Then you wouldn't have to be out there alone, warding off all those pesky bra snappers by yourself."

If you weren't already drifting off, you might take these last words—*warding off all those pesky bra snappers by yourself*—to mean that *he* is responsible for the boys' dismissal. You might be bothered by the fact that once again, and only one match into this tour, Sam is asking you to change your schedule to suit his needs, might register this as a clue that this journey is fraught with peril. But you are too tired to pay attention. And even if you weren't, you are too inexperienced to be anything but optimistic. Perhaps the road forward won't be without its challenges, but surely the hurdles won't be too high; surely there is room for negotiation. You issue a final noncommittal "Mmmm" and fall fast asleep.

A few nights later, you and Sam head outside after a match to sign autographs for the admirers waiting in the parking lot. There is no shortage of Spider McGee fans out here: boys with their fathers, mill workers enjoying a beer and a brawl before the graveyard shift starts, throngs of gangly, dateless adolescent boys. But when you step out a few paces after him, a clamoring mob of your own fans, including a pack of Gorgeous Girls, nearly runs him over in their efforts to reach you.

"We just love you," one of the girls breathes.

Her friend bites her lip for a moment, and then asks, "Do you think maybe I could give you a hug?"

A hug is not an unusual request. You have never denied one to anyone; it has always seemed within the bounds of reason. So you don't think twice—you simply say, "Of course," and stretch out your arms. The recipient treats your gift with the reverence it deserves, enjoying a short, semiformal embrace before disengaging and thanking you for the privilege. But then there is another request, and then another, and now that you've indulged one, how can you say no to any of them? These are the people who've made you who you are, after all.

Sam works hard at staying cool. Still, you see it: the stiffened spine, the set jaw, the glances at the crowd. It seems your meteoric rise is a phenomenon that he has not yet fully grasped. Poor guy. If you had known he would find this so bothersome, you would have skipped it this evening and spared him. You will have to wrap this up, and soon.

Easier said than done. In no time, what began as a small but feverish mob escalates into all-out pandemonium. No one's crossing the line yet—at least there's no more suit snapping—but some of these embraces are lingering and overly firm, and the crowd seems to be multiplying. No one wants to be left out of this experience. This is an event, everyone realizes, and they all want in. When a particularly burly man lifts you off your feet during his long-awaited embrace, it is finally more than Sam can take. He nods to a security guard, who urges the crowd back. While they are being subdued, Sam takes your hand, says, "That's all for tonight, folks," and leads you to the car.

You, of all people, should be understanding. After all, you've suffered similar moments, watching from the backseat of the Hudson while Sam greeted his fans. Maybe you should do something to appease him. And what character might be best suited to that task? A good girl, of course: more dependent, more domestic.

So, tonight, you take on that role by running a tub for him. Sure, your own aches and pains could use some tending to, but tonight, you insist that he go first. And if he lingers for ages, the way he often does, massaging his jutted knees until he's red and pruned, you can use the time to take care of other domestic matters. A quick check-in with your father, you decide, picking up the receiver. No doubt he'll want to chat about that special on Senator McCarthy that's been all the talk. You don't have much to contribute to the conversation, but listening to him might be a welcome diversion.

Soon, you are connected with your father, and, as you suspected, he is eager to talk. But it seems he has a more pressing topic in mind.

"I'm glad you called," says Franz. "I have some news."

In a rambling speech, your father not only confirms what you have come to suspect—that he is involved with Patricia—he informs you that he has asked her to marry him, and that the nuptials will take place as soon as you can be there.

"I know, it is a crazy thing," he says. "But life is crazy. You think it is one thing and then suddenly it is another."

No kidding. In three short months, he has gone from feeling indifferent to Cynthia's mother to proposing marriage. How did this come to pass? You promise to call again when your plans are shored up, wishing him a good night, and then head for the bed. You could use a bath of your own, but talking to your father has left you exhausted.

"Everything okay?" asks Sam, padding into the room in his boxer shorts.

"Sure," you lie. You can tell him about your father tomorrow. If you tell him tonight, he will only want to talk about it, and you haven't the energy. "Tired, is all."

"It's okay to say no sometimes." He slips under the covers and presses into you, his body hot and damp, and kisses a spot on your shoulder. "If you don't, you won't have enough left for anyone else, including yourself."

It takes a minute for you to follow his train of thought away from your father and back toward the events of the evening. He means your fans; those are the people from whom you are supposed to withhold. Maybe he's right. Their need for The Sweetheart borders on insatiable, and the amount you have to give them is already dwindling. Still, Sam's definition of the celebrity-fan relationship strikes you as limited—a fan *gives* as well as takes. You wouldn't pay these prices if you weren't getting something in return. It is with them just as it is with him: a worthy investment in a mutually beneficial arrangement.

"While we're on the subject of saying *no*," he says, "if you're going to cancel Boston and come to New York with me, we should probably tell Joe pretty soon."

"Boston is big bucks," you say. "Joe's not going to be happy if I cancel Boston."

Sam kisses you again, this time higher on your shoulder. "Let me handle Joe."

Is that what you should do? Sure, a trip to the city has its appeal, but so do the crowds and cash that await you in Boston. Besides, Sam has handled a lot of things this trip. In all other arenas, you have certainly proven yourself capable of managing your affairs. This is as good a time as any to practice that skill.

"I don't know." You sit up and rub the back of your neck. You could have really used a soak tonight. "It's a good gig. I don't want to burn any bridges."

"Here." Sam pulls himself up. "Let me do that." He wraps the long fingers of one hand around a shoulder, presses the pads of another firmly into the middle of your back, and runs them along the muscles. You try to stay loose, but the fibers tense up whenever he makes contact.

"Let me know when something hurts."

"There."

He backtracks until he finds the spot and applies more pressure. "How's that?"

"Painful." Whatever this is, he is clearly practiced, but it's hard to tell whether it is helping, and it definitely doesn't feel good. In fact, it is downright awful. "Could you do it a little more softly?"

"I could, but that wouldn't get the knots out." His hand moves over your shoulder blade. He stops again when he gets your signal, brings a fresh stab of pain to this area, too. "Trust me. You're going to thank me tomorrow." He grips both of your shoulders in his hands, runs his thumbs alongside your spine toward your skull. "Tomorrow, you will follow me anywhere."

"You think so, huh?"

"Yes. You will come with me to New York, and we will have a time."

He kneads the scruff of your neck as he says this, opening new pockets of hurt. At the beginning of this trip, his hand on your neck was pure pleasure. It reminded you of your place in his life, in the larger world. This—this is different. But you could be reading too much into this. He has been doing all of this a lot longer than you have. Surely he knows what he is talking about. Maybe the pangs you now feel are the first buds of relief.

There is probably nothing to worry about. What has he done, really? Kept a few fans at arm's length? The truth is, you could probably use a little help in this department. You should go. Boston can wait. You can practice running your own life another time. This is the Big Apple we're talking about. You have never been, and now, you can go at the top of your game and on the arm of the man you love. Of course you will have a time. How could you not?

On the bedside table, the minute leaf on the alarm clock flips over. You could look, but you close your eyes instead, let your still-sore body jostle to the rhythm of his touch. You don't need to know the time. You already know that tomorrow is on its way.

NINETEEN

New York proves to be a busy time for Sam, which means for you it is a lot of sitting idly by and wondering if you didn't make a bad call. Thankfully, at the end of it, there is one monumental perk: you get to be on television. And I don't just mean some local newscast. Today, you are the celebrity guest on your favorite game show.

That's right, Gwen. Today, *you've* got a secret.

How many countless hours did you and your father sit in front of the Philco to watch this program? How many times did you both cover your eyes when the white-lettered secrets appeared on the screen so you might play along with Kitty and Bill? How often did you watch Garry Moore guide the panelists past pitfalls the guests unwittingly opened up? *Yes, his work* has *included some writing, but that's not the most relevant aspect of it.* And you couldn't begin to count the times your father responded to the sponsor's slogan—*Winston tastes good, like a cigarette should!*—by reaching into his pocket for his own pack of smokes and savoring one himself.

Is that what he is doing right now, only on Ms. Riley's sofa? Maybe he is shaking out two cigarettes, one for Wally, one for himself. Maybe one arm is already occupied with clutching his soon-to-be wife, Ms. Riley—Patricia—about the shoulders. Or maybe he isn't even watching. Maybe he is off in another room, rocking the little turnip to sleep. You can't quite conjure up a scene; none of this exists for you outside of letters and phone calls. The whole thing is still beyond your imagination, to say nothing of your comprehension. The commercial wraps up and the flat-topped, bow-tied Garry Moore walks over to the curtains to greet you, a stack of cards in his hands and smoke drifting from his own half-smoked Winston, its butt pressed tightly between his lips.

"Let's welcome our next guest, shall we?" he says from his mouth's outer corner.

Time to get your head in the game, Gwen. You will be home for the wedding soon enough and can take it all in with your own eyes. Perhaps then it will become real.

The sound of applause brings you around, sets off the physical reaction that's become your new nature. You've lost the penny—let it slide off your chin months ago; in its place a wink and an air kiss—but the apple stays clutched in your shoulder blades. No longer do you mind the silhouette and sway this pose creates. In fact, you've come to like that feeling, to exaggerate its effect, to have new respect for its power. This is what you do; this is who you are.

You assume the position and then parade through the curtains, waving to the studio audience. Don't forget to blow a kiss to Sam, who sits in the middle of the front row, his arms crossed. This appearance has put him out of sorts. When Joe floated the idea and offered to make the call—if you had to go to New York, where you couldn't pocket a purse, then you should at least get some publicity out of it, he figured—Sam had been all for it, anxious to make good on his promise (*We'll have a time!*) and prove that sacrificing the Boston gig was worth it. And the show's producers loved the idea. They are in the novelty market, after all, and you are nothing if not novel. No one's going to guess your profession, not in a million years. But shortly after you arrived at the studio, when they explained what they had in mind for the end of your appearance, Sam wanted to pull the plug. It was too late for that, you told him, wishing he could just relax for once.

Now, Garry ushers you over to your seat on the stage. It's grown warm under the lights, a welcome change from the otherwise drafty studio and still-brisk New York air. "Folks," he starts, "we're not going to tell you our guest's real name because that could be a giveaway. So, for the evening, we'll call her Leigh Kramer."

When the stage manager asked you to come up with a pseudonym, the first thing that came to mind was your actual name, but you quickly scrapped the idea: that secret, you prefer to keep. You also considered this one—Gwen McGee—to alleviate Sam's anxieties over this performance and demonstrate your love. The last thing you need is for you and Sam to arrive at your father's house tomorrow knotted up with tension; it's not as if this wedding business isn't going to be strange and awkward enough. But something kept you from doing this. Instead, you fashioned a new name from your old one by shedding half the syllables and editing the ones that remained.

"So, Leigh, if you'll please whisper your secret to me—"

This is history, Gwen! What a moment! There you are, playing along with the charade, putting your lips in close proximity to Garry's ear just to *psst psst psst* into it while you hold up your hand as a shield. And then, on the screen for everyone at home to see: *I am a professional wrestler.*

More applause, just as you were expecting, but something else, too: laughter.

You look out into the crowd, dazed. How dare they condescend to you! You'd like to see any of those square pegs give your life a go. Is there even one among them who could strut her way into a jam-packed auditorium? Who could catch her opponent's head between her legs and flop her over not once, not twice, but *three* times in less than a min-

ute? Garry adjusts his bow tie and gives you an uncomfortable smile
and a pat on the hand before he drops his eyes and clears his throat.
"All right, folks, let's get on with it. Now, this secret has to do with
Miss Kramer's profession. Okay, let's start with you, Bill."

Bill, a younger flat-topper with a long skinny tie and thick-rimmed
glasses, is the leftmost person seated behind the panel adorned with—
what else?—the sponsor's name in white type, bookended with two
large plastic replicas of its signature product: boxes open, wares displayed.

"Fine, fine. Miss Kramer, does your profession require you to use
your intellect?"

"Yes," you say, defensive, but Garry butts in. "Well, sure, you need
brains like you would for anything, but I wouldn't call it a brainy profession, no."

"So, would it be fair to say it's more of a physical job then?"

"Yes."

"There," says Garry. "Now you're on to something."

"You use your hands then?"

"Yes."

"And what other . . . body parts would you say you use?"

This time, the laughter has a bawdy edge that makes you squirm.

"That's enough out of you, Bill," says Garry, wagging a finger. "Alright, Jayne, let's move on to you."

Jayne, the next panelist, intertwines the fingers of her white-gloved
hands and presses them to her chin. "If you don't mind my saying so,
Miss Kramer, your secret sure did get a reaction out of this crowd. Is
there something a little silly about what you do?"

"*I* certainly don't think so."

"No, no, of course, and none of us do, either," says Garry, "but it's
probably fair to say that some might find it a little . . . *unusual*."

"Unusual, eh? Well, you are a very *tall* woman. Lovely, too, of
course. Does your height play some role in your profession?"

"I guess you could say so."

"I know," butts in Henry. "She uses her hands and her height. She must be a shelf stocker."

This gets some snickers from the crowd. This time, the audience's reaction seems less coarse but more spirited, and you sink a little deeper into your seat.

"Settle down now, Henry," says Garry. "You'll get your turn. This is Jayne's turn now."

"Yes, Henry, *please*. Miss Kramer, are you a model?"

"No."

"An actress?"

"No." But this is certainly a preferable line of questioning. At least you are starting to be taken seriously.

"A basketball player?"

More laughter. Hmm. Maybe not.

"No."

"No, but you're headed in the right direction," says Garry. "Let's move on to you, Kitty."

"Right direction, huh?" asks Kitty. She leans forward and extends you the kindness of her bright smile, as if to apologize for the others. You always did like her. "Miss Kramer, are you some kind of athlete?"

"Yes."

"Are you a runner?"

"Well, I am, but—"

"But that's not really what we're after," says Garry. "I don't want to lead everybody down the garden path."

"Fine, fine. Are you a gymnast?"

"Uh, yes, that too, but once again—"

"Once again, that's not getting at the main gist of it here."

Kitty furrows her brow, puts on her thinking cap. "A swimmer?"

"Wrong, wrong, wrong." Moore puts a finger in his collar and pulls. "Okay, Henry, why don't you take a shot at her?"

"Don't mind if I do." Henry stands and moves as if he's going to come toward you.

"Sit down, Henry! I'll say, what's gotten into you boys tonight?"

"It's okay, Mr. Moore," you answer, regaining your poise. "I can handle Mr. Morgan."

Now, a different noise from the audience: a long, low, collective *whoaaaaaaaaa!*

"You heard it right here, folks. Miss Kramer says she'd have no trouble taking on our friend Henry. I'd venture to guess she could take on just about any man, for that matter. There. That should be another clue for you, Henry."

"Do you usually take on men, Miss Kramer?"

"No."

"I see. Other women, perhaps?"

"Yes."

"And when you do this, do you often wear considerably less clothing?"

More snickering.

"Actually, yes."

"Would you consider providing me with a demonstration in"—he checks his watch—"six more minutes? In my dressing room, perhaps?"

"All right, all right. Have you guessed it or not, Henry?"

"Sure, I've guessed it. Why, she's the future Mrs. Henry Morgan!"

It takes several minutes for Garry to collect himself and rein in his audience as well. Even Kitty has a hard time concealing her amusement.

"That's enough, you mongrel. Leigh, tell them what you do."

"I am a professional wrestler."

There's no more laughter now, just polite applause. Before this moment, the sound of applause has never meant anything to you other than earnest admiration. This is the first time it has the sting of derision.

"That's right, folks," Garry continues. "Kramer isn't her name, it's Davies. Miss Gwen Davies, also known as The Sweetheart! Wrestling aficionados can see her next on Saturday, April 3, at Turner Arena in Washington, DC, when she takes on Screaming Mimi Hollander."

It's over now, the questioning. If only that were it. But now here comes the part of the show when the person with the secret displays her talent and encourages the other panelists to give it a go. Today, that means you'll have the supreme pleasure of showing off a few basic moves. Toward that purpose, Garry escorts you out of your seat and back toward the curtains, which are pulled back to reveal—you guessed it!—a wrestling ring.

"Now, folks, Miss Davies has very graciously agreed to show us a few tricks of the trade. So, Gwen, why don't you climb on up there." Off come the flats, and up onto the apron and over the ropes you go. "That a girl. Now, Gwen, I don't want to put you on the spot, but you did just tell us you thought you could take Henry here."

"Sure thing, Mr. Moore. As long as Mr. Morgan isn't afraid."

"Afraid?" says Henry, hurrying out of his loafers so he can join you in the ring. "Wild horses couldn't keep me away." Once inside, he poses for the crowd. A hand stuck between the buttons of his shirt claps against his chest: *be still, my beating heart!*

"Ready?" you ask.

"Sister, I was born ready for this."

First things first. Henry slingshots himself off of the ropes, but you quickly get him in a headlock and flop him onto his back with a loud smack.

"You all right, Henry?" asks Garry, extending a microphone at Henry's face.

"Oh, yeah," he says with faux breathlessness. "I got one question for you, Miss Davies. Was that as good for you as it was for me?"

While the audience does its part, Henry elbows himself up, flips onto all fours and then returns to his feet. He's only just recovered when you stoop to grab him—one arm around the waist, one through the legs—and lift him off his feet, holding him against you like an infant, your hand resting boldly on the crack of his ass, which sets off a fresh bout of laughter. And for your last trick of the evening, you plant a foot in front of you, kneel down, and drop him across the top of your knee.

All of this was rehearsed beforehand, of course. These stunts are theatrical, but still, a person has to know how to go about them without getting hurt. Henry Morgan was on the receiving end of your backbreaker at least a dozen or so times this afternoon in preparation for this moment. When it is over and the audience's response has died down, he gets in one last joke (also scripted)—*I'd say that calls for a Winston!*—and then rolls under the ropes, throws his legs over the apron, lands feet first, and brushes himself off while the other panelists huddle around him in mock sympathy. But what the viewers see next is clearly not part of the act. Just as the credits start to roll, a figure— another man, tall and long-limbed—steps into the frame, reaches through the crowd of panelists, and taps Henry on the shoulder. Henry turns around, and there is Sam, fist cocked, ready to deliver an unscripted knuckle sandwich right in his smartass choppers.

There are plenty of girls who would be charmed by such a gesture. Under different circumstances, you might be one of those girls. But not today. Not after the last few weeks. Until this moment, Sam has managed to toe the line. Now, he has finally crossed it.

The fight starts right outside of the studio, in front of the heavy black door out of which you have both just been tossed. Once the show went off the air, it took a while for things to get settled. Jayne and Kitty backed away while the rest of you clustered. Voices were raised, necks and faces went red, arms and hands waved. Eventually, Morgan and the producers decided not to press charges—they just wanted Sam gone, and fast—and the security guards escorted you both back to your dressing room to gather your things, hurried you down the hall, and dumped you unceremoniously out into the alley.

The buttons of your coat are undone. There was no time to fasten them inside and now the cold is creeping in, so you work on remedying this while you throw the first stone. "This was a big day for me, Sam."

"I know. I'm sorry." He's working on his own coat now. "I just couldn't help myself."

From his tone, you can tell that he hasn't yet registered just how upset you are—that you are frustrated by his actions not only today but over the last few weeks. You will have to be more pointed, more direct.

"That's happening a lot. It's becoming a real problem."

It is the first time you've ever mounted any kind of serious challenge to Sam, and so even after you've buttoned up and fully protected yourself against this tail end of winter, you feel yourself tremble. Sure, you could handle yourself in the ring, but this kind of confrontation is unsure ground. Sam, on the other hand, does not hesitate to meet you head-on.

"What *should* I have done, Leonie? You heard what that guy said, the way the crowd responded. He's up there throwing raw meat to a pack of wild animals, and guess who's the meat? I'm supposed to let that go? I'm supposed to sit in the middle of the feeding frenzy and let it happen?"

"I'm perfectly capable of taking care of myself. I'm pretty good at it, actually."

"If you want me to apologize," he says, getting louder, "you can forget it. If I think you need protection, I'm going to protect you."

"You're overprotecting me, Sam." You don't raise your voice, but you give it grit. "You are *smothering* me."

The word comes effortlessly. Before this moment, you would not have characterized your feelings this way, but as soon as you say it, you realize it is true. From both ends of the alley comes the noise of the New York streets: the whiz of cabs and their impatient horn blasts, the call of street vendors, the jingle of bicycle chains, and the chatter and hurried steps of passing pedestrians. Not that you can hear any of that. All of it is drowned out by the deafening silence of a long, angry pause.

"What are you saying, Leonie?" His voice doesn't crack, exactly, but there is something different about it. "Is this it? Are we done?"

"No!" You cup your hand over your eyes and squeeze. "That's not what I mean."

"What then?"

"I don't know." But you do know, don't you? You need a little time to yourself, a little space. It's okay to want this, Gwen—it's not an unreasonable request. It's just that you are going to have plenty of it soon enough. In less than a week, Sam will point his convertible toward the faraway Heartland while you catch up with Mimi in DC and make your way back down south. The best thing would be to just put this fight on the shelf, enjoy the time you still have left, and let your frustrations dissipate in the cooling waters of separation. "Can we put this on hold for now?" you ask. "I don't want to fight at my father's house, and especially not with the wedding tomorrow."

Sam puts his hands into the depths of his pockets. "Maybe you should go by yourself then."

It is unclear to you whether this is a test of sorts, but once the offer is on the table, its appeal is overwhelming, and you cannot resist.

"Maybe I should."

As soon as you see his reaction—there's that same hangdog face from the night you met him—you regret giving in to this impulse. If only you could rewind, end this whole stinking mess. But now, you've started down this road, and you don't see how to get off it. "For my father's sake," you add, hoping this qualification will soften the blow.

"Well, then." Sam toes a bit of loose asphalt, and then kicks it against the building. "If that's what you want. That's what you want?"

You don't say a word, letting your silence do the talking.

"Fine. I'll just go pack my things." Sam turns and heads up the alley. "No sense sticking around if I'm not going with you," he calls over his shoulder. He's headed in the wrong direction—your hotel is *thataway*—but you don't have the heart to tell him.

TWENTY

Franz answers the door wearing the bottom half of his Christmas pajamas. There's more flesh on him than there was last time you were here, to your great relief. There are other improvements, too. He's not clean-shaven, of course—it's almost midnight—but he's got himself a tidy haircut, a healthy color to his skin. He squints to get a better look.

"Leonie?" he says. He stops scratching his chest long enough to grab your arm and yank you into the house. "What are you doing here? You said you weren't getting in until tomorrow."

"Change of plans." You rest your suitcase where the television used to be and slump down into the couch, into the darkness. "It's okay. Go back to sleep and I'll explain in the morning."

"Go back to sleep?" Franz shuts the door. "My daughter shows up on my doorstep in the middle of the night and she wants me to go back to sleep?" He fumbles around in the dark, finds a lamp, and turns it on. It's the same old room it's always been, except now there are ghostly rectangles where family pictures used to hang, and a row of cardboard boxes against the far wall.

Franz's head jerks as if he's suddenly remembered something. He returns to the door and opens it again, looks out. "Where's Sam?"

Somewhere on the road, you suppose. After the fight, you went for a walk through the city streets; when the cold got to you, you stopped for a cup of coffee. It was good medicine. By the time you paid up, you were ready to ask him to stay, to talk the problem through rather than avoid it. But when you got back to the hotel, he was already gone. You tell your father that he's not coming.

"What do you mean?" Franz says, closing the door again. "I thought Sam was driving. If there's no Sam, how did you get here?"

"I took the train."

"All by yourself? At night? Without someone to pick you up?"

Exasperation creeps back under your skin, into your blood. You should have known your father would react this way. Why is it that all the men in your life seem to think you need their protection?

"Yes, Father. I do it all the time, you know."

"That's supposed to reassure me?" Franz drops beside you on the couch. "Too bad. I was prepared to like the guy after what he did tonight. That was him, right? On the television?"

"Yes, that was him."

"I thought so! He hit that jerk"—Franz punches his hand; the smacking sound causes you to flinch—"right in his ugly mouth. Good for him!"

"Right. Good for him." Forget it. You don't have the strength for anything more than this note of sarcasm; you can't bring yourself to argue the points on this matter again. This subject—Things That Gwen Davies Handles Just Fine on Her Own, Thank You—has grown tiresome.

"What's with the sour face?" he asks, tousling your hair. "What? You don't want to tell your father?"

"Not really." What could he possibly say? Even if you *could* bring yourself to talk to your father about your *boyfriend* and your *feelings,* he'd just side with Sam.

"So, we're playing Leonie's Got a Secret, are we?" Franz presses his hands together, holds them up to his nose, and inhales. "Okay. The secret has to do with why her boyfriend, Sam, did not drive her to my house but instead let her travel by herself in the dead of night. First question: Is it because he is afraid of your father?"

This warms you up, and you smile despite yourself. "No, of course not."

"Is it because he is as big a jerk as Henry Morgan?"

"No," you say, and make a little noise—not a laugh, but along those lines. What's come over your father? Here he is, not only worried about those feelings you are loath to discuss, but insisting on being a support to you even when you've given him an easy out. It's puzzling, but pleasantly so. "Don't head down the garden path."

"But you had some kind of fight, am I right?"

Now he's getting somewhere. "Yes."

"And is the subject of this fight something you want to talk about with your father?"

"No. Not really," you say. You're not ready for sleep, but you put a hand over your mouth and yawn. "I'm too tired. We should get some rest. You especially. You're getting married tomorrow."

"I am, aren't I? It's crazy, right?"

It sure seems crazy to you. You'd like to poke around, ask questions, but you're not sure how to approach it, or if you even really have the right. You don't live here anymore, and it's his life. The man's been a widower for fifteen years, and Ms. Riley is a fine woman. If this is what he wants, who are you to question it?

"No," you lie. "I don't think it's crazy."

"Then you're crazy."

Franz sounds considerably less playful when he says this. He stares ahead at the boxes and their long shadows. Tomorrow, he's going to take those boxes next door, to his new home. This is more historic than your television appearance. This is your father on the precipice of reinvention, a man who didn't think his life could change. It's only natural for him to have some ambivalence, right?

Franz reaches across the coffee table for his smokes and shakes one out of the pack. To light it, he brings a match quickly and briefly to life before killing it between wetted fingers. "Tell you what. I'll just sit here for a minute and smoke a cigarette while we don't talk about your stupid fight or my crazy wedding, okay?"

And with that, the two of you sit in silence, Franz taking long pulls on his cigarette, until, finally, you go for the easy joke.

"Does it taste good?" you ask.

Franz, falling back into the old pattern, doesn't miss a beat. "Yes," he says. "Like a cigarette should."

There will be no more inquiries into your professional and personal travails on this trip. No one even seems to register the remarkable fact that you are here. No, everyone is wedding-centered and moving-minded. Franz's boxes have to be carried next door, and then Cynthia and Wally's belongings will move in the opposite direction. Since you are here already, Franz decides, there is no reason not to go over to the courthouse first thing in the morning and get this over with. Time's a-wasting.

The plan is to meet on the courthouse steps at eleven sharp. You, your father, and Ms. Riley wait in the designated spot, stiff in your Sunday best, but even after a good twenty minutes, Cynthia and company have yet to arrive.

"I knew we shouldn't have left without them," says Ms. Riley, her lips pinched.

"They'll be here," says Franz. "Harold probably held them up."

Ms. Riley's frustration disappears at the mention of her grandson's name. "You got to see this kid, Leonie. He's a real sweet baby. Hardly ever cries. I'm telling you, my daughter doesn't know how good she's got it. And your father is so good with him!" Ms. Riley has a dreamy grin on her face. "Harold's favorite is when your father puts on the radio and then picks him up and kind of dances him around, you know? One night, Cynthia and I got in from work, and you know what we found? A big pot of stew ready to eat, Tony Bennett on the record player, and your father dancing Harold around the room. I'm telling you, I fell in love"—she snaps her fingers—"just like that."

Can that even be called love? It sounds like a decision that has more to do with stomachs than hearts. Before this moment, you were sure that posing for Monster was the right thing to do for you and your father. You got to keep your life, and he got just enough help to stay afloat until his ship came in. Now, you wonder if you haven't accidentally nudged him onto the wrong ship. Perhaps you have only saved yourself.

"There they are," says your father, pointing.

It's Cynthia, all right, starting up the courthouse steps, Harold bouncing on her hip. Wally is still a good dozen steps or so behind her, walking at a pointedly slower clip. His face is expressionless, but one thing is clear: he is in no hurry.

"Okay, okay." Ms. Riley looks on for a minute, exhales, and then wheels around to face you. "Now. No more of this Ms. Riley business." She tweaks your nose between her thumb and knuckle. "It's Patricia. Pat. I don't expect you to call me Mom or anything."

When Cynthia finally reaches the top of the stairs, she catches her breath, and says, "We did it! Our plan worked!" She reaches for your hand and squeezes, which doesn't produce the same effect it might have once upon a time. Now, you're just annoyed with her for holding up the ceremony. "Remember how hard we tried to get these two together?" she continues. "Okay, so it took ten years, but here we are! Aren't we, Harold?"

Harold stares at you from the safety of his mother's hip. You give him a weak smile, which seems to interest him for a minute, but then he looks past you, checks out the action happening at your back: his grandmother straightening your father's tie. The minute he sees your father, he holds out his arms and kicks his legs.

"Not now, Harold! You'll get spit-up all over Pop's suit." Cynthia wipes his mouth with the diaper she's draped over her shoulder.

Pop? That's a new one.

"Can you go any slower, Wally?" Pat yells down the stairs, which prompts Wally to do exactly that, lifting his leg by microscopic degrees, as if trying to free it from quicksand.

"Oh, brother," breathes Pat.

Franz opens the heavy courthouse door. "Let's just go," he says. "He'll catch up." He ushers Pat in, and Cynthia follows, pausing briefly to let Franz tickle Harold under the chin, which makes him laugh. You know that you should find this endearing—heartwarming, even—but honestly, Harold was a lot easier to love when he was in Cynthia's belly, when he wasn't wriggling his way into your family.

Everyone has made a point to tell you what a good baby Harold is, how he almost never cries, but it seems today is the exception. The minute the party steps in front of the judge, Harold's lower lip pokes out, his chin trembles, and a wail escapes from his lungs that could tie a knot in any woman's fallopian tubes. The judge tries to go on with things for a while, but before long, the cries have escalated to a point that they can't be ignored. He folds his book closed and waits for some semblance of peace to resume.

"Give him here," says Franz, holding out his arms. As soon as Harold is in them, he quiets down. For the rest of the brief ceremony, Franz holds Harold's back against his chest, keeps a firm hand under his bottom, and softly clucks into his ear while Harold chews on Patricia's outstretched finger. When it is time to kiss the bride, Franz twists Harold over to the side and leans forward, and Patricia hops up on her toes and meets your father's mouth with her own. The kiss is brief and tidy, no more than a brushing of the lips.

Is your father's marriage to Pat strictly one of convenience? You will never be able to answer this question with complete confidence— it is impossible to know what really exists between two people—but it does serve many practical needs. Pat gets her daughter's family right where she wants them: close, but not underfoot. On top of that, she gets a man who makes her life a little easier, who knows he is lucky to have her and acts like it. In return, your father gets economic security; he gets to keep his house, even if he doesn't get to live in it anymore. Sure, taking on the household responsibilities while Pat earns the paycheck requires some pride swallowing, but he probably thinks it's better his wife pay the bills than his daughter (which, let's be honest, is convenient for you, too). This probably does not seem like enough to a young woman with her whole life ahead of her, but in time, you will come to appreciate the value of noises in the home, a warm body in the bed.

After a celebratory lunch comes the business of moving. Everyone's boxes are shuffled over to their respective new homes easily enough. The real job will be hauling off Franz's old couch, which has seen better days. It is slated for donation to the church and needs to be loaded on the back of Wally's truck and carted over before the office locks up at six. This will make room for the new one that is waiting for Cynthia and Wally at the furniture store. The menfolk prepare to tackle this chore, but you insist on taking over your father's role.

"It's your honeymoon!" you argue.

There's that, and sure, there's a little residual concern for his health packed into your reasoning. The memory of him hunched over on the sidewalk, struggling for air, is still fresh. It will also keep your mind off Sam, who has been running in the background of your thoughts all day.

Your father scratches his head and says, "I don't know. It's pretty heavy."

He's right—on top of being ugly, that old couch is a monster—but obviously he doesn't realize whom he's talking to, so you flex a bicep to remind him. "I think I can manage."

All of the other players have stepped back and let the tug-of-war go on without them. None of them are sure what their role in this discussion should be, or if they even have a role. After all, you've only been a family for, what, five hours now? The first one to step forward is, to your great surprise, Wally. Even stranger: he takes your side.

"Come on, Franz. We watched her pick up a grown man last night and throw him on the ground. Surely she can handle one end of the couch."

"Wally," says Cynthia, a note of caution in her tone. But this warning comes too late: Franz is ready to throw in the towel. He shrugs his shoulders and says, "Okay. If you think you can handle it. We'll have dinner ready for you when you're done."

After they head next door, Cynthia goes into her new bedroom to put the baby down for his afternoon nap, leaving you in the living room with your new brother-in-law and advocate.

"I guess we better get to work," he says.

Getting the couch into the truck is physically demanding work, but coordinating the task with Wally goes smoothly enough, with none of the tawdry once-overs from your last encounter. Perhaps he's not such a bad guy. Ms. Riley may consider him trouble, but you know a thing or two about heels, and you are prepared to give him the benefit of the doubt. Once the couch is roped down, the great mass of it weighing down the bed of the truck, Wally motions for you to get in. You've already got the door open and a foot on the well when a voice calls out to you.

"Leonie, stay here," the voice says. "I'll go."

It's Cynthia. She's standing on the curb in a pair of dungarees and saddle oxfords, her hands on her hips.

Wally laughs. "You?"

"Why not me? The baby's down. Leonie can stay here, keep an eye on Harold, visit with her dad a little more. She won't be here long, you know."

"Think about it, Cynthia." He starts counting on his fingers. "We still have to get this thing out of the truck—"

"I know. I can do it."

"You're nuts," Wally counters. "Look at Leonie and look at yourself. Now, which one of you do you really think ought to go with me?"

Cynthia says, "Why don't we let Leonie decide?"

How is it that you have managed to get yourself tangled up in another one of Cynthia's love spats? Truth be told, neither option—(a) go with Wally, or (b) watch the baby—is terribly appealing. Harold is probably harder to handle than Wally. Sure, he's out for the count now, but what if he wakes up and needs something? You know, baby stuff: a bottle, a clean diaper. You can swing a little domesticity when you have to, but this? This is way out of your league. Still, you know whose side you want to be on, which one of them is the real force to be reckoned with, so you choose accordingly.

You should have opted for moving. Dealing with Cynthia's objections would have been preferable to the sweat you start working up fifteen short minutes after they leave, when Harold begins crying his eyes out.

He is a good baby. What a crock.

How *does* your father do it every day? You decide to find out and head next door, honeymoon be damned. Before you can knock, the door swings open and Franz appears. It is more than a little strange seeing your father in the Rileys' home—his home now.

"I was on my way," he says. "I could hear him through the walls. But what are you doing here? I just heard the truck pull off."

"Cynthia went with Wally. I got put on baby duty."

He bends over, tickles Harold's chin. "How's that working out?"

Harold answers for you by stretching his arms toward your father and shrieking like an injured cat. "I need help," you say.

"Come on, turnip." Franz lifts the baby out of your arms, drapes him over his shoulder. "It's okay. Pop is here."

That's all it takes. Within seconds, Harold's cries soften into a whimper. You thought this would bring relief. Instead, you feel a stab of possessiveness that puts you even more on edge.

For the next two hours, you struggle to make yourself useful, to no avail. First, your offers to help Patricia unload boxes and find places for your father's things are gently rebuffed. This is her territory; these are her decisions. Meanwhile, your father single-handedly cares for all of Harold's needs, which includes a diaper change, a warm bottle, and a lullaby that puts him soundly to sleep, releasing Franz long enough to assemble a meatloaf and pop it in the oven. All of this seems a monumental effort of organization, patience, and persistence, but every time you ask what you can do, your father says, "I've got it under control!"

"There must be something," you say. "I'm just sitting here while you two swirl around me."

"Here," says Patricia, dragging a couple of boxes into the living room. "Tell me what to do with these things."

The first box contains the flotsam and jetsam of Leonie Putzkammer: a stack of paperbacks, ribbons signifying various achievements, yearbooks, random school supplies, and the records you didn't take to Florida when you took the record player. "Let's see what you have there," says Franz, and you hand him a pyramid of 45s and 78s. Everything else is just odds and ends from your childhood, and a few of your mother's things, too, possessions—not quite trash but not quite treasures, either—that were swept into the dustiest corners of trunks, drawers, and cabinets, where they'd remained for years, decades, untouched and unneeded.

None of this stuff has any real purpose for you anymore, nor any memory or emotion attached to it, but it frightens you to think of it gone forever. What you have wanted more than anything was *change,* to shed this old life, but the idea that the old life would no longer be waiting here for you is hard to accept.

The second box is full to the brim with more of the same. Unsure of what else to do, you sift through it and assemble a small pile of things that appear precious and compact enough to fit in your suitcase: costume brooches you can't remember your mother wearing, photos with water spots on half of her face, a plastic Kewpie doll and baby's blanket that could only have belonged to you, a silk scarf you can tie over your head the next time you ride in Sam's convertible. But then, at the very bottom, under all those layers, you spot the wide brown O of the brim on an upside-down hat. You try not to get too excited. So far, it is just a hat. But when you remove the balls of yarn from its crown and pull it out, you can see that this is it: the Musette, as perfect as your memory of it. I doubt you even realized you were looking for it, but of course you were. You place the hat on your head and put everything else back in the void of the box. There is no need to fake sentimentality for the other stuff when you have the one true thing.

Harold begins to stir. "Right on time," says Franz. With speed and efficiency you can barely believe, he changes the baby's diaper and scoops him out of the bassinet. "Have I got just the thing for you," he says. He slips one of the 45s out of its sleeve and places it on the turntable: Patti Page. "Not bad, huh?"

Harold certainly seems to agree. Franz sings along with the record and twirls him around the room in their well-rehearsed waltz. As he does, the whimpers become hiccups, and then giggles. Pat steps into the doorway and leans against its frame, a hand over her collarbone, a thankful smile on her face. And just how do you fit into this picture? It's not clear yet. You were not prepared for your usual roles, however undesirable they might have been, to be so quickly and totally taken over. Amazing, isn't it? You may be skilled in the arts of theater and adaptation, but you have no idea what character to play.

. . .

Cynthia, on the other hand, has a few suggestions.

"I hurt all over," she says upon her return. "Do you think you could help Wally unload?" Wally, acting the slowpoke again, gets out of the truck just in time to hear this and rolls his eyes, but you say, "Sure thing, Cynthia," eager to do something other than take up space. Besides, the work is easy enough, and dinner is all the better for having made yourself useful. During the meal, she leans over and whispers, "Why don't you come camp out on our couch tonight? Let them have the place to themselves."

Makes sense to you. It is your father's honeymoon, after all, and it hasn't been much of one so far. But Cynthia has an ulterior motive.

"Leonie," she says later, helping you stretch last night's sheets over her new couch, "do you think you could do one more thing for me?"

"Maybe." You've been siblings less than a day and already she's maxed out a year's worth of favors.

"Do you think maybe Harold could stay out here with you tonight?" She bats her eyelashes a little. "It would give me and Wally a little . . . you know. Privacy."

Privacy? How much privacy could they really expect with you in the adjacent room? You peek down into the bassinet, which, for reasons that are now clear to you, has been rolled into the living room and parked by the couch. There he is: the little turnip himself. He's sleeping on his stomach, his fist pressed against his mouth. You have already spent much more time with Harold than you care to. But Cynthia, master of getting her way, senses your hesitation and is ready with her defense.

"He's a really good baby. Probably sleep right through the night. And if he doesn't, well, I'll run right out. You won't have to do a thing. You don't mind, do you, Sis?"

"I don't think it's a good idea," you say. "I didn't do so great with him earlier."

"Please, Leonie." This time, all the honey has dropped out of her voice. There is something urgent in her plea. This isn't Cynthia the Snake Charmer. This is Cynthia the Desperate. "We need this."

They need something, all right. Life is a grind: long hours at work, endless chores, sleepless nights. Resentments are building. For the next few years, every dispatch from home will describe the destruction of their marriage: she will spend too much money, his eye will wander. Surviving these disasters will take more than anything you or I can give. Still, it is a call for help, one you cannot ignore. You look up at the ceiling and sigh, resigned. "He can stay."

"You're the best," she says, throwing her arms briefly around your neck before skipping into the bedroom.

Wally doesn't follow immediately behind her. Instead, he stands in the doorway for a spell, staring at you with something of a dumb grin. Maybe the first impression you formed of him was the right one. You understand that people will make assumptions about you based on your figure, but whatever Wally is reading into it is far from any message you are trying to send. For the first time in a long time, you can sympathize with Sam's need to run interference when he can.

For a minute, it seems like Wally might say something, but before he can, Cynthia calls, "Wally, come *on*!" It hurts to hear her hit that same note of desperation, and to see the way he turns his eyes away from you toward the bedroom before he waves his good-night and disappears, but at least it is over and, finally, you can be alone. Sort of.

After the door is closed and the mattress springs begin to groan, you stretch out on the couch and attempt to ignore the sounds of their efforts by flipping through the stack of magazines on the coffee table. They're mostly Wally's magazines: *Motor Trend, Hot Rod, Popular Mechanics, Sports Illustrated*. Nothing you care to read. You should call Sam soon, but you won't tonight. What you really need is sleep. That is the only way to put an end to this day, to keep your mind from drifting in unpleasant directions, like whether a certain other couple is enjoying marital relations this evening.

Soon the cries of an infant summon you to duty. Harold. For all of my life, I have tried to love that little turnip. I have done auntly things. When he came to visit in the summer, I filled the pantry with indulgent snacks—MoonPies, Slim Jims, pork rinds, cheese curls, Coca-Cola in glass bottles, and, to go with the Cokes, bags of Tom's peanuts—and let him eat to his heart's content. The rest of the year, I sent cards on birthdays and holidays with crisp bills tucked inside; little outfits and various sports paraphernalia; posters, albums, and other memorabilia autographed by rockabilly and country-western stars. And I *do* love Harold. Perhaps it has not been in the natural, innate way that Franz did, but over time, I found my own way. This is all anyone can ask of family: that they try their damnedest to act like one. And that's exactly what you do when you lift Harold out of his bassinet, hold him against you—one hand on his back, the other under his bulky bottom—walk him over to the radio, and turn it on: not so loud as to disturb anyone, but loud enough to dull the sounds coming from the bedroom, loud enough to soothe the crying infant. That's what you're doing when you hold his head against your chest and let out a long, low *shhhhhhhhhh*; when you begin to sway, the way your father did with him earlier, the way he surely must have done with you once upon a time. That's what you're doing when you tuck your resentment away, stroke his head while his cries subside, turning into little hiccups, and whisper, "There, there. There, there."

TWENTY-ONE

The following afternoon, after taking the morning train to DC and checking into your hotel room, you gear up in ring attire, wrap your coat around yourself as tightly as possible, and take the elevator to the lobby, where a legion of platinum-haired ladies in trench coats is waiting for you. In another one of his half-inspired, half-cockamamie stunts, Sal Costantini asked Vicky Darnell to assemble all the local Gorgeous Girls for a photograph he can use to publicize tomorrow's big event: your grudge match with Screaming Mimi Hollander.

You understand why this bout has to happen, but there's nothing you dread more than squaring off with Mimi. At least your fan club is here to bolster your spirits. This has got to be more Gorgeous Girls than you have ever seen in one setting. More sizes, shapes, and colors, too: petite to Amazonian, boyish to zaftig, porcelain to bronze. One of the girls—long strawberry-blond hair, hooknose, and athletic build—stands a full head above the crowd, so she is the first to spot you and the photographer stepping out of the elevator. She taps the shoulder of the girl to her left and says something into her ear, which starts a game of telephone until all eyes are fixed on you.

This is why you hurried here, why you kept this morning's good-byes short and sweet. You don't just know this role—you relish it.

Even if you hadn't already met Vicky, you could have guessed that she would be the one holding the clipboard, commanding the brigade with the efficiency of a drill sergeant. Her acne is worse than you re-member; she tried to tamp down the redness with pancake makeup to little success. When her attention is pointed toward you, she smiles and offers only the shyest of waves. This tugs at your heart. You so enjoyed how free she was with her affections last time you met. (Your fans don't often swoon.) The attention she has shown your character has been in-strumental to your success, but more than that, it felt to you like friend-ship. It shouldn't, really, and if your life were richer, maybe it wouldn't. You had so looked forward to more of the same, not only from her but the other girls as well. Instead they follow Vicky's lead and keep their distance, acknowledging you only with smiles. And so, instead of the full embrace you imagined, you and Vicky share an awkward hand-shake. "It's good to see you again," you tell her, an earnest truth despite your greeting, and she says, "You, too," before she introduces you indi-vidually to each grateful girl while the photographer taps his foot.

The photographer wants to take the picture outside in front of the arena, beneath the marquee. His plan is to place you at the bottom step and pose your multiples behind you. It is late afternoon and the light-ing is terrible, but he hopes to make up for this with a semiartful shot: Athena at the Parthenon, ascending into infinity. This works for you, so you and your blond army follow him to the corner of 14th and W.

You and Vicky bring up the rear, and as you walk, she gathers cour-age and begins conducting an unofficial interview. She is less concerned with wrestling and rivalry than she is with other, more trivial affairs, like where you shop. Other questions include *What was it like being on I've Got a Secret?* and *Is Spider McGee a good kisser?* You answer each

one with patience and enthusiasm, slathering on the kayfabe for max-
imum effect. Eventually, you reach the arena. Vicky stares up at your
name on the marquee, sighs, and says, "Your life sounds dreamy."

You could go a lot of ways with this. You could avoid a response
altogether. It isn't really a question, after all; it's a statement. *Your life
sounds dreamy.* Or you might test the waters of real friendship and let
her in on the most surprising revelation of your transformation: this
life is far from what you thought it would be. But you have been doing
this long enough to understand that Vicky does not want reality. She
has no desire to see the complicated young woman you are most of the
time. Besides, she has gone to a lot of trouble. You owe her something,
don't you? No, don't burden her with the truth. Don't tell her that your
life is dreamy for only a couple of hours a day, at best. Don't tell her
how much those hours cost you.

"Yeah," you say. "It kind of is."

The photographer claps his hands to get everyone's attention.
"Okay, ladies," he says. "I need to get a better look at you before I put
you into spots. You know what that means." When no one rushes to
shed her outer layer, he snaps his fingers a couple of times. "Let's go,
let's go. We're burning daylight." After a collective startle, the girls
brave the cold and their insecurities and take off their trench coats, revealing their swimsuit-clad figures.

First and foremost, the girls are human, and so their bodies have
all the normal, reasonable deficits: old white stretch marks, new purple stretch marks, cellulite, knock-knees, bowlegs, flat feet, duck feet,
legs like tree trunks, legs like twigs, crooked teeth, teeth smeared with
red lipstick, droopy bosoms, imposing shelflike bosoms, nonexistent
bosoms, downy chest and stomach hair, faint mustaches, hairy moles,
birthmarks, jutted jaws, cleft chins, freckles, dark circles, back fat, front
fat, unruly corkscrewed hair, flat limp hair, hair with split ends, too-
short hair, and lots of platinum hair with dark-black roots. And because they are human and teenagers to boot, and because it is too cold

to be standing around in a swimsuit, their shoulders hunch forward, their arms fold around chests and torsos, their heads drop.

I wish I could tell you that you aren't mentally cataloging all of the more unfortunate features or, at least, that you also register the plentiful number of exquisite ones: heart-shaped faces, perfectly set dark eyes, lovingly manicured nails, spotless complexions, huggable middles and caress-able curves, elegant noses, plump lips. I wish I could say that when you look at them, you see how they are all just as complicated as you. Instead, you come to this disappointing conclusion: The Gorgeous Girls are not terribly gorgeous.

At least you have the decency to keep this thought to yourself. The photographer is not nearly as delicate. "Oh no," he says, under his breath but just barely. He lets the camera drop to his side. "No, no, no. This is *not* going to work."

Vicky sidles up to you and the photographer, and you search her heavily made-up face, which is several shades darker than her rapidly goose-pimpling body, for signs that she has overheard him. If she has, she is keeping it to herself. "Are you going to arrange us, or should we just figure it out ourselves?"

"Hmmm," he says, brain spinning, eyes wide and frightened. "I'm not sure yet, Miss—"

"Darnell. Vicky."

"Vicky. I'm rethinking things. Now that I see all of you, you see. Hmmm. Is quantity the way to go? I wonder. I need to think. Here, let me start with Gwen." He grabs you by the arm and leads you roughly, hurriedly to the initial step, where he wants you to stand. "Don't worry," he says in a whisper. "There's no way I'm going to let all those dogs in the photograph."

While your own thoughts haven't been much kinder, this strikes you as unnecessarily cruel. "Those *girls* went to a lot of trouble to be here."

The man snorts. He lets the camera hang around his neck while he kneels to direct you into the stance he wants, and you comply, too shocked to do otherwise. "It's okay," he says. "I'll be the bad guy."

Before you can reply, he is on his way back toward the crowd, rubbing his hands together, apparently ready with his excuses. From your position, it is hard to hear just exactly what it is he tells the girl-huddle, but you make out *composition* and *essence* and *resolution* and *desirable,* and watch in horror while he handpicks five girls he finds suitable enough for the picture, whittling his imagined infinity down to a row of stunned bridesmaids.

The operative word here, Gwen, is *watch.* Despite your horror, you do nothing beyond standing, stony and silent, in your pose as the girls who didn't make the cut pick their trench coats out of the pile. Many of them—rattled and disappointed but still loyal—stay to watch the shoot; a dozen or so others pick up their purses and walk out. One of the selected girls shows her solidarity by exiting with this smaller group and loudly declaring the happenings *bullshit* and you a *goof.* Another spectator, wiping her eyes with the heel of her hand, rethinks her loyalty and joins them. While the photographer leads the four remaining girls up the stairs to position them, the deserters cross back over W street, where the whole group of them are stopped by a woman whose face you can't see but whose shape you recognize instantly.

How convenient that Mimi should be passing by at just this time! What could she have *possibly* been doing here? She stops to speak to them, and the girls respond with angry animated motions, pointing back toward the arena, toward you.

This must be hard for you to watch—the fury and bruised esteem of your fans, not to mention the smug, self-righteous look you can just imagine on Mimi's face. But when you shift your gaze back to the thirty or so girls who stay, your eyes fall on an even more painful sight: Vicky.

You know all too well the rejection she is feeling. You should have protested. That's what a real champion would do, anyway. She wouldn't have just posed.

One night later, just before the match, you stand at the back of the arena awaiting the announcer's call. This has now become so routine that it sometimes borders on dull, but tonight, you have all the old jitters: cotton mouth, butterflies, goose pimples, etc. For the first time since your very first match, Mimi will be in the opposite corner. You hoped to speak to her before now, take her temperature, but she was too preoccupied with some activity in her dressing room. From the sound of it, there were multiple people in there with her. You don't know what that is about, or what kind of retribution she might have planned for you, and the anticipation is brutal. Making matters worse is this business with the Gorgeous Girls. Before the match, you sweet-talked Sal into upgrading their free tickets so they'd be closer to ringside. This is small compensation, to be sure, but you hoped it would salve any still-smarting wounds and lessen some of your guilt. Now, you are panicking. What if they don't come? What if the botched photo shoot has turned them all against you? What if you have to look down at a series of empty rows—ringside, no less!—all the while pretending nothing is out of the ordinary, keeping a silly grin on your face? Because you certainly can't make your fears known to your audience.

Costantini plastered cards with your image in every storefront in every working-class neighborhood in the city. For those who might have missed these, there was also the picture of you in today's paper, looking confident and queenly. Now, this dank, drafty area is teeming with fanatics who answered the call and have come to cheer you on. It hardly matters that you dread tonight's stroll down the aisle more than any since you ceased to be a taunted and maligned heel. You have a job to do.

And so, once you are summoned—*Ladies and gentlemen, please welcome the sweetheart of the ring, Gwen Davies!*—you step into the aisle and get to work. You cut a slow and gracious path through the outreached arms, the giddy smiles, the cardboard signs (*Sweetheart, Be Mine!*), the tokens of affection (single roses in cellophane), the unintelligible jumble of adoration: *love, dropkick, legs, gorgeous, pin, hold, face, touch, bombshell, win, love, love, love.* You answer your fans by squeezing their hands, mouthing *thank you*s silently but with exaggerated slowness, pretending not to see the flicking tongues or the hands cupping imaginary breasts, accepting the acceptable tokens, and pressing your lips to the ends of your fingers and blowing kisses at worthy targets—the man who holds both of his children aloft so they can see you through the crowd, the couple whose sign says they drove fifty miles to be here. Best of all, when you reach the front row, you find twenty-odd Gorgeous Girls, Vicky included, elbowing one another, clasping hands, bouncing up and down, and making a satisfying amount of noise. What a relief; they are going to give you a second chance. Some of them are, at least. After you make your way into the ring, you point to the blond-haired, red-mouthed girls (*I see you!*) and quickly shed your robe, climb onto the turnbuckle closest to them, and stretch out your arms, welcoming them back into the fold with one large embrace: *Take me, I'm yours.*

The noise dies down and the announcer, holding a microphone suspended from the rafters by a long black cord, summons your opponent—*Screaming Mimi Hollander!*—to the ring. Mimi appears in the aisle and marches past the revelers and their taunts, her head aloft, jaw set, eyes blank. This, of course, is not out of the ordinary. Here's the unusual part: she isn't alone. Shortly after Mimi appears, a group of women fall into step behind her and follow her through the crowd. There are eight of them, all dark-haired and clad in black suits.

Now you know what Mimi was up to in her dressing room, don't you, Gwen? She was schooling these girls. Those shuffles and furtive whispers were all part of Mimi's crash course in the art of the heel. Now, she is parading her pupils out as a supporting cast of evil sidekicks. The effect, you have to admit, is awe-worthy. Perhaps their heads are not held quite as high and mighty as their leader's, but they are still convincingly wicked: their fists resting defiantly on their hips, their mouths drawn closed into steely, resistant puckers. And that's not all they've learned. When the spectators direct their surly energy toward them, those insults, the same ones that would so easily weaken your resolve, pump them up. Chests inflate. Dark energy rises.

Amateurs, perhaps, but better heels than you ever were.

It's only as they come toward the ring, toward you, that you begin to realize these aren't just random women. Your first clue: the one directly behind Mimi is wearing a wig, and the girl behind her has hair so asphalt-black it could only be artificial. But *why*? Wouldn't it have been easier to just recruit dark-haired girls? Take a look at the next girl, Gwen. Recognize her? Sure you do. It's the tall girl from the lobby, the strawberry-blonde who spotted you and whispered to her friend: *It's her!* And there's the friend behind her. You know her, too, don't you? She was also at the shoot. And when she made the cut and her friend didn't—when her friend bundled herself in her coat and hurried out of the park before she could leak a public tear—she did what you should have done: declared it bullshit and walked away. And now here they are tonight, in solidarity with Mimi, in defiance of you and all that you represent.

Mimi climbs through the ropes and takes the microphone from the "stunned" announcer while the troop forks off and marches around until they have the ring flanked. "Ladies and gentlemen," Mimi growls. "You think Gwen Davies is pretty goddamn gorgeous, don't you?" The crowd screams their answer, an undeniable affirmative. Mimi strolls closer to the Gorgeous Girls' VIP section and stares down. "I know you ladies think so. What is it you call yourselves again? The Gorgeous Girls, right?"

The girls take the bait and scream their unflinching fidelity. Vicky puts her fingers in her mouth and whistles.

"Well, ladies, you're right. Let's face it: Gwen is gorgeous. But there's a lot more to grappling than being gorgeous, and tonight, I am going to kick her gorgeous ass."

This uncorks the crowd. The jeers, hisses, and invectives that follow produce a din that shakes the walls. One could argue that this passion is born òut of love for you, but when you see the way Mimi works them, the way she gets the lot of them eating out of her hand, you see the problem with this argument. They don't hate her because they love you; they love you because they hate her.

Now you understand what Mimi tried to explain on that bus ride to Tennessee: the heel is the *show*.

"And just so you know, y'all aren't the only entourage in town. I brought my girls with me tonight. Allow me to introduce the Go-to-Hell Girls. Ladies, tell them what we think about all this gorgeous nonsense."

The girls hop up on the apron, two per side, and hang one-armed off the ropes. They are no prettier than they were earlier in the day. They have the same wide noses, the same thick thighs. The heckling is merciless. Nevertheless, they are radiant in their go-to-hell glory, each brazenly extending a finger to the crowd.

This might have been the end of it if it weren't for Vicky. Perhaps she handled yesterday's disaster with grace, but it appears this mutiny has pushed the limits of her tolerance. If she must go to hell, it seems she plans to take a few girls with her. She hops out of her chair, leaps to the ring, and yanks the wig off the first girl she can reach. The wigless girl jumps on top of her, and that's all it takes. Soon, girls from each side rush into the fray.

You can't exactly just stand and watch this happen, so you scramble out of the ring and into the melee. The girls are unskilled in the art of self-defense but filled to the brim with anger, so the battle hovers some-where between school-yard rumble and barroom brawl: chairs over-turned, fistfuls of hair grabbed, blouses snatched open, faces scratched with long, manicured nails. You wade through the bodies, try to gently coax the girls off one another, but they're not having it.

This is your first rodeo, but Mimi and the ref, who followed you out of the ring, are riot veterans. They are all too knowledgeable about what can happen if this doesn't get nipped quickly, so they cut through the girls with purpose and force, neither hesitating to employ submission tactics when necessary. The ref sticks to bear hugs, while Mimi hooks them around the back or under the arm. While they do this, you continue working your way to the middle, where the de-wigged girl lies on her back, covering her face with her hands as Vicky straddles her and uses both arms, one after the other, to slap the girl repeatedly. When you reach Vicky, you take her shoulders in your hands and say, "Hey, hey, hey. Stop it. Stop it," but the inertia of her fury is too over-powering: she wheels around and turns those windmilling arms against you. She strikes you once across the face, and that's enough. When she reaches out to hit you again, you grab her by the wrist. Vicky's face prunes into a silent cry, but you stay resolved and keep her in this hold, the same one you used against that predator in Oklahoma. In your wildest dreams, you couldn't have imagined using it on the president of your fan club.

"I'm going to let you go," you say to her, even-voiced and holding steady in your squat despite the jostling crowd above you. "And you're going to get off of her and stop this nonsense. Got me?"

Vicky's mascara-smeared eyes squint into hard, flat lines. She nods her agreement, so you release her. When Vicky steps off her victim, you extend your hand down to help the girl up. Instead of accepting it, she adjusts the strap of her bathing suit, which has slipped off in the bat-tle, and then gets herself up onto her feet. Large swatches of hair have escaped from her strawberry-blond bun. Her face pinks, and there's a small dot of blood under her eye at the end of what appears to be a scratch. She wipes her eyes with the back of her arm.

"Are you okay?" you ask.

The Go-to-Hell Girl swallows one last cry and nods, so you turn your attention to Vicky, who is massaging her wrist. "What about you, Vicky? Are you okay?"

She lifts her eyes to meet yours. "How could you do that?" Her voice is emotionless: not sad, or hurt, or angry.

How could you do that? It's a perplexing question. What is she really asking you, Gwen? Does she mean the wristlock? The photo shoot? Or is she referring to something else, something larger? You have no idea how to answer your biggest fan.

The three of you stand there for a minute while the riot peters out. Eventually, a pair of cops cut their way through the spectators, many of whom are still standing on their chairs, hooting and pounding their fists.

Later in the evening, you and Mimi share an otherwise unoccupied holding cell, waiting for Costantini to finish the paperwork that will get you both the hell out of there. For reasons that are murky at best, the cops decided that you and Mimi were guilty of instigating a riot and hauled the two of you—and no one else—off to the pen. At first, you were furious, and then, you have to admit, a little pleased—there was something exciting about the prospect of a little scandal and notoriety—but now, you are just tired and cold. You're still wearing your suit, and the bench you share with Mimi feels icy beneath your thighs.

"I don't see why I have to be here," you say, crossing your arms and rocking for warmth. "You're the one who marched in those girls."

Mimi squints her eyes and rubs her forehead with the heel of her hand. Is this weariness or exasperation? "Yeah, well, I only did it 'cause you were so lousy to them."

"Don't give me that," you say. Mimi has always been self-interested to the end, and the one good thing you could say about her was this: at least she didn't pretend otherwise. This is hardly the time for her to start acting as if her concerns were larger than herself. "It wasn't about those girls and you know it."

She hugs her knees and turns her face toward you. "Then maybe you should tell me what it was about."

You draw your knees up to your chest too and hold them. In your attempts to stay warm, both of you have contorted yourselves into the smallest shapes possible. "Oh, I don't know. Same thing it's always about—you sticking it to me."

"Me? What have I ever done to you?"

This baffles you. She really doesn't seem to know. If it weren't for all of the problems she'd caused you—the money, the pejorative *champ*—you might still be her partner. Before you can pick up your jaw to say as much, she continues: "You know, I really thought you were going to be different. You weren't too stubborn to learn, and you learned fast. You thought on your feet. You took a punch without crying. You've got a helluva dropkick. And you were hungry. I could tell. You really wanted it."

Listening to Mimi list your admirable traits might have softened you up if it weren't for the last couple. What does she mean you *were* hungry, you *wanted* it? No need to use the past tense; nothing's changed. "I still do."

"No, you don't. You want fans."

Well, yes. Of course you want fans. That's what this has always been about. The sensational suit, the outrageous persona: why else would you do these things if not for fans? "What's wrong with that?"

"You really don't get it, do you?"

No, you really don't. It seems clear to me now—almost painfully so. It is not just about the championship. Anyone can get a belt, and anyone does. It is about the skill. The knowledge. The history, and the fellowship. It is about the ability to walk into the blowing winds; it is life on your own terms. I wish you understood this, but you don't. Not yet, at least.

Mimi turns away, and the two of you sit on the bench, rubbing your limbs for warmth. Eventually, the guard unlocks the door and slides it open. Sal stands behind him, hands in his pockets, rocking on his heels.

"Ladies," he says, smiling to beat the band, "that was phenomenal! Any chance you can do that again on Wednesday?"

TWENTY-TWO

In the run-up to Wednesday's bout, the only other in his territory, Costantini floods the airways. *Last time these two went head-to-head, they both landed in jail,* says an ominous voice. *Trust me: you don't want to miss the mother of all grudge matches.* These are not the truest words ever said, but they are probably truer than Costantini knows. Before DC, you might have considered this series of matches with Mimi as being slightly more than theatrical. Now, everything is different. This next fight is as scripted as any, with you its predetermined winner, but the rivalry is real as rain.

The fight occurs in an outdoor ring set up on some fairgrounds somewhere in—where are you now? Maryland? Virginia? The stars are so densely clustered in this region of your map, they bleed into one another. Wherever it is, it seems nearly perfect at first glance. The evening sky is the special lavender of twilight. Picnic blankets have been spread; children chase one another. But it's much too chilly for an outdoor event. It is hard to muster the swagger of a sex symbol when it is all you can do to keep from snatching one of those blankets and throwing it around yourself. How on earth will you get your grip on the ropes with fingers this numb with cold? How secure are those ropes, anyway? You don't place much faith in this mat, which sways beneath you as if it's floating on water. It wouldn't surprise you if the whole shebang collapses at the worst possible moment.

The ref, looking crisp and slick in his white T-shirt, calls you both to the center of the mat to go over the rules. It's the usual no-brainers: no knees, no hair pulling, no choking, no leveraging the ropes. "What about hitting?" says Mimi, her glare fixed on you. "Does it have to be open fist?"

There is no need for her to ask this question; you both already know the answer is no. She clearly means to intimidate you, and she is succeeding. Sure, wrestling is more performance than athletics, but that doesn't mean she can't rough you up in the process. You return to your corner and lean into the ropes to loosen your quickly tightening muscles, your confidence as shaky as the goddamn ring. When the bell rings, your heart sinks into the toes of your Green Goddesses. Given your druthers, you'd rather climb out than take a step toward Mimi, but you don't have much choice: all you can do is turn around and attempt to hold your own.

Mimi doesn't waste any time. In short order, she is on top of you, taking you by the head and shoving your face into the mat. Thankfully, this flips the switch on some instinctive defense mechanism deep in your brain. *Sweep her leg.* Before you know it, she's on her back. You spin around, pulling her leg with you into a toehold, and arch your back in an attempt to pin her shoulders. Her arms flail about with more animation than she really needs to avoid the pin.

It's something to be grateful for, you suppose: at least she's still willing to put on a show.

Try the ropes, Gwen. Go on—the ref's not looking. Put your feet up there. Get some leverage. Of course, as soon as you do, Mimi gets you into body scissors and crab-walks you both into the center before rolling you all around the ring. You have to get out of this before she makes you too dizzy to operate, but her thighs are nutcrackers, locked on your rib cage and threatening to snap you in half.

The ref breaks it up, but the relief is only temporary. As soon as you get to your feet, Mimi socks you with a right hook, and then, while you are still staggering, a left that connects just right of your chin and forces you onto the mat, flat on your back, your face on fire. Has she knocked your jaw out of the socket again? No, you don't think so, but the pain still sears, and you roll onto your side, your knees tucked in, your hand cupped around the throbbing corner of your face.

Briefly, you glimpse, between the ropes, a threesome of Gorgeous Girls: eyes wide, fingers pressed to mouths. Terrific. Maybe you should just go ahead and die. You're in the right position, after all. While you're still curled up on the mat, Mimi executes a step-over leg lock, and part of you considers releasing the tension from your shoulders and letting them press into the mat. Sure, you're supposed to win this match eventually, but right now all you want is to end your humiliation.

Don't give in to this impulse, Gwen. Keep those shoulders up. Kick out of it. Fire one of those Green Goddesses right into her gut. Road-work has given you legs that are more than just photogenic, you know. Watch her fly backward and hit the mat. Sure, some of that is theatrics, but some of it is *you*. Mimi is undeniably fierce—your jaw will attest to this—but you, sister, are no slouch.

Mimi leaps at you, and you flip her over your shoulder. Listen to the roar of your contingent as the flat of her back claps against the mat. Watch her squirm. And just where are the Go-to-Hell Girls tonight? Back in their girdles and swing skirts, no doubt. Not that Mimi would have tolerated the foolishness of a visible fan base for long. When she staggers to her feet, it is just as she wants it: all on her own steam.

This is your chance to win. This whole rig is shaky at best, and the safety of those ropes is questionable, but you'll have to make it work. Atta girl. Up on that top rope. Lean forward and make it fast.

If Mimi was ever genuinely dazed, she recovers shortly after you leap, just seconds before you will rain down on her with the foe-vanquishing Bombshell. And while this shouldn't prevent her from allowing your blow to connect and deliver the defeat that is rightfully hers, this is not what happens. Instead, she backs out of the way, causing you to crash unceremoniously and somewhat painfully on the jerry-rigged mat, which feels like concrete.

While you try to wrap your head around what just happened, Mimi puts the sole of a boot against your wrist, bears down on it, and then squats to look you in the face.

"Sure got a lot of fans out there tonight," she says, her eyes locked on yours. "Let's show them what you're made of."

This shouldn't throw you. Holding your own against Mimi will be no minor feat—her skill set is solid gold—but you are more than just glitter. You can execute a number of legitimate holds; you can land a kick and a forearm blow that would knock a small horse off its hooves. You made Sam drop like a hot rock, didn't you? This last thought gives you the strength to kick her off and send her stumbling backward into the ropes, which allows you the time and confidence you need to get on your feet and meet her gaze.

Mimi uses the ropes as a catapult and comes at you with a running kick that sends you flying backward and then ricocheting back toward her before you can blink. Some part of you understands that you need to use this inertia against her, but you realize this too late to build on to it with your own gusto, and the move you attempt—an unimaginative clothesline is all that comes to you—is weak, obvious, and easily avoided by a forearm blow that wallops you in the chest like a length of pipe. While you stumble around, attempting to stay out of her reach while you catch your breath, she stands in the center of the ring, patient and collected, hands resting on her hips.

"That's it?" she says. "After all this time, that's the best you've got?"

You're burning now—with rage and shame. Focus, Gwen. Direct

these emotions into a rally. Let them fill you with the superhuman strength you need to topple the giant. Haven't people in desperate circumstances found the strength to lift cars and boulders?

Oh, if only that were how the world actually worked. Instead, panic ensues, which causes you to resort to catfighting. You pull her hair, take swipes with your fingernails, and claw at her suit, which stokes the audience—whistles and hoots abound—but only causes her to laugh. While your hands are tangled in her wiry hair, she takes hold of your wrists and presses her mouth to your ear.

"This ain't exactly the school yard," she says, her breath hot, "but if that's how you want to fight—"

Mimi squeezes your wrists, forcing you to release her. As soon as you do, she throws your arms down, rears back and slaps you hard across the mouth with her open palm, and then again with the back of her hand. Your jaw shivers with new pain.

The response from the audience is unanimous: their voices blend into the low moan of disapproval. Mimi is undeniably the superior athlete, but this wins her no converts. Exposing your truth, your core—perhaps you are not all style, but substance seems to be in short supply—does not sway this crowd. Their faith in your character is blind and unconditional.

While you are curled into a comma on the mat, your back turned to her, Mimi squats down beside you and takes your arm.

"That's enough," she says, her voice softer. She pulls your arm back into a hammerlock and eases you up to your feet. "Your turn. Go ahead and flip me."

Mimi's had her fun. She's asserted herself enough to feel satisfied and is ready to get back to the business at hand—helping you stage a face-saving victory. And you do as she says. She plays along nicely, releasing her grip on your arm as you reach back to grab her, spring-boarding off the mat and over your shoulder, smacking the mat with her hand as she lands.

You should accept this for what it is and go along; you should just get the pin and get the hell out of there as fast as you can. But you are smarting in more ways than one. The fact that even now, when it is your time to shine, she is the one calling the shots is more than your hot head can handle. And so, when she staggers up, you grab her by her wiry head of hair and thrust your knee into her sternum as forcefully as you can. Do you hear a crack? In your imagination, perhaps, but the sound is redeeming, as is the praise from the audience: a loud *Hot damn!* slices through the less articulate noises of the crowd. For a second, as Mimi falls back, landing gracelessly on her rump, you're feeling good, as if you might be able to pull this one off after all.

Mimi looks up at you, her breath quick, her hand spread across her chest. Her face shifts quickly from surprise to realization to determination. She says, narrowing her eyes, "You really don't know when to quit." Before you can answer, she's off the mat, and she comes up swinging—first with a right, which you dodge, and then another with the southpaw, which connects in just the same place it did earlier. How is it that she can always zero in on your weaknesses? Your jaw already feels larger than normal. You can just imagine what the next couple of days will be like—milkshakes for breakfast, lunch, and dinner, and plenty of ice packs.

While you are stumbling around wincing, hand cupped to your face, Mimi gets one hand on the back of your neck, another through your legs, and lifts you onto your side, your belly pressed against hers. She puts her hand around your throat and keeps a loose hold—not choking you, but showing that she could. Her hand there, against your jugular, makes you go cold. Finally, she drops down to her knee, draping you over top of it. Your body folds like a lawn chair. You tumble off and roll away.

You have two choices here. You could admit defeat and let her win. This is the logical choice. There is very little fight left in you, and she has answered every one of your assaults with a resounding thumping.

261

But you haven't relied on reason this entire match. Why start now? Why not throw your all into one more last-ditch Hail Mary maneuver? Sure, a sleeper hold is probably against the rules, and it will definitely be outside of Mimi's personal code of ethics, but it is the only physical advantage you have over her other than your appearance, and fat lot of good that has done you these last two nights. Better make it good, because this is it. This one will have to take her out.

It is your big gun, Gwen. Go for it.

It works like a charm, just like it did the last time. In short order, Mimi hits the mat with a thud. But the sight of her—eyes closed, face slack—hits you even harder. Panicked, you drop to the ground and grab her shoulders. You're not thinking about a pin any longer; you simply want to make sure she's okay. The ref misunderstands your motives and yanks you off. He checks her pulse with his ham-knuckled fingers and you swallow air, your throat dry. But this is not the worst of it. That would be the sight of the audience standing in their chairs, roaring at the sight of the vanquished villain.

Wolves, the lot of them.

Thankfully, the ref says, "Pulse is steady," and, as if responding to his voice, Mimi stirs beneath his touch. Now that the drama is over, the ref turns to you, staring daggers. He motions to the announcer and yells, "DQ!" If he was expecting a fight, he won't get it; there will be no argument from you. Not with this guy, not with Joe, who will call later tonight to order you both back to Otherside to straighten this mess out, and not with Mimi. Moments from now, when you turn to her in your shared dressing room and offer your sincere apologies, she will tell you that you have finally gone too far, and that she is done with you. She will say this in a voice so still and quiet that it cannot be misunderstood. There is nothing arbitrary about the line you have crossed. There will be no more rivalry. Even that bond has been severed.

· · ·

Later in the evening, when you return to your room at the motor lodge, you call Sam. There is no telling what he might say, but you are desperate to hear a voice other than the one inside your head. You let him talk first, and he is noticeably cool. His dad is looking into booking him in some of the Western states soon; do you want him to look into booking you, too?

"Of course," you say, incredulous.

"I thought I should check first," he answers. "You know. I don't want to *suffocate* you."

While you have not unraveled all the complicated feelings you have for Sam, there is a lot you want to say to him. You want to say *I'm sorry.* You want to say *I miss you.* You want to say *Sometimes I have to swallow my jealousy, so why can't you?* and *Sometimes I think you're the only person I have in this world* and *You're almost perfect, but I need you to be just a little bit better* and *Are these things you should work on or are they things I'm supposed to learn to live with or are we supposed to meet in the middle? I've never loved anyone else and I don't know how it works.* But after the bout with Mimi, you have neither the energy nor wherewithal to pick up any of those strands. Instead, you sink onto your bed and begin to cry. "I can't take this right now, Sam," you say. "I've had a terrible week."

"Why?" he asks, dropping the too-cool-for-school act and heading straight to five-alarm. "What happened?"

You tell him everything—the debacle with the photo shoot and the Go-to-Hell Girls, the lesson Mimi was so intent on delivering tonight, and your pathetic attempt at retaliation. To your relief and surprise, he doesn't dispense judgment. He simply listens, asks for your coordinates, and says he'll be there as soon as he can. Sometime in the wee hours of the morning, his car rumbles into the unpaved lot and parks in front of your window, where you have been sitting for the better part of four hours, waiting. When he starts toward your door, you open it.

"I didn't think you'd still be up," he says, pocketing his keys.

"I couldn't sleep."

"No, I guess not." He nods toward the room. "Let's go inside and talk about it."

He is working hard, Gwen. You can hear the forced control in his voice; you can see the way he's avoiding your eyes. No doubt there is part of him that is glad for what has happened. He is as critical of your character as Mimi, if not more so. You suspect he would like to hear that you have learned a lesson—that you will do things differently from now on—but he knows better than to ask as much. For this, you are grateful. You are only just beginning to understand that Mimi is right: that while you might enjoy some privileges, you are not powerful. Real power cannot be so easily reduced. Even if these ideas were fully formed, you would not be ready to say them out loud to anyone, and certainly not him. So after you usher him into the room and close the door, you swallow hard and whisper, "I don't want to talk."

Sam, surprised and sober-faced, sets down his suitcase. "You don't?"

"No." You begin unbuttoning the flannel top of your pajamas. Talking is the last thing you want to do right now. What you need now is to know that the world is not so different from the place you imagined it to be. That you can still make things happen, that you can get what you need. That the formula still works.

TWENTY-THREE

Two days later, in the blistering heat of the late Florida afternoon, Sam's Crestline finally turns off the highway and rolls down the long stretch of road that leads to the Pospisil School for Lady Grappling. Mimi occupies all of the backseat, a rolled shirt beneath her head, her face fully shrouded by a scarf. She was understandably reluctant to share a lift with you, but Joe's imperative loomed large and the price was right, so here she is. There has been little from her on this drive other than the shifting of her body weight or the occasional request for a pit stop, and you have not solicited anything more. Only now, as the car decelerates, do you dare to speak to her directly. It seems a risk worth taking, given what you have seen.

"Look, Mimi," you say. "Isn't that Johnny's car?"

Mimi sits up. Her eyes widen as she takes in the Hornet, which is parked in front of one of the cabins.

"I didn't know he would be here," says Sam.

"Me neither," says Mimi. "Which means he's gone and done something stupid."

Sam pulls his car alongside Johnny's, and Mimi scrambles out before it's even parked. She bangs on the door closest to where the car is parked. "Johnny, open this door!" She keeps up this racket for what feels like forever while you watch through the windshield, too stunned to act.

"What does she mean by 'something stupid'?" you ask Sam.

"I think we're about to find out," he says. He steps out and props himself against the hood of his car. It's not clear if he is preparing to intervene or just wants a better view, but you follow suit, unsure of what else to do.

After some time, Johnny comes to the door, rubbing an eye. Before he can say a word, Mimi shoves him to the ground. "What the hell do you think you're doing here?" she yells. You turn toward the sound of footsteps. It seems she's attracting a crowd now; wrestlers and vacationing fishermen alike take tentative steps toward the commotion, craning their necks. A fruit fly leans against her doorjamb, a hand covering her mouth, and The Angel of Death jogs over from the gym, sweat sparkling on her bald head. Sam, on the other hand, isn't moving a muscle. This is still Mimi and Johnny's fight.

"I warned you," Mimi says, spitting out the words.

Johnny, still sprawled on the ground, makes no effort to protect himself as she raises a knee, poising herself to stomp him in the stomach, but then a noise comes from the back of the room—the hesitant cries of a just-waking infant—and she stops cold. It seems this is the sign Sam was waiting for. When he moves in, you do the same. Sure enough, there's Junior, prone on the comforter, pushing himself up by his fat little baby arms, his oversize head full of mashed curls. Johnny clambers off the ground and scoops up the child. After whispering a few comforts to his son, Johnny walks the two of them over to Mimi and says something quietly to her, but then looks up and takes in the two of you just behind her, and then the crowd beyond.

"I didn't leave her," he says, bouncing Junior on his hip, his voice booming so that all of you can hear. Everyone is already in on their soap opera, he seems to have decided. He may as well straighten out the facts. "She left us."

"Show's over, folks," calls Joe from the back of the crowd. "Go on. Back to your business, everybody." He makes his way around a pair of fishermen, waves the fruit fly back into her room, and shoots a steely glare at The Angel of Death, who returns a humble smile before heading back to the gym. These small gestures carry the weight of authority with even the tourists; in ones and twos, all the bit players recede from the scene.

Joe points a finger at Johnny. "So now she's here. You have tonight to figure this mess out. I want to hear your plan first thing in the morning. I'm talking first thing. Crack of dawn. And then I want to talk to you"—he turns his finger on Mimi, and then on you—"and you. Meet me on the dock at nine o'clock. Do not, I repeat, do not keep me waiting. Is that clear?"

You and Sam exchange glances. You had made a tentative plan to accompany him to his next few bouts, with the understanding that the plan would have to be abandoned if Joe had already rebooked you. From the look on Sam's face, he is ready to admit that it's a lost cause, and that you will just have to hold out hope that you can join Sam for some of his Western tour. Better to mind your p's and q's now than to risk that.

"Clear," you say, the sentiment echoing all around.

Later that evening, Sam stands against your bedroom wall, a glass pressed between it and his ear. As luck would have it, most of the cabins were full, and Betsy had no choice but to put you up in the room next to Johnny's, handing over the key with an apologetic smile. There is little more than cheap wooden paneling separating your room and his, which means the many rounds that he and Mimi have gone this evening have spilled over into your space. You and Sam have tried to give them their privacy, first with a long meal and then a stroll among the buildings. Now the mosquitoes have chased you inside, where the fight is impossible to ignore. Sam has dropped this pretense and put a glass up to the wall.

"I wish you wouldn't do that."

"Come on. Don't tell me you're not curious."

"Of course I am, but it's not my business."

"No? Okay, then I won't tell you anything."

But what could he possibly tell you that you can't hear for yourself? He hardly needs that glass; you can make out most of the details from where you are sitting, and with very little effort.

"It just makes more sense for Junior to stay here, with you. He's too little to be on the road, and besides, you're done with this tour. You said so yourself."

"I said I'm done fighting Gwen. I didn't say I was done fighting."

"It's just for a month."

"Just a month? Are you listening to yourself?"

"What if you just kept the gigs where you don't have to stay overnight? You can ask one of those new girls to watch him on match nights. Hell, they'd probably think you were doing them a favor."

"I don't understand why you can't take him back to your mother's."

"And I don't understand why I have to keep telling you that it ain't gonna happen. She's not exactly my biggest fan right now."

"And I am? You're not exactly asking for peanuts here, mister."

"Please, Mimi. I can't afford to cancel this tour. I really need you now."

"What kind of idiot do you take me for, Johnny? You think I don't know what you're doing? You think I don't know how this plays out? First it's a couple of bookings, then one tour, then another, until taking care of Junior is my whole damn life. Until I'm just like Lacey. And then what? Then you get bored of me, too."

"Is that it? Is that my big plan? I ruined Lacey's life, and now I'm going to ruin yours? Jesus, Mimi. How can you think so little of me? I know I messed up. I messed up. I get it. But I love you. I messed up because I love you."

For a long while, nothing comes from the other side of the wall. It isn't hard to picture the scene over there: Johnny standing over the bed, Mimi lying across it, the baby asleep beside her, the whole room damp with tears and sweat and hazy with cigarette smoke. You feel a need to fill the vacuum created by their silence, and so you tiptoe over to Sam, press your ear not to the wall but to his shoulder, and lace your fingers through his. He puts the glass down and looks over at you, gathering his thoughts.

"I can't believe Lacey left," he whispers. "I knew she knew. But I didn't think . . ."

His voice trails off. Instead of finishing his sentence, he squeezes your hand, leans his head against the wall, and sighs.

"One month," says Mimi from the other side of the wall, her voice muted but crystal clear. *"I'll keep him this tour. But after that, it's over. And I don't just mean Junior. I'm talking about us."*

"Mimi—"

"I'm serious, Johnny." Mimi sounds as calm and resolved as you've ever heard her.

"I don't get it. Why now?"

"I told you what this was. I never signed on for anything more. I'll help out now because you're in a spot, and I helped get you there, but I don't owe you anything more than that." A door opens. *"I suggest you start figuring out what you're going to do when this tour is over,"* she says, and then the door closes.

You and Sam walk silently over to the bed's edge and sit side by side, staring at the paneled wall as if it's a screen that has only momentarily gone blank, that might roar back to life any second so that the story can play out to some more satisfying resolution. You are desperate to hear some truth that is greater than the ones you have learned tonight—life is messy, love is fragile, and in the end, everything is bound to get messed up. But there are only the sounds of footsteps muted by carpet, of water running in the sink, of drawers opening and closing. When the room finally goes quiet, Sam pats you on the thigh.

"That will never be us, will it?"

"You mean Johnny and Lacey or Johnny and Mimi?"

"Either. Both."

"No," you say, but you are not so sure. You have proven yourself capable of outrageousness time and again. More importantly, you have something in common with the two women at the heart of this calamity. You understand that personal and professional ambitions don't always align. These have already caused a number of rifts in your short relationship with Sam, the last one mended just days ago. You don't know what lies ahead. The only givens are that tomorrow, you will endure another lecture from Joe and say good-bye to Sam yet again. There is no telling how long this next absence will last, when you might fight again, or how either of these things might affect the other.

The next morning, you cross through the empty parking lot—Sam and Johnny are both well down the road, headed toward their respective matches—and arrive at the dock at the preordained time. Mimi is already there, her legs dangling over the end, one arm propping up her body, the other securing Junior to her lap. She acknowledges your arrival with a quick nod before returning her attention to the water.

Waves slap against the dock, delicately at first and then with increasing momentum. You hear the motor before you see the boat, which curves around the bend in the river, slows down, and idles up to the dock. Joe, dressed in a flannel shirt and looking older than ever—when did he get all those liver spots?—lifts his hat and silently lassoes the rocking boat to the pylon.

"Morning, Gwen," he says. "Mimi. How's motherhood treating you?"

Mimi blows a few fallen strands of hair out of her face more forcefully than necessary. "Sit on it, Joe."

Joe chuckles. Perhaps he is taking some pleasure in Mimi receiving what probably seems like just deserts.

"Let's put this mess aside for now and talk business." He hoists himself out of the boat, groaning with old-man effort, and situates himself between you. "It seems you two have decided that you can't be in a ring together. I am inclined to agree. Recent evidence does suggest that it is almost always a catastrophe. So I have split the remaining matches between you and booked new opponents. Gwen, you'll get the Carolina bouts that are coming up, and Mimi, you'll take a little break and then cover the Georgia ones. I am, however, going to ask the two of you to keep one match I just booked."

"Go on," says Mimi.

"It's all set for next month, in Memphis. Winner heads to a title bout."

You turn to Joe. "What title?"

"*The* title." Joe holds a hand over his eyes, shielding them from the still-rising sun. "I told you. All things come to those who wait."

Mimi nods. You can tell she is trying not to look as excited as she feels, if only because you are doing the same. The Women's World Championship: it hardly seems possible. It was less than a year ago when you opened Joe's letter with its implicit promise—*with hard work and a little luck*—and that glossy of Mildred Burke and the belt, which you promptly tacked up behind your bedroom door. It isn't hard to go from that image to one of you in the same pose, wearing the same belt. You need that belt. That belt would validate just about everything.

"You want to tell us how you finagled that one?" asks Mimi.

It is not like Joe to explain his backroom dealings to the talent, but this is not your average backroom deal. It seems this one was negotiated by the reigning champion herself. Mildred was the one who stopped by on her way back to Atlanta one morning; Mildred was the one who made the pitch. Joe could book one of his girls against her (for a match Mildred was slated to win), and—for a price, of course—she'd job the match but act like her opponent shot it. Yes, Joe would have to take some heat from the NWA for insubordination. There would probably be sanctions—difficulty booking his new champion, perhaps—but Mildred convinced him that the fury would die down quickly, that it was worth the risk. Everyone would be relieved to have this whole championship matter resolved, she said, and ultimately, all they would care about was selling tickets. Joe had certainly proved that his girls could do that.

"I don't get it," you say. "Why now?"

"Why?" says Joe. "Better me than Billy, that's why."

It seems Burke had finally agreed to wrestle Wolfe's champion, June Byers, sometime during the summer. Mildred wasn't born yesterday. She knows June will shoot the match and probably win. So, according to Joe, she's decided to take what she can: a fraction of her deposit on the belt, and the satisfaction of sticking it to her ex-husband. Joe makes it clear that he didn't exactly leap at the prospect of doing business in just this manner, but after he and Leo chewed on it for a night, he decided the opportunity was too good to pass up. Yesterday, he made the calls: one to Mildred to confirm, and the other to the Memphis promoter to schedule two matches.

Mimi grows quiet. "Does that mean—"

"Yes." Joe does not hesitate to make eye contact with her when he says this. One thing you can say about Joe: he's no chickenshit. "I went back and forth. I was not particularly keen on the idea of rewarding either of you after these latest high jinks, so I decided that I'm not going to decide. I'm going to let you two fight it out."

Even this is not enough to bring you back to earth. Sure, your odds aren't good—you know full well there is little hope of besting Mimi in the ring—but the possibility of victory, however slight, is sweet. Besides, even if you don't win, the fact that you are being given this opportunity speaks well of your popularity and your manager's opinion of you. A fight of this magnitude will only get you more attention, bigger purses, etc. Even if you lose, you win.

"Unbelievable." Mimi tilts her head backward, stares up at the sky. "You're going to give her a shot at the title? After everything she's done?"

"I made one mistake," you say.

"One mistake? You make nothing but mistakes. You *are* a mistake."

"Is that right?" You are willing to grant Mimi some outrage, but you have your limits. "What about all the people who pay money to see me? Are they mistakes, too?"

Mimi's eyes narrow. "I sell as many tickets as you. And I've got seniority."

"Yes. But you've also got a scandal sitting in your lap," says Joe.

"Quit sermonizing and start being practical," Mimi spits back. Junior startles at the force of her words and begins to cry. "Don't you think people are going to figure out what happened?" she says more softly, bouncing Junior on her knees. "They'll say, hey, if Joe doesn't have to play by the rules, why should we? They'll shoot every match. Now which one of us do you think has a better shot of hanging on to this thing?"

"Please," you say. "Look at you. How are you going to go on the road and defend a title?"

"This baby is not my responsibility."

Junior's cries grow louder. Mimi clucks in his ear to soothe him, which undermines her argument. "You sure about that?" asks Joe, his voice suddenly quiet, but it hardly seems necessary.

"You're making me jump through hoops for no good reason," says Mimi, equally quiet. "You know I'll beat her."

"You think?" you ask through your teeth. The salt is new, but the wound is old. "Then what are you so worried about?"

Joe sighs. "Ladies, there is no point to this. I've made my offer. Take it or leave it."

"I'll take it," says Mimi, "but I still say it's lousy."

Joe hoists himself up and stands over you, Mimi, and Junior, hands in pockets. "Don't act like I'm doing this to you," he says to her. "You want the belt? Well, then, go get it."

"I'm sorry to interrupt," says a voice from behind. It is Betsy, her pumps dangling from her fingers. She must have slipped them off so the heels wouldn't slip through the cracks in the planks, which explains how she could walk down the dock without alerting anyone to her presence. She couldn't look any more out of place here, in her high-necked blouse and nylons, a pair of reading glasses hanging from her neck. With her free hand, she tucks a windblown tuft of hair behind her ear. "I have some sad news and I didn't think it should wait."

Betsy hardly needs to say more. There is only one kind of news that follows a statement like that, and the look she gives you—urgent, intent—is clearly meant to communicate something about the secret that you share. You can easily guess the rest. The next words she will say are unnecessary; she has already delivered the message.

"David Henderson is dead."

TWENTY-FOUR

On the day of the viewing, The Angel of Death drives you and Mimi out to the Henderson homestead. Joe, not wanting his friend to suffer the indignity of a skimpy wake, made it crystal clear that any girls who were in town should be there or suffer his wrath. You and Mimi are full up on that at the moment, so you've put your animosity aside so that you can both take advantage of this one transportation option. That does not mean she has any intention of making small talk. On the drive over, she sits in the backseat with Junior on her lap, looking grim in a high-necked black dress, her hair subdued into a neat bun, refusing to breathe one word. So be it. If that's how she wants it, that's how it will be. At least, that is how it is until the car is parked, when you have to watch her struggle out of it, wrestling with both the baby and an enormous bag of his belongings. It wasn't so long ago that Harold and his accessories—how is it that people so small need so much stuff?—was giving you similar fits. When the bag slips off her arm and falls onto the ground in a heap, you reach for the straps.

"Here," you say. "Let me get that."

Mimi motions for you to hand it over. "I got it."

"No, you don't." You hoist the bag onto your shoulder and motion toward the house. "After you."

For half a minute, Mimi stands there with her hand outstretched, unwilling to let even this stand, but then Junior hurls his bottle to the ground. It rolls toward your feet. You pick it up, wipe off the nipple, and shove it into the bag.

"Fine," she says. She slams the car door closed with her hip and heads up the road.

When Joe spots your party entering the house, he hurries over, thanks you all for coming, and tickles Junior under the chin. "There's coffee and cake in the kitchen," he says. Mabel goes straight for it, but Mimi says, "I think I'll just pay my respects first." She hikes Junior up on her hip and heads to the living room, where the coffin is displayed.

This eagerness on her part strikes you as peculiar, and while you'd rather have a private moment of your own to say good-bye, you tag along, feeling tethered by the bag but also a little curious.

"Did you know him well?" you ask.

"Not really," says Mimi. "I'd seen him wrestle a few times when I was a kid, so I knew who he was before Joe introduced us."

"So he's the reason you're Screaming Mimi Hollander?"

"I've always been Mimi Hollander. He just added the Screaming part. Pretty lazy if you ask me."

Henderson's coffin, along with dozens of wreaths and floral arrangements representing nearly every wrestling promotion, has been set up along the blank wall he used as a backdrop for most of his photo shoots. The thing is practically a submarine. When you get to it, you expect Mimi to say a quick good-bye, but instead she lingers, scanning the crowd. When she finally trains her eyes on something, you follow them to the corner, where Joe stands talking to three familiar-looking men in suits. Southern promoters, you think, but you couldn't identify them any more specifically—not by name or region. At this point, the whole country is a blur. The foursome seems deep in conversation; about what, you can only imagine. When Joe finally looks over from the corner, Mimi says, "Okay, good, he sees me," and then finally leans over and looks down at Henderson.

"Rest in peace, you old pervert," she whispers before heading off.

Now it's your turn. This is the first time you have ever been to a viewing. If such an event was part of your mother's burial, the adults involved had the good sense to keep you away from it. Even now, it strikes you as a strange ceremony. What is left of Monster Henderson seems far removed from what you remember of the man. It is hard to connect this body to any real sense of loss. Seeing it here, like this, a new prop against an old backdrop, only connects him to your real fear.

Just for my personal collection, he said. *No one sees them except for me.* It never occurred to you to wonder what would happen if the man up and died.

The only person who might answer that question is Betsy, who walks toward the sofa, two plates of cake in hand. This is not the time to talk, of course. In addition to all the other people now roped around the room, Mimi and Junior have taken up residency in the nearby wingback chair from where Henderson once described to you the conditions of his deal. Still, it seems a good idea to stay close, so that you might take advantage of any opportunity that opens up, so you drag a dining-room chair into the circle. Betsy takes her seat on the sofa next to a man wearing dark, oversize sunglasses and greets you with a toothy smile.

"Hello, Gwen. Mimi. Nice of you to come."

She gently rests one of the plates on top of the man's hand, and, after some initial fumbling, he takes it from her. This is the first time you've seen Betsy's husband, if that is in fact who he is. Was he a wrestler once upon a time? You figure so from his physique. He is neckless, shiny-bald, and barrel-chested with softened pectorals that show through the jersey knit of his shirt. When you settle into your chair, his head turns toward you.

"I see we have company," he says, although it's clear he can't see you or anything else for that matter. His gaze is too low, too far to the right. Trachoma, perhaps? You've been warned about unsanitary conditions and instructed to avoid others' towels, to keep your face off the mat as much as possible, but can't say the message ever really hit home until now.

Betsy hurries to finish her bite. "Mimi, Gwen, this is my husband, Hank—"

Mimi snaps her fingers. "Hank Mahoney! I knew you looked familiar. I saw you wrestle here at the armory. I couldn't have been this high"—she holds out her hand to indicate the height of a second grader, but, apparently realizing the gesture is meaningless, retracts her arm, blushing her apology—"I mean, I was just a kid."

"You must have been. That was a lifetime ago," says Hank, patting his wife on the knee. "Betsy's the real champion, putting up with me all these years."

Betsy squeezes his hand in response. "Hank and Monster go way back."

"Way back," says Hank, and then launches into the history of their relationship, beginning with a match in Tampa that left them both with broken arms—"We drove to the ER together, and then to the bar! You should have seen the looks we got!"—and ending with the other morning, when Hank and Betsy arrived at Monster's house for breakfast only to find the paper still on the porch and the coffee unmade. These are the stories this man needs to tell because of the real loss he feels. You feel like a trespasser here, crashing the gates of others' grief. It is a rare thing you and Mimi have in common—she nods along, but her eyes are glazed.

Junior starts sucking noisily on his fist. "He's getting tired," says Mimi.

Can this be right? It hardly seems possible that she has learned to read this baby in just a few short days. True, you had less than twenty-four hours with Harold, but every attempt to meet his needs was a disaster. You are hard-pressed to believe anyone could master this game in less than a week, least of all Mimi. And yet here she is, humming into his ear and stroking his back to good effect.

"Would you like to put him down?" asks Betsy. She slides her plate onto the coffee table and motions to the spare bedroom. "He's welcome to the guest bed."

"That's okay." Mimi brushes a sweaty tuft of hair off his forehead. "I doubt we'll be here much longer."

"Are you sure? He's such a big boy. He must be heavy."

"Well," says Mimi, easing herself out of the chair, "yes, now that you mention it."

Betsy rises to help, but you are eager for the chance to slip away. "I can help her."

You follow Mimi to the guest room, where she eases Junior onto the bed. She pulls his shorts up over his diaper, his shirt down over his back.

"The first time, I just thought we were going floundering," she says, still staring at Junior. "I never meant to let it get this far."

It takes a minute for you to understand that the *we* is her and Johnny, and that she is offering some kind of explanation. What is not clear is if she is talking to you, Junior, or someone or something else—herself, the universe. If there is a right way to respond, you don't know what it is. You have no resources for this and no idea what she might need from you, if anything. All you can do is wait until she offers a clue, or else releases you.

Mimi looks around the room; on the bedside table, she eyes something that makes her do a double take. She taps on the spine of this title: *Sexual Behavior in the Human Female*.

"Check this out," she says. "Regular scientist, this guy."

"I guess." You mean this to sound nonchalant, but you can hear the quiver in your voice.

"He had plenty of experiments going, from what I hear. You know, when I first came here, to the school, there was this other wrestler. Red hair, that's all I remember. Anyway, she had just bought herself this new robe. It was super fancy—fur trim, big gold fringy things on the shoulders, you name it. Didn't make any sense to me. The rest of us were dirt-poor. So I asked her, how come you have money for something like that? You know what she told me? That she made a wad of cash by letting ol' Monster here take some nudie pictures. How do you like that?"

"That is shocking." It is a struggle just to get the words out; your mouth has stopped producing saliva.

Thankfully, the baby stirs, which gives you a precious excuse to leave the room. While Mimi rifles around in the diaper bag for something that will calm him, you slip out and collect yourself on the other side of the door. Your pictures may well be somewhere in this house, waiting to be discovered. Betsy is still on the couch, where you left her. You will just have to hope that the preoccupations of the people milling around nearby will offer you enough privacy so she might settle your mind.

"Hello again, Gwen," says Betsy. At the mention of your name, Hank perks up.

"So," he says, placing his untouched cake onto the coffee table before relaxing back into the sofa. "You're the famous Gwen."

He is not making reference to your wrestling career; of that much, you can be sure. No, he knows. He definitely knows. It shouldn't mean much—not to you, at least. It would be hard to imagine a safer person to keep this knowledge than Hank Mahoney, the blind husband of the woman with whom you shared your scenes. But knowing that somebody who wasn't there is aware of the pictures makes you even more anxious to pin down their whereabouts.

"I don't suppose—"

"I'll take care of it tonight, dear," she says. "There's nothing to worry about."

Her response is unusually abrupt; clearly she does not want to talk about this. Not here, not now. Still, you need to be sure you understand correctly. "You're going to destroy them?"

"Yes," she says. "We'll have a fire tonight. How does that sound?"

"Where are they now?"

Betsy nods down the hall, toward the room from which you just emerged. "In there. Under the bed."

Under the bed, just inches away from Mimi. All it would take is a little curiosity on her part, and she could ruin you.

"Of course," says Betsy, "you're welcome to them, if you'd rather."

No, you wouldn't rather. A fireplace roast sounds just about right. But now that Mimi's been in the room, you need more reassurance than Betsy can offer. Your safest bet is to destroy them yourself.

Before long, Betsy is summoned to some hostess duty or another. When, finally, Mimi slips out of the room and wanders into the kitchen for a cup of coffee, you have the opening you need. You close the door as quietly as you can, but of course the baby makes a noise. There is no room for failure with this one—you have got to soothe him, and fast. You try rubbing circles on his back, just like Mimi did earlier. This does the trick. He settles into a comfortable position, his knees bent so that his rump sticks up in the air, and falls soundly asleep.

You feel around behind the dust ruffle and find the box there, just as Betsy said it would be, shoved well past the margin of the bed. You slide it out and find it full of manila envelopes, all of which are carefully sealed with an abundance of tape and ordered alphabetically by surnames. After a quick glance over your shoulder to confirm that the door is in fact closed, you begin finger-walking through them, moving from front to back: Blackburn, Channing, Doolittle. No Davies. You feel a quick chill of panic, which is quickly eased by the realization that these might not be ring names but actual family names. Perhaps all is not lost after all.

Now here's one you recognize: Hubbard. Mabel Hubbard? *Really*?

You can't imagine the Angel of Death agreeing to such a thing, or Henderson asking. Apparently the man's tastes ran long and wide. But then, there it is, in the back, peeking up over the rest—Putzkammer. Holding the envelope in your hands makes you feel panicked, but also curious. You have half a mind to slide the photos out right now, take your first peek, but that would be careless. It is enough that you will be able to leave with them. You fold the envelope once, and then again, before shoving it into your clutch, giddy with relief. You hadn't realized how much weight those pictures had added to your worries until just now, when it lifts.

On the drive back to the grounds, no one says a word except for Mabel—now there's someone you will never see the same way again—who yammers on about her upcoming gigs. Many of the dates and venues she mentions are ones that would have been yours and Mimi's, but she seems none the wiser. That or she doesn't care. Either way, it serves as a reminder of the things that have passed between you and Mimi. This time, when Mimi climbs out of the parked car, the diaper bag is strapped sideways onto her body so that it can't possibly slip off. She needs no more help from you, or anything, for that matter. When you say good night, she acknowledges you with a glance, and then heads for her room.

That's all well enough and good. You have your own business to attend to.

Your first instinct is to set a match to the envelope without even looking inside, but then something gets the better of you. At the very least, you should confirm that you have gotten what you set after. In the privacy of your room, you flip on the light, slip a finger in the opening beneath the flap, and tug. Sure enough, there you are—Betsy Mahoney and the famous Gwen. I can only imagine what other people would think if they saw these pictures. I don't believe anyone in your life or mine—not Joe or Sam, not Sis or the Turnip, and most certainly not Franz—is capable of understanding what was happening in that moment, how important it was to you and Betsy to be seen in this way, by this man, whose appreciation for your sexuality did not diminish his esteem or your dignity. For you, it was a beginning; for her, a woman whose husband can no longer look at her in this way, it was something lost restored.

Here is the thing that triggers a short but Technicolor flood of memories—shaking Henderson's shockingly large hand at your first meeting; spending the evening in the backseat of the Hornet, getting lost in *The Price of Salt*; drinking tea in his home, which he served with remarkable refinement and gentility; discovering something in his gaze that made the whole world shift. One of the more vivid of these is when, toward the end of your photo shoot, Monster asked you what you thought of *The Price of Salt*. The truth was you hadn't finished it. You'd abandoned it shortly after Sam made you lose all concentration. But instead of saying this, you heeded Betsy's advice to maintain Monster's fantasy and said, *I liked it.*

Me, too, he said. *Especially the ending. The world needs more happy endings.*

These words stay with you as you walk out past the cabins to the wooded area, dig a shallow pit with your hands, and drop the flaming envelope inside. Tomorrow, you will resume what is left of your tour. Beyond that is a possible meet-up with Sam on the West Coast and a definite head-to-head with Mimi for a shot at the most coveted trophy in women's wrestling. It seems that you are headed toward your happy ending, thanks in some small part to David Henderson, who not only took these pictures but was considerate enough to see they were returned to your hands. Grief catches in your throat and stays lodged there as the photos turn to ash. For the rest of your life, you will feel grateful for this moment of sadness, this sense of loss. Without it, the loss of this man might have seemed little more than an event that led to other events. No death should be reduced to so little.

TWENTY-FIVE

Three weeks later, you walk across the water-guzzling green lawn of the El Rancho Vegas, past the lake-size pool, and on to the Opera House, where you are wrestling in a series of special girls-only matches against a masked opponent billed as Fury Hysteria. A few days ago, after you met all your obligations in the Carolinas, you boarded a plane for the first time in your life and made your way here. Recently El Rancho's owner, Beldon Katleman, spent a mint trading out the resort's western decor, which mostly attracted local yokels and residency-establishing divorce seekers, for snazzier stuff in order to compete with the Flamingo and the Desert Inn. Now, he needs an act salacious enough to lure patrons southward down the Strip. He dreamed up this experiment after catching your performance on *I've Got a Secret*. When he called Joe to make the arrangements, he requested you by name.

Well, sort of.

"I think they called her The Sweetness or something," he'd said. "You know who I mean. The blonde. The one with the legs and the jugs."

And that's the limit of his interest in you. It's why most bookers hire you, of course, but the fact that you have been hired for a very specific purpose has never been this explicit, this, er, naked. There is hardly even the pretense of sport in the advertisements, the costumes, or the recommended choreography. And while one might say there is more honesty in this transaction than most, you sorely miss the little lies that make all of this seem better than it is. Without them, it is much harder to hold on to the strings you've been grasping since DC, the ones that allow you to justify your persona to the Gorgeous Girls, to Sam, to yourself.

It is a sleazy gig, but you can hardly blame Joe. He would have been happy to take a pass, especially now that Memphis is a go. But you were eager to catch up with Sam, who was already booked for the week in California, and the money Katleman offered justified the cost of a cross-country plane ticket. Now, it is almost over; this is your last night here as a hired hand. And not just that—Sam will arrive tonight. He's supposed to get in sometime after his last match (too late, thankfully, to catch your performance; you can just imagine what he might say). After that, it's one more night here in Vegas to rest and regroup, and then you're back on the road together, wrestling your way across the country to the big night. You are desperately ready to see him, and yet not ready at all. In all your phone conversations, you have yet to make clear what is at stake in Memphis. You half expected one Pospisil or another to clue him in, do your dirty work for you, but so far, nothing doing. It seems you are just going to have to tell him yourself.

It is not going to be an easy conversation; that much you know. There's been little talk of long-term plans, but Sam is clearly on a mission to get you both off the road. He will not see any advantage to more attention or bigger purses. There is no way to break the news that he won't take as hostile, and no way to avoid having a fight or, worse, having to make a terrible choice.

The stage manager knocks on your door. It is time to leave your concerns behind you, to be revisited after the match—and this whole sleazy gig—are over. When that time comes, you can rehearse ways to share the big news.

You and your opponent, whose room is across from yours, exit at the same time. Fury is short, thin but loose-skinned, as if she's recently lost a great deal of weight, and probably a decade older than you. Her stomach is scored by a long, faint brown line. Her suit is surprisingly smaller than yours, the halter top low-plunging, the briefs cut below the navel. The suit is black, like her boots and her mask, which covers half her face and the top of her head.

"Ready for one more night of slap-ass?" she says.

"Am I ever." You search the exposed part of her face for some sign of familiarity. You are quite certain you might recognize her if you saw her without her mask, but you haven't been able to catch her coming or going, as you've been keen to do ever since the first match. At that initial meeting, while the two of you waited offstage to make your entrance, you asked, *Where have I seen you before?* Not anywhere she could think of; she knew of you but seemed sure that you hadn't met. Still, you gave her a brief summary of your career, so if there was a point of crossing, she might find it, but she didn't—it seemed she was just returning to wrestling after retiring prematurely and before your time. Still, you couldn't help but be curious.

The stage manager puts his arms around you both and says, "Ladies, let's try to give 'em something special tonight, shall we?"

"Maybe you should explain what you mean by 'special,'" says Fury.

"Oh, I don't know. Perhaps something a little more—playful. Fewer holds, a little more rolling around. You know. More like—"

"A pillow fight," she volunteers, stony faced.

"If you like," he says, his smile broad.

"If that's what you want," you say, "then you don't need professional wrestlers."

"Maybe not. I'll keep that in mind for next time. But if you could just indulge me for one more night, that would be terrific." He claps you both on the shoulder. "Thanks, ladies. Break a leg."

When he is gone, you turn to Fury. "Can you believe this guy?"

She sighs. "I can't afford to upset anyone. I just signed on to do two more weeks of these. I need the room for that long and I can't pay for it without this job."

Fury follows the stage manager down the hallway and takes her mark. You have half a mind to go right back inside your dressing room. The silliness of this week has made all of the most defensible claims for your profession difficult to remember. But there is something about her sigh that makes you swallow hard and follow her down the hallway.

Fury Hysteria is called to the stage before you, and she enters the ring with a wry smile and a convincing, hip-slinging strut, all traces of defeat left backstage. Once she's through the ropes, she begins juicing the crowd with some calisthenics that make the roundest parts of her body shake and jiggle. Seeing that smile, you feel better about tonight, about her. Like you, she knows the score. Perhaps this is the only attitude to have, you think. The way to keep these acts from being degrading is to insist that they aren't and act accordingly.

Like many of your matches, this one begins in ref's hold, but one that is decidedly more intimate: instead of firmly holding each other's shoulders, your hands are at the back of each other's necks, your faces close together. A kiss, it suggests, is imminent. But there can be nothing so straightforward, of course.

Instead, Fury reaches back and slaps you good. She makes contact, and there's a bit of a sting to it, but, as you fall back and against the ropes, you make a face designed to assure your audience that this is largely for dramatic effect, just part of the spectacle.

Before long, the two of you are in the requested position: horizontal on the mat, arms embraced, legs entwined, your bodies barrel rolling over one another, all of which has very little to do with any actual wrestling maneuver. (Just try to imagine Sam or Johnny in such a position.

Can't do it, can you?) When, finally, it seems the whoops and catcalls are wearing thin, you decide it is time for this silliness to end, so you roll on top and sit up, your arms pushing hers down by her side. She offers little resistance.

While you are in this position, it occurs to you that you could pull off her mask here, in front of the audience. It would be a fitting end to this series, wouldn't it? You reach down and grab the tip of one of the ears in your fingers.

Suddenly, Fury is alive and dead serious. She grabs your arm, forces it back with a steeliness you didn't know she possessed. "I don't think so," she says, and puts her legs around you, rolls you to the side and over, until she is on top, but only briefly. You easily roll her off and over. From your respective corners, the two of you get up slowly.

It's time to get this over with. Then you can get out of here and move on to the bigger and better things that await you. You leap at Fury's bottom half where, instead of simply taking her by the waist, as you might ordinarily, you thrust your head between her legs and force her onto her back. Once she is down, you somersault over her and land a bit more provocatively than you intend with your briefs on her chest. Your instinct is to scramble backward. You can maneuver enough to turn around so your back is facing her, but that's as far as you get. She musters enough strength to twist until your shoulders are pinned to the mat.

"How about that?" she says after the ref calls it, her voice barely audible above the din. She looks out at the audience, as do you. Because of the stage lights, it is impossible to see faces, but you can hear their loud approval. A much more earnest smile breaks out on her face. "Maybe I still got a little something." But the smile is short-lived, disappearing after she sees the ref's gesture for her to adjust her top. Somewhere in the melee, it became twisted, exposing part of her breast, and, realizing this, she turns away to shield herself. On any other occasion, such an occurrence might result in a fine, or renewed threats from the local athletic commission, but tonight, it is exactly the special something the stage manager had been hoping for, and his smile picks up where hers left off.

Later, when you hear a knock on your dressing room door, you've only just returned to street clothes. It is still early, and you haven't begun to rehearse your speech to Sam. You are too busy rehashing tonight's match. When you open the door, a young man gives you a suspicious look. "Are you—" He looks you up and down. "Geez, lady, I hardly recognized you. You sure look different."

No doubt. The lightweight slacks and ballerina flats you are wearing are a far cry from The Sweetheart's pencil skirt and stilettos. You want to enjoy your last dinner here in the famed Opera House, not hide away in your bungalow for yet another meal; and to ensure that you'll dine without interruption, you've reserved a table for Leigh Kramer—your *Secret* identity—and donned your most androgynous duds. You've even gone so far as to hide your trademark hair under the Musette. After all these years in storage, it deserves a night out. The whole ensemble feels surprisingly good, effortless even. You can see yourself spending more time in it. When the boy continues to stand there, stupefied, you clear your throat and ask what you can do for him.

"Right. Sorry. There's a gentleman waiting for you in the dining room. He asked me to take your stuff back to your room." He points to your satchel, inside of which your Sweetheart accoutrements are packed safely away. "Is that everything?"

"Yes," you say, handing over the bag and following him down the hallway, which has quickly crowded with be-feathered dancers exiting the stage after their just-completed dance number, and into the recently froufroued dining area. How long has Sam been here? Not long enough to catch your act, you hope. As if tonight's conversation isn't going to be difficult enough. Speaking of which, you should be spending these precious minutes thinking about just what you might say, not fretting over an event that you can't possibly change now.

The young man points you toward a far corner, but it still takes a minute of scouring to find Sam. There he is, sitting alone at a table in the front-center of the theater. "Sit, sit," he says when you reach the table, and stands to pull out the chair beside him. If he saw your performance, surely there would be a note of sourness—and, more likely, he would have something to say about it—but instead, he is smiling intently. Perhaps he arrived too late. "Are you hungry?" He motions for the waiter, but waves off the menu he is offered. "You want a steak? They're supposed to have a great filet here. Two filets, medium rare, and a martini for me. You want a martini? Two martinis."

Sam is a marvel, a flurry of action: you have no idea what's going on with him.

"Hope you don't mind this table," he says. "Normally, I don't like to be so close to a stage, but it seemed a bit more private." He cocks his head to one side, makes a face. "You're awfully quiet. Everything okay?"

"I guess I'm just surprised," you say, leaning across the table.

Sam claps his hands and rubs them together, causing the flame on the tea light to flicker. "I've got news."

"Really?" Sam's giddiness fuels your own sense of playfulness, so, in the absence of any clear game plan, you mimic his gesture. "So do I."

"Do you? Okay. Ladies first."

"Mine can wait," you say, stalling. "Let's hear yours first."

The drinks arrive. Sam plucks an olive from its toothpick and crunches it to smithereens. "I'm going to lose."

Lose? What does he mean, *lose*? Lose the *belt*? "I'm sorry? Is that good news?"

"Are you kidding? It's *great* news. I'm a free man. I can sleep in my bed, cook in my kitchen. I can start taking over more of Pop's end of things." He reaches across the table, takes your hand. "I can settle down."

And there it is. You cup the back of your neck with your hand and force a smile; it's clear that there's no way this is going to go well. How would that work, you zigzagging across the country while he stays hunkered down in Cleveland? You take a sip of your martini for courage, but it only makes you nauseous. You should know better than to drink when your stomach is empty and your head is scrambled.

"I might not get to see much of you anymore," you venture, eyes glued to the tablecloth.

Sam squeezes your hand. "You would if you came with me."

You retract your hand to your lap, where he can't get to it. "You mean quit."

He is clearly surprised by your resistance, but he presses on, dips his head down low, forcing you to meet his eyes. "Yes. I'd like you to stay with me and let me take care of you."

Of course he would. He's already imagining it: the ball games, the deviled eggs. You move to speak, but your stomach lurches forward, so you press your lips together and attempt to compose yourself.

I think you better spit it out, Gwen. Trust me: this is not going to get any easier.

"I can't do that, Sam. Not yet, anyway."

"What do you mean?" he says, rearing back. "Why not?"

"Because," you say, finally looking up, "I could *win*."

Thankfully, the waiter appears, slides plates in front of each of you and asks you both if you'll need anything else. Sam still has most of his drink, but he asks for a second regardless. When the waiter leaves, he says, "Win what?"

"The women's belt. The real one."

"How? I thought it was out of contention."

"Joe worked it out with Mildred. The Memphis match with Mimi is a run-up, and whoever wins that match will wrestle Mildred for the title."

"A shoot?" Sam lets out a low whistle, which garners him cranky glares from nearby patrons. Not that Sam notices, mind you. "I guess that settles that, then."

"Thanks for the vote of confidence."

"I'm just saying. She wants it, and she's a real pro."

"And I'm not?" you ask, anger rising. Suggesting that Mimi is likely to win is one thing—none of the local bookies would give you reasonable odds, and no one knows your limitations better than you—but this language is intentionally loaded. *She's a real pro.*

"Come on, Gwen. What were you doing tonight? You call that wrestling?"

Well, that answers one thing, doesn't it? "That's not fair. This is a one-time thing."

"You bet your boots it is. And don't think I won't have a few words to say to Joe about it."

"I don't need you to talk to Joe for me," you snap. "Why are we even talking about this? I thought I was sharing some good news with you. You could at least *pretend* that you're happy for me."

"Sure. I'm happy for you." Sam does not make eye contact when he says this; instead, he stares blankly at the stage curtains ahead of him. Finally, he drains his cocktail, sets down his empty glass, and cracks the knuckles on both of his fists. "I just think maybe you should consider the downsides."

"Consider the *downsides*?"

The waiter, just dropping off Sam's drink, raises an eyebrow at your curious outburst, but Sam waves him away. He snaps open his napkin and lays it over his lap. "Let's just eat our steaks, watch the show, and finish talking about this later."

It is clear that this evening is a bust. There is nothing for you to do but push aside the rest of your martini and sit silently in the darkness as, finally, the stage lights go up and the curtains pull back, revealing the Most Fabulous Girl in the World. Before the performance is over, the smoldering, heart-faced Lili St. Cyr, suspended over your heads in her golden cage, rids herself of her sequin-spangled outfit, and, in the process, drops a pair of rhinestone-adorned knickers into your lap.

The next morning, you tuck your hair into a bathing cap, slather on a healthy helping of Coppertone, and head out to El Rancho's oversize pool for a dip. You are gearing up for a serious conversation with Sam, but your mind is still clouded by the events of the last half day. As you descend the stairs, it seems the water doesn't even have enough crispness to snap you out of your sleepiness, let alone cool your head.

Neither you nor Sam has breathed a word about the belt since dinner. After the performance, Sam suggested the conversation remain on hold—after all, you have only this one night together in Las Vegas—while the two of you head to the casino so he might try his hand at the tables. But you were less than thrilled with the prospect. You didn't want to put off the conversation; you wanted to come to some resolution. This was *your life* being bandied about here. In the end, Sam went to the casino alone, and you stayed in the room, cogs afire, until you eventually fell asleep. When had he returned? You couldn't say.

Now, you wade to the middle of the pool, where it is still shallow enough for you to stand. What you would like to say to Sam, assuming you can say such a thing in a rational, convincing way, is that where he sees downsides, you see advantages. Maybe you *can* zigzag across the country while he stays in Cleveland. That way, he can revel in the team sports and housekeeping that you find so stifling, and you can enjoy the perks of being Gwen Davies without the guilt that his presence inspires. Every few weeks, when those pleasures, and the absence of each other, wear thin for you both, you could come to Cleveland for a spell: not too long, but long enough. You might even strike a deal with the Pospisils to make Cleveland your permanent base. This seems a fair compromise. Sam will not be immediately sold, of course—he will want a more conventional arrangement, one that he doesn't have to explain or defend to others—but perhaps he could be convinced.

And if he can't? What will you do if he proves unwilling to accommodate your persona and your profession? I know you don't want to think about it, Gwen, but it is a real possibility. You should be prepared to make a choice.

In the short time you've been here, the pool has grown crowded with mothers and children left to entertain themselves while the fathers gamble in the casino. Everyone here seems unaware of or indifferent to your presence. Almost everyone, that is. A few yards away, a girl has been stealing glimpses of you between handstands. When, from your crouched position, you offer a smile, she cautiously wades over.

"Are you that wrestler?" she starts.

You put a finger to your lips. "Yes, but I'd like to keep that quiet, if you don't mind." You've left a note for Sam asking him to join you after he wakes; the last thing you need is for him to stroll out here and find a swarm of fans.

"Oh. Yeah, sure." The girl squints against the sun and bounces on her toes to keep her head out of the water. "I guess I shouldn't ask you for an autograph then."

"I could have the waiter bring one over to you. How about that?"

"Yes, please," she says, smiling her relief. "Thank you." She dips her head back to soak her hair, and then slicks it back and wrings out the ponytail. "I like your suit."

It is not clear to you if she means the conservative bathing suit you are currently wearing or your trademark red wrestling suit or if it even matters. This may simply be the kind of empty compliment that shy girls offer as they attempt to make conversation. But hearing these words out of this girl, her own suit clearly purchased by a sensible parent, reminds you that Sam is not all wrong: there are downsides to winning the belt, even if they aren't the ones he imagines. Having fans like—

"What's your name?"

"Serena."

—like Serena muddies the picture considerably. Vicky Darnell and the Go-to-Hell girls were the first to point out the harm a character like yours could do. Knowing that prepubescent girls might be watching shows like last night's is enough to give you pause.

"And where are you sitting, Serena?"

Serena crouches low before springing up out of the water and pointing to an umbrella at a far corner of the pool. You follow her finger to the other side of the pool and find, walking along the perimeter of the deep end—a graceful, attention-generating stride despite his certain hangover—the person for whom you've been readying your speech.

"Okay, Serena," you say, wading toward the ladder, "consider it done."

When Sam spots you climbing out of the water, you point toward your tote on one of the deck chairs, and he sits down in the one next to it. By the time you arrive, he has placed an order with a white-uniformed waiter. "How'd you make out last night?"

Sam groans. "Don't ask."

A waiter arrives with Sam's drink: a tall glass of hair of the dog. "Anything for you, Miss Davies?"

"Just a favor."

After the waiter leaves with an autograph for Serena, Sam props himself up on his elbow. "You know," he says, squinting, "it's reasonable for me to have mixed feelings about your news."

"I know. But Sam—"

"Please." Clearly he has been doing some rehearsing of his own. "Just hear me out. Yes, I would like you to be off the road and closer to me. I would like to have a regular life with you. But it's not just that. Think about all the creeps who've come out of the woodwork since you started this Sweetheart business. If by some miracle you win, it will only get worse. And if I'm in Cleveland, I can't watch out for you."

You sink further into your chair; your body feels heavy. How can you make him understand that you are aware of these problems—Sam doesn't even know the half of it—but they are simply no match for the rewards? You take a deep breath and try to make what you are about to say as agreeable as you can.

"Look, I know how you feel. I get it. Sometimes I feel that way, too. But if there is no Sweetheart"—go ahead, Gwen: admit it—"then I don't know who I am."

Sam begins to say something, but thinks better of it, closes his mouth and his eyes and rests his head against the back of the deck chair. While you wait for him to form his response, you turn your attention to the other side of the pool, where a woman takes a seat in a lounge chair. You don't recognize the face, but her shape and skin tone are unmistakable. This is the woman you've been wrestling these last few nights.

There'd been a moment last night as you were both going back to your dressing rooms when it seemed she might remove the mask, but if the thought had occurred to her, she must have changed her mind. Instead, she only offered you a sad smile. "I turned my life upside down to get back into wrestling," she said. "To do this."

This is the first time you've seen her since then, and, even without her mask, you are no closer to knowing who she is. Still, you can't help but sense that you know this woman. You must have wrestled her before, but when?

Something clicks when you see how she drapes her legs over the arm of that deck chair, the way she kicks off her mules and lets them fall to the ground. And those freckles—don't you recognize those freckles? Imagine her a little heavier, her hair a little longer. Now here comes the final puzzle piece, expertly balanced on the tray of the waiter who delivers it to her waiting hands: a Tom Collins, topped off by a maraschino cherry, which she promptly fishes out of the ice and plucks from the stem with her teeth.

Lacey Bordeaux here, clear on the other side of the country. But why shouldn't she be holed up here, establishing residency like so many others? Her recent actions certainly suggest she's eager to unload Johnny as soon as possible. It's not implausible, just as it's not out of the realm of possibility that Katleman, having learned about her colorful past, wouldn't offer her this gig, her first in over a year. Without the protection of her mask, you can see that she looks bad: there are bags under her eyes, she's drinking too much. She is here to start over, but it is hard for you to believe she will get much further than where she is now. Word of what she's done will get out, and the NWA promoters will lock her out. She has chased one mistake with another.

Your first instinct is to tell Sam, but then you think better of it. Lacey seems intent on hiding, and who are you to out her? Besides, you aren't eager to steer the conversation away from the one at hand. If you don't want to be caught in the same trap that took Lacey out, you will have to be honest about what you want. You can't worry about how he will react, or whether you will be able to maintain your relationship with him.

"I want to be with you, and I want to be the champion, too," you say. "Please don't ask me to pick one."

Sam rolls onto his side and opens an eye. After a long pause, he says, "You might have to, one day."

You could take this opportunity to deliver some of the speech you've been readying, lay out your plan forward, but there's nothing in his tone or expression that suggests he will be receptive. Better to simply accept the extension he is offering and use it to build your case. You are sure you can get what you need if you can just make the right argument.

"But not today?" you ask, grateful for this gift of time. In your heart of hearts, you know what your choice will be, should it come to that, but you are far from ready to make it and still hopeful you won't have to.

Sam reaches for his glass, tips it against your arm, and runs its icy base down the length of your muscular bicep, stopping at the crook of your elbow before returning it to his lips. "No," he says. "Not today."

TWENTY-SIX

The rest of the tour—ten cities in ten days, from one coast to the other—is an exercise in patience and endurance. Thankfully, you and Sam have enough of both to make it to the last stop: Memphis, the site of the most significant matches of both your careers—the end of his title run and quite possibly the beginning of yours. The two of you arrive early at Ellis Auditorium, equally eager but for very different reasons. You are met by a representative of the Memphis promoter, who escorts you both under the building's terra-cotta cornice and down the pink marble hallway to get your first look at the auditorium. As the man walks you along, he tells you it has an electric stage that can move from one end to the other in a brisk twelve hours and rise from the first floor when the occasion calls for heightened drama. When he tells you this, you imagine a wrestling ring ascending from the ground like a green shoot springing from the earth, triumphant, and, in the center, you: fists on hips, chin aloft, legs firm, stomach taut, hair coiffed, lips red, smile confident and knowing, every ounce the champion.

But that would have been too perfect. No, when he waves you into the arena, you find the stage already in position, the ring assembled. Both sets of curtains have been drawn back, joining the north and south halls to accommodate the thousands of fans, who are already snaking down the aisles and taking their seats: ringside for the well-heeled; for everyone else, floor level or balcony or, should the fan's skin tone happen to be too dark, the nosebleeds. But you are not going to complain about the stage. It will be drama enough just to make your way down the aisle of such a stately venue. Tonight it will be filled to capacity: the noise deafening, the head count staggering.

When you arrive in the women's dressing room, Mimi is already there, still in her street clothes, sitting at a vanity and finishing a hamburger she brought over from Palumbo's. When she hears the door open, she does not turn around. Instead, she looks straight ahead into the mirror, where she meets your reflection with a hole-boring stare and an overly broad smile. You give her a brief nod and pretend to busy yourself at the other vanity, but already, she is under your skin. The stare is menacing, to be sure, but it is the smile that rattles you. There's only one word for it: smug. She can't wait to get through this fight. She knows she will win. She's anxious to see the looks on the audience's faces after she annihilates their hero, but more than that, she wants to hurry up and get on to the next one, where she'll secure her rightful place in wrestling history.

That smile has been taunting you for the last twenty-four hours. Yesterday afternoon, when you and Sam arrived at the Peabody, Mimi was already there, entertaining Junior in the lobby. The two of them stood by the fountain, pointing at the ducks. She hadn't noticed your arrival—she clearly had her hands full—and so you might have easily made it up to your room without an encounter. But seeing Mimi like this, well-intentioned but way out of her element, softened your feelings toward her. You left Sam to finish checking you both in and crossed the room to her. You understood that you couldn't make amends, but you were hopeful that you might at least improve the tenor of this competition.

"Hello, Mimi."

Mimi turned and made eye contact, then froze in surprise, but her expression melted into something more hostile—her eyes roving without apology, her cat's smile teeming with canary feathers. That look made it harder to be there, to say what you wanted to say. But you'd made this much effort. You had to follow through.

The minute you opened your mouth, a red carpet rolled out from the elevator, toward the spot where you were standing. This prompted a flurry of activity, and a crowd quickly gathered on all sides of the carpet, elbowing the three of you away from the action, obstructing your view, in order to position their cameras. A Sousa march—the *last* thing, you suspected, a woman with an excitable infant wants to hear—began to play. Mimi turned her attention to Junior. And then, the reason for the hoopla: Mr. Pembroke, the duckmaster, stepped out of the elevator, strolled down to the fountain, gently prodded his ducks from its waters, and marched them back up the carpet—single file, no less!—and into the elevator, which would return them to their palatial estate on the rooftop.

"Quack!" Junior shouted as the line waddled past.

Mimi looked at him, surprised. "Yeah, ducks say *quack*. Good job, buddy." She pulled him close, her fingers tickling his rib cage; he clung tightly to her and laughed. "How 'bout that? You know, I've been trying to get this kid to say *Mimi* for weeks, and now, out of nowhere, he's saying *quack*?" She shook her head.

"Oh, I don't know. It looks like you've figured out a thing or two."

"Yeah, well. My duties are officially done tonight." She kissed him quickly, and then turned her attention to you. "So tomorrow, I will be free to destroy your hopes and dreams."

There was something reassuring about this cockiness; it smacked of her usual derision, which eased the way for you to say what you'd come over to say. "I know my chances of beating you tomorrow are slim, but I also know that any chance I have is because of what you've done for me." And with that, you extended your hand. "Good luck."

Mimi looked at you sideways, as if looking for some indication that she was being set up. But this was genuine appreciation, long overdue. Still, she didn't take your hand. She might have lightened up a bit, but she wasn't eager to accept your good wishes, or to offer any of her own. When, finally, the crowd that had gathered for Mr. Pembroke's ducks had dispersed, she tilted her head up at the elevator dial—the ducks were back on the roof, the numbers were descending.

"I better get Junior back upstairs," she said.

You stood there in the quickly emptying lobby, your hand still held out, as she crossed the room and disappeared into the elevator. Refused yet again, just like the first time you met her. You expected her to shake your hand. It took a minute to recover from the sting and gather yourself, and then you turned your attention to Sam, who had just finished his dealings with the hotel clerk and stood a few yards away, dangling your room key.

Mimi's next move was even more surprising. When, finally, the elevator arrived to take you, Sam, a bellhop, and a cartful of luggage to your floor, the operator opened the sliding door, and, after a pair of men raced out, there she stood, balancing Junior against one shoulder, her satchel hooked over the other. She murmured something under her breath, rifled around in the satchel, and pulled out a stack of mail.

"This was in your box in the office," she said, holding it out to you. "I brought it for you."

"You didn't have to," you said, staring at her, semifrozen. You weren't particularly keen on extending another vulnerable hand. "I'm going back to Florida after this."

"Yeah, well, it was just sitting there, so I grabbed it." She rearranged Junior on her hip. "So take it already."

"Okay, okay," you said, and did as commanded. "Thanks."

When it didn't seem as if you were going to move, Sam put his hand on your back and ushered you into the elevator. Everyone rode up in tense silence, broken only when you reached Mimi's floor and she stepped out and turned around. She began to say something—her mouth yawned open, her finger pointed—but she stopped, put her hand down, pressed her lips together, and began again. "I have done a lot for you," she said. "I hope you remember that tomorrow." And then she instructed Junior to wave to the nice man and the pretty lady. The operator quickly slid the door closed—no time for monkey business— but not before you saw that smile again, even more assured than it was before, if that was possible. She beamed at you as Junior waved.

In the lobby, that smile was faith-diminishing, and then bamboo-zling, but as you headed up to your floor and entered your room, you decided it was nothing short of infuriating. *If she expects me to just roll over,* you thought, dumping the stack of mail on the desk, *she is sadly mistaken.* She might have visions of wiping the mat with you, but your visions were equally clear: you were going to wipe that smug look right off her face.

It is a big night, and ordinarily, you might labor over your hair, your makeup, your suit, your boots, making sure every inch is picture-perfect, but Mimi's presence in your dressing room is unnerving. You cannot afford to be unnerved tonight—this will be the biggest match of your career thus far, one that will play significantly in your personal history and the history of your sport—so you forgo the usual rituals and hurry through your routine before taking your mark by the auditorium entrance to watch the show.

The main event this evening is the World Junior Heavyweight Championship—Spider McGee versus Baron Michele Leone—but tonight's card is chockablock full of performances of all stripes. In addition to your match with Mimi and two others on the card, there has been a magician, a pair of banjo-picking twins, and now, a group of baton twirlers and tap dancers, who are so busy shuffling and spinning their hearts out that they barely notice the crew's attempts to whisk them out of the ring. After much charm and cunning, the stagehands manage to send the girls up the aisle so they can set up for the musical act, the Blue Moon Boys, who will soon take to the ring to play a few standard bluegrass numbers as well as their current radio hit. The band's lead singer told you the name of the song earlier in the day, while the two of you were making a promotional appearance at Lansky Brothers—a men's clothier, popular with the heppest of cats—but it didn't ring any bells. Now, as you stand backstage, you can't even remember what he said. How could you? As soon as the crew breaks down their set, the announcer will call your name and you will step into what is sure to be a defining moment. You will be able to fill in this detail later, of course, when the song becomes a national treasure and its performer an icon. I suppose this is another tragedy of the evening—that you are too busy writing yourself into the history books to appreciate the history that is happening right in front of you. This one, at least, you will be able to laugh about.

As you lean against the wall, dreaming of glory, Sam steps out of the men's dressing room clad in his briefs and boots, his soon-to-be-lost belt draped over an oiled shoulder, and gives you a pat on the rump.

"She's not going to know what hit her," he says.

This is not exactly a wholehearted gesture of confidence or support, but it is a long way from where he began. And you have to hand it to him: the man has been a sport. He was at Lansky Brothers today, too, as were a photographer from the *Daily News* and six hand-selected members of the Memphis branch of the Gorgeous Girls (no more open calls; they'd certainly learned *that* lesson). You were all there to hype the event, and hype you did, thrilling customers in the most brazen fashion: straightening ties, fastening belts, and even borrowing some tailor's tape to measure the inseam of the dark-haired singer, who'd blushed in response. Every time you checked your periphery to get Sam's reaction, his discomfort was visible, but, to his credit, he showed enormous restraint. He was willing to play his part, it seemed, which left you free to play yours. And as you did, the photographers shot roll after roll, taking pictures that might have appeared in the next day's newspapers and wrestling magazines if the unfortunate event that was soon to occur didn't render them wholly unsuitable.

But you don't know about that yet. Right now, as you and Sam stand with your arms around each other's waists, looking out at the ocean of people, listening as the set wraps up and mindlessly bopping your heads along to the beat, the outcome is unknown; anything is possible. There is every reason to believe that you and Sam will have a long, happy relationship, which will be balanced by your long, happy career, free of compromises, beginning with a surprise victory tonight. For once, the people out there in the crowd aren't the only ones pre-pared for anything to happen.

Before you know it, it is upon you—the moment of reckoning. Mimi is in her corner and you are in yours, your attention sharply focused despite the low roar of the crowd. Your best shot, you have decided, is to come out guns a-blazin'. If it comes down to who has more stamina, Mimi will win, but if you come hard at the beginning, you at least stand a chance of catching her by surprise or forcing her hand. This is the only way: a fast win, an early win. And so, as soon as the bell rings, you drive toward her.

As might be expected, Mimi stops you with a ref's hold, but, pro-pelled by your go-for-broke strategy, you twist out and flop her onto the mat with a snap mare. Before she can get up, you stomp your foot into her midsection, putting the full force of your desire into the blow. She doesn't make a sound, but she curls like a slug, her back to you. Instinctively, you understand that she is hurt; you have discovered—or, better yet, created—a weakness. Now, you must zero in on this spot. Before she can recover, you race around and give her another kick in the breadbasket. This time, she cannot contain her groan.

Another kick doesn't make for much of a show, but tonight is about winning, not theater. You must take advantage of every opportunity, so you rear back for a third. But before you can make contact, Mimi rolls under the ropes. She may have her vulnerabilities, but the woman knows how to get out of a jam. When you dive on top of her in hopes of an early pin, she snakes her legs around you into the ropes, working them just enough to force the ref's interference and buy herself some precious time.

After the ref breaks it up, Mimi retreats to her corner, shoots you a look—*What the hell was that?*—and then paces the ring, studying you. She seems stunned and unnerved—good signs. You better act now, Gwen, while she is still bewildered, because once she figures out that you are neglecting her warning—that you aim to *win*—she's going to come at you like a hammer.

You lunge, but it's too late: in no time, Mimi puts you in a headlock and drops you both onto the mat. It is well within her capacity to roll you onto your back and pin your shoulders, but you know how to handle her. You snake a leg over her neck, and, careful to hold her under the chin and not on the throat, lock her into a head scissors. Mimi twists forcefully, heaving you onto your backside, but you manage to keep her head clamped. She thrashes about, more panicked than usual, perhaps because it leaves her midsection exposed and she senses that you have honed in on this vulnerability. It is difficult to hit her from this position, but you manage to get in one chop, and another harder one. Then, while she is still reeling from this last hit, you roll onto your stomach, cross your ankles, and press down on her shoulders with your shins. It's working—the ref slaps the mat once—but she twists, gets a shoulder off. You are so close, you sense, and, seeing the rope just in front of you, you reach out for it, hoping to steal that extra bit of leverage it would give you. But, just as your fingers brush it, you drop your hand. Mimi already thinks you have come by your station in a less than honorable way. Better to lose than for her to always second-guess your right to the title. Instead, you concentrate your energy and bear all the pressure those roadworked legs of yours can muster onto her shoulders.

The ref hits the mat again, and then again and again. First fall: Gwen Davies.

The response from the crowd is instantaneous: a roar of approval accompanied by the shaking of seat backs, the stomping of feet on chairs, the piggybacking leaps of Gorgeous Girls onto their escorts. You scramble off the mat and climb up the turnbuckle to take it in. Yes, it is loud and boisterous and spectacular, but the way you experience it is more than sight and sound. It is the force of their collective desire: they all want Mimi defeated. If you can't do this, you are going to let all of them down. The notion of disappointing them fills you with fear. If there was ever any doubt—if your want of a victory tonight ever wavered, if Sam's concerns or your own occasional ambivalence ever really made you question its merits—it is gone now, blown away by the winds of their desires. You want to give them what they want, what you have implicitly promised every time you have winked an eye or blown a kiss.

There is only one way this can end. You don't just *want* to win; you *have* to.

One down, one to go.

As soon as the bell rings, you charge again, anxious to work fast, to act before Mimi has time to think or catch her breath. This time, you manage to get her in a chicken wing and apply much more pressure than theatrics would dictate. She may have been unsure of your strategy earlier, but this, she reads loud and clear: you are doing your damnedest to take this fall, too.

"Is this your idea of gratitude?" Mimi hisses back at you.

You suck in your breath and then exhale, low and slow. "I don't owe you tonight."

"You sure about that?" Her nostrils flare. "After what I did for you?"

"What exactly do you think you have done for me?" you ask, giving her wrist another yank.

"What exactly—" When she turns her face toward you, you can see that it is clammier than it should be this early in the match. Perhaps your plan has paid off; perhaps she is more injured than she is letting on. "I could have *destroyed* you," she spits.

"*Destroyed* me? I think you overestimate yourself." You give her wrist another little yank. "You want to win? Then win."

"You're on," she says, and then sets you straight with an elbow to the stomach.

This blow knocks the wind out of you, but, sensing you don't have much time, you come back with a kick—not your usual imitation roundhouse, but one that makes full contact—and, landing one, attempt another. It's too predictable. The second time, Mimi grabs your leg, drops you flat on your back, and dives on top of you. Desperate, you lock your arms and legs around Mimi and roll the both of you under the ropes and over the apron until you both thwack down onto the announcer's table.

"What do we have here, folks?" he says, scrambling to get out of the way. "Ladies and gentlemen, you won't get this kind of excitement anywhere else. This is no-holds-barred, going-for-broke grappling at its best. And this is just the *women*!"

Both you and Mimi scramble to your feet, rush to adjacent sides of the ring, and climb in. Luckily, you get to your feet just a hair ahead of her, enough time to attack first. You maneuver her into a full nelson and, once your grip is locked, toss her side to side to get her dizzy. You're running out of gas, but you have to act, so you jump up and put her in a body scissors, using your weight to drag her down to the mat. Mimi comes alive, presses back, nearly pinning your shoulders, but you manage to roll back, lifting her up with your legs, and slam her force-fully onto her seat. She doesn't make a noise, but you are well aware that the maneuver is hard on the torso, and so, your hold still secure, you roll back and drop her again, and she moans. Still, she has enough in her to roll onto her side, and then her abdomen, push up on her fore-arms, and twist until she is on top of you. You struggle with everything you have left, but she still manages to work her way up to her feet, your legs in her arms. Your eyes go wide—she is clearly wounded, her face braced, but by the sheer force of her will, she begins to spin.

It is not the first time you have been on the receiving end of the Hollander Helicopter, but it is the most punishing. This time, instead of hurling you safely within the confines of the mat, where you might land on your back with little damage, Mimi launches you into the turn-buckle, lacerating your shoulder blade. Before the ref can see the blood and call time, Mimi drags you, wincing with pain, into the middle of the mat, where she applies just enough force to secure the pin.

The audience groans with disapproval, and as you slouch over to the corner so the ring doctor can stop your bleeding, you feel your con-fidence waning, doubt creeping in. It is one–all—anyone's game—but you can't help but wonder if you have missed your chance. You lean against the ropes while the doc presses a towel against the cut for what feels like forever: long enough, you are sure, for Mimi to refresh and re-group. You try to push these thoughts out of your mind, but with every moment that passes, you feel your victory slipping away.

Sure enough, when the doc signals that you are ready and the bell rings, Mimi springs, whipping you into a hammerlock and then run-ning you around the mat before flopping you down. As soon as you get to your feet, she fires a judo chop into your chest that knocks you back into the ropes.

Everything hurts. It will be over soon if you can't do something now, Gwen. If there is still some small well of resources for you to tap into, this would be the time.

As it turns out, there is: mercifully, you come to your senses quickly enough to harness the momentum and bounce back with a flying leg scissors. One foot lands on Mimi's chest, the other hooks behind her knee, sweeping the veteran wrestler onto her back. This move signals a turning of the tides, which the audience endorses with hearty, full-throated glee. You hear someone scream, *Take her out!*; still another yells, *Make her bleed!* Bolstered by their faith, much sturdier than your own, you manage to grab one of Mimi's legs with one arm and her torso with the other, lift her off her feet and drop her back over your knee. Mimi rolls onto the mat, limp with pain, and the crowd goes wild. They make their collective wish known, loud and clear: *Drop/the/ Bomb/shell! Drop/the/Bomb/shell! Drop/the/Bomb/shell!*

You would love to oblige them—for your victory to be as poetic as all the choreographed ones before it have suggested it might be—but sadly, you cannot. The Bombshell is a stunt. If you are going to win, you will have to rely on tactics that are less artful but more effective.

This maneuver, the most infamous of your career, will pass in a flash and occur before you can give it a first thought, let alone a second. For those not in attendance, the only evidence will be articles from the *Daily News* and *Wrestling As You Like It*, neither of which will mention the prematch interviews but instead will focus on this moment, describing it in one as *malicious* and the other as *positively criminal*. In this tiny capsule of time, brief but eternal, you forgo not only your signature finishing move but all semblance of entertainment, not to mention sportsmanship, by rearing back and planting a Green Goddess squarely in Mimi's abdomen.

Wrestling As You Like It will describe Mimi's subsequent scream as *earth-splitting*. The *Daily News* will use this more ominous word: *deathly*.

As soon as you hear that sound, you know something is terribly wrong and drop to the mat, where your opponent lies folded in half. "Mimi," you say, searching her face; "Mimi," you say again, listening to her quick, shallow breaths. Before you can say anything else, the ref is on top of you, pulling you away. You have no choice but to steady yourself and take in the scene from a distance. The ref, the ring doctor, and Mimi, quiet now but for those breaths, her pallor graying, take up the foreground; behind them is the audience. *Take her out!* they cried. *Make her bleed!* Now that you've done what they asked you to do, they have all clammed up. All around you, people stand and stare, their hands over their mouths.

You cannot move. More and more people rush past you toward the injured wrestler: Joe, Johnny, and who knows who else. Again, someone yanks you backward; this time, it is Sam.

"Let's go," he says. He holds open the ropes, but you don't budge. "Through the ropes!" he barks. "Now!"

This does this trick: you move slowly, but at least you move. "Jump down," he says, and you do. This seems to be working: concrete directions. "Walk faster," he commands, and the two of you barrel up the aisle, past the audience, still stunned, and march right into the grasp of two policemen, on-site to provide security, who take over the orders.

"This way," says the elder of the pair, covering the right flank as the four of you hurry out of the auditorium: down the pink marble hallway, under the terra-cotta cornice, and into the squad car.

TWENTY-SEVEN

Early the next morning, these same two cops are in your room, on the phone again. This is how it has been all night, the two of them holed up in a motel room with you and Sam, the phone ringing every couple of hours. *Don't bring her in until we know something. Just stay there, make sure she doesn't blow out.* At long last, they can deliver the final update.

"Good news," says the older cop.

After the sergeant's last call, many hours prior, you'd learned of hemorrhaging and understood that Mimi had been rushed to the operating room for an emergency hysterectomy. The word sounded serious enough, but you hadn't been entirely sure what it meant and had to ask for an explanation, which the officer had given with a stutter and more than a little pink in his cheeks. Still, in that moment, the finality of what this meant hadn't been of much importance to you. You could only focus on her condition and the images it conjured—a gurney being rushed down a corridor, feverish doctors and blood-drenched gowns—and the most immediate concern: would it be enough? Since then, you

have remained in a fog of the past, replaying the events of the evening—
no, the last year—on a continuous loop, focused on the moments where
the story might have gone differently. You should have gone home when
your father asked you to. You shouldn't have gone to Florida in the
first place. You shouldn't have given Sal Costantini your name or any
reason to remember it. You shouldn't have joined Cynthia on *Band-stand*. Yes, that is where this whole thing went wrong. That's when you
developed this miserable itch. The officer tells you that the worst has
been avoided. Surgery has gone as expected and without complication;
Mimi's condition is serious but stable. The relief that washes over you
is so complete that you almost don't hear the rest: according to the sur-
geon, a confluence of factors—a congenital abnormality, previous med-
ical procedures, and a decade of trauma to the area—had contributed
to her weakened uterus. You aren't entirely to blame. The cops have
been instructed to let you go. There will be no charges.

Before they leave, the younger of the two officers shakes your hand.
He has trouble hiding his disappointment. It's clear by his expression
he looked forward to the possibility of booking a minor celebrity. The
elder seems more sympathetic. He pats you on the shoulder. "Quite a
relief, I'm sure," he says.

"Yes," you say, thinking of Mimi. Only later will it occur to you
that he was referring to your own narrowly avoided catastrophe.

Once they leave, you are on your own. You will have to repeat all of
this for Sam. He's gone out to fetch coffee and (at your insistence) the
morning paper. Since leaving the auditorium, he's left your side only
one other time, after the squad car pulled up to the Peabody, where he
had to walk through the lobby still in the barest of his regalia, pack up,
and check out of both rooms, and then bring everything to the agreed-
upon meeting place, a nearby motel where you would be safe from
scrutiny. He paid for these actions with an ignominious defeat—the
commission declared a forfeit and awarded the belt to his opponent—
but this news didn't seem to faze him. If his feelings for you are at all

shaken by what has happened, he is keeping it convincingly to himself. His only concern has been for you; he has provided every comfort he could. You are sorry he wasn't here to hear the news. You don't want him to suffer any longer than necessary.

When the phone rings, you know right away who is on the other end. Only one other person knows where you are. You don't feel ready to talk to Joe, but Sam's not here to do the talking for you and you don't want to put him off.

"Have you heard?" he asks.

"The cops were here. They said she had an operation, but she's going to be okay."

"And they told you that it wasn't your fault?"

"Yes, they told me."

"Okay. Now you tell me."

"Tell you what?"

"Say, 'It wasn't my fault.' "

Those words douse you like a wave—you had not expected reassurance from Joe—and leave you awash in gratitude. You have to press your eyes and your lips closed to stave off the emotions. When you regain composure, you say, "It wasn't my fault."

"Good. Now we have to decide where to go from here. I don't think there will be any problem sanctioning a fight against Mildred, but if we are going forward, I will need to make my case to the commission soon."

This shouldn't surprise you. For your entire relationship, Joe has been coaxing you up off the mat only to urge you on. Yet this time it sets you upright. You thought you were coming in to safe harbor, but this has sent you adrift again. After all this time, you are still unsure whether to read Joe's strategy as exploitation or as tough love.

"You still want me to win the belt?" you ask. "Even after what happened?"

"Well. I want *someone* to win the belt, and it's not going to be Mimi now, is it?"

"No, I know, it's just . . . people are going to feel differently about me now, aren't they?"

Joe does not say anything else for a long time. Perhaps he is carefully choosing his words, or maybe he is hoping you will realize what is inevitable before he has to say it. "Yes. The next time you step into a ring, it will be as a heel."

It is not until you hear that final word—*heel*—that you understand. If you intend to stay in the business, the only way forward is to capitalize on the assault, to build a new, reviled persona around it. The thought of this makes you ill. Being a heel was unbearable before—the ominous glares, the insults and epithets, and, most terrifying of all, the terrible silence before and after every match. Wouldn't this treatment be infinitely more painful now for being deserved—a routine persecution for your crime?

But worse than what might lie ahead is what you must leave behind. What he is really saying is that the persona you have forged, the one on which you have gambled all of your relationships, is gone forever. No matter what you do next, The Sweetheart is dead. You are quite certain there is no way you can go into the ring without her. You need the love she inspires; you need the pulse and thrum of it. That sound that rushes in and fills the hollows inside you. Sure, it smells of kayfabe, but damn if it doesn't feel like bona fide affection. Maybe if you were still at the beginning of your career, just stepping out of Joe's DeSoto and onto the shell-strewn ground for the first time, your stars not yet drawn on a map but still twinkling above you, you could be different. Now you know what you want, and you know you can't get it as a heel.

"I can't do that, Joe. I wish I could. But I just can't." And then you put the phone back into the cradle.

The room is too quiet now, too full of your thoughts, so you turn on the radio for noise. This is not quite enough to distract you, so you open your suitcase in search of your book; but when you lift the lid, you find, piled on top of your clothes, the stack of mail Mimi gave you last night. Sam must have swept it off the desk into your bag. Surprising, you think, dumping the letters onto the bed and sorting through them, that he would notice it in his hurry and preoccupation. You certainly hadn't. In fact, you forgot about the mail almost as soon as you threw it down; you hadn't so much as skimmed its contents. You were focused, after all: your eye was on the prize.

Most of the pile appears to be fan mail, which you simply can't stomach right now. You give each envelope a cursory glance before tossing it aside, stopping only when you spot your father's handwriting. Thankful, you tear into the envelope, but right away, your heart sinks. The letter is largely a report on Harold and all of his adorable and hilarious antics. If this were not bad enough, he fails even to say that you are missed. He hardly mentions you at all, except to say this: *I have decided to stop worrying about you so much. You have proven that you are happy and that you can take care of yourself.* It is unclear if he means this with pride or sadness or even if he really means it—perhaps he is trying to convince himself—but you read it as a severance. You have drifted too far from the shore to swim back. You don't know what you are going to do now, but one thing is clear: there is no going home.

After that, there is more fan mail, but at the bottom of the pile, there is a manila envelope. There is no address and no postage, only a name: *Betsy Mahoney.* The color of the envelope, its size, its heft: it's all too familiar. Only the name is different. If there is any color left in you, the sight of that name would be enough to drain it off. You grab your room key to tear into the package. *Betsy Mahoney.* Another set, filed under another name. It had never even crossed your mind. There they are: the pictures, the ones you didn't think existed anymore. Why are they here? How did they get here? Lucky break that Sam isn't around. Lucky, too, that Mimi didn't get curious. There's no telling what she might have done if she knew what she had.

Or did she? *I have done a lot for you,* she said when she handed over the stack of mail two days ago. And last night, in the ring: *I could have destroyed you.* You turn the envelope over and inspect its closure. Sure enough, its security has been breached: the original seal has been broken and the envelope resealed with additional tape.

So she had seen them. And then she gave them to you; she just handed them over without ultimatum. She could have easily assured herself a victory last night if she had used the pictures as blackmail. You wouldn't have hesitated to job the match in exchange for them. Everyone, yourself included, might be better off if only she had used her discovery as leverage: not the emotional leverage of gratitude, which she hadn't been above using—and which, had you realized what was in that envelope, would have been enough—but *real* leverage that would have left you without options. Years from now, she will tell you this was her original intention, but after her encounter with you in the lobby, she couldn't pull the trigger. She might have acted like a heel, but when it came down to it, she played it straight. And you put her in the hospital. This knowledge burrows inside of you and lodges itself so surely that it will never be extracted. For the rest of your life, you will wish that you had understood this sooner, that you had acted differently not just on that infamous evening but so many other times.

You gather up the photos and the rest of the letters, sweep them into the bottom of your luggage, and then curl up on the bed. You pray that Sam will take his time, get stuck in traffic, get lost for a while. You don't have the stomach for the comfort he will surely want to offer.

The key in the door startles you out of what might have been slumber. How long have you been asleep? Not long, surely; Sam is just returning. He nudges open the door with his toe, precariously balancing a paper bag and a cardboard box holding four cups of coffee, and you jump up to help him.

"Where's the black-and-white?" he asks.

"Gone," you say, taking the box from him and setting it on the nightstand. "More coffee for us, I guess."

You give him the same news the cops gave you, in the same flat tone.

"She's okay, then?"

"As okay as can be expected."

"So, that's it? You're free to go?"

"I guess so. Let me see that paper."

Sam seems to be carefully considering what he should do or say next. You fish the newspaper out of the bag yourself. It is already turned to the page you want. The article is barely a column and is not accompanied by a picture. *Positively criminal,* you read. You sink onto the bed and hang your head between your knees.

"What now?" Sam asks.

"Your guess is as good as mine," you say to the carpeting.

"Should I call Joe?"

This is not the time to feel the old resentments. Still, you can't help but stiffen when he says *I* instead of *you.*

"I've already talked to him. He still wanted me to fight on Saturday."

"And?"

"And I said no."

You do not look up to see Sam's face when you say this, but you can imagine that it is as neutral as he can make it. After a long silence, he ventures, "Then what are you going to do?"

"I don't know. I haven't gotten that far yet."

"I guess you know what I would like you to do."

"You still want me to come with you?" you ask, finally daring to lift your head.

"Of course," he says. "You're still my sweetheart. That's all I care about."

You do not deserve Sam's second thoughts, and yet here he is. It is both humbling and burdensome to be the object of such certainty when you are so unsure of yourself. But it is also an enormous relief. Every-thing else is up in the air, and yet he is still here.

It is too much. You have to wipe your eyes with the heels of your hands.

Sam stays where he is, gives you the space and time to have this mo-ment, pays just enough attention to assure you that comfort is available should you want it. When it seems you've pulled yourself together with-out this, he says quietly, "Just think about it, okay?" After you nod your assurance, he politely steers the conversation toward lighter fare.

"Coffee's getting cold." He examines the four cups, selects two, and hands you one. "This one's yours. I hope it's got enough cream for you. I told her to go heavy."

Sam hops up to take a seat on top of the dresser and blows across his coffee. "Let's just stay here for a little while, okay?" he says. "I don't have to be home for a few days. We don't even have to leave this room if you don't want."

"You don't have to stay."

"I *want* to stay." Sam jumps off the bed, grabs the paper bag, and reaches inside, pulling out a pair of MoonPies. "Hungry?"

Not only did he make sure your coffee was prepared the way you like it, he also brought back a favorite treat. You think of Patricia, the way she talked about that pot of stew your father made, with new understanding. You take one of the MoonPies and open the wrapper. "You thought of everything. What else you got in there?" When he seems to hesitate, you try again. "Don't hold out, Sam. What else?"

"Just some smokes and—" He pulls out a small box and hands it to you. Gold, with a little crown on front. *Miss Clairol Hair Color Bath,* it says. *Sable brown.* "There was this beauty salon next to the corner store, just opening up for the day, and it occurred to me. I just thought you might want to look a little less . . . conspicuous."

You stare at the box in one hand, the MoonPie in the other, for a long while before putting both down on the bed. Can this really be necessary? If it is, it means another piece of you is gone, that you are steadily disappearing. But maybe this is a way to pay penance—by getting rid of The Sweetheart, bit by bit. You can hardly expect to absolve yourself with a bottle of hair dye, but you need to make a gesture, and for now, this is all you have. "Let's do it," you say. "Now. Before I change my mind."

Sam proves to be surprisingly adept with hair color, his gloved hands carefully separating your locks and then brushing them, root to tip, with the dye. When, finally, it is time to rinse, Sam issues a few directives as he eases you beneath the tub spigot, but the rest of the operation is mercifully silent. He does not speak again until after you have toweled off and gone to the mirror to examine his handiwork. "You look beautiful," he says, talking to your image as he stands behind you, gripping your shoulders. It is not only how he sees you but also how he wants you to see yourself, which he further demonstrates by stooping to kiss you on the temple, but it does not make you feel any better about the woman who stares back at you. It's you, all right, but it is not any woman that you know.

"Beautiful," you say, "but not gorgeous."

TWENTY-EIGHT

The next day, late in the afternoon, you ease your way down the hospital corridor—long but not nearly long enough—a pitiful bouquet of daisies in hand, approaching Mimi's room with more than a little trepidation. There was talk of doing this yesterday, and then again today, but you resisted it, put it off, until finally, there was no more time. Today's visiting hours are winding down, and tomorrow, Sam has to start driving back to Cleveland. If you are going with him, this is your last chance. He would be by your side if only you had let him; instead, he is waiting in the parking lot, as you insisted. This is something you have to do alone.

The door to the room is cracked open. The scene you find is much like the one you have imagined: Mimi draped in a gown and lying, eyes closed, in a hospital bed, a doctor's clipboard with all of its horrific details hanging from its foot. There is another bed in the room. The sheets are rumpled but it is empty; for the time being, she is alone. You set the flowers on the nightstand and pick up a pen to leave a note—you shouldn't wake her—but she opens one eye and then the other.

"What happened to your hair?"

Right. You are a brunette now. It still catches you by surprise every time you pass by a mirror. "It wasn't my idea."

"Hmm." It is hard to know what she thinks about it, if anything. She may simply be groggy from all the medication.

"I didn't know about the pictures," you say. "Not until after."

Mimi laughs and then winces. "I guess not."

"How did you get them?"

"At the wake, when I was getting Junior to sleep. I dropped something on the floor—I don't even remember what—and it rolled under the bed. I found the box and had a hunch. I just meant to be nosy. I wasn't even looking for you. But then there you were."

There is enough room on the side of her bed for you to sit comfortably without disturbing her. This is your first instinct—to put yourself in this spot, to close the space between you—but you resist it, choosing instead to hover by her feet. "I don't know what to say."

"Me neither." She takes a few shallow breaths before her face slackens.

"Can I do anything?" You mean for it to be an earnest question, but, in your nervousness, it sounds stiff and meek: a formality.

"You've done enough, thanks." Her eyes dart over to the bedside table and settle on the plastic pitcher. She props herself up on her elbows and rolls toward it, but you are already there, filling the cup. When you offer her the straw, she puts her mouth around it, albeit grudgingly, and sips. "Oh, I'm all right," she says. "There's nothing wrong with me that won't be better someday."

"They told me you won't be able to have children."

Mimi shrugs her shoulders. "That doesn't make any difference."

But of course it does. However unlikely or undesirable motherhood might be for her, it used to be her choice to make, and now it's not.

"We're back," booms a man's voice, and you turn around just as Johnny storms the doorway, a diaper bag hanging from one arm, Junior held aloft with the other. He doesn't recognize you at first, but, after a double take, he makes a face. He cuts his eyes at Mimi, nods toward you. "Should she be here?"

"It's okay." Mimi presses the fingers of a hand against one eye, then the other. "She's leaving soon. Why don't you walk Junior around the floor one time."

"Yeah, sure." Johnny picks the baby up, tosses him, howling, into the air, and catches him. As he walks past you, Junior slung roughly over his shoulder, he says quietly, "She's tired," and waits for you to nod your understanding before he leaves.

When Johnny is well down the hallway, Mimi says, "He's been like that the whole time. You should have seen the fight he put up to get me this room. It was one for the books."

In these words, you can hear the pride, but also the tender feeling—not just devoted, but resolved. You aren't sure whether this is a result of the accident or something that happened before, but when you hear her say this, you understand that she has made a decision: she will not walk away from Johnny after all.

"So go ahead," she says now. "Say whatever you need to say."

For the past two days, you have rehearsed the various ways you might ask for forgiveness, all of which, you now realize, are lacking. A new thought comes to you. It does not have the beauty or depth you would like it to have. It will not restore her; it will not redeem you. But it is true, and, as the tears you blink away will attest, it is a thing you need to say.

"I'm a heel."

Mimi raises an eyelid. Her mouth settles into something of a smile, and it seems like she is going to say something, but then a serious-faced nurse pops in to check Mimi's vitals. By the time she is gone, the moment is, too. Instead, Mimi says, "Joe tells me you're not going to wrestle Mildred. You know that don't help me any."

Yes, you know. It also doesn't help Joe, and it definitely doesn't help Mildred Burke, who is destined to lose the belt to June Byers if she can't job it to you. "You think you'll keep wrestling then?" you ask, heartened by the prospect.

"That's the plan. Give me another sip of that water, would you?" she asks. This, you are only too happy to do. "I'm going to be fine," she says, licking her lips. "You're the one to worry about."

"Yeah, well." Perhaps she means for you to reassure her, to let her in on the latest plan for reinvention spinning around that newly dyed head of yours, to hear your confidence in it. The problem is this: you don't have confidence, or a plan, for that matter, and you don't have the stomach to fake it. The last thing you want to do is tell her a lie, so you leave those words—*Yeah, well*—hanging in the air until she falls asleep.

The waiting room near the hospital entrance is not at all comfortable, but it has the advantage of possessing a trash can, so it is the perfect place to sit and clean out your purse while you bide your time. You just couldn't bring yourself to stroll through those sliding glass doors—not just yet. Sam's longer, broader, glass-half-full view of things has served you well these past few days, but you are not yet ready for another dose of optimism. You need a minute alone to think, to sit inside the wreckage and assess the damage.

While you are still slumped in your seat, gathering your resources, the doors open and in walks Joe. He stops to mop his brow with a handkerchief while you hold your breath, but it's no use: he spots you. He stands there, hands in pockets, and waits for you to come to him, which you do with more than a little hesitation.

"Good of you to come," Joe says.

"I don't know about that." Joe stares at you for a long while, waiting for more. Perhaps he thinks that you owe him something. Perhaps he wants more explanation, or at least some pleasantries. You would like to oblige, but these are more than you can manage. The best you can do is this apology: "I'm really sorry, Joe."

"I know you are, kid. I am, too."

"You had this whole thing worked out—" You don't dare think, let alone say, the rest of the sentence: *and I blew it for all of us.*

"I did. But you know what? I'll just have to work something else out."

"You will?" This is both reassuring and disappointing. If a championship can go forward without you, it means you were never as instrumental as you imagined. "What?"

"I don't know. I haven't gotten that far yet. If you've got any brilliant ideas, I'm all ears."

"No, not really."

"That's too bad." He slips off his glasses and runs his handkerchief over the bridge of his nose. He asks, "What about you? What's your plan?"

"Can't say I have one."

Joe returns his glasses to his face and nods his head in a matter-of-fact way. He pulls out his money clip, counts his dough, and performs a few mental calculations before peeling off a couple of bills—enough to cover all that he owes you and then some—and then another and another just like it. When you open your mouth to protest, he takes your clutch from your hands and stuffs the bills inside: this is not negotiable.

"You have stuff in Otherside you're going to want back," he says. "I can send it to you, or you can come get it. Whenever. There's no rush." He places his heavy hands on your shoulders, and for once, you don't mind them there. "If there's anything to talk about, we can talk then."

You would like to tell him not to hold his breath. You will never feel ready to open up to him, let alone wrestle again—not under the new terms. But you sense that he already understands this, so instead, for only the second time in your life, you dare to kiss him. Later, you will decide that it is this gesture, the way it hurls you backward in time to that first peck on the ear, and the story Joe told you in that moment, that will give you an inspired idea, one that has the potential to not only fix his immediate problem but also change the course of history for all involved, including him.

"I have the answer," you say. "I know who can fight Mildred Burke."

"I'm listening."

"What about the best wrestler you've ever managed?"

The look on Joe's face makes clear he is deeply suspicious of this idea, that perhaps he even entertained it himself and dismissed it. He is not a man who welcomes scandal, and Lacey, who is likely still at El Rancho, where you left her, will come with one that will cast its shadow in all directions. But in the year you have known him, he has grown less averse to risk, more willing to change with the times. These trends will only continue; before the decade is over, he will sign his first African-American wrestler and make Mimi his business partner. Whether he is ready for that kind of risk today remains to be seen, but it seems to you if there is anyone worthy of a risk, it is Lacey. She has paid her dues and then some. Maybe some could begrudge her the title, but not you, and certainly not Mimi.

"I don't know," he says. "I don't even know where she is now."

His face might betray his doubt, but in those words, you hear a man who can be convinced. This can't be easy for you, Gwen—selling Joe on a champion other than yourself—but it is your best chance. You can't make it right, but you can do one right thing.

"Luckily for you," you say, "I do."

In the parking lot, Sam leans against the Crestline, arms crossed, and talks to Johnny. It is a relief that they have found each other. Otherwise, the sight of Sam waiting in the Memphis heat—hair damp, shirt bibbed in sweat—might make you cringe with guilt. When the men catch sight of you, they shake hands and part ways. Johnny brushes past, acknowledging you only with a slight nod, but Sam springs into gentlemanly action, helping you into the passenger side before climbing behind the wheel. He rests his arm on the back of the bench seat and asks, "Do you feel better?"

"About Mimi? No. Not really. But I'm not sure I want to."

"Sounds to me like she's doing okay," he says, cranking the engine. "Johnny says she's already talking about touring together and buying a travel trailer so they can take Junior on the road. Speaking of which, I saw Joe walk in."

"Yeah, I spoke to him."

"Did he give you any grief?"

"No." You feel quite certain you have convinced him that Lacey should win the belt. You briefly consider sharing this news with Sam, but if you do, then you will have to tell him about seeing her in Vegas. You can only imagine what he might say if he discovers that you saw her and said nothing to him. This is hardly a conversation you want to have now.

"See? What did I tell you?" Sam puts the car in reverse, looks over his shoulder, and eases off the brakes. "Just you wait, Leonie. This story is going to have a happy ending for everybody."

"Everybody but me," you say.

"You're thinking about this all wrong. You're not down. You're just in between. That's all."

Here it is again—Sam's finger pointing toward the bright side. This is not what you need right now. In time, his optimism will seem like prophecy. Good news will trickle in from every corner, and, while you will never quite believe that this was all meant to be, you will settle into the idea that everyone got the life she needed, including you. But first, you have to grieve. For all her faults, The Sweetheart was one of the few things in this world that was yours, and now she is gone.

"Maybe I don't want to be in between. Maybe I want to be where I was."

Sam adjusts his grip on the steering wheel and stares ahead. When he's gathered his thoughts, he turns and says, "Leonie, don't you see? You were already in between."

It takes a moment for this to arrive to you as fact. At first, it seems like much of Sam's version of events—intended to cheer rather than honestly evaluate. But you can hear first how this is different and then how it is right. Remember the debacle in DC, the soul-grinding performances in Vegas? Maybe you *were* already in between. Maybe you had already taken the first steps toward something else.

"If I'm in between, then what's next?" you ask.

"You're not supposed to know," says Sam. "That's the problem with in between. That's why it feels bad. But in my happy ending, you and I go back to Cleveland and build a life together."

Maybe that *is* the answer. Now that everything else is in tatters, perhaps your best shot at happiness is to put aside your reservations and take a chance on Sam's somewhat flawed but true-blue affections. Sure, he can be overprotective, but this is born out of a deep and abiding concern for you, isn't it? Hasn't he proven that he will be a loyal defender and protector? Besides, what else are you going to do now that the life you imagined for yourself has made like a banana and *split*? Going back to Philadelphia is not an option. And if you can't go home, then really, what else is there? All signs point to Sam. You just have to take the first step.

"Okay," you say. "Let's do it."

Sam brakes hard. The car jerks to a halt. "Say that again."

But you can't bring yourself to say those words one more time. Instead, you take his hands off the wheel and into your own. This is it: you have made the choice. It is a good choice—the only choice, really. It gives you both a place to go and a person to go with. That is more than a girl in your circumstances should ask for. Someday, you are quite certain, you will thank your lucky stars.

TWENTY-NINE

It is late morning in Memphis when you head out for a run. In a few short hours, you and Sam will start out for Cleveland so that he can begin his transformation from wrestler to promoter and you can begin your new lives together. You suit up and slip out as quietly as possible, careful not to wake Sam as you leave. You don't want to have to explain what you are doing.

After a few stretches under the awning, you set out, headed north on Second Street, past the one-story brick buildings of Film Row toward the downtown high-rises. It is a bad time for a run. The heat is stifling; the occasional breeze provides minimal relief and brings with it the unfortunate smells of the Wolf River. Still, it feels good to be out here—on the concrete, under the neon. The wide sidewalks are dotted with newsstands stocked with comic books and vendors with baskets full of vegetables. Above you, the lines for the trolley cars form an electric web.

It doesn't take long for you to find a rhythm, feel your muscles awaken. In the last year, this body of yours has developed many abili-

329

ties, but running may be the one you have most fully mastered. You can run until your legs turn to rubber, your lungs burn. Just a little longer, you will tell yourself, but once that's done, you decide you can go a little longer still, and again and again.

A few blocks into your run, a pair of trench coat–wearing, brief-case-swinging businessmen rubberneck as you cruise past. You continue onward. Your body no longer creates a debilitating self-consciousness. It has been your rocket ship. With it, you have enraptured strangers, inspired young women, paid for your father's mortgage, bankrolled your own independent existence, and brought auditorium after auditorium to its knees. You have a new and wholly merited respect for its value. But Sam is right—you were already starting to see its limits. You have withheld too much of yourself, reduced yourself to too few colors: platinum blond and Fire and Ice red. It is high time you broadened your palate.

What you are less sure about, now that you've had some time to think, is whether it is better this way—your persona quickly and unceremoniously put to rest. Sam certainly thinks so. In your conversation last night, he maintained that this clean break is better than what might have happened otherwise, you growing further enmeshed in something you clearly had ambivalence about. You'll grant him this—it is certainly more efficient. But better? Had the story been allowed to unfold gradually rather than suffer this abrupt ending, you might have someday packed The Sweetheart away with other items you'd outgrown. Now, you wonder if you aren't forever doomed to see her as something precious that was lost, a gem that slipped out of its setting.

You turn left and pick up speed as you run past the loan offices and shoe stores on Beale Street, attempting to distance yourself from this idea. That is the last thing you need to take to Cleveland. Sam is not a consolation prize. The man deserves better. What a silly girl you've been, wasting so much time bemoaning his flaws when you should have been examining your own. Overly ambitious. Shallow. Self-centered.

Hardly the kind of person to merit his loyalty. You should count your-self lucky. You *are* lucky. Because even if the two of you aren't perfectly suited, what couple is? The ones you've examined most closely—your father and Patricia, Cynthia and Wally, Mimi and Johnny—all seem built on compromise. It is a happy ending you are after, not a perfect one.

Another turn puts you onto Main Street, where scores of fashion-forward ladies in heels and gloves stroll the sidewalks. You can't help but notice the looks you get from them: the snickers, the raised eye-brows. Not that you blame them. A big, sweaty, red-faced woman in shorts and tennis shoes does tend to stick out in such a venue. On an-other day, you might take the hint and turn around, but you suddenly can't breathe. *You're fine,* you tell yourself. *Just keep going.* But you can't move. You can't go another step.

The awnings over Goldsmith's department store offer some respite, so you press your forehead against the cool display window and stare ahead while you wait for the spell to pass. From the other side of the glass, a group of mannequins stare back. One is clad in a floral-print, tea-length dress with an oversize bow. Another models a lemony-yellow suit with a long pencil skirt and cropped jacket, still another a red dress with bolero sleeves and a belted waist. One even sports a pair of light-weight slacks. And then there are the swimsuits. There is a jet-black suit made of waffle nylon, a second with gold embellishments and two small hip pockets, and a final one that gives you pause: a one-piece suit with a modest neckline and the new higher-cut legs in an uncanny shade of green.

As you take in the picture, your attention shifts from the manne-quins to your reflection in the glass. You are as shocked as ever by the dark-haired girl who stares back as you, but once this fades, you find it is not followed by the usual feeling of loss. For the first time, you see possibilities. You cannot imagine Gwen slipping into any of these frocks, preparing for a day at the office or a day at the beach or a first

date or her debut as a heel, but this girl—well, why not her? So you
can't be The Sweetheart again. There are so many other women you
could be, more even than what you see in front of you—ways of being
you can't imagine, that have yet to be invented. Just a year ago, you
knew nothing about wrestling, and now look at you. You are young and
in between.

There is nothing wrong with what Sam wants. He wants what many
people want. He wants to put on a suit and tie and go to the office. He
wants to sit in the stands and watch his favorite teams. He wants to
take his children to those games the way his father took him. At the end
of the workday, he wants to sit around the dinner table and eat the beef
brisket his lovely wife has prepared for him. He wants Leonie. He is a
good man who wants reasonable things, and by all means, he should
have them. The problem is that he thinks this will make you happy, too.
This is not selfishness on his part, just a fundamental misunderstanding. The truth is he simply doesn't know you well enough. And perhaps
you've been too willing to adapt to suit his moods and needs. But now
it is time for you to stop pretending.

You will not go to Cleveland. In that life, you drown, and you take
him with you.

There is a tap on your shoulder—an older woman in white patent
leather heels and a belted pink dress, two sullen adolescent girls by her
side. "Are you all right, dear?" she asks.

"Yes," you say. "It's just—I just realized that I have to break up with
my boyfriend."

"Well, I feel sorry for that poor boy." She offers you a monogrammed handkerchief from her matching white purse, and you run
it over your eyes before mopping your forehead. "You know what you
should do? Go in there and buy yourself something pretty. That's what
I always do when I feel bad."

"I don't think I'd know what to buy."

"Oh, I bet you could find something." She gestures at the window display. "Go on in and take a look-see." She gives you the once-over before adding, "On second thought, maybe you ought to go home and clean up first."

"Maybe I should," you say, using the handkerchief one more time before offering your thanks and handing it back. The woman pats your arms and says, "That's okay, honey. You keep it."

You close your hand around the handkerchief and let the city settle in around you. You will not go to Philadelphia or Otherside or Cleveland. That means this is not just another blue star on a map. Until a better option comes along, You Are Here. And who knows how long it will take you to figure out your next move? Maybe days, maybe weeks—maybe years. Thankfully, Memphis seems as good a place as any. An electric streetcar rolls past, sending off sparks. You can smell roasting peanuts. And there is this kind stranger, who has sent her girls in to start shopping without her until she is certain you can be left alone.

"Go ahead," you tell her. "I'll be okay."

And you will be, but it will get worse before it gets better. Before you are ready, you will have to tuck that handkerchief into your waistband and head back to the hotel room to deliver the news. Sam will sit quietly on the bed while you talk, his face still damp from a recent shave, his keys in his pocket, his eyes shining. But when you are done, it will be clear that you cannot be swayed, so he will not waste his breath. He will merely nod, resigned to his fate: another round of forlorn bachelorhood. And when the last good-bye has been said, he will put his hand on the back of your neck in that familiar way of his that can feel simultaneously tender and burdensome. Any ambivalence you feel will be merited, but in this moment, you will put it aside. From now on, all of your decisions will be your own. For better or worse, they will not be complicated by his wishes and feelings, which will make you blessedly free to accept this gesture's simplest meaning, to press your face against his shoulder as he says, for the last time, "Leonie, Leonie, Leonie."

After that, there will be doubt. You will wonder if you have been clear-eyed or fatalistic, optimistic or naive. You will hope you have done right by him, that he will go home to the city he loves, do work that he is meant for, and settle into a life that is mostly like the one he wants. I think that is the point, after all. Not to get everything—few people do—but to feel like you got the right things, that you didn't let them slip away. You want this for him as much as you want it for yourself.

"Okay, honey," says the woman. "I'll take your word for it. But I'll be right inside if you need anything. My name's Mrs. Timothy H. Kellogg. And you are?"

What should you say? You're not exactly Gwen anymore, and you're hardly Leonie. While you consider how you might answer, you shift the handkerchief from one hand to the other, flipping it over to reveal its monogrammed corner. There, above the rolled hem and some pulled thread work, surrounded by tiny embroidered flowers, is the letter *K*. And then it comes to you—a name from your past, one that might carry you into the future. At first, you are hesitant to say it out loud. Once you do, there will be nothing ahead of you but open road. But what else can you say? You can't rewind time, and you can't stop it either. All you can do is go forward.

So what are you waiting for? Go on. Tell her my name.

EPILOGUE

That was the first time I introduced myself as Leigh Kramer. I have been doing it for so long now, nearly sixty years, that I sometimes forget I was ever anyone else. This is how I think of you, whenever something like Mimi's invitation gives me cause: as someone distinct from me, someone who could—and did—disappear. I guess I thought it would be different here, in front of the home you left in search of the championship, but it's not. It is all so familiar—the red brick, the arched windows, the unassuming cornice—and yet it feels like it belonged to someone else. A girl I used to know, a girl from another place and time.

When I set out this morning, I didn't plan to walk all the way to the old neighborhood. But here I am, standing on a sidewalk spoiled by handprints and cracked by overgrown oaks, staring at the stoop where Franz, a Winston dangling from his lips, gave his reluctant consent, and the home just beyond it. The one to its right is cluttered with folding lawn chairs and stacks of old tires; the one to its left—the Rileys' home, and then Franz and Pat's place—is boarded up with plywood.

But this one has benefited from some recent improvements. The iron handrail has been replaced, and the door and window sashes have a coat of white paint so new it still looks wet. Just below the house number is a local Realtor's sign. It's for sale.

I take a seat on those steps and a long pull on my water bottle before I work up the nerve to pull the invite out of my pocket. I am surprised to find myself so rocked by it. I haven't suffered from sentimentality—nothing, at least, that would send me out on a hunt like this. I have long been rid of the evidence of your existence: the boots and the stilettos, the pencil skirt and the two-piece suit, the magazine clippings and the photographs. And I have no reason to grieve. The fact that Mimi will now be rewarded for her life's work and take her place among the pantheon of professional wrestling legends only underscores the conclusion I came to long ago: this is how it was meant to be. You weren't supposed to be champion. You had a more important purpose: you made my life possible. And it is much better to be me than to be you. I get to be my whole self—face, heel, and everything in between.

On the other side of the street, a familiar car pulls along the curb. The door opens, and the driver steps out, hikes up his pants, and walks toward the house. Now here is just the person to orient me in time: the Turnip.

"How did you know I would be here?" I call out.

When I say this, he stops in the middle of the street and stares. It seems he is only now realizing who I am.

"I didn't. What are you doing here?" Two boys, biking in his direction, pass around him on either side, which he smartly takes as a warning. He makes his way up to the sidewalk and over to where I am sitting. "Did you walk this whole way?"

"Don't act so surprised. I'm not that old."

"Yeah, well, you're not that young, either."

No, I guess I'm not. Most of my years are behind me now. All the more reason to be satisfied with the life I have led—because it's too damn late to do anything else.

I look at the Realtor's sign, and then back toward Harold, suddenly putting two and two together. "*This* is the house you're thinking of buying?"

Harold smiles. "I take it you don't think it's such a good idea."

"Why would I? You have a beautiful home. You've been working on it for years. It's practically perfect. Why would you give it up for this?"

I'm not sure why I bother to ask him this when I already know the answer. This was his home, too. He lived here with his mother, next door to his adoring grandparents, harboring poorly understood desires and nurturing private hopes, until, at eighteen, he was let loose into the world and started making the decisions that led him to this point in time, when his daughter is halfway around the world living a life he doesn't understand. His presence here says something about the security he felt then and the bewilderment he feels now. For the first time in a long time, I feel something resembling tenderness toward the Turnip.

I mean Harold. His name is Harold.

"Oh, I don't think I could really pull the trigger," he says. "I just happened to see that it was on the market and couldn't help myself." Harold points at the invitation in my hand. "Is this why you're here? This person you're looking for—she's from the neighborhood? Anybody I might know?"

At first, I think about all the clever ways I can answer this so that I might avoid a lie but still keep you a secret (*You met her once, but you wouldn't remember it. You were still an infant.*) but then I realize that is not possible. To omit is to lie. I do not want to lie to Harold. I want to love him as much as Sis does, as much as Franz did, and the only way to bring someone closer to you is to tell the truth. I don't know why I have to keep learning this lesson, but I guess I do.

"The invitation is for me," I say. "I am Gwen Davies."

337

As soon as I say it out loud, it seems true to me in a way that it didn't before. You are not a separate being, someone I could just abandon in front of that window at Goldsmith's. You are the small part of me that, despite everything, and beyond all rationality, still wishes that last match had gone differently, and for reasons that aren't altogether selfless. I don't really understand how we can coexist—me wanting the life that I have, you wanting the life you didn't get—but we do.

"You are Gwen Davies," repeats Harold. "What the hell does that mean?"

"It's a long story," I say. "I am going to need some sustenance to tell it. Take me home so I can eat my MoonPie, would you?"

"The Realtor's supposed to meet me here any minute."

"I can't wait. I'm old. You said so yourself."

"Just walk through the house with me first. You must be curious."

"I'm not. And you shouldn't be, either." I wave the invitation at him. "You should take me home and help me figure out what I'm going to do about this."

"It will take ten minutes. Twenty, tops."

"It is more important for you to hear what I have to say. It might teach you something about parenting independent young women."

Harold studies me for a while, which is just fine. I don't have an angle. I just want to talk, for once.

"Okay," he says, "you win. Let's go."

When we are buckled in, Harold motions for me to hand him the invitation. He studies it for a while. "Mimi Hollander," he says. "Should I know that name?"

"Everybody should know that name," I say. "She was the show."

"Then we should go."

We. I don't know why, but that gets to me. I have to swallow hard before I can talk. "You haven't heard the story yet."

"I know it starts with you being someone called Gwen Davies and ends with you getting this," he says. He hands the invitation back to me and starts the car. "I am pretty sure that whatever you say, I'm going to want to go."

I nod and slip the invitation back in my pocket. Maybe we should go, maybe we shouldn't. That doesn't seem so important right now. At least, not as important as what I am about to do. I start fiddling with the radio. I have a lot to think about before we get back to the house, and I could use some tunes.

"What's that station I like?" I ask, but instead of waiting for an answer, I push all the buttons until I find it, where Bill Haley's "Crazy Man, Crazy" is just getting under way. "Did your mother ever tell you about the time she and I danced on *Bandstand*?"

"Only every time she hears this song. So, about a million times."

"Alright, then. I won't make it a million and one."

"How about you dedicate the song instead?"

Harold is referring to a tradition I began as a DJ for WHER-AM, Sam Phillips's All-Girl Radio Station, where I spun slow, square tunes for the old and unhip. This was the job that helped me find my footing after those first few years of purgatory, waiting tables (the only other skill set I had) and torturing myself with hindsight. At that stage of my life, radio was the perfect fit: the studio combined some of the pleasures of the arena—most notably, a ready, waiting audience—with the privacy and security of the hotel room. One evening, I ended my show with a Tony Bennett song and, in a fit of nostalgia, said, "This one's for you, Father." After that, I finished every shift with a personal dedication to someone who figured in my life. I never offer any backstory, just the dedication and the name.

This song is as good as any to send out to someone I love. It is the one that started it all, and I could dedicate it to many people. To my sister, Cynthia, who led me on the dance floor and said, "Do it, Leonie!" To Joe, who told me to get to work. To Sal, for discovering me, or Monster, for seeing me, or Sam, for letting me go. To my father, as I could almost every song I hear. To Pat, for loving him. It could go to my friend Screaming Mimi Hollander, the meanest bitch that ever walked the face of the earth. And, of course, it could go to you, the girl I used to be and, in some modest way, still am. But it is time for me to get back to the work of being Leigh Kramer, and I can't think of a better way to start that work than to dedicate this song to the man who is sitting right beside me.

"This one's for you, Harold," I say. "Now, please. Take me home."

ACKNOWLEDGMENTS

I found inspiration and information for this novel from the following texts: Bernard Malamud's *The Natural*, Tess Slesinger's "On Being Told That Her Second Husband Has Taken His First Lover," Jeff Leen's biography of Mildred Burke, *The Queen of the Ring: Sex, Muscles, Diamonds, and the Making of an American Legend*, Ruth Leitman's documentary, *Lipstick & Dynamite, Piss & Vinegar: The First Ladies of Wrestling*, and two highly unreliable but infinitely colorful autobiographies by two of those first ladies: Penny Banner's *Banner Days* (with Gerry Hostetler) and Lillian Ellison's *The Fabulous Moolah: First Goddess of the Squared Circle* (with Larry Platt).

Thank you to Hasanthika Sirisena, Julia Kenny, and Lauren Pearson for their help with the early drafts. I am especially grateful to Tony Earley, Joe Regal, and Markus Hoffman for their insights and enthusiasm, and to Emily Graff and everyone at Simon & Schuster. Thanks also to the family, friends, writing communities, and literary journals who helped me become a better writer and gave me reasons to keep trying: my mom, Serena, and my dad, Al; my brother, John, and his limitless wrestling knowledge; the Florida State University Creative Writing Program (2000–2003), the 2007 Sewanee Writers' Conference, *The Mid-American Review*, *The Southern Review*, and *The Greensboro Review*. And I am forever in the debt of my husband, who risked sleeping on the couch to tell me the truth, and who sacrificed his own precious little time so I could have a few more minutes to write. This book was written for my babies, but it would not exist without their father. I love you, Jack.

ABOUT THE AUTHOR

Angelina Mirabella received her master of arts in English (creative writing) from Florida State University in 2003. Her work has appeared in *The Southern Review, The Mid-American Review,* and *The Greensboro Review*. In 2007, she attended the Sewanee Writers' Conference as a Tennessee Williams scholar. She lives in Ithaca, New York, with her husband and two daughters. *The Sweetheart* is her first novel.